Information Agent **Brandon Drake**
is about to learn more than he ever wanted to
know about

INTIMATE FALLS

Brandon Drake never did like the nastier aspects of
the P. I. business, which is why he had navigated a
lateral shift to the high-tech information business. High
challenge. Low risk. No need to carry a weapon. So
long as everyone plays by the same rules . . . .

Enter Julia Hobbs. Pregnant. The father of her unborn
child is missing after a climbing expedition in Yosemite
Valley. Her brother told her that her best hope was his
old friend Brandon Drake.

Together Brandy and Julia find her husband, dead, in
the wrong part of the Valley, and tied to another climber
who hadn't been reported missing yet. All the evidence
points to murder, and an underworld high-tech
information cartel will stop at nothing to halt Drake's
investigation. Nothing.

INTIMATE FALLS

A Brandon Drake Novel
by

Lance Rucker

LOCHENLODE BOOKS • VANCOUVER

INTIMATE FALLS

A Lochenlode Book

National Library of Canada Cataloguing in Publication Data

Rucker, Lance, 1948-
 Intimate falls

(The Brandon Drake mystery series)
ISBN 0-9688274-0-3

I. Title. II. Series: Rucker, Lance, 1948- Brandon Drake mystery series.
PS8585.U29I57 2001   C813'.6   C2001-910154-6
PR9199.3.R76I57 2001

For information address: Lochenlode Publishers
                                  3341 Flagstaff Place
                                  Vancouver, B.C.,
                                  Canada   V5S 4K9

The World Wide Web site address is
http://www.lochenlode.com

Cover design by Lance Rucker and Sophie Spiridonoff

Printed in Canada

Acknowledgements:

Gladys Srivastava, for her endless efforts at protecting the English language from my relentless assaults.

Dr. Scott Paterson, a former brother-in-law who continues to be a brother.

Dr. David Sweet, whose interface with forensic science continues to be as valuable to me as to him.

Dr. Rex Ferris, Forensic Pathologist, an invaluable scientific resource.

"Whenever two rockclimbers tie on to a rope to form a climbing team, they are doing far more than tying their bodies together. Once they are up high on the rock face, they must act in perfect concert. With a special, intimate attachment they have tied their fortunes together. And at the end of their climb, they are bound to share with one another a highly intimate success. Or a highly intimate fall."

One

It was one of those great autumn days when all the golds and reds and browns and the few remaining greens turn the world into a color carnival. In other circumstances, it could have been one of the fourteen thrilling days of Brandon Drake's life. But the day was not ruled by Nature. Nor was it ruled by Man. It was a day ruled by Machine.

One of the time bombs set by the Industrial Revolution was the Computer. It was a bomb set to go off generations later and destined to engulf every island of clock time which had been freed up by all the other wondrous machines created since that revolution. We make machines so that we have time so that we spend time. And spend it how? In rapturous contemplation of our own individual journeys toward enlightenment? In active pursuit of a successful formula for deriving winning numbers for the lottery? In appraisal of the spiritual evolution of our universe? No. In learning how to use the curious intangible development of wizardry and infuriation called "software".

It was Upgrade Day. The day when Brandy's entire mental faculties were focused on the adaptation of his computer usage to a new series of patterns and formats and processes which are just similar enough to the "old" way of doing things as to seem tantalizingly familiar and friendly, but just different enough to confound every decent attempt to shortcut the complete rereading of the new software documentation. And each time there was an upgrade in one of the half-dozen programs which were the basic tools of his trade as an information jockey, the manuals were longer and longer, more and more complex.

On Upgrade Days, wonder and loathing are stirred into the mental pot until confusion bubbles forth, calling for more reading, more wonder, more loathing. Upgrade Days were even worse, in their own sweet way, than the annual personal springtime fest known as "Tax Day", when Brandy pulled together the envelopes and pockets full of the previous year's receipts and spent the day cursing and swearing and hunting for lost information and trying to remember why he'd written off only forty percent of the cost of the carpeting in his sunroom-cum-office as a business expense. It didn't matter that he had been trained as an accountant. Just figuring out and submitting his own taxes each year reminded him why he hadn't lasted more than six months in the family accounting business. But Upgrade Days made him wonder why he moved into high-tech detective work. Out of the frying pan . . .

New software was different than upgrade software. At least new software does new tasks with the jaded machines. New software plays new games, presents new challenges. But upgrades? Upgrades are the modern day equivalent of self-flagellation and self-deprivation of the medieval monks. High-tech masochism. And every time he began the painful process, Drake would grit his teeth and stare at the upside-down diploma mounted on the wall above his computer and ask . . . well, far lesser cosmic questions.

It was in such a mood of high spirits that Drake wrenched himself from his computer to scour the kitchen for an afternoon snack. He was rummaging in the bottom drawer of the fridge, through a pile of recycled cloudy plastic bags and their enclosed remnants of such delicacies as last week's roast beef (no longer rare), a cardboard palette of side bacon, broccoli in its mostly flowered yellow state, a fold of dried out flour tortillas, all of which had broken in two where they'd been folded, and more things below which he had no heart to examine. PB&J won. On sesame white bread. A nearly virgin loaf.

He was still emerging from his upgrade trance and was slowly becoming aware that, standing at the kitchen counter next to the refrigerator, he'd nearly eaten the two sandwiches he'd made for himself. He was considering how thirsty he was for something cool to drink to wash down the snack when the doorbell rang. On Upgrade Days his rule was to ignore the phone and door. People would leave messages or call back or come back, but an interruption in the process of learning an upgrade only intensified the agony. Upgrade Day was zombie day. Brandy chomped another mouthful of bread when the bell rang again. He felt the texture of the cottony fresh bread pressed between his tongue and his palate and the inner surfaces of his teeth, and grunted an animal "humpf" to himself. The doorbell rang more insistently, and he dropped the remains of the PB&J on the sandwich plate on the countertop and shook his head in annoyance. "For cryin' out loud . . ." he grumbled, lumbering through the living room toward the big front door of his condominium.

"Yes?" he demanded as he jerked the door open. He was usually more careful to look through the peephole before opening his door. In the information business, one had to be reasonably cautious, even when one specialized in low-security, no-risk contracts. Not everyone with whom he dealt was so generous in their appraisals of what constituted innocuous information. In the information business, one man's refuse can be another man's gold mine. Or his death certificate. People get real edgy about what other people want to know about them. And sometimes they hold grudges. And sometimes they send gifts to your home. The kind of gift which leaves a few remnants of the door clinging to the hinges and brings ambulance drivers to cluck and raise their eyebrows and carry the remains of the person who answered the door back to their ambulance in a body bag.

The lady at the door was stunning. Intense, wild-haired, and striking, she had deep brown insistent eyes. They wouldn't let go. The more Brandon focused his attention on her, the more striking she became. "Are you Mr. Brandon Drake?" she demanded.

"Yes. Yes. May I help you?"

"I hope so. May I come in?" She marched past him with her eyes lowered before he could respond.

As he watched her stride across his small living room and lower herself onto his grey-mauve couch, still keeping her back to him, he murmured aloud to himself in a deadpan, "Sure thing. Make yourself at home." He clicked the door and locked it. Wondered whether the enchantment was with the demeanor or the hair. It was medium length and curly-frizzed like a science experiment in static electricity. He sat attentively at the edge of the cushioned straight chair directly across from her and faced her, waiting for eye contact or words. Miz Brazen was suddenly very humble. She searched the rug for lint and chewed at her lower lip and wrung her hands. Brandon waited.

Eventually her eyes travelled up to his. The sclera were red, as if she'd been taking drugs or was in a deep trance. Or both. But her words were distinct and clear when at last she finally spoke. "I need to talk," she said.

She was unwavering and silent. The sheer force of the woman's eyes and her intensity shook the last fog of Upgrade Day from Brandon's mind. This was a woman to be committed to. Or to be committed. Or a woman to make love with. Or all of those things. "Well?" Brandy prodded.

"I need to find someone. Someone special. And I want you to tell me how to do it."

"I'm not a missing persons bureau."

"I know. But I've heard about you. And I . . . Will you help me? Please?" Her eyes were more supplicant than her voice, and both oozed real sincerity. Brandon was so startled by the effect that he wondered if he were slipping back to foggy land.

Drake gauged her carefully. It wasn't that anything didn't fit, yet. It just seemed like too *much* to fit. "Mind if I ask a personal question?"

"Anything. Whatever you need to know . . ."

"What's your name? Who are you?"

She flushed crimson. Stumbled for words. "Oh. Of course. I'm so sorry. It's just that I was so determined to have you say 'yes' that . . . Julia Hobbs." She leaned forward off the couch and extended her arm straight out toward him, a downward angle to the heel of her flat hand. Brandon took it, responded with a firm ritual shake, and held it an extra moment to enjoy her textures. A thoroughly sensuous woman. Charged and set and live-wire.

"Glad to meet you. You obviously know who I am."

"Of course. Will you help me?"

He released her grasp. "Probably not."

"What? Why not? Why do you say that?"

"To slow the train. Before I'm hit by it."

She bit her lip and cast her eyes down again. "Oh. A little strong, huh?"

"I like to be swept off my feet, Miss Hobbs, but . . ."

"Julia."

"Okay. But I don't like to be railroaded. Who do you want to find?"

"My husband."

"How long has he been missing?"

"Since he was killed."

"I don't understand."

"He was rockclimbing in Yosemite Valley. He didn't return from a day's climb. But they haven't found his body. And that was nearly three months ago."

"And you want me to find him?"

"Exactly!" She leaned forward into his eyes with a tight, pursed, triumphant grin.

Brandon frowned. "Then I'm definitely not the man to help you. I've never done anything like wilderness searches."

"No, no. You don't understand. I don't want you to find his body. I want you to find *him*. I don't think he's dead. But if he is, I want you to help me find people who *can* find him, because I want to be absolutely sure one way or the other."

"But you don't think he's dead? Why not?"

"Because it's not his style."

"Dying isn't most people's style. Except once per."

"No. I mean, everything they said about what happened . . . it just doesn't fit Farmer at all. Farmer might climb the most gruesome cliff in the Valley, but he *never* climbed alone, and never would he change plans without telling the climbing control people at the Park Information Center. Never. That's why I think he's not dead."

"But you said it's been three months. And you haven't heard anything from him?"

She halted in mid-flight. Eyes back to the carpet.

"If he were alive," Brandy persisted, "don't you think he would have contacted you by now?"

"I know. But, you see, we had an argument the week

before he left."

"Must have been a pretty severe argument if you think he'd disappear like that and not get in touch with you. Not that it's my business, but . . ."

"We've been separated for nearly two years, Mr. Drake."

There was a long silence.

"Forgive me for being the cynical man that I am, but does your reason for wanting to locate either your husband or his remains have anything to do with insurance?"

She shook her head and frowned incredulously. "No! Why, heavens no! I come from a very wealthy family, Mr. Drake. I've never needed Farmer's money. And I certainly don't need his insurance. And the people at Minnesota Mutual have already told me I'll get the insurance if he hasn't reappeared in seven years anyway."

"That's probably true. So, once again forgiving my skepticism, why are you so anxious to find out what happened to your estranged husband?"

"Don't you think my curiosity is justified? I mean, he *was* my husband for five years. And I loved him deeply. And . . ." She noticed Brandon's dubious brow. " . . . he loved *me*, too. We just couldn't live together. That's all. He was a workaholic, and I just got tired of trying to be fitted into his schedule. Unsuccessfully, at that. Farmer and I got along beautifully when we were only together once a week or so. The last two years were the best of our lives together."

"It took you three months to start searching for him?"

"I thought the police would find him. Or that he'd turn up on his own. I should have known he wouldn't, though."

"Why's that?"

"Because he never went overtime on a project in his life, and the one he was working on when he went to Yosemite for the rest was due three weeks later. It went so totally against his grain to be late on a project, I knew then that something was wrong. Maybe he fell and had amnesia, or he was kidnapped . . ."

"Off the side of a mountain?" Brandon asked.

"*I* don't know."

"Three months?"

Julia glared at Brandon for the first time. She sucked in a deep breath and eased it out, the fierceness melting from her expression as she sighed. "Okay. Okay. I'll tell you. I guess it doesn't make any sense otherwise. Because I'm pregnant with Farmer's baby. And I wasn't sure until two weeks ago. I kept thinking it couldn't be. It was the night before we had the argument. Just before he left. And for the past three weeks, all I can think about is 'what am I going to tell our baby?' That his daddy just disappeared? And then I thought I should get rid of the baby, but . . . even though Farmer never wanted to have a child, *I* did. Well, it wasn't so much that he didn't want to have the child. It was more that he knew he'd never have the time to give a child the father-care it deserved. So we'd decided not to." She looked steel solid into Brandy's eyes. "Satisfied?"

"No. That still doesn't explain why you picked *me*, Julia. I was serious when I said that missing persons is not my line."

"Remember Jerry Hambleton? He's my brother. He told me you were graduate school buddies. He said you were good at what you do. Weird, but good. And when I found out you were here in Vancouver, it was like a special message from the cosmos that said 'Go see this man, Julia!'"

"There's nothing more unreliable than recorded messages from the cosmos. I'm glad you came to see me, Julia, but I am *not* a private detective. I used to be, but now I'm an information agent. I help people find information that isn't in the Yellow Pages. Information about industrial research, information from databases, information about corporate affairs."

"Meaning?"

"Meaning I'll be happy to refer you to someone who can search for your husband. But that someone is not me."

"But I don't want someone else. I want you. I . . . I have a strong feeling about you. That you can help me find Farmer. And . . . and those feelings are never wrong. *Never*."

"Julia, there are better people out there who are in the business of locating missing persons and checking police files and that sort of thing . . ."

"Not according to Jerry."

"Jerry is an incurable romantic. A lot of my university buds thought that I gave up a career in drab old accounting to set the world on fire as a buccaneer adventurer of the James Bond genre. But it's not that way. It never was that way."

"He says you've done some of the most impressive detective work ever done in the private eye business in North America. He says you've located all sorts of people in all sorts of bizarre circumstances and . . ."

"All that was years ago. And all blown as fully out of proportion as the size of the trout that fishermen used to catch in the mountain streams. Among other things, I'm completely out of touch with the right kinds of contacts in that business. Especially in California. And you have to keep current to be good at P.I. work. I can send you to a man named Don Beeley, in San Francisco. He could get background on your husband and on the police investigation, and the information would cost half of what I'd have to charge. Not because I'm any better, but because right now, without connections, it would take me twice as long to get the same things."

"I want *you*. And that's final." Brandon was surprised at her suddenly renewed assertiveness. Her eyes confirmed what her tone of voice commanded. Drake had the sensation that if he refused to consent, he should resign himself to having a pregnant Julia henceforth camped on his living room couch. "I don't care how much it costs." She heard the echo of her own voice within her and realized how hackneyed, if not downright ridiculous, her statement sounded, so in the next breath she quickly appended, "Within limits, of course."

She leaned forward on the edge of the couch again, sliding her hands down her calves to her ankles, which she clamped onto so firmly that her fingers blanched. Her complexion paled two or three shades, like a faded Botticelli, and she said in a frail and plaintive voice which was barely more than a whisper, "Before you tell me how much you charge --- or anything else for that matter --- can I have a cup of tea or a glass of milk or something? Anything? I'm feeling a little nauseated."

TWO

On his way to the kitchen, Brandon began to ponder his dilemma. To ponder his dilemma and to ponder the absurdity of the balance sheet on this one. As he leaned back against the Formica edge of the kitchen island and watched the electric kettle urging the water to boil, he began the tallies. He'd sworn to himself a great, long, solemn, private, sacred oath when he began to forge his new career in high-tech detective work, that he would no longer be wooed by anything which distracted from, or delayed, The Transition. He was an information agent now. Partly by declaration, and partly by fact. But what he chose to do from now on was what drove The Transition. He was a full time information agent now. No more garden variety private eye stuff. No more bedroom searches, no more unfaithful spouse cases, no more charity cases, no more guns.

So the left brain said, "No way on this one. It's straight P.I. work. There's probably not a high-tech thread in the whole weave. Refer it to Beeley or Fazio, and get back to work on your computer upgrades," but Brandy's right hemisphere said, "Why not give it a turn? It's a low-risk probe for maybe a week tops, and she says she's got plenty of money to fund the search. Why not check up on it, plan a strategy, and then turn it over to some California people? No skin off your nose."

Why is it that just when you think you've finally gotten a handle on your own personal assertiveness training, along comes another test? Try this on, Brandon Drake. Can you spell "no"? N-o? Look in the mirror and read your own lips. Hmmm. Lips which are saying "Old buddy's sister," and "Damsel in distress. Pregnant, no less. Have a heart, Brandy." Shitfire. It's fine giving seats on the bus to them, but you can't go giving your lifetime to them. This whole thing is not part of the game plan for the new career turn. Bottom line: if you say 'yes' to this one you'll be saying 'yes' to everything else that comes along and then five years down the line you'll still be tracking missing husbands and spurned lovers and wondering why you could never seem to make the break.

This would be a simple Missing Persons Bureau affair, an unsolicited invitation to search for a missing, estranged husband, for an old college bud's sister, at a bad time. There was absolutely no good reason for Brandy to accept the invitation, neither for Mrs. Hobbs' sake nor for his own. And . . . damn, he could already hear himself saying "yes". Damn it, Drake, there are people out there who enjoy this stuff a lot. Real bread-and-butter P.I. types. Your address book is full of them. Beeley lives right in the Bay Area, for God's sakes. Give him a referral.

Then the "X factors" leaped in to upset the logic of it all. Call it Cavalier Syndrome. Or Favor-For-A-Friend Fever. Or Don Quixote Tweaks. Lovely ladies always seemed to have that effect on Brandon. Even pregnant ones. Especially pregnant ones.

So much for his retreat to the cabin in the North

Woods. So much for the month-long R & R so carefully planned as his well deserved, personal reward for the combined strain of the completion of the Waxler contract and for busting his buns with the last of the Upgrade Days for this year. Just from the thought of it again, he could smell the Ponderosa pines in the forest, and hear the limitless sounds of the limitless silence, and feel the vibrations in the handle of his axe as the firewood split beneath its smooth stroke in the cool of the early morning, and feel his harassed body stretching peacefully and carelessly to its happy dimensions in a quiet corner of an otherwise relentless universe. *His* quiet corner. So much for . . .

"Mr. Drake? Brandon?" called a still-feeble voice from the living room. "Where's your bathroom? I . . . I think I'm not feeling too well. I think I'm going to be . . . sick."

"The door just around the corner from the fireplace," Drake called back. "Through the bedroom."

The unsteady staccato accelerando of her footsteps toward the bedroom and the bathroom beyond added a pathetic, heart-tugging urgency to Drake's planned response.

Melodrama in Lotusland . . .

When Julia shuffled carefully back into the living room, Brandy was blowing across the surface of his too-hot tea and watching her. She slumped back onto the couch and unselfconsciously enveloped her own cup and slurped away at her tea.

"Sorry about that," she said tentatively. "It comes in waves. Less often now than it did a few weeks ago, but I guess it's normal. Isn't it?"

"Don't know. No expertise in obstetrics."

"Neither have I," she said plainly. Suddenly Julia's deep brown eyes were infused with fire again and she spoke as if from another psyche. Two Julias. Too much. "So how much will it cost me?"

"I didn't say yes."

"Yet."

"Right."

Julia licked her lips.

"Are you always so forward?" Brandon asked.

"Only when I want something badly. How much will it cost?"

"I see my part of it as under a week. I would have to charge the per diem rate, which is eighteen hundred dollars a day plus expenses." He watched her face closely, hoping to discern a response that would signal her return to her senses and to the alternatives that his left brain had recommended all along. He read a blank. Stun maybe. A lot of people thought detective work was cheap. Welcome to the New Millennium, Mrs. Hobbs.

"So, less than fifteen thousand dollars? Is that what you're saying?"

"Probably, but that's just the initial work. If there's anything further to go on, the California people will start charging their own fees and I can't tell you what those might be. I'm not current on it. Whatever it is, I want to tell you again that it would be less expensive to have them do the whole thing for you. To let them take it right from here."

"Well," she declared decisively, "I still want *you*, and if it comes to further costs I'll worry about that when we get to them." No room for doubt. The Brazen One was back.

Brandy smiled resignedly. Somehow he'd known all along it was going to work out this way. Right brains are always so smart about some things. "Okay, Mrs. Hobbs. I'll give it a cruise-through for a couple of days to see what I can turn up for you. Depending on what I find out, I may have to go to Yosemite myself to find out anything of real value. Without a body, it would still be primarily a Park matter. The Mountain Rescue group might have something, but I doubt the issue has gone much further along yet. The Yosemite Park Rangers are world renowned for their police work. But other California agencies may have been called in, too . . . do you know anything about any of that?"

"Not really. I don't remember the name of the policeman who called me. I have his name and phone number at home. I think he was with the Park Rangers. How'd you know about all that?"

"Yosemite was one of my favorite playgrounds when Jerry and I were in university. I know the area a bit."

Her eyes glittered. "So where do you begin down there?"

"I have a few ideas. Depending on what those turn up, I'll either carry on from there, turn it over to someone I know for you, or tell you I think you're wasting time and money to have it privately investigated. Fair enough?"

"Fair enough. When do we leave?"

Drake winced at her. It had clearly been intentional. No slip of the pronoun. No Babe In Arms, Miz Julia. Well, no Fool In Arms, Mars Brandy, either. "*I* leave day after tomorrow and *I* will go alone or not at all. Claro?"

She pursed her lips. "I could help."

"And in the process of trying to help, you could cost yourself twice as much of my time and money in getting any answers. If there *are* any answers. If you want to play Clue, find somebody else to play with."

"Now, just a minute, Mr. Brandon Drake. Can't you understand that I need to see where this thing happened? That it is a big void in my life just having him disappear and no trace and not seeing the hole he dropped through? Is that so tough for you to understand?"

"Not at all, Mrs. Hobbs. But the facts still stand. Don't confuse your feelings with the things you say you want me to do. I work best alone. If I have questions I can call you at home. When you want to have a nostalgia run, do it on your own time. Sorry if that sounds cold, but I'm a professional."

Her demeanor shifted again. "Okay, okay. What is it you usually do with your clients? Shall I write a check for some sort of a retainer or an advance against expenses?"

"No, that's all right. I'll let you know at the end of the week. Can you leave me some telephone numbers where I can reach you, days and evenings? Tomorrow I'll want to call you and go over the details and get the police contact names you already have . . . things like that."

"Of course. But you know, I could really be a big help to you down in California if . . ." She jerked to a stop. His frown said it all. She wrote the numbers carefully on the back of a piece of note paper she scrounged from her leather patchwork purse. Handing those to Brandon, she climbed to her feet and straightened and tucked in her blouse and picked up her handbag. "Thank you, Mr. Drake. You're being very kind. I'm sure you'll find Farmer."

"I wouldn't want you to get your hopes up. Not if the local authorities haven't come up with any trace. But we'll see."

As she turned to thank him again at the door, Mrs. Hobbs unexpectedly and abruptly smiled the sweetest, purest little-girl sunshine smile. Yet another psyche. Three Julias and counting. And this one reached way up to Drake's shoulders to haul him forward and slightly off balance for a warm and lovely kiss on the cheek and a hug around the neck. "Good luck," she whispered.

As all three of her marched away to the elevator door just down the hallway from Drake's condominium, he shook his head and wondered just how much of Julia was a product of first trimester hormones.

Three

There was always something especially gratifying about the first stages of setting up an investigation. It was always so organized and orderly, to make a simple collection of knowns and unknowns, likelihoods and unlikelihoods, paths to follow up on, people to contact, etc., etc. Very gratifying, indeed.

And it didn't matter that within forty-eight hours of the start of the investigation, whether it was computer database work or hoof work, all that orderliness went straight to hell in a clutter of new information and suspicions and a juggling of priorities. It didn't matter because information people have to thrive on that clutter. If you screen all the incoming information in terms of your initial plans and expectations, eight times out of ten you'll come up empty handed. Nothing will make sense, regardless of how well organized it might be. In the end, the order always returned, even if it often bore no resemblance to the original battle plan. Having that faith kept a man in the investigation business. And kept him alive.

Regardless of this apparent and essential chaos which dogged almost every investigation, the initial set-up was somehow critical for the proper alignment of the accountant mentality with the Creative Muses, those strange creatures which were always on the lookout for the totally unexpected, the absurd pattern, the unlikely fit.

Fresh application of one of the previous day's software upgrades allowed an efficient scan of the Associated Press, Reuters, and California Dailies databases. Total search time today was less than ten minutes for a news search chore that had formerly taken an average of thirty minutes of connect time and which frequently crashed out before anything of use could be downloaded to the safety of Brandon's PC. Before computer-accessible databases, the job would have taken the better part of a day, sometimes more, and most of the smaller California Dailies would have demanded a trip to Sacramento or L.A. or San Francisco to ferret them out.

Admittedly today's screenings yielded very little substance: one two-inch San Francisco Chronicle article from Associated, three Sacramento Bee clippings about the disappearance of the climber, and title references to three Mariposa Gazette articles.

"Solo Climber Disappearance", from the Bee, was two columns, four inches, alluding to the suspected accident, basic search of designated climb site, no sign of climber, suspected unreported change in site plan, Level Two search underway, family contacted in Vancouver, Canada. That article appeared the day after Farmer failed to check in at the climbing registry at the Park Visitor Center, and made credit reference to the article published the previous day on the front page of the Mariposa Gazette (which, owing to the Gazette's weekly publication schedule and limited circulation, was not available on the current upgrade of the California Dailies database).

The Bee update three days later was one column, six inches. Park Rangers and Mountain Rescue completed search of all park trails and major climbing sites, still no sign of the climber except for personal effects left in his Yosemite Lodge cabin and a rented vehicle left in the Lodge parking area. The article credited a local Yosemite spokesman for the Mountain Rescue unit, one Clive Horrigan. The Park Rangers were maintaining alerts to all hikers and climbers in the Yosemite National Park area, and the California Highway Patrol and other major California agencies were assisting the Park Rangers in their search, as well as with their investigation of alternative explanations for the climber's disappearance.

The third article, three days later, rehashed old news in three columns along with a photo of the wife of one of the Bee's staff photographers roped to a ledge on the back side of Yosemite's Half Dome. The article was padded with a comment on solo climbing safety and the necessity for meticulousness in climbers' check-out/check-in procedures. That must have been the beginning of an especially fertile period in central valley news, because no further mentions --- not even honorable ones --- of climbing or of Farmer Hobbs plunked themselves down on the hallowed pages of the Bee thereafter through the late summer and early fall. If there had been a body, or if Farmer had been a famous person, or if the Central Valley drought and the upcoming State referendum on sales tax reduction hadn't continued to sell newspapers, there might have been a followup article about the still-missing computer hardware designer. Might have been, but as of yesterday, there'd not been.

The single two-inch inside filler which graced the San Francisco Chronicle was an abbreviated version of the first Bee article, and appeared the same day as had the Bee lead. And that was all.

The Canadian Press International database was even less productive. The Vancouver Sun tried to make news of its local-boy-made-good in the world of the disappearing, but was thankfully distracted after a weak start. No body, no clues, no pictures, no news.

Brandy spent over an hour on the phone early the next morning with Julia, reassured her he would be in touch in a few days at the outside, sooner if he learned anything significant. He made a hard copy of all relevant information, packed the bare essentials for city-going and for mountain-going and caught one of the early afternoon commuter flights to San Francisco. It had been less than two weeks since one of the first earthquakes of the new century had rumbled the Bay Area to its knees, and the peculiar effects on transportation and communications within San Francisco and the Santa Cruz areas convinced Brandy that he'd be better off doing his door-knocking and friend-visiting at the *end* of his Yosemite foray, not at the beginning. Most of the Bay Area systems were operational, and B.A.R.T. was running again, but a few areas were debris-littered war zones around which the local population still hadn't quite learned to move their traffic and daily lives smoothly. A few more days were bound to help.

The Budget car rental agent was from Tampa. Flown in to the earthquake zone to help out. Things were a bit slow in Florida, anyway. They must have neglected to tell the big man that Northern California Octobers can sometimes be cold and rainy. Or perhaps his Tampa wardrobe included nothing but thin, brightly colored sport shirts and thin, pale polyester trousers. Florida Polyester pointed to the assigned sub-compact and Brandy hauled his two carry-ons out through the rain. He made the mistake of loading the trunk before he climbed in to start the car up. Inside, it smelled like a dirty ashtray. The car reeked as if it had just been returned to the rental agency by a four-pack-a-day nonstopper. The

thought of sitting in that stench for five minutes, much less
for the four-hour drive to Yosemite, was more than Brandon
needed.

Back at the desk, Florida frowned incredulously.
"It's smoky?"

"That's right. Sorry, but I'm a non-smoker."

Florida rolled his eyes benignly and shrugged. "Wish
I was so sensitive." He turned away, his hip pocket bulging
with a cigarette pack, while he checked the computer to find
out what else he could offer. "Not sure if I have anything
else in that class."

"In that case, you can give me a free upgrade."

Florida frowned at Drake again. "Say what?"

Drake held the tip of his finger to a stand-up cardboard
sign on the countertop which declared:

"IF YOU'RE NOT OFFERED A BUDGET-
RITE FREQUENT-CUSTOMER APPLICATION
FORM, HAVE A FREE UPGRADE ON US."

Florida grunted and grimaced and clicked a few more
keys. "Okay. Got one. A-13. It's a mid-size. Just a sec and I'll
clear the other one."

A-13 was a Chevy Corsica six. Very nice. Not very
gutsy, but not heartless either. The automatic gizmos were
not too annoying in either their placement or their action,
and in a few minutes Drake had done his routinely meticulous
checkout of exterior and interior --- an old habit with car
rentals --- and was on his way east across the San Mateo
Bridge. The traffic was dense for an early afternoon, but
considering the shutdown of the Oakland Bay Bridge during
the earthquake and the resultant diversion of trans-bay traffic
to the other bridges, and considering it had been over a year
since Brandy had driven in the Bay Area to know what to
expect anyway, he was surprised how little difficulty he ex-

perienced making his way through the rain toward the East Bay, the Central Valley and the Sierra Nevada beyond.

Yosemite in late October could be either summer or winter, but odds were good for some coolness and some wetness. Rain on the coast meant fair odds for some snow in the foothills. But only odds.

The drive was mostly drizzly until a real torrent broke loose at Oakdale while Brandy had stopped to pick up a few snack foods and trail foods and other odds and ends of creature comfort for his day or two or three --- whatever it took --- in Yosemite. Although he had reservations at the Lodge, the valley restaurants were not open on the twenty-four hour schedule on which his hunger operated when he was travelling. Odd metabolism, but after forty years he'd finally learned to accept it. And to prepare for it. Standing in the meager shelter of the awning outside the supermarket, watching other shoppers attempting to hop and wade ankle-deep through the raging streams which had been trickling gutters only twenty minutes earlier, Drake looked from one grocery bag to the other in his arms and wondered if this stop had been one of his best plans of the day. During the next easing of the rainfall cacophony, Brandy made a break for the car. Distracted by the unavoidable ankle-deep left-foot soaker, he missed the first hint of a joggled slumping of the armfuls of groceries as the paper sacks disintegrated. Small-"e" ecology bites back. The door fell open and the odds and ends tumbled into the car guided more by luck than by Drake's backhanding technique. Three of the oranges tried to roll away across the roof before he could corral them into the back seat. One missed the pattern and made it to the puddle in which the car was parked. Brandon rolled his eyes, shook the drips from his brow and hair, and awkwardly squeezed his wet body into the driver's seat. Pisser.

By the time he got through Groveland, everything except his socks had dried in the warm exhalation of the

Corsica's heaters. As afternoon dwindled into evening, Brandy used the monotone veil of rain and sleet for a visual and mental backdrop, to plan how he might best and most efficiently dissect fact from the tangle of rumor and lore which would unavoidably have grown around Farmer's disappearance in the Park three months earlier.

Climbers are a particularly clannish group. It seemed best to probe that group, either directly or indirectly, to try and glean any insights unknown to date by the authorities. That was an option Brandy wished to keep open anyway. Tomorrow he could assess the organized climbing activities which were still persisting into late autumn in the Valley. Then he would know better what entry or guise might be most productive. The key to this part of the investigation seemed to lie in quiet, unobtrusive fact-gathering. No aliases were in order here, but there were certain advantages to beginning in the dark and allowing the local "experts" to bring you to the light. They would spin tall tales and exaggerate the size of the brutes that got away, but they might also haul out the speculation skeletons and the rumor wagons, too. The police would have the straight story, and others could fill in any remaining gaps. If there was new territory to be identified, unorthodoxy and cleverness were where smart money was to be invested.

There was snow falling on Big Oak Flat Entrance Station to Yosemite National Park. The wizened old Park Ranger propped up in the booth in the oversized Smokey hat rasped, "Tioga's closed. Valley's open. Got chains? Never mind. Prob'ly won't need 'um. It's just a fresh dusting. Tomorrow I don't know, though." Litany complete, Brandon handed the man the twenty dollar vehicle fee and drove on along the clear wet roadway through the white terrain up past Crane Flat and down along the twisting roadway high above the canyon of the Merced River. The stone retaining walls along the road were less reassuring than they had

probably been to the drivers who had more slowly and carefully negotiated these routes just after their completion by
the Civilian Conservation Corps in the Thirties and Forties.

Soon the twists and the grades evened out through
the forests and Brandy began to recognize the landmarks of
Yosemite Valley. No matter how many times as a college
student Brandy had come here, arrival in this valley
continued to be an intensely awe-inspiring, almost religious,
experience. A museum of natural monuments which men
could climb on, build under, and write about all they wanted,
but still remain insignificant before. Yosemite is beautifully
humbling. Always.

It was completely dark when Brandy pulled into the
Lodge parking area and stretched out the muscle knots in
his legs and back and arms with a stroll across the Lodge's
huge lounge, past the massive fireplace, to the main desk.
The lovely young woman across the reception counter
beamed immediate recognition at Brandon's name and with a
twinkle in her eye replied, "Oh, of course! Cabin 43. Your
wife already checked in earlier. Just a little while ago. She
said you'd probably need a second key. Here you are. Have
a nice stay in the valley, Mr. Drake." Brandy beheld the key
in his hand as if he'd never before seen one. "And . . .
congratulations!" the desk clerk added with a wink, "It must
have been awful to start off an anniversary holiday with car
troubles, but now that you're here, I'm sure everything will
be just perfect! If you need anything, just call us!"

Cabin 43 was a stunned stroll across the Lodge's
huge lounge, past the massive fireplace, with a pin-up smile
to hide the rush of anger, out the great doors, back to the
still-cooling, still-ticking rented car. The snow-rain mix taunted
him, aimed for his nose and eyes. Cabin 43 was a brief spin
around the one-way driveway, turning past the valley floor

pine until the brights reflected 4-3 beside the fourth cabin in the row. The Chevy crunched to a halt on the gravel between two other rented cars with California plates.

Anger had been replaced by uncertainty. Maybe it was a simple case of error. Another Drake? Or a similar name, perhaps. Poor memory at the desk, maybe? No need to jump to conclusions. Maybe it would have been best to challenge it right there and then at the desk, rather than to bite the lower lip and say what Brandy had long since learned to say whenever the facts suddenly drop-kicked him in unexpected ways. "Of course," he had said, neutrally. You could always recover later from a flat "Of course". No one in the English speaking world knew what "Of course" meant. And everyone was always ready to assume you were agreeing with them.

The lights were on in 43, but no one was moving around in the main room. Craning off the low front porch, Drake could just make out through the curtained windows a woman lying across the bed. She lay on her back and seemed to have fallen asleep with a large white towel draped across her torso. Voyeur tightness of Brandon's throat gave way to renewed anger as the woman rolled her head away from the windows and gave Brandy a good view of her profile and her electric frizz of clean hair.

In a rush of vengefulness Drake silently opened the outer door, slid his key into the lock, gave it a hard, angry twist, and shoved the big door inward. The outer door punctuated his arrival with its locking clank. The woman on the bed sat up with a lurch, one wrist pushing hair from her sleepy brow while the other arm flailed out to gain some balance against the too-soft mattress. She was wincing and frowning and straining through the sleepiness to remember who and where she was, and to recognize the tall, thin man who had just barged into the bedroom. The towel fell down to her lap, baring her chest.

Her mouth opened to say something, but before

her neuronal clutch could ease out to engage her mind to the oral apparatus, Brandy seized the lull. His voice boomed: "My per diem fees are *significantly* increased if I am expected to marry my client, *Mrs*. Drake. So nice that you announced to all of Yosemite village that I was about to arrive. This has probably blown virtually every chance I may have had to get certain types of information about your husband, *but* if there's anything I can get you, *dear*, don't hesitate to give me a call."

"Wait a minute," she slurred, still half asleep. "Wait a minute." Both hands clutched at the electric hair, pushing it against the sides of her head. The towel still lay in a heap on her lap. "You've got to believe me . . . I never meant to have it happen this way. It was all a *big* misunderstanding." She took a deep breath and stretched her eyes and struggled to clear the fog in her brain. "Wait a minute. What time is it?" She searched her bare wrist. Frowned. Looked around for a clock. Looked back at Brandon. "Let me remember . . ." she fumbled. "I know . . . When I checked in this afternoon, before I requested a private room I just asked to find out if you were here yet and, I guess, the woman at the desk assumed . . . I mean, I didn't really *say* we were married."

"Who did?"

"*She* did. And I guess . . ." Julia's voice waned to an almost inaudible thinness. "I guess I just let her go on thinking it."

"Great! Good planning! What next, Mrs. Drake?"

She cast her eyes down toward her lap and glimpsed her own dark coffee-and-cream nipples, very exposed and very erect in the cool cabin air. She startled and grabbed the loose edge of the towel to cover herself. She glanced up self-consciously to see if Brandon had noticed. He seemed oblivious. He was still glaring at her face.

"You're mad, aren't you?" she asked.

"Not yet, but I'll simmer down in a few minutes.

Right now, I'm still *raging*!"

"Oh, dear," she said ruefully, "I guess I wasn't thinking about everything. I mean, I didn't see what difference it could make. There are two beds in the cabin here, but I can understand if you . . ."

"I told you two nights ago what you could do to help. You could have stayed available to the telephone, at home in Vancouver, ready to answer questions when I have them, managing to stay out of my way."

"So do you want me to leave? I just wanted to see . . . where it all happened."

"Right."

"I . . . I'll go up to the office and get another room. Right now. Is that what you want?" Without waiting for an answer, she started to gather herself up from the bed.

"Oh, sure. And did you rent a brass band you can lead when you go marching through the lobby? In case anyone staying at the lodge is sufficiently deaf that by tomorrow morning they won't have heard all about the holidaying couple in 43 who didn't even spend their first night in the valley together without taking separate rooms? I mean, why didn't you tell them you're pregnant, too?"

She was an echo in the distance when she replied, "I did."

"You *what*? Jesus, Julia!"

Julia clutched the towel to her breasts and burst into huge sobs. She howled undecipherable laments through the muffle of the fluffy folds and Drake just stood in the center of the room, feeling like a bully and wagging his head in helpless frustration.

"I was just standing there at the desk," Julia whimpered. "I got another sick wave and . . . she looked so concerned and nice I explained that it happens all the time, but less now, and then I had to explain that . . ." After many long moments Julia sucked in two sobs. Her face contorted in a parody of the mask of Greek tragedy. Through reddened, puffy cheeks she sobbed, "It's not like I . . . What can I do? I blew it. I'm sorry. What do you want me to do? Drive back to San Francisco? I'm . . ." She tried to inhale, but it came in sob-catches again, until the final word could be crooned out of a solid base of convincing self-pity. ". . . sorry."

Brandy closed his eyes firmly to rebalance himself, to deal with the unbelievable, the ridiculous, and he managed to step back just far enough from the scene there in the cabin in Yosemite to appreciate it for all its absurd humor. When he opened his eyes again, she was still sitting on the bed with the towel clutched to her bosom, watching him, waiting for his reaction.

"Tell me something," Brandon said calmly.

"Anything," she whispered.

"Is there enough hot water for a nice long bath for Mr. Drake, or did Mrs. Drake use it all up?"

"Does that mean I should stay?"

"We'll talk after I take my bath. I'm cold and damp and dirty and hungry, so please just leave me alone until I feel more human. Okay?"

Four

By the time Brandy had extricated himself from the tiny tub, and dried and combed and shaved and brushed the various parts of his body to the clean, lively tingliness that he had so craved to feel as his deserved reward for a long day of travel, the Julia debacle was fading to a level of mild situation comedy. She was presumptuous and absurd, but there was something ingratiating about her style, too. And she was the sister of an old and good friend. What the hell?

He sashed the terry-cloth robe securely at his waist, pulled open the bathroom door, and stepped into the main room of the cabin. Julia was sitting on the edge of her bed, in a conservative dark burgundy dress, frizzy hair held back neatly with combs, her eyes as modestly and tastefully made up as could be expected to obscure the redness and puffiness from her earlier cloudburst of tears. Her hands were folded on her lap.

"Feeling better?" she asked, tentatively.

Brandy smiled and looked around him. The room was

neat and tidy, his suitcase had been unpacked, and the only sport jacket and dress shirt and tie he'd brought with him were hung on the hanger at the back of the closet door. "Did someone call a valet?"

"Peace offering. And you said you were hungry, so I thought we should go out for supper as soon as you're ready. The only place open now is the formal dining room over at the Ahwahnee Hotel, and they'll only be seating for another half hour, so I thought I'd be ready. I just made reservations for us." She stood up and walked toward the front door. "I'll wait over in the lobby for you, if you wish. So you can get dressed in private. Okay?"

Brandy nodded and smiled. "That won't be necessary, but suit yourself." He unsashed his robe and began to dress. Julia hesitated at the door, her back to Brandon. "That could get a little inconvenient for us, don't you think?" he asked. "I assume it's not a big issue with you, or you wouldn't have considered sharing the cabin with me."

"But I wouldn't want you to think . . ." Julia began to protest.

"If I were really bothered by having you watch me dress, I could always go into the bathroom. I grew up in an open-door family, too. Why don't you just sit back down. I'll only be a couple of minutes."

Julia turned around self-consciously. "Okay. I just don't want you to feel . . . Wait a minute!" she exclaimed. "How did you know I came from a -- what did you call it? -- an 'open-door family'?"

"Your brother was my roommate in the co-ops at Berkeley. Remember?"

"What else do you know about me?"

Brandon raised an eyebrow at her. "Lots!" She frowned. He grinned. "Truce?"

"Truce!" Julia grinned back. "Okay. But *do* hurry. I can't eat much in the mornings these days, so by evening I'm starving!"

They were seated in the cathedral-like dining hall at the Ahwahnee by the maitre d', who brought the formal menus for them to read by candlelight. The dining room was surprisingly full, considering the season. There were couples of varying ages, and several family groups, many of whom chattered in low voices in foreign languages. Brandy heard snatches of German and French on the way to their table.

Brandon dug into his right breast pocket for his half-lens granny-style, nose-perching reading glasses. Badge of presbyopia. Don't leave home without them. There are alternatives to glasses, any of which can help people over the age of thirty-five to deal with a combination of low light and small print, but restaurant waiters get visibly upset when patrons pull flashlights out of their pockets and handbags in order to see their menus. As an old friend of Brandy's once pointed out, if presbyopia were the only curse of aging which Brandy ever experienced, he had no reason whatsoever to bitch. And it was. So he didn't.

He looked up over the tops of the granny-rims to see Julia suppressing a giggle. He frowned. She couldn't contain herself.

"You look so . . ." she groped for words between giggles, ". . . so *professorial* in those!"

Brandy shifted the glasses further down his nose and continued to stare at her. "I think, dear Julia, that I prefer what a wonderful Vancouver friend named Alexa told me last month when she said I looked *sexy* in them."

Julia put her index knuckle to her lips to steady herself. "Oh, but you do. You do look sexy. Most men do. I mean . . ."

"That's *enough*, Julia. For god's sakes. I'll probably settle for the kindly old professor image a little later in life, but for now . . ."

"Mind if I ask how old you are?" Julia grinned again.

"Same as your brother. In fact, our birthdays are just three days apart."

"Sexier all the time."

"Meaning?"

"Oh, nothing. I've just always had a weakness for older men."

"How fortunate, Mrs. Drake."

"Oh, yes. I'd almost forgotten."

Brandon rolled his eyes toward the ceiling. "How quickly they forget!"

Julia's smile was devious. A wine smile. But she hadn't had any wine. And Brandy became even more convinced that they shouldn't have any wine with their dinner. Wine always held the risk of fogging judgement. At least, for him it did. Particularly about women whom fate had declared his roommates.

They ordered, and while the salads were being munched and crunched, Julia turned serious. "Is it too early to ask? When do you think we'll find Farmer?"

"Yes."

"Yes?"

"Yes, it's too early to ask. And it's more likely to be 'whether' than 'when'."

"Oh, I *know* we'll find him. He seems so close. I guess being here where he was last seen just adds to the suspense, but I have a real sense that I'm going to be with him again soon." Brandon watched her. Her manner was neither funereal nor flippant, but merely matter-of-fact. As if she were commenting on the weather. "Maybe it's too much suspense."

"You've been in the Valley, now. You could go back home tomorrow. I'd make up a cover story at the lodge about a sick relative. Might be best."

The imp returned to Julia's eyes. "Don't worry, honey. Your sweet, pregnant wife won't ever leave you in this great big valley alone!" When she saw the look of resignation on

Brandy's face, Julia burst into another fit of giggles which turned heads three tables away.

As if by tacit agreement, their conversation never returned to their mission in the valley. After a delightful dinner, while they awaited their desserts, the maitre d' was making his rounds and stopped at the Drake table. He was in full battle dress: black tie and dinner jacket. His spray-fixed jet-black hair was showing just a touch of distinguished grey at the temples. He held his hands together, fingers slightly spread, affectedly, like a recent heathen convert who hadn't quite mastered yet the position for praying. He worked the tables, Julia had pointed out during the appetizers, like a politician works a crowd of voters before an election.

"You two look *so* happy together," he chimed, in a forced sing-song voice. "I thought I'd better find out if the speculations of the other guests here in the dining room are correct. People can't help noticing such a *happy* couple, can they? Are you on your honeymoon?"

Julia blushed. Her first real sign of any embarrassment. She began to shake her head in a firm negative reply when Brandy decided to get back some of his own. "Yes. Yes, we are!" he declared proudly.

"Well, how lovely!" the maitre d' interjected, catching Julia's startled gasp before she was able to fumble her way to words. "Congratulations! You really do look *that* obviously happy, the way you talk and the way you look at one another . . . If you don't mind my asking, is this by any chance your first night . . . I mean since you've been *together*?" He rolled his eyes. "You know what I mean!"

"Yes," replied Brandy, smooth as honey. "As a matter of fact, I guess it really is."

The maitre d' beamed at Julia and she blushed even deeper and harder, right down to the open collar of her burgundy dress.

As he wandered off, threading his way through

more tables and more homilies, Julia looked around at the approving faces of the people at nearby tables who had overheard the conversation with the maitre d'. She maintained her forced smile as she whispered, "Thanks a lot, sweetheart. What if he talks to the receptionist over at our lodge? How's that going to look?"

"As if you've been a very *bad* girl, Mrs. Drake."

She pursed her lips in frustration.

"I'm not usually a vengeful man, Julia," shrugged Brandon, "but sometimes . . . I just can't resist. And you have to admit . . . I owed you one."

The rain and snow had stopped speckling the windshield on the quiet drive over to the Lodge.

Julia and Brandy were both so tired by their long drives and by the combination of the grand meal, the cool temperatures, and the altitude that they said little as they prepared for their beds. Their good-nights were unadorned and resignedly cooperative. The truce held.

On his winding way down the dark curve of stairs to the private places of deep, deep sleep, Brandy lingered a moment on the reflection of certain earlier glimpses which, although they had fleetingly evaded his consciousness at the time, now invaded in full concert, replete with detail in sight, sound, and even smell. Julia. His first impressions upon his arrival in the Valley earlier in the day. In all her exposure and nakedness on the soft bed, before self-consciousness (or whatever it was) had caused her to draw up the velour towel curtain from around her well-contoured thighs and hips to cover her ripe and full-breasted chest. It was a nice combination, that natural voluptuousness above, and the not-too-narrow waist just beginning to fill with the first-time pregnancy, still too early to be detected by any real enlargement of the belly. Her light skin tone suggested she'd spent very little time in the sun, or was one of those women who never really tan. Whatever it was, the flashes Brandon viewed and replayed mentally as he relaxed into sleep were of a slight rosy flush across the upper chest and neck, probably from her recent hot bath. Or could it have been a flush of arousal? In the darkness of the cabin, Drake clenched his eyes fiercely to drive the lewd thought away.

No question. Many men find pregnant women erotic. And they *are* erotic. Nothing wrong with that. They always had that effect on Brandy. He sensed it. And he could always detect it as soon as he was in a room with a woman. Even if she was early in the first trimester. He knew other men that could tell, too. Even cerebral Mason, his crazy inventor friend, had admitted to that once.

To make things worse, Julia was one of those special ones who were so honestly and naturally erotic that you had the sense they couldn't help themselves. The effect was entirely beyond effort on her part. But for crying out loud, she was a *flake*. And a client. And looking for her lost husband. And the last thing Drake needed was mixed feelings about locating Farmer Hobbs. There were plenty of other erotic women in the world. Right.

Brandy concentrated on squeezing the Julia images from his mind's eye, but he felt the woman lying in the next bed, less than five feet away from him. He heard her soft breathing. Opened his eyes and saw her lying there, covered by the thin blanket, backlit by the glow of the yellow bulb from the porch light. His mind overlaid her silhouette, breathing softly, with the earlier vision. The frizzy, electric hair. The big breasts, strong nipples, solid wrists and ankles. Not a big woman, but a solid one. The smoothness of her skin and the automatic precision of her fingers clutching the folds of the towel. Once again. In his mind's eye.

Brandy squeezed his eyes tightly again until the

entire visual field was scrambled to a checkerboard of deep azure on a sea green background. For god's sakes, she was *taken*. Let her alone.

Julia's steady breathing was interrupted by a deep sigh. Then she resumed her steady slow rhythm, and suddenly Julia was climbing high on a rock face on one of the craters of the moon, shouting taunts down to Brandy, telling him to hurry up, that the soup would be too cold to eat. Soup? Brandy frowned. Then the other part of him smiled. He watched the eroticism of Julia slip away, just out of sight up the mountain. Let her go at last. Sleep had won.

Good night, Mrs. Hobbs. Tomorrow was another day. An information day, hopefully.

By eight o'clock, when Drake returned from his morning wake-up walk, the remains of the nocturnal smattering of early snow had already begun to shrink to odd patches on the needle-strewn valley floor. The early morning sun felt fine and warm on the bare skin of his face and neck and hands. The sound of water in the basin and the crumple of sheets and blankets on the bed nearest the window said Julia was in the bathroom. The herbal scent of Fa soap and piquant woman-smell competed with the wood smoke and ash aromas which emanated from the wooden walls and from the stone of the small, empty hearth in the corner of cabin 43. An authoritative writch-ritch and swish announced the end of oral ablutions.

A few towel pats later the bathroom door swung open and Julia charged into the main room past Brandon in much the same way as she'd charged past him in his own condo only two days earlier, when they first met. "Ready!" she commanded. "I'm hungry! Let's go!"

The breakfast service at the Lodge was swift and the cuisine basic but satisfactory. Brandy managed to off-balance Julia's a.m. assertiveness just long enough to lay down the ground rules of the day's activities to her as they ate. She seemed to listen attentively and seriously, and only twice asked him for clarifications of what he was telling her.

By the time he jotted his cabin number on the breakfast bill, Brandy was anxious to get outside into the cool mountain air. He had dressed more carefully than usual for the day's projected activities, but the concern had been for supreme outdoor comfort, not for sitting in heated dining rooms. He had pulled his heavy cotton two-way stretch pants, the ones with the big patch pockets, over the skin-thick layer of Thinsulite underwear, and on top of the light cotton turtleneck he wore his old dark plaid Pendleton. Unbuttoned and untucked to keep him cool, buttonable and tuckable as need might arise for more warmth. For protection against the rain and snow which squalled up on no notice in the October mountains, Brandy carried his smooth navy Gore-Tex shell, with its drawstring hood and Velcro wrist adjusters. No gloves. Not for a day hike. He hated filling his pockets with them. He pushed his dining room chair back from the table and relaced his aged dirt-brown hiking boots with their well-travelled Vibram soles.

Putting aside the creature-comfort aspects of his intention to take a nice leg-stretching hike during the day, Brandon's choice of attire mainly addressed ulterior concerns about his ready acceptance into conversation by people who worked in the valley. Hikers and climbers are swept by definite fads in styles of attire, but certain timeless standards transcend trends. Comfort and utility have always been the key. Only the technology changes. The principles remain the same. The invention of Gore-Tex reduced the weight and stiffness of oiled canvas outerwear, reduced the dependence on the life-saving insulating properties of wet wool, but a serious outdoorsman still keeps the wool there, just in case. It isn't token sentimentalism. It's survival. And other serious climbers and hikers recognize the worn-but-well-cared-for signs of what any forced combination of lingo and bullshit would take hours to establish, and would still leave in guarded doubt. Outdoors people have their own clubs with their own uniforms, and it seemed to Brandy a clear advantage to rejoin. He couldn't and wouldn't pretend to be a climber --- his experience with climbing had been only rudimentary, with almost no technical work --- but there was likely to be reasonable openness by climbers toward a non-pretentious cross-over from backpacking and hiking, and Brandy intended to exploit it.

Julia's attire was a different matter. It was outrageous. Which was one more reason for which Brandon's plans called for him to work solo. Still, there were places where an exuberant "wife" could be useful. People are, by and large, less suspicious of couples who ask questions than they are of men asking questions on their own.

They left Julia's car and drove the Corsica over to the village and parked. Just past the post office, Brandy dropped Julia off at the Ansel Adams Gallery while he walked on to the Visitor Center. There were less than a dozen park visitors milling around inside the complex of rooms and exhibits which were designed to comfortably accommodate maybe one hundred seventy-five or so. Various uniformed park personnel floated from corner to corner of the exhibit areas attempting to navigate that fine line between garrulous eagerness to serve the public and competent formality.

A plain young woman stood behind some sort of open Dutch door arrangement to the left of the main entrance, beneath a large sign which read "Hiking and Climbing: Information and Registration." An elderly couple was engaging her in animated conversation. Much head nodding and wide gesturing with arms, pointing at rocky landmarks high above the valley, as if the walls of the Visitor Center were transparent around them. Atop the narrow counter along the wall beside her door there were several racks of small registration slips and a large, open registration book of the conventional Park Service type.

Topographical maps of the park, of the valley, and of the entire northern and central Sierra, covered the long wall above the counter. A smaller sign beside the racks read:

All climbers and hikers must register here. Please advise Park Rangers as to your expected return time and the number in your party, and be sure to check in upon your return to the valley. Climbing and hiking safety is everyone's business.

If the Park Visitor Center is closed, you may check in or out at the registration box attached to the information kiosk adjacent to the main doors.

Another sign advised "Weather conditions in the Park may change suddenly at any time. Please be prepared." Brandy reviewed the pamphlets about the various trails and climbing areas. He chose a few as relevant to his plans for the day.

As soon as the elderly couple in their old hiking boots and bright, new, scarlet gaiters finished with their questions and shuffled away from the Registration and Information lady, Brandy drifted over to where she stood behind her countertop doorway. She wore a Smokey the Bear uniform, no hat, no makeup, and her hair was neatly held up with a dark brown comb. The tag on her left breast pocket flap said her name was Diane Backhaus. She greeted him with a simple smile: "Good morning. May I help you?"

"Yes. I was looking for a nice long day-hike. Are the cables still up on Half-Dome?"

"No. I'm sorry. The storms had been icing them up too much, so the park patrol took them down last weekend. Have you ever been up the Four Mile Trail? It's pretty strenuous, but . . ."

"No problem. That's the one that goes to Glacier Point?"

"Right. You know your way around the valley pretty well." She considered him for a moment, taking in the effect of the seasoned hiking attire on his lanky frame. He was tall and sandy-haired and looked quite fit. Not muscle-heavy. More the long-distance marathon type. His face held a boyish grin, but the grey eyes were unwavering and strangely wise. She gave him a "safe and unpretentious" stamp of approval for the moment. Park Rangers, not unlike policemen, have to be able to make assessments of personality quickly.

"I came here a lot when I was in college," Brandy replied, "but I haven't been up in quite a few years."

Her face became more animated as she warmed to the interaction. With a big smile, her plainness became a healthy sort of pretty. "Be sure and register before you go up, and let us know when you get down from the Point, too. And remember that the days are very short right now. So count on darkness by five-thirty. It could take you nearly eight hours, round trip, depending on your pace."

"Well, my pace is fast, but I like to stop fairly often to spend time just absorbing everything along the way, if you know what I mean."

"The *only* way to do it."

"How long have you been here in the Valley?"

She looked serious. Career mode. "Just under a year. A year in mid-December."

"So you were here a couple of months ago when that

fellow went missing? Some guy from out of country? I read about it in the papers. Sounds like a real mystery."

"Oh, yes. The Canadian climber."

"Found him yet?"

"No. But then most people guess we never will. You see, we're still not sure that it was an unplanned disappearance."

"Really? I thought he was climbing and just never came down. I mean a climbing accident. The papers said he was up there alone."

"Except that nobody ever found any sign of him or any of his technical equipment. And that's unusual. Even for solo climbing. It's not as easy as you'd think to disappear in this valley. And his room --- he had a cabin over at the Lodge --- it didn't look as if he planned to come back."

"What do you mean?"

"The police found only a few of his city clothes there. No extra climbing gear and no toiletries and the maid service said the bed hadn't been slept in for two nights before he disappeared. Looks a little strange."

"Really? What would you make of that?"

"They're still not sure, but there is always the possibility he wanted to disappear, that he never planned on coming back."

"And wanted people to think he'd died?"

"You never know. That happened here once before about eight years ago. My supervisor told me about it. A guy who'd gotten mixed up in some sort of drug thing in the Los Angeles area. He didn't want anybody looking for him."

"And?"

"They mounted a major park search with the Mountain Rescue people, just like we did in July for the Canadian guy, and even found this guy's gear up behind Washington Column, above some rugged rock falls. They had to leave the file open, even though the body wasn't found. Apparently the police called here a month after he disappeared to say he'd been found in Tucson. Dead. He'd been using another name, so they knew it was a planned thing. Only I guess somebody else figured it all out quicker than the police did. Some people do some pretty crazy things."

"And you think that's what the Canadian guy was doing?"

"Maybe. Nobody knows."

"But wouldn't you think somebody would be more clever about what he left in his room, things like that?"

"I don't know. The fellow who left his gear above the Column should have known they'd search the rocks below with a fine tooth comb and not find his body . . . Maybe these people just want to give themselves a little running time. I don't know. But I can tell you it costs the taxpayers a heck of a lot a money to search for them!"

"I bet. Did this guy --- the Canadian --- did he register his climbs here?"

"Oh, yeah. He was good about that. He was a regular in this valley. An amateur, but a regular. I'd seen him for a week or so in the spring, after I first came here. He was down with three other people from up north. Seemed pretty safety conscious. That's another reason it looked so funny to me, his suddenly going on his first solo and then disappearing like that."

"So he was climbing alone?"

"That's right. Let me show you. You might find it interesting to see how we use the registry. We like for hikers and climbers to know about that. It increases your respect for the importance of accurate registration."

Ranger Diane pulled another large volume off of the shelf in the small office behind the Dutch doors and flipped it open to July. She slid her index fingers deftly along the entries until she found what she was looking for. "Here," she declared. "Here are his entries for the four days before he disappeared. See? Group climbs with three other people. All of them regulars. They'd all climbed with him before, but they'd come up a week before him, and they all had to go home to L.A. in midweek. He'd planned to stay on until the end of the week. I was on duty here, on the second day when they went up the lower part of Sentinel from the south side. I remember I asked the guy how it was going for them and he said everything was just great. He was very pleasant. They returned that night at . . . looks like eight-forty-five. I was off duty by then, but there are the signatures. All the other times, they checked out for the climbs before the Center opened by leaving the slips in the box outside the door. And that's what he did the day he disappeared. Most climbers have to do that because they leave so early in the morning. You can tell by the initials which Ranger transferred the entry from the slips to the book for them." She closed the book and hefted it back to its place on the office shelf.

"Is anybody still looking for the guy?"

"Not any more. I mean, we always keep our eyes open when we're out there, but I don't think anybody really expects to find anything now. We haven't heard from the state police in over a month, so I'd guess they're out of ideas now, too."

"Well, I'll keep my eyes open when I'm hiking today." Brandy grinned.

Ranger Diane chuckled. "You'd have to have pretty good vision to see anything from the Four Mile trail. When he disappeared, he was signed out to Arrowhead Spire, just east of the Upper Falls, on the *north* side of the valley."

Brandy laughed with her. "I see what you mean. Guess it's not too likely I'd see anything of him on the south side of the valley. But say, isn't the Arrowhead supposed to be a really difficult climb. I mean, why would somebody pick that as his first solo?"

"Nobody knows why, although everybody who climbed with the guy seemed to agree that he probably had the technical expertise to do that climb. The surprise was because the guy had a reputation as such a safety nut. There's no belay protection for a person on solo, you know."

"Hmmm. People do strange things, I guess. Well," Brandon nodded, "thank you for the trail information."

"That's what we're here for. Be sure and register your hike."

"Right." He turned on the boyish look again. He extended his hand. "By the way, my name is Brandy Drake. And unless you're wearing someone else's name badge, I assume you are Ranger Diane Backhaus. Maybe I'll see you here tomorrow, Diane."

She shook his hand. "Everybody around here calls me 'Dibbie'. But Diane is okay, too. You can call me whichever you prefer."

A group of four adults with a stringy-haired teenage girl in tow shouldered their way through the main doors and looked around to orient themselves to the visitor center. Ranger Diane saw them glance her way and straightened herself reflexively. She nodded back to Brandy and said briefly, and a bit too loudly, "Have a nice stay here in the park, Mr. Drake."

Brandon leaned forward and whispered, "Brandy."

Diane smirked shyly at her own mode change and said, "Okay."

Five

Julia was standing on the wide walkway in front of the Gallery, looking out across the grand expanse of the Big Meadow and the south wall of the valley beyond. The sun was dazzling and the meadow's grasses were now golden and ready for winter. She had her hands stuffed into the pockets of her beige full-length trench coat. Her running shoes were as white as in a Mr. Clean commercial. When she sensed his approach, Julia turned and observed the jiggling laces of his boots vacantly.

"What's the matter?" Brandy asked.

"Nothing," Julia answered too quickly. "It's just . . . you know that feeling I told you about? It's even stronger now. He's up here. Near." She refocused her gaze onto Brandy's face and beamed warmly up at him. New persona. "Find out what you wanted?"

"A few things. Now for the Mountaineering School. Enjoy the photography in the gallery?"

"A lot of it is strictly Turista Commercial, but the Adams stuff is pure genius. Absolutely awesomely *won*-derful! But it's like . . . like his *museum*. Only so much of it you can absorb at a time. Right?"

"Right. Now, remember, give me a full five minutes, and watch for a signal after you come in. In case I change tacks. Okay?"

The full head of fluffy, wavy off-white hair on the man at the Mountaineering School was just a little too homogeneous and perfect for a sun bleach job. And the tan was not what you'd expect on a true albino. This was one of those pitiful middle-agers who every morning stare into their dresser mirrors, anxiously eyeing the rough places and wrinkle patterns and dark spots on the face, dabbing at the meticulously brushed hair, then inspecting the brush for newly jettisoned strands. This was a vain man who carefully avoided looking into the unforgiving eyes in the mirror. A man who clawed after his elusive youth, hoping that undivided attention to the various scourges of age and attrition would somehow keep life from being edged so relentlessly away from him hour by painful hour.

The only man in the log-frame cabin office of the Yosemite Mountaineering School, Whitey slouched on a high stool next to the glass case portion of the counter, leaning against the cash register, listening via a pair of miniature earphones to a portable CD player, chewing a minuscule piece of gum, and studying a supplier's catalogue of climbing equipment. When Brandon cruised through the front door of the School, Whitey gave a self-conscious pat to the front of his coiffure, looked up at Brandon, and eyed him carefully as he approached. After a basic assessment, Whitey didn't bother to sit up straight.

A name plate taped to the side of the cash register said "Phil Lesyk, King of This Place". Brandy wondered if Whitey and Phil were one and the same.

"Help you?" Whitey grunted.

"Yeah. You know where I can find Phil Lesyk?"

The man looked Brandy over more carefully before he answered, "Who wants to know?"

"My name's Brandon Drake. I heard Phil knows more about climbing than just about anyone around. That true?"

"Some people seem to think so. I'm Phil. What can I do for you?"

"I want to know about the rock climbing here in the valley. Anything going on, or is it too close to winter?"

"A few people climbing. You lookin' for somebody to climb with? Most of the regulars are gone, of course. They go south with the ducks and the geese." Canned grimace for canned line. Drake forced a matching grimace. "What's your experience level?"

"Novice."

"Oh," he sniffed, and his smile went lopsided.

"I just happened to be here for a few days and I thought I'd like to learn a little more about basic climbing. Any classes going on?"

"Like I said, most of my instructors have gone elsewhere for the season, where the weather is better for climbing, or they're doing other things for the winter. Rock bums. Doug and Mary are out with the only group we've got, but it's an intermediate group that's been going for nearly two weeks together. They're almost finished. Leaving for L.A. next Tuesday. You don't want to start with them."

"Any absolute beginner classes? It wouldn't hurt me at all to start from scratch."

"Not much call for starter classes this time of year. You have to be already hooked to want to begin in the cold weather. Know what I mean?" He paused and frowned as he continued to size Brandon up. "I do some teaching, but without a group, I'd have to charge you private rates. Fifty-five an hour. And that's only if I can get a hold of

Annie to come in and mind the shop for me here. You look pretty fit and lean. Pretty tall, too. Probably pick up wherever you left off in no time. How many days did you say you were going to be here? Like, how many did you want to climb?"

"Three. After today. I'm already committed to a hike this afternoon. But if there are any other beginners in the valley looking for lessons too --- you know, like other singles or couples --- I wouldn't mind splitting up the lesson time and cutting costs."

Whitey winced. Obviously not the kind of talk he wanted to hear. Brandon's gilded edges were dulling a bit. "Annie might teach for less. She's not full-time, of course, and she's not on contract with the School during the winter months, but maybe we can work something out. Give me an hour or so. She was supposed to leave for New Zealand sometime the end of this month, but I saw her yesterday and she didn't mention anything about pulling stakes yet, so let me see what I can do for you." He picked up the phone and punched in a number. As they waited for the electronic tendrils to reach out across the valley for someone named Annie, the bell on the door jingled.

In bounced Julia. She was a woman whose meekest entry to any gathering was likely to be about as inconspicuous as the arrival of Mick Jagger on stage during a Stones concert. Even in a shop full of the wild and trendy turquoises and yellows and emeralds of climbing ropes and climbing shoes and the plethora of hardware and support gear and sacks in which to store the gear and carry it, Julia was striking. Once inside the door, she peeled out of her trench coat. On the front of her sweatshirt bright orange letters blared out from the Day-Glo yellow background in a way which cowed everything in the climbing shop. The sweatshirt proclaimed "Nooners are for Women of ALL ages". Julia's legs in the shiny fabric of her bicycle-racing-style pink-and-black skin-tight pants produced an effect that was less like walking and more like pulsing. Brandy usually didn't notice clothing much, unless he had a solid reason to remember what someone was wearing, either for later identification or for his own protection. He couldn't believe he'd missed during breakfast the effect Julia was now displaying. Hadn't she taken her coat off? Or had she perhaps changed clothes since breakfast? An altogether convincingly outrageous woman.

She glanced all around the shop until her eyes came to rest on Brandy. He nodded his head quickly to the affirmative and beckoned to her with a crooked finger. Julia strode directly toward him. "Arranged for your climbing yet, honey?" she asked.

"Working on it."

As Julia joined them, Whitey sat up very straight on his stool, raised a bleached eyebrow, licked his lips, and assumed a businesslike tone of voice on the phone. "Annie. Phil here. Got a fellow at the school wants some rockclimbing lessons. Starting tomorrow. He's here for three days. He's had some basics before. I've got nobody free to work with him. When did you say you were off to Down Under?" He cupped his hand over the receiver and rasped directly to Julia, "You climbing, too, sweetheart?"

Julia made a surprised face and an animated "No" expression. She pointed at Brandy. "*He's* the family climber. Not me."

"Too bad," he said, the first hint of sincerity to surface in his conversation. Back to the phone. "Yeah. Really? So you might have to leave day after tomorrow? Well, how about if you give him two days and I'll see if I can set up something else for his last day. Okay? Great. Why don't you drive into the valley and drop over to the school and meet him so you can arrange your times and equipment? Whatever you think you'll need. You can come as you are. No makeup required, sweetkins. He's got a cute lady here right now hanging on his arm. Even the famous Raggedy Annie wouldn't have a chance against this lady." He gave a distorted wink to Julia. "Right. I've already mentioned private rates." He cupped the phone again. "One-twenty for the day, or forty an hour. You okay with that?"

Brandy considered. Julia piped in on cue. "Go ahead, honey. We can afford it. And you'll never know until you've really given it a try. You only live once. Right?" Brandy looked doubtful about it, but nodded affirmative.

"Okay, sweetie," rasped Whitey into the phone. "No, no. That's fine. I'll take care of it. I just thought you might be coming into the valley before this afternoon anyway. You stay home and I'll set everything up. How about he meets you here at seven tomorrow morning? That early enough? I'll outfit him for you." He hung up. "Okay. We'll just do a little paper work. Liability waivers. Standard forms. Then I can outfit you. I should tell you. Annie is one terrific climber. Really knows her stuff. If Annie don't know it, it ain't known. World class . . ."

"What's her name? Her last name?" asked Brandy. He was amused that the woman climber who had been a poor second to Phil earlier in their conversation had now, after the arrival of Julia, become world-class. He wondered which was closest to fact. "I once knew a lady who called herself Raggedy Annie, but I don't remember she was into climbing at all."

"Annie Wharton. Don't know her maiden name. That was her husband's name. He was a climber, too."

"Was?"

"Died . . . I dunno . . . five, maybe six years back. Automobile got pasted on one of those granite faces out Highway One-Twenty. Wet roads. Not even snowing, for god's sakes. And he hadn't been drinking, either. Goes to show climbing isn't as dangerous as people crack it up to be. It's driving that'll kill you." He looked at Julia again, crossing his hairy arms over his chest to show off the muscles of his forearms. "You sure you don't want some lessons, too? It wouldn't cost much more. Climbing families have all kinds of adventure and fun! I could give you some of the theoretical stuff tomorrow morning while Annie and your husband --- are you guys married? --- do their workout at the floor faces. Then I could close the shop for a long lunch and take you bouldering to get you caught up so that the day after tomorrow you could go out and climb right along with him and Annie. I mean, you look pretty athletic. I'll bet you'd come along just fine." He licked his lips. Brandon squelched an urge to kick the stool out from under the obvious sonofabitch. Or to blow him a kiss. The urge welled up to do *something* mean.

Julia looked inquiringly at Drake. "Sounds like fun, hon. What do you think?"

With his back to Whitey, Brandon frowned at her. "I thought you wanted to take it easy this trip, dear."

Julia didn't take the hint. "Oh, I could always see how it goes and stop if it was too much for me. I never mind being a jamtart if I don't enjoy something. You know me."

"Yes, indeed. I *sure* do." Brandy considered the implications. What Julia did was her problem. If she wanted to have to deal one-to-one with Whitey's helping hands as she pushed and twisted her way up the sides of boulder ledges and cracks with him right below her, that was her problem. Furthermore, it would keep her out of Brandy's way. And she might even learn something of use about Farmer's disappearance. Brandon turned back to face Whitey again. "How much more would that cost us? To have both of us doing it?"

Whitey squinted into the nether reaches of the cosmos and computed. "Oh, we *like* to see new climbers get started. Let's say one-sixty for the day, for both of you, and call it even. Annie'll charge the same for the two of you when you go out together the day after tomorrow. How's that sound?"

Before Brandy could whittle that down twenty, which he was sure he could do, Julia torpedoed his whole gambit by throwing her arms around his neck and kicking up her feet and swinging on him, crooning, "Oh, honey. Thank you. This will be *so* much fun."

Oh, well. What the hell? It was her money.

Six

As they walked from the Mountaineering
Shop, Julia said she was hungry.
Very hungry. Then, before his eyes, she began to turn ashen
and then slightly greenish. After a lengthy visit to the Ladies'
at the Village General Store, her color had begun to return,
but Brandy still suggested maybe the hike wasn't such a
swift idea for her. She could rest back at the lodge while he
stretched his legs a bit and poked around in the valley for
more information about her missing husband. Julia protested
that all she needed was a little food in her belly and she'd be
fine. She ripped off back into the general store and emerged
about ten minutes later with a small bag full of the oddest
assortment of yogurts and licorice twists and sweet-and-
sour candies. When Brandy saw what she had at the bottom
of her bag, he let out a loud whoop.

"What's so funny?" she demanded.

"You're so . . . so . . . classic. I mean, it's great. I'm just
very amused. That's all." She dug to the base of the bag and
pulled out a small jar. She wrenched at the lid with a strained

grimace until it popped open and she greedily pulled out a big pickle. Brandy carried a wide grin on his face as he watched her. "I thought you didn't have any money with you this morning."

Julia slipped a hand into the band of her stretch pants and retrieved a credit card. "Desperation is *always* prepared." Brandy smiled more broadly and gave her a paternal pat on the tip top of her head. She crunched away at her pickle and said, "So? Wanna bickle, Mister?"

After a slow stroll back to the car, a momentarily sated Julia stashed her cache on the floor of the back seat and told Brandy she wanted to go back to the lodge now to change into "more suitable hiking attire" before they went for their hike. Still perplexed by her gigantic mood swings, Brandy took a quick pass by Cabin 43.

Julia emerged from the cabin just as Brandy had finished stuffing his coat pockets with some of the trail foods he'd cached in the back seat of the Corsica yesterday.

Brandy had looked forward to seeing what Julia considered suitable hiking attire. Her skin-tight pants still blared their contrasting waves of black and shocking Day-Glo pink. There'd be no losing sight of her on the trail. But she had exchanged her state-of-the-art white jogging shoes and their lime-green laces for well-worn, high-top hiking boots. Brandy had to be a little impressed with that, especially since he'd been wondering ever since she'd come bouncing into the mountaineering shop just how far she'd survive up the switchbacks before the ankle and leg strain would have her pleading to turn back. Her what-did-you-expect grin as she bounded over to him told him she was reading his thoughts. Annoying. Women shouldn't do that. No one should do that.

The Four Mile Trail suggested by Ranger Diane was too long for the remaining daylight hours, and there was a pilgrimage to be done, anyway. Julia had wanted to see exactly where Farmer had been climbing when he disappeared. When she rejoined him at the car in front of the Lodge, Julia pointed up at Yosemite Falls, high above them, and asked what trails went "up there".

"Up where?"

"You know. Up where Farmer went. Call it a sentimental journey, if you want," she said tensely. "I feel half brave and half afraid about it, but it's something I have to do."

"I'm sure we won't find anything up there. And we would have to go back into the village to register the hike, regardless of where we go. Not to mention, it's pretty late in the day to even *hope* we'd make it to the top of the Falls, depending upon what kind of shape you're in."

"I know, I know," she acquiesced. "But I'm feeling restless. Maybe a good long hike will get it out of my system. I don't guess Ansel Adams always registered his hikes, did he?" She looked back up at the Falls and seemed taken to a trance. Her face flattened and her voice dropped into a lower register. It happened so suddenly that even a seasoned P.I. type who thought he'd seen almost every nuance of temperament mankind could swing his way was struck by her eeriness. "He's up there. I know he's up there. I can still feel it. More than ever." Then something snapped free again and she shook her head very hard and bounced off and away toward the foot of the trail, shouting over her shoulder, "Come on, Brandy. I thought you were a *hiker*!"

The Upper Yosemite Falls trail began only two stone's throws away from the Lodge, right across the road. The trail worked its way up through the base of the rockfall just east of El Capitan, that imposing monolith of a glacial sculpture of grey granite which commands most of the valley and whose few cracks and ledges continue to provide new and ever-uglier ways to taunt the world's best climbers. And, occasionally, to kill them.

Brandy and Julia were crossing the first bench, about eight hundred feet above the valley floor, before they said a word to one another. Although he normally had to be especially aware of the necessity for tempering his long stride to make the first mile or so of any hike a nice warm-up for shorter-legged companions, Brandy discovered early in the hike that there was no reason to coddle Julia. She was a very game hiker indeed. The more he tested the limits, the more respect he had for how readily Julia kept pace with him.

Just before Columbia Rock, the trail traversed and climbed along a shoulder of sandy boulderslide, an area which gives way underfoot so often that the Parks trail maintenance people have to devote many hours of work each year just to maintaining some semblance of trail support by building rock-and-chicken-wire retaining walls, most of which disappear with the next shift or slide. Signs warn hikers against lingering there, despite the fact that the untreed openness of the slope affords the first excellent panorama of the Valley for those emerging from the lower, forested switchbacks. Julia pointed to the village. The shops and Visitor Center were already far enough below them to look like toys assembled on the brown-and-charcoal October carpet.

They passed two groups of junior high school hikers, trekking along with overburdened tear-drop daypacks and an assortment of caps and hats. Each group was led by a Ranger guide. Each of the guides, as he passed, said with his terse smile and weary brow that he was eager to get his group back down to the Visitor Center, or wherever they were bound, as soon as possible. Snippets of kid-talk popped up when the groups passed, generally about team sports or television shows or computer games, or quick jibes and digs at one another, things which clearly had nothing to do with the wilderness through which they were privileged to be travelling. It has always been that way with children in the wilderness. In spite of what our romantically distorted memories remind us *we* used to experience in the way of wordless awe and undivided adoration for our wilderness during our own youth. And yet people keep coming back. Maybe that's the best sign. In spite of all the negative impact their growing numbers continue to have on the quality of wilderness.

The Parks people have had to limit the number of hikers and backpackers on many of the High Sierra trails because so many people want to come back. They want to pack all their food and their water purifiers (which until recent years were not required), and their sleeping bags and their ground cloths and their ponchos and their spare socks and underwear and their flashlights and their maps and their toilet paper, and they want to carry all this stuff around on their backs through the rock and ridges of the high mountains for days and even weeks. And they carry their garbage out with them, most of them. People who would complain about carrying a load of groceries from the car into the house in the city. And they keep coming back to do it some more.

The kids had not been up in the high country overnight --- they were definitely not equipped for it --- and it was too early in the afternoon for them to have gotten all the way to the top of the Upper Falls and back down, no matter how early their treks had begun. It was barely noon and the round trip to the top of the nearly 2500 foot high waterfall takes more than seven hours for all but the most aggressive hikers. The kids had probably taken their time getting up to where the trail tucked into the slide area to the west of the Falls, where hikers could take short spur trails right to the base of the upper Falls. There the kids would have listened to a few Ranger stories before coming back down. It made good sense to keep kid-treks short and sweet.

Past the Columbia Rock lookout, Brandy and Julia continued up to where the trail slips beneath the overhanging cliffs and ledges, into a rocky staircase which relentlessly switchbacks its way up the wall. There the views open up onto the world's third highest waterfall --- the Yosemite Falls --- where it comes thundering its way down to the calmly meandering Merced River in the main floor of Yosemite Valley below. From the west wall Brandy was able to point out the Arrowhead Spire, about half a mile east of the Falls above them. It jutted out from the north wall of the valley like one of the flying buttresses of a Gothic French cathedral.

"That's where he disappeared? Climbing that?" she asked.

"That's what he put in the climbing register."

"How do you get to it? It just sort of hangs there."

"The climbers go up this trail first, then across the river and along the top edge of the wall. When you're next to where the spire sticks out from the wall, then you climb down onto the narrow saddle of rock which connects the spire and then you climb straight up the spire."

Julia squinted up at the spire, then back at Brandon. "You really must know this place well. Where did you learn all that?"

"Don't be too impressed. I read it in that book I was browsing while the guy at the mountaineering shop was getting his act together for the paperwork on our climbing lessons."

Agape at the spire again, she shook her head disdainfully. "Fools. They're all fools. They have to be. That's straight *up*! Crazy. I can't believe anyone would climb that alone. Least of all Farmer. He only did foolish things when he was trying to impress me, and he would have known this one *wouldn't* have impressed me."

"That's not the worst of it. That climb is included in the list which have already been free-soloed."

"Meaning?"

"Meaning at least one clown has climbed up that spire alone and without any ropes."

"Sweet Jesus."

"You still want to go up there? To see it up closer?"

"Can we get that far today?"

"I doubt it. You're a pretty good hiker, Julia, but we got a late start."

"Then maybe we should save it for a day or two, until after we find out more from the climbing people. Going all the way up there doesn't seem so important right now. I don't know why. Does that seem strange?"

"No stranger than anything else you've laid on me so far."

She frowned. "You sure know how to make a person feel unwelcome. You know that?"

Brandon bit his lip. Maybe he'd been too hard on Julia. Maybe it was important for a woman to see the place where the father of her baby had last gone. Maybe that was only natural. And maybe Julia's unusual resources could be brought to bear on the fact-gathering. She'd kept pretty close to Brandy's instructions at the mountaineering school. He felt oafish as he looked at the crazy lady who sat on the rock and stared, tight-lipped, at the sheer mountain face. He chastised himself for all his life's cruelty, intentional and accidental, to women and to small animals, and to shorter and fatter kids at school. If you can't say something nice about someone . . .

Julia's voice interrupted his self-abasement. It was tensely controlled, with an edge of urgency. "I want to hike some more. Now. Hard. Maybe another hour or two. Then we can turn around and come back. Okay with you?" Without waiting for his reply, and without another word,

Julia led the way up the strenuous switchbacks straight up toward the top of the Falls, for nearly an hour of that special brand of Sierra aerobic training which closely approximates marathon stair-climbing in skyscrapers. The exhaustion effect was undoubtedly intensified because this was their first day in the mountains, newly arrived from sea level. The high altitude compromised their unadapted lungs' capacity to alleviate oxygen deficits.

Julia seemed driven. Brandy was beginning to feel weary. He was in fair physical shape, and prided himself on an exquisite staying power when the chips were down, but Julia's pace up the mountain was well beyond masochistic. Brandy hung in there until she had exhausted herself so thoroughly that something finally broke loose. Glancing up in time to see her face as she plodded around a sharp switchback ahead of him up the trail, he noticed that tears were streaming down her cheeks. He guessed she'd been crying for a while already, because her face was well smudged and smeared with trail dirt from her hands and sleeves as she had wiped away the salty water. As they approached the next switchback, Brandy called forward for a rest stop. Julia sagged heavily down onto a rock ledge, bowed her head, and turned away.

Still huffing from exertion when he reached her, Brandy suggested as casually as possible, "Time to go down, now? I don't know about you, but I think I've had my fitness training for the day."

She kept turned away from him, trying to keep him from seeing her face, still huffing and puffing heavily with the effort to regain oxygen.

"Hello?" Brandy tried.

"Okay," she rasped. "But you lead."

Without pause or rest, they switched their way back down to the green bench where the Upper Falls comes roaring down to its base, where the trail works its way through the denser woods before heading west around the shoulder of the Falls hollow for the return back down to the valley. It's a different set of muscles for coming down steep inclines than are needed for climbing up them. Some hikers prefer descent, usually arguing that it requires much less work than ascent. Long-limbed hikers, however, usually prefer the up-hills because the strain on ligaments and tendons of controlling descent is almost horrific for them. Not to mention what happens to the hikers' toes: unless you lace up your boots so tightly that the circulation is cut off at the top of the foot or the ankle, the toes are crammed into the tip of the boot with each (often excruciating) stride. Gangly Brandy was very glad to come to a relatively flatter section of trail.

The spray from the base of the Upper Falls serves to keep all the trees and undergrowth lush. A hiker who lingers in that area is soon saturated by the fog-like clouds of humidity from the backspray. Julia produced a bandana from her jacket pocket and wiped her face. When she saw the heavy dirt smeared on the bandanna, she shook her head pathetically. "I must be pretty cute."

Brandon laughed. "Probably like the first finger-painting you ever did."

"Why didn't you tell me?"

"And ruin good art?"

"I want to go nearer the sound. It seems so . . . powerful. Is that all from the water?"

"Uh-huh."

"Do we have time for a little exploring?" she asked, the first signs of her glow returning at last to her voice.

Brandy looked at his watch. "Four forty-five? Sure. An hour, maybe, so long as we make fast tracks after that for getting back to the head of the trail."

She leaped to her feet and led the way down several

of the many unmarked trail spurs which headed down through the rock and dense undergrowth from the main trail in the general direction of the thundering water. As they climbed up onto the spray-soaked boulders at the end of one little trail, the noise mounted in intensity from something like heavy radio static to a deafening roar. Julia hopped up on the highest wet-topped boulder and leaped nymphlike from there to yet another rock which was even closer to the edge above the river. Still forty or fifty feet from the face of the granite over which the falls descended, they were about as close to the falls as the shifting and furiously back-eddying pools would allow them to get. Throwing open her arms to the saturating spray, Julia stared upward into the continuous flow of the falling water, trembling, enduring some special thrill. It was a fourth Julia, and Brandon found himself more fascinated by her reaction than by the rumbling waterfall.

After many minutes of such suspension, Julia slowly turned and brought her attention to Brandy, who squatted on the boulder behind her. Her gaze held an odd offering of revelation, but Brandy still wasn't sure what to make of it. It was a special moment's gift, mysteriously wrapped, and then it was gone.

"What's the matter?" Brandon shouted above the din.

"Something is happening," she shouted back. "I don't know what it is, but . . . let's go!" She grabbed his hand as she leaped past him off the boulder and Brandy slipped and nearly fell twice on the run back up the trail to catch her. She was a woman possessed. They were both quite out of breath when she found another trail spur which headed toward the wall immediately beside the falls. Actually, it was less a trail than it was a space between two large boulders which rimmed the main trail. Brandon bounded after her, Alice pursuing the White Rabbit.

"I want to go to the edge," Julia whooped over her

shoulder.

"The *what*?"

"The edge! I want to press my ear to the rock at the bottom of the falls. It must be the *power* of it. Come on!"

Brandy clambered along behind her, watching her peer around the tenacious trees and the precariously perched boulders alongside the rumbling torrent of the falls. This was no trail at all. And it didn't look like there was any chance of getting all the way to the rock wall beside the falls. Brandy looked up and saw the more than two thousand feet of vertical granite. He shuddered. Then he heard a scream. In spite of the background rumble, the acoustical curtain seemed to part for that scream. And then she screamed again. Brandy lurched forward to get to her, stumbled over some rock hidden in the wet undergrowth above the river's edge, and saw Julia half crouched with her forearms crossed in front of her forehead, as if to protect herself. She stared down the boulder slope toward where the sidespray of the falls continually filled the shallow ravine with clouds of thick, cold, pulverised water droplets.

Brandy worked his way around the boulders and through the undergrowth, back into the thunder and the icy shower until he reached the place where Julia was perched atop of a small, flat rock ledge. He grabbed her arms and shouted above the din, "Julia! What is it? What's the matter?"

"There!" she exclaimed, pointing directly below them. The color of the saturated, faded clothing blended too well with the wet rock and undergrowth, but the small red climbing bag was still bright enough to stand out, and just at the base of the boulder on which they were standing a thin yellow snake of woven climbing rope could be glimpsed as it threaded and curled its way beneath three months of foliage to where it was still wrapped and tied around the remains of a climber. Brandy turned her away for a moment to steady her. "It's him!" she shouted. "I know it's him! It's got to be!"

Seven

Brandy shook Julia free from the first waves of her hysteria and commanded her to stay on the boulder while he went down for a closer look. Taking care not to lose his footing on the slippery slope which led from Julia to the body of the climber, Brandy worked his way down along the loose climbing rope.

When he reached the body, he was glad he'd left Julia back on the rock. Even in the refrigeration of the base of the falls, the insects and the small animals had mutilated the remains. Most of the corpse had been completely skeletonized. One leg had been pulled loose from the other remains, the large femoral bone gnawed in half by some small creature intent on the nutrition of the marrow encased within. The portions of the skeleton which had been protected by the mist-dampened clothing were slightly better preserved and were still recognizable as human. A white climbing helmet lay about four feet beyond the body, bowl up, harness still snapped. It must have been lost in the fall or, possibly, pawed loose from the dead climber's skull by some foraging animal.

The initials "E.F.H." were on the climber's chalk bag. Brandy pulled it loose and shook some of the stiffness from it. Mold covered the side which had been lying toward the ground. A tentative pawing search through the tangle of gear still held fast to his waist sling turned up an assortment of climbing hardware, mostly carabiners and chocks and small pitons, the non-stainless steel parts heavily oxidized from prolonged exposure to the mists of Yosemite Falls. A closer inspection of the chalk bag's contents revealed an inside protected flap, where Brandy found Farmer Hobbs' driver's license and his American Express card. And that was it.

Three months is too long a time for a body to remain on one patch of ground. From the moment of death, the earth begins to reattach and reclaim, as a reminder of the illusion of any sort of exclusivity which *Homo sapiens* might wish to assign to its precious corpora, individual or collective. Only the bones are resistant to the claim, and even they eventually yield to time and the forces of entropy.

The black webbing harness on Farmer's torso was still tied on to the yellow climbing rope, as if it mattered. Applying even what little rudiments of technical climbing knowledge Brandy possessed, he felt safe in concluding that as a solo climber, Farmer could have gained only the most minimal belaying effect and safety from the rope. Protection is tough enough on these rock faces even with a partner to belay you. Brandy looked up at the sheer wall which extended forever upward from where the corpse lay. The body was nearly a half mile west of where Farmer had registered to climb that day. Animals may have prodded and dragged Farmer's body a few meters but not likely much more than that, given the restraints of the climbing rope tangled in the dense foliage.

Julia looked anxiously toward Brandy, her forearms

still crossed at her forehead. With the identification cards clutched between his fingers, Brandy nodded a solemn, sympathetic confirmation. She crumpled onto the top of the boulder. Her sobs were inaudible above the din, but her chest visibly heaved as she gasped her anguish. Brandy fought his way up the slope, his hand again sliding along the soaked and weathered climbing rope. Before he had managed to work himself all the way back up to where Julia was, he stuffed the cards into his pocket and picked up the yellow rope. On impulse, he gave it a shake and a tug. The clatter of metal brought up a small tangle of chocks and pitons --- the strangely-shaped truncated blocks of metal and cabling and rockscrews which climbers use to fix their climbing ropes to the tiny cracks of the walls as they climb --- still attached by carabiners to the climbing rope. There were four chocks and one piton cabled on. He pulled again and saw where the rope snaked over another large boulder and back down along a notch to the right of where Farmer's body lay. Curiosity prevailed. Brandy kept pulling the rope until it jammed. He worked his way carefully down to the hang-up and as he eased himself up over the V-ledge of rock, he reflexively sucked in a massive lungful of cold mist at the sight below him: the remains of another climber!

The second body seemed to be in much better shape than Farmer's, perhaps because the precarious angle of the slab of granite which was its final resting place had made it that much safer from predator animals. Behind Brandy, Julia was unsteadily crawling off the edge of her boulder, still convulsive with her sobbing misery, but showing every sign of intending to come down the slope to join Brandy. He scrambled back part way up to her, shouting and using sign language to indicate to her through the roaring din that there was someone else down there. Also dead. Could she stay put on the rock? He was torn between a sense of his humane duty to provide solace to the widow and his keen desire to find out more about the climbers. When he reached her he put a steadying hand on her shoulder and shouted, "Stay here! He wasn't climbing alone! There's someone else down there! I'll be right back!"

Brandy looked up to try to map the trajectory of the fall. It must have been a straight drop from the ridge of rock next to the top of the Upper Falls, with a final glancing bounce of one or both of the tethered climbers off the bell-shaped shoulder of rock next to the bottom of the falls, a hundred feet or so above where the bodies now lay. Somehow they had come to rest on this overgrown, boulder-rimmed slope adjacent to the base of the falls, with one climber on one side of the rim of boulders and the other climber on the rim itself, just meters above the swirling waters.

At the V-notch between the rocks on which the second climber lay, Brandon strained from side to side to get a better view of the corpse below him. It seemed to be in better shape than the mostly skeletonized remains of the other body. Brandy tugged at the rope to test if he could bring the body up to him, but it just wrenched and contorted like a stiff sack of grain in response to his coaxing. Either some part of the body was wedged where he couldn't see it or some piece of gear or clothing was hooked to the rock surface on which the body lay. He reluctantly slid up over the lip of rock and carefully worked his way down to the remains, trying to rely for his balance as little as possible on the soppy, weathered yellow lifeline. He slipped twice, cursed, and continued with his tentative mini-steps.

The second body was female. The relative proportions of the pelvis and the narrow dimensions across the shoulders and hands were confirmatory. Her distorted face and exposed skin were withered and wrinkled and partially mummified. The exposed skin had a whitish tinge to it. A long mildew-darkened blonde braid of hair was matted to a distorted, partially crushed cranium, the only sign of damage to the body.

Except for the small, single, ankh-shaped wire earring still attached to something at the side of what had been her head, she wore no jewelry. But then, most climbers don't. For practical reasons.

During the private investigation days, Brandy had seen more than his share of dead ones, and if he hadn't seen how both climbers were tied on to the rope in solid belaying knots and harnesses, he wouldn't have believed that this second body had been here for as long as the other body had been at the other end of this rope.

The rope was still double-looped and tied securely to the second climber's waist. Even alive, hers had been a slim waist, judging from the diameter of the rope loops and the twisted climbing harness.

Brandy tugged on the rope lead again to shift the woman's remains, but the resistance suggested he might break the corpse apart before he could get it to move that way. As he tried various means to dislodge it, he considered that the woman's corpse might have been here for more than a few weeks. Brandy tipped forward for a different vantage on the woman's body, and his foot slipped out from under him, sending him thumping painfully to his knee on the wet rock beside her, and as he grabbed at the climbing rope for balance it jammed tightly through the notch on the lip of the slope above him. He cursed out loud and scrambled to regain a balance independent of the deteriorated rope. There was still ten feet or so of granite ledge protecting him from a long, last dip in the icy waters of the raging Yosemite River. Nobody liked narrow margins when he could avoid them. But now that Brandy had already assumed the risks of getting down to the woman's body, his curiosity again overwhelmed his fears, and he was soon securely rebalanced on his feet.

The woman's chalk bag was wedged beneath her

sprawled remnants. Brandy nudged her with the toe of his climbing boot to try to dislodge the bag. The sopping, weathered fabric of the nylon-spandex Capri pants, once skin-tight but now baggy and very wrinkled in places, was very like a two-day-old helium balloon. It tore easily where he pushed at it, and peeled loose in an ugly, gummy way from the wedge of rock on which she lay. Only the slightest hint of fetid odor --- more like ammonia than like the distinctive aroma of decaying flesh --- joined the persistent, cleansing, gusting spray from the falls.

Brandy reflexively pulled his head back from it, then slowly stooped down and groped clumsily through the climbing hardware at her waist. There was much less than Farmer had had on him, so either she was the leader and belayer at the time of the fall, or she had been on belay while Farmer lead, and she had just started up after him, to clean the wall of all the hardware Farmer had laid down as protection for the fatal pitch. Given the limited amount of protection still attached to the rope, it seemed more likely she was the leader, and Farmer the clean-up partner. Which meant she would have been anchored at the time of the fall.

Brandy felt carefully at her waist, following the harness and belaying loops with his fingers. He fished a broken end of nylon webbing from under her. Sometimes, he knew, climbers use sewn-through slings as part of their belaying anchors, and sometimes they prefer the flexibility of being able to adjust the lengths and tie them off. The sew-through of this woman's broken sling was quite workmanlike, and certainly hadn't failed. The frayed end of the sling may have been altered by three months of weather, or it may have been chewed apart by an animal since the fall.

Brandy couldn't make much of it. He knew some basics, but when all was said and done, his was still a limited expertise in climbing equipment. It would be up to the mountaineering experts to put in their best guesses as to the cause of the fall. And after this much time it had to be conjecture anyway. An already over-used nylon sling, looped over the sharp edge of a rock anchor? Extra stress set off by a footslip and a short fall by Farmer, jerking against his belayer and her anchorage in just the wrong way? How little it takes in the climbing game to turn a minor slip into a fatal error.

Brandy looked at the heavy mold growth which made a grey-green outline on the rock beneath where the woman had lain. It was like the floor outlines the detectives leave at the scenes of homicides after the body has been carted away. Only here it was a parody by Mother Nature. Lest we forget.

Brandy tugged at the woman's chalk bag until it finally let go of the rock enough that he could unclip it from her harness. There was no identification in the bag and there were no pockets in the climbing skin-tights she wore. He looked at her climbing boots, still attached to her feet, wondering if there might be identification there, but the thought was too grisly. It was up to the Park people to find out who she was. He returned the chalk bag to her belt and pushed things back pretty much as he'd found them. Then he stood up and surveyed the cold greyness of death. The stillness that even the symphonic thunder of the falling water could not disturb. And he took a deep breath to feel the contrast of life before he began to cautiously pick his way back up the rocky slope.

Eight

Julia was sitting up when he rejoined her. Her eyes were puffed to bare slits and she clutched her tightly laced hands to her mouth. Brandy helped her off the flat top of the boulder and led her, zombie-like, back through the rocks and brush back to the main trail. It wasn't far, but the going was dense. No wonder the bodies hadn't been discovered sooner.

He sat her down solidly on another boulder at trail's edge and told her to wait. Brandy picked his way back through the undergrowth until he again reached the loop of yellow climbing rope. Pulling up all the slack, he carefully fed out the doubled cord as he backed in the direction of the main trail. The rope was about three yards too short to reach all the way to the trail, so he looped the end up over a young evergreen which was trying to establish itself in the mist. After a few rearrangements, he was able to drag the rope across the higher boughs of the small tree so that it was just visible from the trail. He wanted to feel certain he could direct the Park people to the site. He gave a moment's thought to building a small cairn right in the middle of the trail, to mark the spot even more clearly, but the dusk had cloaked the area so deftly that they couldn't afford another moment's delay. Darkness comes with alarming speed in the Sierra, and Brandy had no desire to spend this night bivouacking in the cold when their warm cabin sat only a few miles away, on the valley floor.

Julia stood up when she saw Brandy return. He took her by the arm and urged her ahead of him down the trail. "Let's go," he said. "We've got to move quickly, now. It's getting dark."

Julia stiffened, spun around, and grabbed Brandon's right arm in a powerful reflex clutch. "My god!" she wailed. "We can't just *leave* him here!"

Brandy let her cling to him long enough to let her hear her own words. As her grip and the wide-eyed tension eased, he said calmly, "Julia, he's dead. I'm sorry. But there's nothing you can do here now. The Park people will bring out the bodies tomorrow. I'm sure of it."

Tears started to roll again. "I knew he was up here," Julia said sadly. "I just knew he was here. I don't know *how* I knew it. I . . . I just knew it."

"It's okay," Brandon reassured her, still unsure what to make of it himself. He took her by the shoulders and gave her a squeeze of reassurance. "It's okay. Come on. Let's go."

She shook her head sadly for a few moments, and then she turned around and without any further prodding headed down the trail toward the valley.

Their trek to Columbia Rock and the criss-crossing down the sand slide seemed more like Keystone Cops animation than hiking. Brandy kept Julia in front of him so that he could watch her, but he stayed close enough to help when she became unsteady again from time to time.

The first of the quartz halogen lights were appearing in the dulling valley below, defining the last minutes of day slipping into night, and putting further pressure on the duo to increase their already exhausting tempo for the final twenty minutes' march to the lodge.

They were part way down the sandy switchbacks in the deep dusk when Brandy heard the rumble. His memory later told him he had *felt* it before he heard it, but it wasn't until he glanced over his shoulder to see the chicken-wire-and-boulder retaining wall two switchbacks above them sagging and contorting under the weight of the tide of fine gravel from the top of the slide that he realized an avalanche was in progress. He lurched forward on the narrow trail into the back of Julia and drove her on toward the switchback turn in the trail just ahead. Confused, she staggered and began to turn around. He hit her with another body block, intending to send her plummeting right over the edge of the sand face, hoping to distance them as much as possible from the center of the slide, but they collided with such force that Brandy had a sudden awful thought that he must have broken her back. His mind flashed on the thought of "life over limb", then on a more sacrilegious expletive of "Jesus!" before the two of them were launched into a mean, twisting, rock-and-roll action which catapulted them into each other, down sandbanks, and against rock ledges, tumbling and spinning and being pushed and pulled and knocked about until it felt as if Brandy's limbs were being torn off his torso by ones and by twos.

Julia had yelped once at the beginning of the fall but Brandy heard nothing from her after that. Just when he thought they might have ridden out the worst of it, after his third bone-whacking somersault, as he was skidding face-first down the surging surface of the descending sandslide, he caught a glimpse of an animate something moving along with him, and he instinctively lunged out to grab what looked like Julia's wrist. He had to try to keep them connected in the darkness. But just then he was hit by another load of sand from above. Still in a fish-tailing belly-skid, Brandy was just able to shake free enough of the sand from his face to flutter his eyes open and see through the darkness and the turbulent dust cloud that it wasn't Julia's wrist but her ankle which he had latched onto.

Another rumble and Julia was wrenched completely free of Brandy's clutches. All further sounds were muffled by the sand in his ears, and in the next moment Brandy was hit from the side by something heavy enough to completely knock the wind out of him. And then everything went absolutely silent.

Drake lay still for a long time. Stunned. He was fairly certain he hadn't lost consciousness, but the sandy silence seemed infinite. An expanding moment. One of those instants before fear, when adrenaline insures that survival reflexes have the first and most unlimited call on the body's full resources. He tried to move, but everything seemed encased. Entombed, more like it. As if he had been dropped into concrete. Everything except his head. His head and his right arm and shoulder were starting to move, although the arm had little feeling in it.

Brandy pulled and surged hard against the restraint, like a horse too tightly cross-tied. He spit out dirt and sand and finally managed to suck in some dust-laden air, but the constriction around his chest limited the amount of oxygen to far less than he knew he needed. Panic was beginning to set in. He flailed with his numb arm until it hit his head. A good sign. Every movement was increasing his freedom. He shook and shook his head, but each time he tried to open his eyes, they filled with more sand and dirt, stinging and mercilessly cutting the surfaces of sclera and cornea and eyelids. He heard the muffled sound of grunting and straining and paused for a moment to listen, until he realized it was himself he was hearing. An animal struggling for basic free-dom of movement. Strain and pull and push and twist, each time casting off more bonds of the soft surface of the newly arranged sandscape.

After his right arm and leg were freed, he clumsily extricated the rest of his body. He had been buried on his side, head down along the slope. He still had sand and dirt in every orifice, but his obscured vision was the worst obstacle to his reorientation. His vigorous shaking of his head and stinging eyes finally stimulated enough tears to permit him to begin seeing through the thick dustcloud around him. He had come to rest about fifty meters above the edge of the treed section of trail toward which they had been descending at the time of the avalanche.

Brandon took a deep breath to shout "Julia!" but the call came out as little more than a rasp. He tried again, with more success. "Julia!" He stumbled around on the soft sand surface, looking for lumps or ridges, intermittently shaking his head furiously to drive out more of the sand and grit. He crooked his head and pounded it with his fist to clear first one ear and then the other. "Julia!" Nothing.

He stood still. Blinked. Against a tree about four yards below him, a large boulder twitched and jerked and slithered. In the deep brown dusty fog the shape looked less like a Day-Glo pink and more a dull grey-tan. Julia was thrashing around to get herself free and stabilized on the sand slope, much as Drake had done, but it was creeping away steadily beneath her, taking her under as fast as she was pulling herself out. Brandy scrambled and stumbled down to her and held her still long enough to let the sand stop moving. When she felt him and heard him shouting at her, she forced herself beyond her consuming hysteria and allowed him to help pull her free. He helped her onto her side and let her cough and sputter until her lungs were clear. She began to make recognizably human sounds.

Brandy tried to get Julia to her feet, but she was unable to put weight on her left leg. Still worried about the likelihood of a second avalanche, he lifted her to carry her, but he immediately lost his own balance in the soft footing and they fell over. On the third try Julia was able to put enough weight on the leg to allow them to half hobble and half drag their way across and down to where the remnants of the Falls trail disappeared into the woods.

Once they were on solid trail, Julia pushed herself away from him to test if she could walk without help. After two or three tentative steps she declared, "I . . . I think it's better now. I'm okay."

"Good. We'll find a comfortable place right here where you can sit and wait. I can hike down and be back with help in an hour or so. You won't have to walk out. They'll carry you."

Frantic with fear, she started to protest. But when she tried to speak, sand fell out of her hair and into her eyes. She shook her head and made faces and sputtered as more fell into her mouth. Then she tried to clean the grit out with dirty, sandy fingers and only made things worse. "Shit!" she complained, punching at her eyes. She winced up at him through the sand and pain. "My leg's okay. It just felt like it had fallen asleep up there. That's all. A nerve pinch or something. But it's okay." She marched around in a circle to demonstrate, showing very little residual lameness, as she continued to struggle vainly to rid her eyes of dirt.

"We were lucky to stay on the surface of that slide," remarked Brandon. "You sure you're okay?"

"Perfectly," she sputtered, spitting out more sand with each syllable. "You're *not* leaving me here!" She stopped in front of Brandy, twitching all around her eyes. "So let's go!"

They didn't stop to get the sand out of their shoes, but the two of them sporadically shook their heads to clear the orifices, and turned their pockets inside out and shook out themselves and their clothes as they tramped down the trails through the trees.

Near the bottom of the trail, they ran into two burly men just starting up the climb, carrying large, bright lights. They were heavily laden with packs, shovels, ropes, and other paraphernalia. One was a uniformed Park Ranger and the other man wore green work fatigues.

In the artificial lights, Julia and Brandon must have been a ghastly sight. "Hello?" the Ranger shouted when he saw them. "Everybody all right here?" They came close and the Ranger extended his light ahead of him to take a more careful look at the two apparitions in front of him. "Jeez, you two sure look like you've had a rough time. You okay? Anybody else in your party?"

"There was a slide up there on the trail, and . . ."

"We know. We were just coming up to check it out. We heard it clear down to the Village. We could tell by the dust it was the sand face. Anybody else caught in it as far as you know?"

"Don't think so."

"Damned trail's always giving out there, but we thought it was in good shape for the winter. We completely rebuilt it this past spring. Did you see anybody in front of you on the trail? Or behind you, maybe? Anybody else who might have gotten caught in it?"

"We were moving pretty fast."

"And it's pretty late for anyone else to be up there," added Julia. "We saw no one the whole way down."

"You want somebody should go down with you?" the Ranger type asked.

"No. I think we're fine. It's not very far, is it?"

"About three, maybe four, minutes to trailhead. But go careful. It's dark enough a person can surely nobble knees on the boulders by the sides of the trail."

"There's a support group getting organized with the trucks at trailhead, about two more big switchbacks and then that flat piece along the base. Here, take a flashlight. You'll need it." He offered an extra light which had been dangling at the side of his pack. "You sure you're okay?"

"Thanks," said Brandy. "We're just shaken. Nothing broken, as far as we can tell."

"What the devil you doing up here this late anyway?"

"We found a pair of climbers up at the base of the upper falls."

"You what?"

"Found the bodies of two climbers. Roped together. Dead. One of them was Farmer Hobbs, the Canadian climber who went missing this summer."

"Him? Jesus! The body musta been in bad shape after all this time."

Julia was standing beside Brandy and she grabbed at his arm to help her balance. He saw her eyes roll up into their lids and she gave out a low moan as she sank to the ground. The two men scrambled and clanked with their lights and gear. Brandy felt for a pulse, but Julia began to come back to consciousness almost as soon as she was on the ground.

The Ranger looked at her pupils in the bright lantern light. "You'll be okay, ma'am, but maybe Jerry should go down the rest of the way with you. You musta had quite a fright with that slide."

"It wasn't that," Brandon told him. "Farmer Hobbs was her husband. We came up to Yosemite to look for him."

"Jeez. You're kidding! Oh, jeez. I'm sorry I didn't know . . . Wait! You actually found the body? How did you know where to look? We searched for weeks. At the base of the falls, you say?"

"Hard spot to get at. Impossible to see from the trails.

It was a bit of luck. If that's what you call luck. You were right. They were in pretty bad shape." He nodded his head toward Julia. "I guess the suggestion was just a bit much on her."

Julia tried to stand up, against the protests of the Ranger that she should stay sitting a while longer.

"Look, I'm awful sorry about this, ma'am . . ." he apologized unhappily. "I mean if I'd only known . . ."

"You couldn't have known," Brandy reassured him. "Please. We'll be fine. I'll help her back to our cabin. You go on. We'll be fine. We're in Cabin 43 at the Lodge when you need us."

The Ranger frowned in the bright light, looked up into the darkness of the trail above them. "Okay. We'll check back with you." He barked into the radio he was carrying as Brandon led a dazed Julia on down the trail behind the wide, bright cone of light shed by the freshly charged flashlight the Ranger had loaned them.

At the trailhead, where the signpost announces the name and the length of the trail, under the bright and welcome junction light for the driveway into the Lodge, two Park trucks were being unloaded by three more emergency workers.

"You sure you're all right?" Brandy asked Julia.

"Just shaken. And gritty and dirty. I think I need a long shower and a good night's sleep. If I can sleep. I'm not going to see some doctor so I can blubber all over him about Farmer, so put that out of your mind. I don't even want to go through the story tonight." She looked at the men ahead anxiously. "Okay?"

Brandy understood. Skirting the edges of the lighted area to avoid the distracted workers, the bedraggled pair walked the short stretch along the main road and into the

Lodge.

While Julia went inside, Brandy took off his clothes in the darkness behind the cabin. He shook out six or seven pounds of sand, put his torn jacket and his pants back on and stumbled inside. He inspected his scratches and sore spots carefully in the mirror on the wall between the beds. Some time later, Julia shuffled out of the bathroom and slid between the sheets of her bed and sniffled a few tears. "Just let me sleep, please," she whispered. "Just let me . . ." and the heavy, slow breathing said nobody's brass band could have kept her from sleeping now.

Brandy washed his hair three times, until no more sand rinsed out, long after the hot water had given out. He knew his night was far from ended. One part adrenaline mixed with an equal part of compassion convinced Drake that he should take a walk. Not too far nor for too long a time, but far enough and long enough for him to unload some of the stress hormones and nervous aftermath of the crisis just past.

He left a note for Julia on the smooth spread of his bed, in case she woke up and wondered what had happened to him. As he closed the door to the cabin and heard it softly click behind him, he listened to the night sounds of the valley, and wondered exactly where he should go and what he should do first.

Brandy decided he should contact the Valley authorities, at least to let them know the details about the corpses at the base of the Upper Falls. It was particularly important to let the Rangers know where to find the climbers' bodies. Now that the slide had blocked the main access trail, the Rangers might have to bring workers down from Tuolumne Meadows. Or fly them in by helicopter to retrieve the remains. So many details. Details which could wait until

morning. Except that it is a curse of the accountant mentality
to be unremittingly obsessed with details.

The men at the makeshift emergency trucks across
from the lodge told Brandy where to contact the Park officer
in charge for the evening. Brandy retrieved the Corsica from
in front of the cabin and drove to the village, where he filed
a full report on what he had seen on the mountain and exactly
where they would find the remains of the two climbers the
following morning. No, he was not working as a private
investigator. He was a friend of the family and was merely
helping Julia Hobbs locate her husband. They were just
lucky. If that's what you call lucky. Or maybe she's psychic.
Or both. Yes, they were both available for a positive
identification in the morning. Yes, they would check in with
the main Park office at ten o'clock.

And as Brandy walked away from the Park Ranger
night station feeling well bureaucratized, he made a quick
call from the payphone in front of the Village market to his
own number in Vancouver to let his melodious and
ever-ready answering service operator, Karen Perrin, know
he would be on his way home a bit earlier than anticipated,
possibly tomorrow.

Those mundane tasks out of the way, he headed
straight over to the Mountaineering School to cancel Julia
and himself from their classes for the following day. Details,
details. Hopefully this would be the last item he would be
attending to tonight. After which he would go back to Cabin
43 to fill his empty bed with his exhausted body. He checked
his watch. Seven-thirty and he still hadn't eaten. No wonder
he felt so awful. Which meant he needed to make one more
stop. For food for two. Even if Julia had said less than an
hour ago that she wasn't hungry, she might wake up hungry.
Then she'd be S.O.L. unless Brandy brought something home
with him. Another hour and a half and everything in the
valley would be closed up until morning. Maybe he should

just take her the bag of trail food from the Corsica.

There were still plenty of details to occupy the too-alert buzzing of Brandy's left brain.

And dear Julia. Brandy had a funny feeling that, in spite of her request for solitude and space, she might appreciate having someone on call for later in the night. Someone in the next bed. Someone to talk to, to share the bad dreams with, to cry with, and maybe to remind her she was going to come through this ordeal just fine.

Nine

The lights were still on in the Mountaineering Shop. Brandy peered through the window displays but saw no activity inside. The door jingled open and Brandy jarred it into another good jingle when he closed it heavily behind him. No response. Lights on, nobody home.

The stool behind the counter was vacant. The fluorescents on the ceiling gave all the colorful clothes and daytime displays of the shop an anemic, bluish, ugly pall.

"Phil?" Brandy called. "Phil?"

"Not yet," replied the abrupt, but muffled, voice of a woman from somewhere behind a high stack of unpacked cardboard shipping crates along the back of the room. "I'm not interested in a *fill*, but I'd sure love to have my oil checked. And if you brought that bottle of wine you keep promising me, you bastard, I might even change my mind about the *fill* before the night's over!" In the midst of wild fits of giggles, a tiny, red-haired nymph popped up from behind the single box at the end of the row of crates, like some animated Jill-In-The-Box. "How the hell have you been, you . . ." And she stopped, mouth agape. Her round face, with enormous eyes surrounded by long, dark red eyelashes, was full of the shock of seeing someone unexpected. "You're not Dave!" She bounced out from behind the boxes and the hanging racks of climbing gear, wiping her tiny hands on her old worn coveralls, a bundle of energy coming to see Brandy full-face. "I'm sorry. I thought you were . . . someone else. What can I do for you?" She stopped and squinted.

There were only two faces like that in the world. One belonged to a doll, the famous Raggedy Ann. The other belonged to someone Brandon had known once upon a long time ago. It couldn't be, he reasoned. It couldn't. But there were only two faces like that in the world. And he'd wondered this morning about the coincidence of names, but the last name hadn't matched then.

"Raggedy Annie Bentley?"

Her eyes bugged out and the thin line of mouth opened to a parody of a lipsticked "O". "Brandy Drake? Dandy Brandy Fucking Drake?? Well, for cryin' out loud!" She leaped forward without warning into his arms, wrapping her legs around his waist and spinning him around. He struggled to keep his balance which, with the pain of his afternoon avalanche wounds, was no small task, and the two of them careened into a rack of climbing harnesses before Brandy could catch a support rail and balance himself. Like a wind-up woodpecker, Annie kissed him over and over and yelped and howled and Brandy just sputtered and tried in vain to make sentences like "What the hell are . . . ." "When are you . . . ." "What kind of . . . ." until she finally peeled herself off of him and slid down to ground level.

"For god's sakes," she gasped up at him huskily. "I sure never expected to see you again. Not like this, anyway."

"What the hell are you doing here, Annie?"

"Working for a living. Or as near to working as I'm ever likely to come. I'm still a rock bum."

"So it *was* you. You're the climber working for Phil!"

"*With* Phil," she frowned reflectively. "Ohhh, my God. Are *you* the one who . . . I never even thought to check the name on the roster for tomorrow, and I was damn near half asleep when Phil called this morning."

She bounced over to the counter and flipped up the top page of the clipboard. Her face lit up, red in the cheeks, short hair awry, eyes like big buttons surrounded by the tile-white sclera and sparse long eyelashes, eyebrows halfway up the forehead, her thin-line smile bracketed by parenthesis creases. Raggedy Annie incarnate. Only her shape was like nothing the doll could ever dream of having. At half an inch under five feet, she had a definite overabundance of girl-goods. Ample Earth Mother hips, and breasts which strained quite unequivocally at her faded Yosemite T-shirt and the top buttons of her coveralls.

"Are you really the one I'm supposed to teach tomorrow?"

"That was the plan."

"Ha! That should be a rip."

"Actually, that's what I came to talk about. Things have changed."

"Well, you're not going to stand me up now, are you? Not after you've come here to get my hopes up. I mean, we don't have to go climbing, but I'm sure not letting you out of my paddy-paws without a few hours to catch up on whatever the hell you've been doing for the past ten years."

"Twenty."

"Shit. Like I needed somebody to remind me."

"And why not? You really haven't changed much, Annie."

"Except that when I was twenty-one, you may remember, I had the face of a thirteen-year-old girl. And at forty, I finally have the face of an *adult* thirteen-year-old girl. Hell of a curse to go through life as a girl, isn't it?"

"You fishing for compliments?"

"Probably. It says here on the roster there are two of you, Mr. Dandy-Brandy, and Phil said whoever you're with in the valley is a looker. Your Significant Other?"

"Nope. I don't have one of those. Not any more. You?"

"Not at the moment. Actually, I had two who couldn't stand the heat, and the third one didn't live long enough to find out that he couldn't stand it. Killed in a car crash."

"Yeah. Sorry to hear about that. Phil mentioned it."

"Did he? Well, Phil's an asshole. Are you tied up tonight? We've got a lot of catching up to do."

"I can't tonight. The lady I'm with is pretty distraught and I guess I've had a bit of a day of it myself."

Annie put on a clownish grin. "But I thought you said she wasn't . . ."

"A client. She's only a client."

Annie took Brandy by the forearms, leaned back, raised her brows, and tilted her head up high as if trying to look down her nose at the man who stood nearly a foot and half taller than she. "Tell me another one!"

"Not a line, Annie," Brandon said, smirking at her. "Legitimate. Believe me. The lady really is a client. We found her dead husband up the mountain, and then we were caught in an avalanche. So maybe tomorrow, after they bring the body down and get the whole mess cleaned up . . ."

Raggedy Ann suddenly transformed into a serious face, lips tight. "Dead husband? What are you talking about?"

"The climber who disappeared this summer. The Canadian. We found him."

"Farmer Hobbs?"

"That's right. Did you know him?"

"Holy shit! Where was he?"

"At the base of the Upper Falls. On a rock ledge not far from the trail."

"No kidding? I led one of the search teams. We

combed the whole North Face for nearly a week and found dick-all. We looked everywhere. At the base of the Falls? But he was supposed to have been . . ."

"At the Arrowhead Spire. I know. But he wasn't, obviously. And he wasn't alone either. A young woman was roped on with him."

Annie's fingers dug hard into Brandy's forearms and her jaw dropped open. Her face stiffened in such a still-frame of awful anticipation that it was an obvious strain for her to enunciate her words. Her voice, though still coarse, rose considerably in pitch. "Who was the woman?"

Brandy looked at the glazed eyes, unsure of how to answer. "I don't know. She didn't have any identification on her."

"What did she look like?" Annie persisted, barely more that a whisper.

"Not like anything I'd want to talk about. After three summer months lying in the weather . . ."

"Jewelry? Was she wearing any jewelry?" Annie was growing more tense by the moment.

"Not really," Brandy reflected. "Except for an earring. But only one." Brandy watched Annie's eyes widen as he continued with his details: "Some kind of wire ankh or something. I don't know why any woman would climb wearing such a rope-snagger, but . . ."

Annie's fingers tightened like vice-grips on Drake's arms. Her eyes opened so widely there seemed to be no lids. She was catatonic. Her mouth opened in a dry scream. "Oh, god," she rasped. "Oh, god . . . oh god . . . oh god . . . oh dear god . . ."

Annie's hands went limp and she staggered back away from Brandy. He stepped forward to grab her to keep her from falling over the packing boxes behind her, but he wasn't quite quick enough. She tripped, rolling limply back and to the side and slumping heavily toward the floor. Brandy grasped her by an upper arm to help her to a steadier seat nearby at the counter, but she shrugged him away. She fumbled against the boxes and pushed herself into a half crouch. All the while she continued chanting the "Oh, god" mantra.

"Annie? What's the matter? Are you all right?"

"No . . . " she looked up into Brandon's eyes as if he were a complete stranger. "No. All wrong. It's all *wrong*. I . . . Oh, god!" She screwed up her face with a wild twist and erupted into a keening wail. "Chrissie!" she called, hoarsely. Tears welled up in the rag-doll eyes. "It can't be. It can't be. Chrissie is in South America. Tell me she is. Somebody tell me she is. She has to be. It couldn't have been Chrissie." She pounded both sides of her head simultaneously with her fists and keened again, "Chrissie!"

Brandon grabbed Annie's wrists and snapped her arms down in front of her to break the hysteria. He shouted, "Annie! Annie! It's okay! It's me. Brandy Drake. It's me!"

Her arms shook convulsively and she surprised Brandon with her strength. After the tremors subsided she took a deep breath. "I can't believe it," she whispered through the rivulets of tears. "I just can't believe it."

It had been a hell of a day, and Brandy felt as though he were entirely out of his league trying to deal with such intensities of feelings. Out of his cosmos, maybe.

"Who is Chrissie?" he asked.

She continued to tremble, ignoring his question. Annie rattled on from behind a fixed gaze. "The note was in my house when I got back from Nepal in July. The day after Farmer disappeared. She left it with the key. Like always. So I never thought . . ." she began sobbing. "Oh, Chrissie . . ." she moaned, pitifully.

"Maybe it isn't this same woman you seem to think it is. Maybe . . ."

"It's her. It has to be her. It couldn't be anyone else.

Oh, Chrissie . . ."

"I'm sorry, Annie. I didn't think. I mean, if I had guessed you might know the woman . . . "

"Where are they? The bodies?"

"They didn't bring them down yet. It was almost dark when we found them."

"Tomorrow. I have to call Jack. I'll go up with them in the morning." She sniffled and shook her head miserably. "Oh, Chrissie."

"Annie. Is there anything I can do?"

She looked at him as if seeing him for the first time. "No. No . . . I'll . . . I'll be all right. I just want to be alone for now. I think I can handle it better if I'm alone."

"Okay. I'm sorry, Annie. I really am. Are you sure you're going to be all right?"

She nodded.

Brandy continued: "I guess . . . I . . . Chrissie must have been a very close friend of yours."

Annie stared vacantly at Brandy for a while, considering. Then she met his eyes clearly and said with a touch of pride, "She was my lover."

Ten

By seven o'clock in the morning, the funereal gray of a cloudy woodland dawn pronounced a welcome end to an all too discomfiting night. Uneasy sleep, interrupted by a sleepless roommate, makes a night last forever. Every time Brandy was able to relax and unwind enough to doze off, Julia would shuffle from her bed again, click the latch of the bathroom door, and Brandy's conscious mind would hang him in limbo until she finished. With a concluding flush or a gargle or a choking cough, she would open the narrow bathroom door, switch out the light, shuffle back to her bed, rearrange her cool sheets around her, and pretend to sleep again.

Restless, restless night. Several of the interludes included pitiful arias of alternating sobbing and retching, all of which carried all too well through the paper thin walls. After responding to the first such episode and swinging open the door to find Julia kneeling before the throne, arms encircling the porcelain rim, heaving from a long-emptied stomach, Brandon respected her rasping refusal of his offer to help.

A long bastard of a night.

By eight o'clock in the morning, he and Julia were pumping down their second cups of coffee, and by eight-thirty they were answering the relentless salvoes of questions launched by the District Ranger, one Ranger David Jervis. Ranger Dave. He was trying to be polite. So maybe he wasn't being cruel. Maybe he wasn't really pressing her too hard. Maybe it was just the cumulative effect of the past, horrendous twenty-four hours.

Ranger Dibbie --- she of the Information Center --- cruised through the Ranger station with the current trail register under her arm. She reported to the District Ranger that all hikers and climbers registered to the falls trail had been accounted for.

Dibbie closed the book and tilted her head as she addressed Brandon. "I can't help but wonder, especially after our discussion yesterday, why you went up the Falls trail. You were looking for that climber, weren't you? The one you asked me about?"

The District Ranger raised a surprised brow.

"Yes, we were," Brandy admitted. "but we didn't expect to find him."

"How did you know where to look?" Ranger Dibbie persisted.

"We didn't. We were just going up to look at where he'd been last climbing. I never expected we'd find him."

"*I* did," Julia interrupted, "but not . . . like that."

Nobody had anything to add. The Rangers looked at one another and traded skeptical shrugs.

El Portal district had sent two Rangers to support the three rescue climbers from the Valley unit. They had been on the trail picking their way up past the slide area just before daybreak. They carried a field forensic kit and a full complement of technical climbing equipment. The helicopter which lives during the climbing season up at the Crane Flat Fire Lookout had been summoned from Fresno. It was standing by in the village for the pickup.

By nine-thirty the remains of the two bodies had been located, examined, photographed, bagged, and brought down by helicopter to the Village Dispensary. The rear examining room of the Dispensary had been turned into an impromptu morgue. Doctor Ellis, the valley's doctor-on-call, had been summoned to perform the first post-mortem examination. A coroner was on his way up from Fresno by car to complete the full autopsies. Ranger Dave asked Brandon to come in to verify that the remains which had been brought down were those which he and Julia had discovered the previous afternoon. Chain of evidence. A formality in case there were ever any insurance questions.

Decomposed bodies don't travel very well. Like white wines. Mercifully, Julia was not asked to view any organic remains. Formal identification, for her, was of personal effects only: Farmer's helmet, climbing shoes, and the identification and credit cards which Brandon had turned over to the Rangers and sworn to have found on the skeletonized body, were brought out to Julia in the reception area of the Dispensary. That was hard enough on her. Ranger Dave had already told them that absolute identification of Farmer's remains would be confirmed using his dental records, which the park Rangers had had on hand since just after the disappearance. The tentative identification of his climbing partner would be similarly confirmed, but not until her records could be obtained. So far, so routine.

While Ranger Dave took the widow aside to ask a few further questions about the post-forensic arrangements for Farmer's remains and so forth, Brandy managed to steer aside Doctor Ellis for a few private questions. Brandy tried to keep his voice in low tones so as not to risk upsetting Julia any further. He was not normally quite so sensitive in matters of death, but Julia still seemed understandably fragile.

"There's something I don't understand, Doctor. How could two bodies tied together be in such totally different condition? I mean, there was almost nothing left of him, but *she* was . . ."

"I know, Mr. Drake. I was baffled myself this morning after they brought them down. So much so that after I examined them I put in a call to Dr. Michaelson, Chief Coroner for the State, in Sacramento. When I described what I'd seen, he told me that the woman --- Miss Peacock was her name, as you know --- the woman's body has exhibited classical signs of adipocere formation."

"Meaning? I've never heard of that."

"I'm not surprised. Although I haven't done what you'd call a lot of post-mortem examinations, I've done as much as most rural G.P.'s, and I'd never had an opportunity to see it before, either. It's a spontaneous form of preservation without mummification, due to changes in the fat tissue of the body. I don't know if you got close enough to notice the ammonia smell she exuded, but that's one of the characteristics of the condition. It usually takes about three months or so for the adipocere formation to occur, and it is most usually associated with bodies which have been exposed to damp environments in certain controlled, usually cool, temperature ranges. The team said her body was lying on a rock ledge in the back-spray of the falls, so it's not surprising that . . ."

"But Hobbs was in the spray, too!"

"Yes, but because of his location in the foliage, his flesh may have been devoured by small scavengers rather quickly, before the adipocere formation could begin. She was up on the north-facing rock ledge, I'm told."

"True."

"Well, we had a very hot, dry summer, and there may

have been as much as a few degrees difference in the temperatures in which the two bodies lay, due to the cooling breeze and mist in the bowl at the base of the falls. Also, I'm told that the condition occurs more commonly in women, because they have a higher percentage of fat tissue than men, generally."

"But Miss Peacock was supposedly quite fit," Brandon argued.

Ellis shrugged. "Perhaps, but remember that women's hips and breasts and thighs are more fat-laden than men's, Mr. Drake. There must have been enough fat to allow it to happen. It certainly helps us confirm the time interval since their deaths. Amazing that no one else had been able to find them." The doctor paused and observed Drake for reaction. Seeing none, he added, "And that you and his widow *were* able to find him. I'm told by the Rangers that you hadn't been searching for long?"

"That's right. I guess we were just very lucky. If that's what you call lucky. She found the site. We were on our way back. She said she just 'sensed' him. Is that too weird for you, Doctor?"

"No. Weird, but not *too* weird. We talk about having five basic senses --- touch, vision, smell, taste, and hearing --- but in my experience there are a lot of folks who have a lot more stations they can tune into. When we can't explain things away with the five basics, we just clear our throats and sweep them under that rug called 'intuition'. Every day, psychics turn up missing children in the middle of wide open stretches of wilderness, and I'm sure those people have a lot less invested in their connection with those missing children than your friend Julia had in the father of her unborn child. Listen, maybe I've been in this business too long. I'm constantly amazed at people. The police may have trouble with people 'sensing' things, but not me."

"Thank you for your time, Doctor."

Annie arrived just as Brandy and Julia were leaving. She met them on the porch of the Dispensary. Yet another member of the Puffy Face Set. Brandy could guess what kind of night she'd had, too. Annie reached up to give him a sad hug. She introduced herself to Julia as an old friend of Brandy's, a more recent acquaintance of Julia's late husband, and as a close friend and roommate of Farmer's last climbing partner.

Annie grasped Julia's flaccid hand in both of her own and showed a brand of compassion Brandy would never have credited her with. She said all the right things to Julia, and with an undoubtable sincerity. Annie told Julia how sorry she was about Farmer. She had known him only briefly, mostly through their mutual climbing friends in the Valley. She'd never actually climbed with Farmer. But all the serious rock people in the valley liked him a lot, and everyone respected his complete sense of safety in climbing. The news of Farmer's death was going to be sadly received by everyone.

Nobody had known that Chrissie was up with Farmer in this last tragic climb, Annie explained. Everyone had thought Chrissie was in South America climbing in the Andes. She'd left a note as usual to tell Annie where she was headed and to say she'd be back at Christmas, as she'd done every year for the past four years. All Chrissie's gear had been cleared out, which is why nobody had been looking for her. Rock bums were like that. Real tumbleweeds.

Julia's voice was weak. "Farmer never mentioned anyone named Chrissie. Did . . . did they know each other well?"

Annie smiled a lopsided smile. "They'd climbed together once or twice before. Chrissie was one of the best climbers in the valley. People were always wanting to climb

with her. Nobody ever expected her to end it on a rock face.
It must have been just one of those bizarre flukes of
equipment. Or just one of the human errors. That's why they
stay in climbing, honey. That's part of the real spice of
climbing, even for safety-conscious devotees like Farmer
and Chrissie. Non-climbers never understand it. Calculated
risk is the name of the climbing game."

The door to the Dispensary opened and Ranger Dave
called Annie in. She gave Julia a tense hug and disappeared
into the frame building, with her head lowered.

By noon, Brandy had finished packing into the
Corsica and had completed the checkout routine at the Lodge
desk. He returned to the cabin to help Julia carry her things
out to her rental car. The car door was open, and the front
door to the cabin was open wide as well. Brandy was
squelching slight pangs of guilt at his growing nags of
annoyance that Julia was taking so long to finish packing
her things. *Cut the lady some slack, Bran. She's been through
a lot.*

Suddenly shrieks of pain creased the air.

Brandy leaped to the porch and sailed through the
doorway. Julia lay on her still unmade bed, doubled up, arms
wrapped around her middle, writhing from side to side. Her
open suitcase lay overturned between the beds, contents
askew.

"Help me! Somebody help me! Please!" she wailed
pitifully. Her eyes were clenched shut in pain. "Oh, no! Here
it comes again! Oh, no!"

Brandy held his fingers to her wrist and then to the
arteries of her throat until he could feel her thready pulse.
Then she wrenched herself away from his grasp and began
to writhe about on the bed again. Her waves of grunts and
moans and sharp cries were coupled with agonized clutches
of her fists low on her abdomen.

Brandy shouted out the door to a woman who was

walking out of a neighboring cabin, and she ran off toward the lodge lobby to call for medical help.

Brandy knelt beside Julia's twisting, turning agony, and put a hand on her shoulder to reassure and steady her. "You're going to be all right, Julia."

"Oh, God! My belly! Here it comes again!" she shrieked.

Brandy slid the flat of his other hand onto her abdomen and spoke to her in a low voice, nearly a chant, slower and steadier as he proceeded. "Take a long, even deep breath and let it out. Easy. That's it. Let the muscles in all the other parts of the body go still. Very still. Now take another breath. Slowly. Easily."

Julia listened to him. Forced herself to open her chest and her diaphragm. "It's still *coming*," she warned, weakly.

"Let your belly be cool and comfortable," Brandy droned on, ignoring her fears. "The pain belongs somewhere else. Not to Julia. Let it go. Let it go. You are taking back control of your body. Deep breathing and deep concentration on absolute stillness. That's better."

Julia's chest shuddered as she took another deep breath. Her eyes fixed on the ceiling as she concentrated on controlling her breathing and letting go of the pain. Brandy could feel the easing of the spasms. "That's better, Julia," he encouraged her. "Good. That's it. Slow down the breathing *even more*."

It was almost fifteen minutes before the same Doctor Ellis who had presided over the identification at the Dispensary arrived to take charge of first aid and to examine Julia. He pronounced her stable enough to be moved, and directed the ambulance team to take her to Fresno. He would go with them, and Drake could follow in his Corsica if he wished. But only if he drove later, Ellis warned. Too many people made the mistake of trying to keep up with the ambulance. The ambulance drivers knew the roads and Drake didn't. They didn't need an auto accident to compound the emergency.

Ellis was caught by Brandon's impassive steel-grey eyes and sensed that this was probably an exceptional man. Without any verbal challenge, Ellis reconsidered. On second thought, Mr. Drake could follow directly, if he wished.

By four-thirty in the afternoon, about an hour and a half after Julia was admitted to Fresno General Hospital, Ellis came into the waiting area of the hospital and found Brandy standing tall in the center of the background hubbub of broken fingers, baseball uniforms, and dog-bitten ankles, interrogating the rigidly officious head nurse on Day Emergency. The doctor noticed with special and private amusement that Drake was actually getting answers from the old war horse. He interrupted and pulled Brandon aside.

"Mr. Drake? I'm sorry I didn't have time to tell you more back at the Lodge, but . . ."

"I understand. How is she?"

"Just fine. Her condition is fully stabilized now. As you may have guessed from what I said back in the Valley, I thought she was about to miscarry. That can be touch and go for a while, and I thought she might be better off with the back-up facilities down here in town. It's always a risk to move anyone in that condition, but I felt it was the lesser of evils in her case. I'm not sure why it happened, but it stands to reason that she was so shocked by finding out about her husband, or the trauma of the tumbling you both took in the slide up on the mountain . . . well, you get the picture. From what she described to me on the way down here from the Valley, and from the bruises on her arm and hip, I'd guess you two took quite a beating up there yesterday. It could have been any of those things. Or none of them. Anyway, she aborted no more than half an hour ago. I'm sorry."

Brandy absorbed the news with a grim expression. Maybe, thought the doctor, he had read this man wrong. Maybe he should have worded the news differently. It's hard to know how people will take that kind of news. But Mrs. Hobbs had said on the way down out of the mountains, in the quiet period between spasms and contractions, that this man was a good friend of hers. Ellis waited.

Drake shook his head sadly and said in a philosophical tone, "Sometimes, these things work out for the best."

Ellis nodded solemnly. "I gather you two are *very* close friends." He waited, but Drake didn't respond. Ellis flipped open the metal chart-holder in his hand and scribbled a few unreadable notes. "I'm suggesting they keep her here for a day or two for observation. Probably be fine tomorrow but we'll just have to see. We did a D and C. Everything was routine. I'll be going back to Yosemite shortly with the ambulance team, but Mrs. Hobbs will be under excellent care here. Dr. Warburton will be in charge of her. He's on staff here."

Brandon maintained the unreadable expression. Unnerving fellow, Ellis thought. Maybe he was in a bit of shock himself. "Mrs. Hobbs is still pretty fatigued. Mild shock, though there wasn't much bleeding. She said she wants to see you. As soon as possible."

For men, the intimacy of breeding is a fleeting one, and they come away from the encounter empty. By design.

Women come away from the breeding encounter full. They carry a physical, cellular component of the union, and if it is a successful breeding, they will carry a new body. A third body.

Hence, men cannot have the same sense as women about a miscarriage. Men, if they think about a miscarriage, imagine that it must be a lot like the monthly menstrual discharge, a magnified version of the usual outflow of blood and tissues which the system uses to clear itself of another egg and its supporting structures. With a miscarriage, they reason, the only difference is that the egg is fertilized by another cell and that it has grown and developed a bit further in the world of the microscopic.

Men are not being cold and unfeeling. They are only applying reason within the bounds of their personal experiences with the process of breeding and procreation. They may never be able to closely empathize; but even so, the grandest of them will do what men do best for their part of the post-breeding process. They will provide shelter and protection.

There at Julia's bedside, as she dozed and rested, Brandy sat and squeezed her weak, cool hand until her breathing became slower and deeper and more even, until at last she fell asleep.

Shelter and protection. By instinct.

Eleven

The manager at the Yosemite Lodge drew a map to get Brandy from the Valley to the house in Foresta where Annie lived. It had seemed like a forever drive back up to the Park from Fresno, but there was nothing Brandy could do down there. When Dr. Warburton had come by for his evening rounds, he had suggested Brandy get some rest. With her sedative on board, Julia would be sleeping for at least twelve hours now. So Brandy had decided to return to Yosemite for the night.

After confirming the Foresta instructions, Brandy got back into his Corsica and drove west out the Northside Drive, up the Big Oak Flat Road toward Tioga Pass, maintaining careful vigilance lest the Foresta turnoff elude him.

The cones of white light from the Corsica opened up holes in the moonless blackness of the Merced River valley night. The highway was devoid of road lights, except at the junction where Highway 120 rises from the Merced Canyon. Occasional reflections glittered from mica chips in the granite faces of blocks which had been mortared together long ago in hopes of guarding against fatal swerves of far older and slower automobiles than the roadway now served.

Brandy was far too weary to enjoy the solitude or the beauty. But he also felt that certain gut-level calm which always attends the end of a hunt, the conclusion of a case, the close of a chapter, and he was anxious to take care of the last bits of unfinished business before he could let himself relax into deep and well-deserved sleep. If he really let himself go now, he was sure he could sleep for two days non-stop. So he wouldn't. Not yet.

Tomorrow he would be meeting the man from Julia's rent-a-car company. The man was taking the bus up from Sacramento just to retrieve her car. Then Brandon could check in on Julia at the hospital in Fresno and either escort her home or tread water for another day or two, visiting friends in San Francisco until the doctors considered Julia fit to travel.

Basically it was Cleanup Mode. Bits and pieces. Odds and ends. In the information business, it paid to be fastidious. And not just in the monetary sense. In fact, it looked unlikely that Brandy would be billing Julia for anything more than expenses on this case. Partly empathy. Partly because he could afford not to. After the net earnings from the last three industrial searches had been carefully squirreled away, he was already set to spend about two months on rest-and-relaxation in his cabin in the North woods. No sense getting greedy about life.

Foresta is an anomaly. It was originally planned as several hundred wilderness cabins and seasonal homes in a neat mountain subdivision, but the National Park service had other ideas. As the Yosemite Park expansion surrounded and engulfed the privately owned parcels in the largely undeveloped tract, the Park bought out enough of Foresta's individual owners of undeveloped property to leave a community which looked, on the revised maps, like a random collection of homestead islands connected by an odd latticework of unimproved dirt roads and gravel laneways winding their ways across the needle-strewn floor of the subalpine coniferous forest.

Finding Annie's cabin in the dark, even with the help of her verbal instructions and the hand-drawn map, was no small order. After three Back-To-Go maneuvers, Brandy finally edged the Corsica to a stop behind an ancient grey Volvo sedan next to a tall A-frame house. In the deep forest silence, the Corsica exuded heat, paint smells, and irregular ticking sounds as it began to cool.

Annie stared up at the gaunt, tall figure cast in the yellow light of her back porch. Her smile was weary, but welcoming. She was dressed in olive-green coveralls, with well-worn pink crocheted woollen slippers on her feet. "Oh, Brandy," she sighed heavily.

She pulled him into the kitchen, and closed and latched the door behind him. Reaching up to stretch her tiny arms around his lean chest, she buried her doll face in the belly of his sweater. "I've been *soooo* miserable today. I've been a widow too many times in this life already. This is just about, without exception, the *worst* day of my life. Thanks for coming back to see me."

When she released her hold on him, he steadied her at arm's length to survey her face and then smiled sympathetically. "You said you wouldn't let me out of your paddy-paws without a catch-up. 'Member?"

"I know. But that was a century ago." She turned and he followed her through the kitchen and past a dining nook into the cathedral-ceilinged living room. "I've spent the whole day walking around this house like a zombie. The telephone has been ringing off the hook with everybody everywhere wanting to know exactly what happened. I got so tired of having to go through it all so many times that I finally disconnected the ring and put it on the answering machine.

So I've been running around the house, cleaning it and washing the sheets and every other damn thing I could think of to try to stay very busy. You'd think I was expecting a visit from the Queen of England. But most of all I've been missing the hell out of Chrissie. I mean it's crazy when you think about it. Before I knew what really happened to her, I didn't miss her nearly so much. She wouldn't have been back here for another month anyway. She would still be climbing in South America instead of . . . " She took a deep breath and stared at Brandon. "Instead of dead." Her lower lip began to tremble. "I guess it'll really knock my props out from under me when she doesn't show up at Christmas. I was a little surprised I hadn't gotten any card from her in the last month. I thought she was gone for the season. Like usual. In May, when I left for my trip to the Himalayas, she said she'd see me in December. She always came back north for Christmas. I hated not being with her for seven months. We both hated it. And I missed her a lot. Especially when I came back home and everything was all closed up. And I miss her a lot now, too. *God*, how I miss her!"

Climbing gear was strewn across the wide flat cushions covering the bed-like benches lining one of the long walls of the A-frame. Some of the gear spilled onto the adjacent wooden floor. Annie swept a gesturing arm toward the tangle of equipment. "This is Chrissie's stuff I found over at Cam's place. I couldn't think of any better medicine for me than sorting out all her junk right away, so I went over and got it this afternoon. There wasn't much there. Just the shit she was taking with her to the Andes. It was all packed. Like she'd been all set to go right after they came back from that . . . from the . . . the last climb. But they were obviously sleeping together there. They hadn't even made the bed."

"Do the police know that?"

"They couldn't have missed it. They already took pictures and cleared out most of the stuff, but they left a few things. There . . ." She pointed at a large cardboard toilet-paper carton at one end of the collection. "Those are Hobbsie's. Not much there. I guess they already found the rest of his stuff at the Lodge back in the summer. Where he had the room. But there's some clothes and his bathroom kit there, so . . . you can take them to his wife if you want. You decide. She seemed nice. Maybe it would be better to just forget about that and let her go on thinking they just climbed together. I wouldn't know. Tact was never my long suit."

"As well I know."

She forced a grin. "Not that it was your long suit either, buddy."

"Why wasn't Chrissie registered on the climb?"

"Could be because they didn't want gossip to get out of hand. Rumors in the climbing world are hard enough to deal with in the best of times."

"Okay. But then why weren't they climbing at Arrowhead, where the register said the climb was? Farmer was supposed to be such a safety nut."

"I don't know. They must have changed plans on the way up to the starting point of the climb. That happens, and no one wants to come all the way back down to change the registration. We'll probably never know exactly what happened." Annie's eyes glazed over. "Except to know they're both dead now."

"Who is Cam?" Brandy asked.

"Friend of ours. Owns a cabin down at the other end of Foresta. But he's hardly ever there. That's where Chrissie and Farmer must have been staying for the week Farmer was here. I figured it out as soon as I found out about them being together on the climb. They did it once before that I know of, too. Maybe more. Chrissie wouldn't have told me about it, of course. I guess they were trying to be discreet. The Lodge is pretty public, and my place here . . . well, I guess there was always the possibility of me coming home a few days early

from the Himalayas. Chrissie never wanted to be tacky with
me. Mutual respect. We had an understanding." Annie's
eyes started to water. Her mouth dipped deeply at the corners.
"I never thought to go over to Cam's and look for . . . I mean,
when I found my house closed up as usual, I just assumed
she was gone to South America. Everything normal. I
remember feeling a little relieved that Farmer had been
climbing alone when he disappeared. I had wondered if
Chrissie would get any news down south and give a call to
find out what happened. Down there, the news is practically
non-existent. They could declare a nuclear fucking war and
nobody down there would know about it until it was over."
Annie banged her fist against her forehead in frustration.
"Shit! How was I supposed to know? She always left things
so neat."

Brandy put a hand on Annie's shoulder. Her lip
trembled. "*God*, but it hurts to use the past tense . . ." she
said woefully.

Brandy took her by both shoulders and gave her a
squeeze.

"Is it going to be like this all night?" she asked,
plaintively, warding off tears. "If so, I'm going to be a hell of
a great date for you."

"Grieving is special, Annie. You do it any way you
want to do it."

"Well, you just leave when it gets too heavy for you.
Promise?"

"Okay. Have you eaten anything today?"

"Only some soup. You hungry, too?"

"I'd enjoy a bite."

"You *angel*, you."

It broke the doldrums for Annie to get into her familiar
kitchen. In no time, she whipped up a hearty meal. More
than Brandy thought he could possibly eat, but he was
wrong. Annie insisted that he fill her in on the Life and Times

and Careers of Brandon Jennings Drake, post-degree and post-retrorocket freedom from the Berkeley orbit. They laughed and gibed at one another and recited old jokes and played a few rounds of have-you-ever-heard-from. After a belly-warming fill, they piled the dishes in the sink. Annie insisted it was tomorrow morning's therapy to leave them there.

"Oops. I almost forgot," she added. "Want some wine?"

"I'm not much of a wine drinker usually, but given the extenuating circumstances of the past twenty-four hours, I'll make an exception."

"I probably shouldn't drink any either. It wouldn't take much for me to make a jackass out of myself. This smiling little Annie doll you see before you is hanging off the edge by the tippy-tips of her little fingers. One glass and ol' Annie, ol' reliable, responsible, Mother-of-the-Earth Annie, may come to pieces before your very eyes and have a big flashflood of a cry."

"Which would be fine with me. A good cry never hurt anybody."

"Randy Brandy, you're a sweetheart. I hoped you'd say something like that. The glasses are in the cupboard to the left of the sink."

Balancing glasses and a full bottle, Brandy followed Annie back into the living room and watched her bank three huge logs in the fireplace. Near the bottom of a liter of California red and in the aftermath of an equal volume of salty tears, Annie lay quietly on her side on one of the cushioned couch-benches, her head propped on Brandon's knee. They stared at the flicker above the coals in the large cauldron-like firebed in the center of the living room. The newer sticks popped and the smoke curled its way up into the hood and on up the chimney stack to where it passed through the peak of the thirty-foot ceiling.

Neither of them had spoken for a long, long time.

"Was it Farmer's baby?" Annie asked.

Brandon nodded silently.

"Too bad. Or maybe not. I guess it depends on your perspective, doesn't it?"

There was more silence. Brandon wondered if Annie were falling asleep. Leaning back against some bolsters, it was hard to tell whether her eyes were open or closed unless she blinked.

"Did they figure out what caused the fall?" he asked.

"Equipment failure, looks like. Broken belay sling, maybe." Annie continued to stare at the fire. "Everything else looked okay."

"They let you see it all?"

"They always do. I'm the specialist, remember? Annie's the name, climbing's the game." She closed her eyes. "But I wish I hadn't seen this one. Shit."

"Don't they call in outside experts? Forensic specialists? That sort of thing?"

"Not for climbing accidents. They call in climbing experts for that. And when you're in Yosemite, you can usually come up with the best in the country without dialling a single long distance call. Some of them are Rangers. Some are Mountain Rescue. Some are freelancers, like me." She opened her eyes again.

"Greg Hawkins thought Chrissie was probably shortcutting," Annie continued. "That she hadn't used a sling, and maybe Hobbsie slipped while he was cleaning the wall, and she couldn't hold him. But I know better. Greg is such a presumptuous asshole. He never even climbed with her. Thinks all women are beadbrains. Jesus. So they were all standing around looking at the equipment and the way Chrissie and Hobbsie were rigged and Clive Horrigan agreed with me. I've never --- and I mean *never* --- known Chrissie to cut that kind of corner. And Hobbsie. Hell, he was a regular

Grannie when it came to safety procedures. The nubies would laugh at him when he would come all the way here from Canada and then cancel a big climb if the weather looked the least bit bad. They thought he was a real pussy about it. But he didn't care what they thought. I'll give him that. He just didn't care. He was adamant."

"Whoa! If Farmer was such a stickler for safety procedures, why was he registered as climbing solo that day?"

"I told you, they were probably just trying to be discreet."

"A Ranger told me that he'd been climbing with other people the couple of days before, and Julia said he would never have climbed solo. And now we know that Chrissie was actually up there with him. At least for the last climb. What gives?"

"Hell, I don't know." She narrowed her eyes as fury resurfaced. "But Greg thinks they were cutting corners. Shit! They might have made a climbing mistake, but neither of them would have cut a corner. Not one like that."

"What did Phil think?"

"Phil? He wasn't there today. He would have been, if he'd been around. He's a real gomer for seeing dead climbers. A real morbid sonofabitch. He'll be pissed off that he missed it. Haven't seen him since yesterday when he called me in to the shop. One of the clerks from the Village Store usually stands in on Fridays, so Phil probably won't be back in the valley until tomorrow. If you ask me, Phil probably got horny after seeing Hobbs' wife --- he was really taken with her --- and went down to Merced to try to get some ass last night. That's about his speed. He has to go out and get some strange, if he wants anything. No woman here in the Valley would get within ten feet of the dirty old jackass.

"Anyway, one goddamned broken sling, and two goddamned nice people smack a big rock. It's probably not a bad way to go, but I can't get away from the basic awfulness of losing her . . ."

"Is it unusual for a sling to break like that?" Brandon asked. "That one on Chrissie's harness looked pretty frayed to me, but I didn't know how much of that was from three months in the weather and how much was . . ."

Annie frowned. "What are you talking about? The sling's long gone. It's probably still around a rock or fastened to a piton somewhere up the face at their last belay point. Unlikely to turn up. Or at least it's unlikely ever to be identified. Mainly because there are hundreds of pieces of protection left on the walls of Yosemite every year. People don't bother to carry them out. Damned pigs. Inconsiderate climbers. Because you certainly can't trust anything you find up there, so all you can do is leave it or lug out somebody else's garbage. If we'd actually found a sling on Chrissie we wouldn't have had the big argument about whether or not the cause of the accident was equipment failure. It would have been obvious."

"Well, there was some sort of nylon webbing, the tube-shaped stuff, looped through Chrissie's harness. She was lying on it. I couldn't pull it free from under her."

"And you said it was frayed? Not a closed loop?" Annie rolled off the couch and stumbled unsteadily in an ethanolic haze around the fireplace to the snarl of climbing equipment laid out on the bench on the other side of the room. She returned with a sewn nylon loop and handed it to Brandon. "Like this?"

"Except broken apart."

Annie crinkled her rag-doll brow, wobbled her head in the negative, and sat down beside Brandon. "Can't be. Clive and Devon wouldn't leave anything behind like that. And they wouldn't have missed it, either, when they first arrived up there. I even hiked up there this afternoon --- I had to see where it happened for myself --- and saw the

places they'd marked. There was no equipment left up there.
I would have noticed. I think you must have seen something
else. Anyway, if the sling had failed, it would only confirm
my theory about what must have happened with Chrissie
and Hobbsie. It's all academic. I really don't think we'll ever
know for sure. All we end up with is a lot of uncertainty. It's
like that after a lot of climbing accidents." She dropped her
head back into Brandon's lap and sighed. "I think I'm
depleted. Really depleted. Mind if we change the subject
again?" Another long silence was invaded only by crackle
and popping from the vaporizing moisture deep in the largest
log.

"Let me tell you something," Annie suddenly blurted
out, sitting upright beside Drake again as she spoke, so that
she could face him squarely. "There's a big temptation for
me to haul you off to bed for an all night cuddle. A mighty
big temptation."

"I'd probably be too exhausted to do anything more
than just that," replied Brandy, deadpan.

"All the better, my Randy Brandy. Because now that
I've all but issued an invitation," she added, nodding
knowingly, "in honesty I don't think I could handle company
tonight. Much as I might want it. Call me a fickle female, if
you want. Is that okay?"

"Better than okay . . ."

"I'll make up the guest bed down here by the fire."

"Nice of you to offer, but I've still got a cabin over at
the Lodge."

"No way, sweetheart! I have a real 'thing' about
drinking and driving. These mountain roads are deadly in
the best of conditions, and I guarantee I won't let you get
behind the wheel of a car with half a bottle of vino inside
you! Husband Number Three was mashed against one of
those cold stone walls out there, and I don't want to have
anyone else I know doing the same."

"You weren't watching, my lovely Raggedy Ann. I only had one glass of your precious vino, and that was nearly three hours ago. It was a great wine but, as I told you, I'm not a wine man any more."

"You mean I put away almost the whole damn bottle by myself? Little me? No wonder I almost propositioned you. Good god!"

"So I'll be off and away now." He got to his feet. Annie put her arm around his hips and leaned close as she walked with him toward the back door, bumping table and counter and doorframe along the way. He opened the door and plunged into the cool October mountain night. When he stepped down from the porch to the second step, Annie tugged on his arm to turn him around. Even two steps above him she had to reach up slightly to encircle his neck with her tiny arms. She gave him a warm, moist, lingering, wine-flavored kiss and whispered, "Thanks, Brandy. Thanks for helping me forget. And for making me remember. Thanks more than I can ever tell you. I know what a selfish, rotten goddamned woman I am. Always have been. Never claimed otherwise. Which is why I'm especially grateful. You are more friend than I deserve."

Twelve

Julia was out of the hospital the next afternoon, and Brandy was there to retrieve her. He drove her straight to Oakland International, returned the Corsica to the rental people, and flew home with Julia to Vancouver.

Three days later, a courier service arrived with a cashier's check for fifteen thousand dollars and a thank you note. Julia. Dear, sweet, off-the-wall Julia.

He would never have asked for the money. Even though she'd originally agreed to pay it to him. He wouldn't have asked. Not after the wringer she'd been through in Yosemite. But he also knew better than to object to her paying. In the hill country of eastern America, where Brandy had been raised, it was an important rule of life never to be beholden to anyone. So he understood why Julia had paid out what she owed. A deal is a deal.

All but two thousand of the money was divvied up and swifted away into the Cariboo Cabin Fund to buy more time when it was needed. The R&R survival funds.

And that might well have been the simple end of one of Brandy's stranger cases, if it hadn't been for the curious call five days later.

At about ten-thirty on Thursday morning, Brandon was staring at his computer screen, surrounded by barely cipherable software documentation, trying to figure out how he could coordinate the macro functions on his new telecom package to begin multiple searches of the Compuserve databases in some sort of overlay which would be effective enough to reduce his network connect time by maybe half to three quarters. He was less concerned about the financial savings --- the clients always paid the tab on that one --- than about the reduction of search time required to do the hundred-odd chores he had to perform on-line each month.

The out-of-the-blue telephone call was so unexpected that he had to buy time with several ritual salutations before he figured out who was on the other end of the line. The connection was only so-so.

"Annie? Where are you?"

"At home in Foresta."

"I thought you were leaving to go back to Asia right after you sorted out Chrissie's things. I thought you'd be in Nepal by now."

"I agreed to help manage the Mountaineering School until they made arrangements to replace Phil."

"Replace Phil? Where did *he* go?"

"To the morgue. He's dead. That's what I called about. I didn't know if you'd heard about it yet."

"No, I hadn't. Talk to me."

"After he didn't show up at the school Monday, Dave went up to his cabin looking for him. No sign of him. Then his car was found up at the Lodge. And are you ready for this?"

"I guess so."

"First thing this morning, the trail maintenance people dug him up. Literally. At the base of the avalanche that hit you and Hobbsie's wife. He was really deep under it. They were almost finished digging out the footings for the new retaining wall for the middle section of the trail when they found him."

"Really?" There was a silence on the line as Drake absorbed the implications of what Annie was telling him. She must have already reasoned it out. He wondered what answers she'd come up with. "I swear that Julia and I never saw him up there. Not before, not during, and not *after* the slide. There was no one else on the trail. Which was to be expected. Remember, it was almost dark. What the hell was he doing up there? He must have been very near us to be caught in the slide. It wasn't all that *big* a slide area. It just came down *fast*."

"Right. Well, that's what puzzled Ranger Dave. Which is why I think you'll be hearing from him in the next short while. But that's not really why I called you. There's something else which might be especially interesting to you, private eye type that you are."

"I don't know how you're going to beat what you've just told me, m'dear. I admit to being quite shocked already."

"Try this: in Phil's jacket pocket he had a sling. Failed. Broken. And I want you to tell me the color of the sling you said you'd seen on Chrissie's harness when you found her."

"Dark red, I think. But it was hard to tell. It was pretty shot from being pinned under her body for the three months."

"Well, it wasn't in any better condition after being in a jacket pocket under a sand slide for six more days, either. Can you come back down here? To the valley?" She paused. "I have a few things I want to talk over with you. There's something fishy about this whole damned mess."

"Isn't this a police matter, Annie? Shouldn't you be

talking with the Rangers?"

"Yeah. Probably. But I can't tell them what I'm not sure about yet, and I don't want you to talk to them about any of this either. Please? As a friend? At least until I have a chance to talk to you? If Dave calls before you leave, just tell him what you told me --- that you didn't see Phil on the trail --- and leave it at that. Okay?"

"That's a pretty strange request, Annie. What the hell is going on?"

"Please, Brandy. Just come on down."

"And what's Ranger Dave going to think about my timely return to Yosemite?"

"I'll tell him I called you this morning. I already told him we were old friends. You can come back to spend a couple of days helping me pick up the pieces. As a friend. I'm sure you've faked your way through worse, haven't you?"

"And what will Dave make of the mysterious phoenix sling?"

"Not much. I don't think he's put it together that it was Chrissie's protection. I mean, Phil was a climbing instructor. You'd expect him to have climbing stuff in his pockets. Right?"

"Annie, you're not making good sense. If the police make the connection . . ."

"Look, even if they put two and two together, even if they happen to ask you about the sling, just say you can't remember. Easy, huh? You can always remember later on, you know."

"Annie, it'll take me a day or two to finish up some things I'm doing here and . . ."

"Jesus, Brandy. What do I have to do? Get down on my fucking hands and knees and beg. I *need* you. Right *now*! I'm counting on you, Brandy. You'll understand when you get here and I can explain it." There was a serious, disturbing edge to Annie's voice. "I can even pay you for the trip back down here. Just *come*. Please."

Paradoxically, Foresta felt darker and more ominous on a cloudless early November afternoon than it had a week earlier when Brandy had arrived in the black shroud of night. There had been more snow during the week, and the landscape had settled into sleep with its winter shroud. The main roads were still mostly clear, but packed snow and ice made Foresta's back roads and driveways a challenge to navigate.

"I'm scared. Really scared," Annie rasped as soon as the two of them were seated across from one another at the kitchen table. They were separated by a huge ashtray. Annie wore dark blue coveralls and the same floor-worn woolly slippers as she had been wearing the week before. Her uniform. She was smoking a cigarette, but the house reeked of grass. Somehow Annie looked incongruous with a standard sized cigarette in her fingers. Unnatural. She had rarely smoked at Berkeley during the wild and woolly Sixties. Not even dope. And she certainly hadn't lit up anything during the private evening she'd spent with Brandy the previous week, so he knew what he was seeing wasn't chronic compulsive behavior. And he noticed that Annie held the cigarettes as if smoking wasn't a habit for her. As if it were a momentary sanctuary. As if it didn't feel particularly *good*. Just safe.

"When I called you about the sling they found in Phil's pocket, I was just plain scared. Scared because there's just a whole lot of shit from the past that I wouldn't want to have coming up from the murky deeps. Really heavy stuff. Take my word for it. And I thought about having the police snooping around about Chrissie and me, and I just thought about how that would be pretty horrendous. But the more I thought about it, the more pissed off I got, too. I mean, I realized somebody had actually tried to *kill* Chrissie. Or maybe she just got in the way of somebody killing *him* --- you know . . . Farmer --- but that doesn't matter. They killed my beautiful lover, and she's just as dead and gone, whether she was the real target or not."

"Wait a minute. Slow down, Annie. Go back to Part One. I can see why you might think there was something funny about the way Phil died, but what makes you think Farmer and Chrissie were anything but an accident?"

She leaned forward toward the table, burying her head between her fists. "Stop. Hold it. Hold on, hold on. Before we go any further with this, you have to promise me that you will keep everything I tell you an absolute secret."

Brandon frowned. "I can promise you that only so long as you can assure me I won't have to violate any laws by doing so."

"Well, goddamn you anyway! What happened to client confidentiality and all that shit? I thought you were a Private Eye."

"In the first place, there is no such protection for private investigators. Second, I'm not one of those anyway. I told you about that last week. I'm an information agent. I collect information for people. Usually from computer databases. That's it. Got it? I don't even have a California license any more. So anything I do in this state is without any authorization. Strictly on my own. Just like any other Joe Citizen visitor to this state. Third, you're not my client. You're my friend."

"What good is that to me?" she moaned.

Brandon raised an eyebrow. "I don't know. But if it's of no use, just say the word and I'm out of here."

She lifted her reddened eyes to focus intensely, if unsteadily, on his face. "I don't want to tell anybody about any of this, damn it! But I'm too afraid not to. All I know is that I can't tell the police what I know. But I need to trust

somebody, and I trust you already." She bit her thumb and
then her lip. "What if I just tell you about hypothetical things
--- things that maybe never even happened --- and you can
tell me what I should do? What you would do if you were
me."

"I've already told you my guidelines, Annie. Don't
try to parlay our friendship into some kind of immunity. If
you've got a conscience problem, go see a priest. Or maybe
it's a lawyer you should be talking with. I don't know."

"How about if you listened to what I have to say? All
of it. As a close friend, which you are. What if when I'm
finished, you understand the importance of keeping certain
things confidential, even if the law might say I should report
them, and you agreed that certain things should be kept
secret? Would you have to blab them to the police then?"

"I've been in situations," chimed Brandy, "when each
and every course open to me incurred some technical
illegality or another." Funny how some responses come from
brain lacunae, little bubbles of memory, such that they don't
have to be considered as matters of conscious thought.
They just roll out, as naturally as burps. The caveats of
self-protection and legal integrity come from private
investigators as naturally and instantly as soothing,
nurturing phrases come from caring parents. Verbal
boilerplate. "Eventually," he continued, "most everything
comes out anyway, I suppose, but I never promise protective
silence before I know what it is I'm expected to keep to myself.
Is that clear?"

"That's pretty goddamned Goody Two-Shoes,
Brandy."

"No, ma'am. That's survival. So you can quit dancing
with yourself. You won't get a better prior commitment from
me. And frankly, Annie, any verbal assurance of mine
wouldn't be worth a coon's eye to you anyway. Don't you
realize that? From what you've told me so far, I don't think I

want to know what it is that's bothering you. Sorry, but my life has quite enough melodrama and intrigue in it already." He rose from his seat and leaned over to rest a reassuring friend's hand on hers. She made no attempt to pull away. Her distress was palpable.

She frowned and lit up another cigarette. She snubbed it out immediately. A frantic ritual.

"They're dead," she said. "It was no accident. Obviously, somebody killed them."

Brandon wagged his head at her. "How, suddenly, does Miz Annie know that it was no accident?"

She pushed herself angrily up from the table and pounded down with her fists next to the ashtray. "Brandy, for Christ's sake! I know my climbing gear. I may not have my shit together in too many other departments, but climbing is my game! I saw that sling Phil had in his pocket. It was weird the way it had come apart . . ."

"And Ranger Dave or some of his forensic people will be able to figure that out well enough to make the connection, too. Right?"

"Probably not." She pursed her face into a stubborn button, and plumped back down into her seat. "Not after Dave asked me about it and I told him it was defective protection some climber had hauled off El Cap last week and brought into the school. I told him I remembered Phil stuffing it in his jacket pocket --- that same jacket --- the week before the slide. I just couldn't remember if Phil had said who brought it in."

"So you lied to Dave?"

"For a good reason. I told you."

"Annie, Annie, Annie . . . I don't know why you're doing this, but if you're right, then just let it unfold. You don't have to keep secrets. Leave investigations to the police. They're usually pretty good at it. Nothing could be important enough to risk implicating yourself in a possible murder by lying about what you know."

Annie snubbed out her newly lit cigarette, lurched from her seat, spun around and flung her fists down as she stalked three quick steps away from him. "Jesus, you're so fucking naive! I thought you'd been around more than that."

"Exactly what is it you're scared of from your Great Dark Past?"

Still facing away from him, she covered her face with her hand. Her voice lowered. "I don't want to talk about it. It's not important."

"It must be, to convince you to try to muddy a police investigation like this. Given your expertise in climbing gear, you could provide just the kind of detailed information to the police that could clear this whole thing up in a day. If there was a murder, you could be an important part of solving it. So why the mystery?"

She turned to face him, wide eyes strained and bloodshot, tiny fists clenched tightly. She stood there speechless for a long time, as if she were at the crossroads of a major decision. "Come with me," her throat tightened and rasped. "I want to show you something." She marched straight down the dark hallway to a windowless add-on storage room. As she clicked on the switch inside the door, light surged from a single incandescent hundred-watt bulb set in the middle of an unfinished ceiling. The room was full of all sorts of climbing gear. In spite of the overflow of equipment, there was the obvious orderliness of a conscientious professional. Annie climbed up on a low stepstool to take a handful of nylon tube slings from a wide hook on the wall. "Here," she ordered. "Take a look at these."

"They look like large slings. At least that's what I think they are. I'd guestimate they're about the same length and gauge --- the same thickness --- as the one I tried to pull out from under Chrissie. This red one could even be the same color."

"It is. Look at them more closely," Annie demanded.

Drake carried them down the hallway and out into the brighter light of the living room. He inspected them more carefully. There was heavily reinforced stitching where the loop was sewn closed. He tugged at them in various ways. Looked all around the full length of each sling in turn.

"I don't know what you're getting at," Brandon shrugged. "These look just like the kind of slings I'd guess any climber might use for belay anchorage. Stout loops. Tubular nylon. Sewn end to end. They look new, or nearly new. Good condition, anyway. Assorted colors. They look okay to me. Am I missing something? Is there something wrong with the stitching, maybe? If there is, I can't tell. My granny-glasses are in my jacket in the other room. Furthermore, I'm not a technical climber. So I'm not the one to judge."

"That's true, you're not. But I can tell you that even an expert climber wouldn't notice that anything was wrong with these slings without being very suspicious and knowing exactly what she was looking for. Even super-safe climbers like Hobbsie and Chrissie wouldn't have picked up on it. Hell, it even had *me* fooled."

"So there *is* something wrong with them?"

"Look just next to the final stitching line, where the edge of the overlaid tubing layer hides the main loop fabric for about a millimeter or so. Twist the fabric like this and take a better look at it. What do you see?"

Brandon strained to see what Annie was pointing at. "It looks a little rough. That's all. Why?"

"Because somebody somehow cut and weakened it there. I'm not sure what they used. Something like a very fine, very sharp wire. Bent into a tiny hook, maybe, which could be pushed through the nylon from the flap side and used to cut and weaken the sling from the inside, leaving very little to show on the outside, and that covered up by the flap of the sew-through anyway. I wouldn't swear that was exactly how it was done, but I do know these slings have been tampered with." She glared challengingly at Brandon.

"So you're saying somebody could *make* a sling that was more likely to break, and that it might have been done to the sling which failed in Chrissie's fall. Isn't that a bit hypothetical?"

Annie pointed to the loop in Brandon's hands. "That was one of the slings I brought back from Cam's. The ones you saw me sorting out last Sunday night when you were here? *I* didn't even catch what was wrong with them. I had already checked them and chucked them into my gear room. I couldn't tell whether they were Hobbsie's or Chrissie's --- they were in a pile of mixed gear on the floor in the bedroom between their stuff --- but I assumed they were Chrissie's, so I took them for myself. I would have started using them like my own if Phil hadn't been killed. Every one of them from Cam's house --- there were three they didn't take up with them on their last climb --- every one of them was like that."

"How about the other slings Chrissie and Farmer were carrying with them? The ones on their bodies? Are they in the same condition?"

"I haven't figured out a way to check without raising Dave's suspicion, but I'll bet they are. I'd put some very big money on that bet."

"But there are other explanations for what you've found out here. Maybe Chrissie happened to notice the same things about these slings and that's why they didn't use them. Maybe what you've found is a machine error on this run of slings. A poor sewing machine. One with a bur on the needle. Quality control is never one-hundred percent in any business. Have you never seen any defective climbing equipment before?

"I think you're letting your emotions run away with

you. And that's not a sexist slam. In the rock climbing world, you may be in the habit of relying heavily on your intuition and your hunches. Your survival may depend on it. Well, I rely on mine, too. But in my business, it never pays to jump to conclusions. When certain explanations fit a little too well at first, they sometimes can distract you from getting at the real facts."

Annie slumped onto the couch cushions beside the stone-cold fireplace.

"You still tracking me or are you too stoned?" Drake asked. Annie looked up, mixed anger and terror trying to explode through her face.

Brandy continued. "Drake Basic Rule Number Six says: no matter what is proposed, doubt it. A little creative doubting saves a great heap of effort chasing false trails and saves you from overlooking the real explanations for things. Cheap insurance. So just unwind a few minutes and humor me with some basic background on this. Okay?"

Annie was stone-faced.

Brandy scowled. "Look, dammit. If I was willing to come all the way back down here to play good-old-buddy-in-time-of-need, you can damn well pay out a little courtesy."

Annie's hands began trembling. "Maybe I can't trust you."

"Too late for that concern. When did you discover all this about the sabotaged climbing equipment?"

Like an old piece of machinery too long without oil, Annie began to slowly creak out her next words. "After I talked to you . . . the night before last." She stared down at her hands and seemed struck by the shaking loops of the slings she still held. "And I've been like this ever since." She hurled the slings to the floor and leaped to her feet, bellowing, "For fucking out loud, Brandy! *I* could have used one of those things on my next climb! How do I know they weren't intended for me, anyway?"

"How easily would these slings break?"

Annie took an uneven breath and continued, "They probably wouldn't snap loose under *light* stress loads, like a tugback or a gradual loading. But it's hard to say. The ones I brought back from Cam's place are all strong enough that you could probably get started onto a solid belay without a failure, but beyond that it's anyone's guess."

"Who have you told about this?"

"Nobody. Except you. And that's where it's going to stop."

"That's crazy. Absolutely crazy, Annie. If you're wrong about your suspicions, you've got to find out for sure so that you can let this all go and get on with your life. And if you're right, you can't let somebody get away with it. I've known you well enough to know you'll never have a sound night's sleep until you've helped find out who it was and see them get their comeuppance. Am I right or am I right?"

"Yeah," she said, looking up into Brandon's face. "Yeah, okay. Of course you are. But I don't want the police to do it. I want *you* to find out who did this thing to Chrissie."

"No, Annie. You're talking like a real lunatic."

"Which I am. I'll help you find out what happened."

"I won't be party to this. I can't begin to understand why you'd have a moment's hesitation about what you should do. If you won't go in to tell the police all you know, I'll do it for you."

"Fucking hell, you will!"

"Annie, you've given me no justification whatsoever to keep any of this stuff away from the police. Quite the contrary. Face your own facts. What you've got here is important. Very important. So tell them about it yourself. Otherwise . . . hand me the phone so I can do it for you."

"Even if it meant that I would probably spend the rest of my life in prison and that whoever really killed Chrissie and Hobbs might go free?"

There was a sharp knock at the back door. It was the familiar knock of a visitor who, without the benefit of doorbells or buzzers, knew how to apply a good set of knuckles to a solid rural door. Annie jumped reflexively. Then she shuttled quickly out to the kitchen, Brandy close behind.

Ranger Dave Jervis had to duck slightly to clear the door. Odd that Brandy hadn't remembered him as a particularly large man. But he was. Enormous. He was in uniform, sans Smokey hat, just as he'd been when they'd met during the identification of Farmer and Chrissie a fortnight before.

Thirteen

"**A**fternoon, Annie," the Ranger said in a smooth baritone. "Mr. Drake?" He shot out a gigantic hand in Brandon's direction and gave him a strong handshake. The tips of Brandy's fingers barely extended around the lower edge of the Ranger's hand. "Hoped you'd be here. I tried calling you in Vancouver, but your secretary said you were back down here in the Sierra. When I checked at the Lodge, they told me when you'd arrived, so I guessed you might be out here visiting in Foresta. Would've called ahead, Annie, but I was already coming out here anyway. Mind if I ask you a few questions, Mr. Drake?"

Annie and Brandon traded uneasy glances at one another. She looked back at Ranger Dave, who began idly sniffing the air. "Like some coffee?" she asked him.

"No thanks. I only have a few minutes. I'll make it quick."

"Well, it won't slow you down any if we sit while we talk, will it?" Following Annie's lead, the two men migrated to the table and sat down. The Ranger heaved himself into the space next to Annie, across from Drake. He sniffed the air again, and looked around the room curiously.

"What can I tell you?" asked Brandon.

"Well, I guess Annie probably told you about Phil Lesyk, did she?"

"Yes, she did. Ugly way to go."

"It probably wouldn't be near the top of my list. Did you know he was on the trail with you and Mrs. Hobbs?"

"No. In fact, I find that hard to accept. It was getting so dark, I wouldn't have thought anyone else would have been up there. If we hadn't made such a late start and then the discovery of the bodies up there, we sure wouldn't have been up there ourselves. We didn't see or hear anybody. But, then, we were moving along as fast as we could to get down. It's possible he was behind us, I guess, but if he was, he must have been hiking along at least as fast as we were."

"But you *did* see him earlier in the day?"

"Yes. At the Mountaineering School. We made arrangements for some basic climbing lessons."

"But not for that same day?"

"No. He told us he wasn't available. That he had to stay at the shop."

"So what do you think he was doing up there on the mountain?"

"I can't imagine."

The Ranger looked over at Annie's reddened eyes, then back at Brandon. He pulled a plastic bag from his jacket pocket, withdrew from it the tattered, moldy remnants of red-black nylon tubing, and placed it on the table in front of Brandy. "You recognize this?"

The mold had left white and grungy patterns where it had dried. Brandy picked it up and felt its stiffness, looked at the broken ends and noticed the same relationship to the sewn seam which he'd just seen on the slings Annie had shown him. He looked at Annie. Her eyes enlarged as she turned to see if the slings she'd thrown to the living room floor were visible from the dining table. She reached for the nearly empty cigarette pack beside the ashtray, accidentally knocking a book of matches to the floor.

Brandon turned the moldy nylon strap over again in his hand. "No," he lied. "Should I?"

Ranger Dave shook his head. "I didn't know. Just thought I'd check. We found it in Phil's jacket. Annie wasn't sure she knew where it came from. I just thought it was worth a try. It was a long shot." He looked over at Annie again. She lit up a cigarette.

"Anything else you can think of, from the conversation with Phil at the school? Anything at all which might help me figure out what the hell he was doing up there in the avalanche?" Ranger Dave's manner was cool and persistent.

"No," Brandon replied. "I'd never met the man before that afternoon, of course, but it all seemed like business as usual. When he arranged the climbing lessons for me, I didn't even twig into it that the instructor he'd matched me up with was an old friend of mine. I didn't know Annie was here in Yosemite until that night, after the avalanche, when I went to cancel the lessons and Annie was there minding the shop."

Dave's big eyebrows crested. "Oh?" He stared at the black and orange glow of the tip of Annie's cigarette as she took her first long drag. He stuffed the broken nylon sling back inside the plastic bag and into his pocket.

"I'm curious about something," said Brandon. Annie tensed as he continued. "Have you figured out why Farmer Hobbs wasn't climbing at Arrowhead, like the climbing register had said? And why Chrissie Peacock was up there climbing with him? I gather she wasn't on the register at all."

"Well, we've been working on that. I got back to all of the group he'd been climbing with up until the day before the fall. According to the other climbers, Farmer seemed really psyched up for his first real solo climb. None of them knew Chrissie Peacock was climbing with him, that's for sure. They were all as shocked as Annie was. The other climbers all told me that he talked most of the previous two days about how the solo was such a big challenge for him. Which has surprised us all along . . . I guess you heard how safety-conscious he was. He'd said he was glad someone had challenged him to get into another whole league of climbing, as if the idea hadn't occurred to him until he arrived in the valley for the week; but nobody remembers him saying who it was he was talking about. Maybe it was just a figure of speech.

"Chrissie hadn't been seen climbing anywhere in the valley during the week," Dave continued. "Everyone who knew her assumed she'd left for Peru that week. But we found her luggage at a friend's house. Nobody noticed it because the house had been closed up for the season while the owner was up at his home in Seattle." Dave glanced over at Annie sympathetically. "Chrissie was all set to travel. She had her return air ticket to Peru. She was scheduled for a flight from Los Angeles the day after the accident. She didn't come into any of the valley shops or visit with her friends during the week. She'd already told everybody goodbye for the season. I guess she must have changed her mind at the last minute for some reason. It's just a fluke, and it wouldn't have mattered much, I guess, because we couldn't have found them any sooner knowing Chrissie was there, too.

"Tell me, Drake. What brings you all the way back to the Park so soon?"

Brandy glanced at Annie. Her eyes were defocused on the plain wooden wall in front of her as she apprehensively held the lungsful of smoke. He smiled wistfully and said easily to the Ranger, "Annie and I had a lot of catching up to do. I had to escort Julia Hobbs back home to Canada, for obvious reasons, but I promised Annie I'd return." Annie closed her eyes heavily and exhaled. "I had some business to take care of last week and now . . . here I am!"

"Nothing in the way of business here, then?" Dave probed.

"Heavens, no. Strictly R & R. Why do you ask?"

Dave laughed in his deep, rich baritone. "It's my business to be nosy. Maybe I'm just envious. I'm sure none of my friends would travel a thousand miles just to see me." He stood up and zipped his jacket. Drake and Annie got to their feet, too.

Drake smiled, cocked an eyebrow at Ranger Dave and added in a proud lilt, "There have been times when Annie's and my friendship has been *well* beyond what anyone would call basic."

Dave drew back and looked down at where Annie stood beside Brandon. She took Brandon's hand in hers. A coy smile covered her face. The Ranger nodded acknowledgement and said, "I see. Well, sorry to disturb you folks. Have to be on my way. Let me know if you think of anything about Phil."

Annie squeezed Brandon's hand hard until he replied, "You bet."

"Oh, yeah . . ." the Ranger added in afterthought, "Annie? I've been wondering how Chrissie had been getting to and from the valley. She didn't have a car here, I know. At least nothing registered in her own name. You know anything about that? How would she have been getting around, during that last week?"

Annie looked surprised by the question. "She always used *my* car. At least when I wasn't here. Only I don't know how much good it was for her this time."

"Meaning?"

"When I got back, I found a note in it from her. Said she couldn't start it. Had Freddie come by once and have a look at it, but he couldn't start it either. It needed a new

distributor rotor, but she didn't have it repaired. I did it when
I got back. I'd guess she was bumming rides from others
around here, to get to and from. It's not usually too tough to
manage in the summer. There are always people coming and
going along the main road. Maybe Farmer was coming out
here to give her rides for the week," she said vaguely, but
she winced and frowned under the load of the double
entendre. Everything seemed to echo in slowed motion, as if
the sound waves were passing through sludge. Maybe it
was the dope. Maybe it was the misery.

"I see," said Ranger Dave. "Okay. Just wondered.
Had to tie up some loose ends. Thanks."

After Dave's truck had bumped out of sight down
the rocky secondary road into the forest, Annie snubbed
out her cigarette in the kitchen sink. It fizzled as the hot ash
hit the standing water droplets. Annie laughed a strained
laugh. " '. . . *Well* beyond what anyone would call basic'?
Thanks a fucking heap, Mr. Brandy-Wine Your Most
Venerable Drakeness. You handled *that* situation like a boar-
bear in a china shop. I'll have a lot to do to live that one
down, but it's worth it."

"What do you mean?"

"I mean you insinuated we were lovers about to get
into some serious hanky-panky here for old times' sake."

"So? Is Sweet Annie's reputation around here so
fragile it can't handle that?"

"Of course not. It's just that . . ."

". . . that it's a small community here? Well, that was
all I could come up with on short notice to explain travelling
all the way back down here to provide solace to you."

"It was great. I'm just going to have to be careful.
That's all. You see . . . there have been times when Annie's
and Ranger Dave's friendship, too, has been 'well beyond
what anyone would call basic'."

"Oh." Drake smirked and shrugged and then led

the way back to the living room and started wadding paper for the fireplace hearth. He felt the small, coverall-covered woman padding along in her pink slippers behind him. Without looking over his shoulder, he said, "Now, you better start talking, my sweet friend. I need to know everything you're all gassed up about, everything you've done, everything Chrissie's done. The whole show. And I want it fast and direct. No editorializing. No bullshit. After that, I'll tell you exactly what I think you should do about it. Deal?"

"Do I have a choice?" replied the tentative voice behind him.

"No," added Brandon, loading kindling and logs above the grate. "Oh, and one more thing. No more smoking until we finish. It's not helping you one bit, and it stinks, so it's beginning to make me irritable."

"The cigarettes or the dope?"

"Both. So come back to earth now and tell me the whole story."

"Anything else, sir?" asked Annie, still behind him.

"Yes. Matches."

Fourteen

"**S**o where do I start?" Annie asked, lighting the paper Brandy had accordioned carefully between the long kindling pieces.

"Wherever you want."

"That's just it. Everything about the whole goddamned mess is so frigging scary to me now, I don't want to think about *any* of it, much less talk about it."

"How about starting where we left off?"

"Last Sunday night? I can't remember what we talked about. All I remember is getting very drunk and holding a sobbing wake with you. But even in that state, I doubt if I would have told you anything about . . ."

"No. I mean where we left off when you said nobody should be so straight, when you told me it wasn't fair that the first and only guy to take the tiny Raggedy Ann doll seriously as a *real* woman with *real* feelings, was majoring in accounting."

Annie's expression was a caricature of incredulity. "For Christ's sake! That was twenty-three years ago. If that's where you want me to pick up the story, this could take some time ... I thought you said you didn't want any side-tracking."

Brandon poked at the fire until the crackling flames licked the wood as if they needed no more help, and then he settled himself into a thick bank of cushions. "I changed my mind." He cocked his head impudently to one side and grinned. "*I* don't have any other appointments this afternoon. Or this evening, either. Do *you*?"

Annie took a deep, deep breath and let out an audible sigh. She perched herself at the edge of the bench, equidistant from Drake and the fire.

"Okay. Berkeley, 1968. So ... you want me to begin from that remark I made about how straight you were?"

Brandon continued to grin at her, but said nothing.

"Well," she began, "I'd already decided by then *never* to fall in love. I mean *really* in love. I said I thought it would interfere with sex too much. Love needed to be free and wild. Which is why you scared the hell out of me, by the way. You were perfect for me in so many ways, Brandy, but you were so *goddamned stable*. And intense. And deep, too. And that was kind of wild in its own way. But I didn't want to find out about that. And I didn't want you to find my weak spots, either. I guess I was afraid my wings would be clipped if I got too close to you."

"We were pretty close from time to time anyway, you've got to admit."

"Yeah, and every time that happened I'd make extra sure you knew I was still a free agent. That you couldn't hold on. That I was a big bundle of little woman just too, too horny for one Brandy Drake to handle alone. You remember that?"

"Bert and Greg and Tariq?"

"And others, too. For a while there, most of 'em were bedded down just to keep you at a distance. But most of 'em couldn't stand the heat. The story of my life. One or two nights and they were gone. In fact, you were about the only boy who could go at it as long as I could. Which was another thing that bothered me about you. Maybe we were too much alike."

"Maybe."

"So after you lost interest, I looked at myself and what I was becoming and . . ."

"I didn't lose interest, Annie. I lost patience. You were pretty brutal about those other guys, you know."

"I know. It was intentional. I wanted you to back off. You really scared the shit out of me. Only I didn't call it that then. I said you were smothering my Janis Joplin spirit. Slug back the Southern Comfort and let the fast life roll." Annie caricatured a Happy Face. She had an amazing repertoire of caricatures, by anyone's standards. "And *then* you went and did the worst possible thing. You *forgave* me my miserable tacky trespasses and were willing to become my friend! The only guy who could keep up with me in the sex department and he wouldn't come near my bed. For a long time I thought you did it to get even. Did you?"

"No."

"Well, you might as well have."

"Then you moved to the Southside and set up house with that hippie who owned the paraphernalia shop."

"Owned? *Managed* it. Hell, Vinny never owned a nail to hang a shirt on. Still doesn't, probably. Yeah, I lived with him for about seven months, then I dropped out of school and went to live with some friends over in The City. The Haight was a disaster already. It wasn't safe on the streets there in broad daylight. So we rented a place over in Noe Valley. That was when my Dad died. He was pretty old, and he'd been sick for about a year. He'd kind of considered me his only prop and comfort since Mom died, when I was eleven. Only I hadn't been much of anything for him during his last couple of years, because I was busy doing so many drugs and so many other crazy things to myself I couldn't bother getting down to San Jose to visit him. I'd resented everything about having to be his little girl, and the short of it is that I felt pretty goddamned guilty when he died.

"I blew most of the first of the inheritance. I don't even remember exactly what I blew it on. A lot of little things. It was over $20,000 but it disappeared fast. Fortunately for my little raggedy ass, my Dad had been a smart old sonofabitch. I got an allowance of $6,000 every six months for the next six years. Not enough to live a regal existence on, although I could have just survived on it in those days if I'd wanted to. The main part of the inheritance --- and I didn't know exactly how big it was until it was released by the trustees on my twenty-seventh birthday --- came after I knew how to handle money a little better.

"Smart Dad. Smart enough to know what I was going through, I guess. I don't think he knew about the drugs, but I'm not even sure about that. I would have managed to blow the whole wad if I'd gotten my hands on it right when he died." Annie bit her lip. She looked self-consciously over at Brandon and winced. "You want some wine?"

"No. And neither do you. I want this story unfogged. Continue."

"I may want the wine more as we go on."

"I'm sure. No way. Continue."

"Nice guy. So, where was I?"

"Floating through the end of 1969 on $12,000 a year plus whatever you might have earned. Did you work, too?"

"You gotta be fucking kidding. And you're beginning to sound like an accountant, too. Better get a handle on that, Brandy-dude. Of course I didn't work. Might have sold a little product, something like that, but remember I was into freedom."

"Weren't we all?"

"That's when I ran into Farley Cruikshank. It must

have been some kind of hormonal nesting instinct to latch onto someone and settle down, because he was really a loser. I think I knew that at the start, but sometimes you just do these things, don't you?"

"Where'd you meet him?"

"Ready for a cliché? At a Crosby, Stills, and Nash concert at the Winterland. What a joke! We'd both gone with other dates and we were both stoned, and afterwards we went to his house and fucked all night. He lived at the edge of the Fillmore. A month later we were married. A barefoot flower wedding. On the Presidio. In one of the restricted areas of the Presidio. Illegally trespassing, naturally. On the government land. It was a flip-the-bird-at-the-military thing. In the spirit of protest, right? God, we were so self-indulgent in those days."

"How long were you married?"

"On paper, for a year and a half. But we quit living together after about six months. But that's another story. Nineteen seventy-two, I got into serious climbing. I took a week here in Yosemite at a special seminar in the late spring and I was hooked. I shifted gears and did a solid one-eighty turn with my life. I was still a selfish brat, but at least I wasn't pissing on everybody I knew just to prove how important I was. After that, I spent every penny I could lay hands on coming up here and climbing. In the winter I had to work to make money to climb in the summer."

"So let me guess. Your second husband had something to do with climbing?"

"I thought *I* was supposed to be telling this story. No. As a matter of fact, I met Gordon in Bangkok."

"Gordon?"

"Oliver Gordon, but everyone just called him by his last name. He was a pilot. Small company jets. For oil companies. But I didn't meet him until '74, and a lot more happened between the Dawn of Climbing and the tryst with

Gordon. You getting impatient?"

"Heavens, no! Carry on, lady. At your own pace."

"I have to at least get some water. I'm drier than a sand dune. You want anything?"

"I'll take some fruit juice if you have any."

Annie returned with two glasses of orange juice in her hands, somewhat steadier than she'd been earlier, but still slopping the contents of both glasses liberally.

She sat heavily into the cushions next to Brandy and took another deep breath. "Ready for Part Two?"

Brandon nodded ceremonially.

"As I said," continued Annie, "I lived, breathed, ate, and slept climbing. Most of my Bay area friends abandoned me, except those who bought product from me. And even *they* minimized the contacts. I'm sure I bored the shit out of anyone who wasn't similarly infected with The Climbing Bug.

"In less than a year, I had moved up to serious technical climbing. Everybody laughed at me because of my size, but that only made me more determined to overcome my special obstacles. I have half the reach of most climbers, and I have these weird and crazy body contours --- all tits and hips --- which I always thought God must have given to me as some sort of parlor joke to entertain the angels. So I had to do a lot of work to customize my climbing style to suit my special talents. Why are you looking at me that way? I *do* have some special talents, you know. And I don't mean *those* kind of talents. Jesus, you are *still* a pervert!"

Annie dipped fingers into her juice and giggled as she flicked droplets at Drake. She slugged back another gulp and went on. "Anyway, when climbing gets into your system, you can't get rid of it. It's worse than drugs in some ways.

"I was really putting a lot of money into travelling. Yosemite was great in the spring and summer. Best climbing in the world. But by the second full season the Andes and the Himalayas had the allure of the exotic names. It was just too attractive to say you've tackled Annapurna and K-2 and Everest. And I went to Alaska. And I spent a month in the Alps."

"Miss Globetrotter."

"Right. And that's why climbers are such naturals for courier work."

Brandon perked up. "Courier work?"

"That's right, sweetie. Big stuff. That's how a lot of us, including yours truly, manage to support our habits. Climbing habits, that is. One of the guys I travelled with --- that second year I lived out of a suitcase, the year before I met Gordon --- was carrying for the Really Big Bucks. Jerry. When I asked him how he could afford all the travel, he told me about the sideline. Said it wasn't government secrets or anything like that. Nothing the CIA was ever going to be interested in. Just industrial stuff. Helping to give American capitalism a little jolt in the ass. He even said the door swung both ways. That little companies in the U.S. used the same pipeline to buy stuff about their competitors in Asia and Europe. The rules of Free Enterprise said somebody was going to bring the information out anyway, so why not make a little coin on it?

"Jerry said they sometimes shipped transistors and computer chips and things like that, but usually it was just papers and microdots. He said the worst thing that ever happened to anybody who carried the stuff was that the customs people found it and confiscated it. If that happened, the Pipeline --- that's what everyone called it --- would just ship new stuff by another route.

"What makes climbers so ideal is that we travel all the time, to a lot of places which are drop-off and pick-up nodes of the Pipeline, and so we're familiar faces to the border authorities. We carry lots of bizarre equipment which can be altered slightly to carry small goods, and we can easily make transfers and pickups and deliveries at both ends of the

Pipeline without attracting much attention."

"And who pays the bills? Who organizes the thing?"

"I never knew. I only knew the names and faces of two contacts above me. And later I figured out that three others I had climbed with were also doing it. I think it's a *big* outfit. Big, but careful. So anyway, Jerry introduced me to Rolf."

"A recruiter?"

"Right. And he told me everything Jerry said was true. About there being no risk and about the money. It wasn't enough to retire on or anything, but it was enough to keep me climbing in royal fashion. I guess they knew just how well to pay us to keep us on the hook. And it got me away from drug dealing. And Gordon was happy about that, too."

"Your husband."

"Yeah. We married the year after I started carrying. In early '76. By then I had squirreled away enough to buy this cabin in Yosemite. Well, to put a down payment on it. Gordon and I would spend a few weeks a year here. When he was on holiday. And . . . did I say he was a pilot? Right. Well, we'd come here and I'd climb in the mornings, and then the rest of the time . . ." Annie's eyes defocused fondly up toward the loft above them.

"How long were you married?"

"Until Eighty. He couldn't handle it after the shake-up."

"Meaning?"

"I'll get to that. It's easier if I keep things in order. Those first two years I knew Gordon seemed like paradise. Even though I was travelling almost nonstop, and even though I didn't see my husband more than every couple of months, for two or three days at a time, I felt really . . . stable. Really grounded. I made three or four carries a year. Nepal, Peru, Switzerland, even Iceland once. Sometimes I managed to double-end it and carry both ways on a trip. Plus, by that time I'd started teaching climbing in the Valley when I was here. So I was thinking about retiring from carrying. Retiring from the Pipeline.

"The travel was starting to lose its luster. I wanted to spend more of each year around here. All things considered, Sierra climbing is just about the best there is.

"Gordon made good money. As much as we needed to live on, especially if I didn't need to travel away so much for climbing, and especially with my inheritance. That was '76. I got the rest of it then. The inheritance. It wasn't Easy Street For Life, but I was able to pay off the house here and sock another good-sized chunk away in banks and bonds. Safe stuff. The trustees helped me find the right kind of things. One of them wanted inside my pants, so I probably got more advice than most of the firm's other clients. Gordon used to get pissed off at how often the guy called when he was home, but then . . . Gordon couldn't handle much heat in the kitchen."

"You sound proud of that."

Annie scowled at Brandy. "When I want a fucking shrink, Brandy-ass, I'll look in the Yellow Pages."

Brandon smiled.

"Where was I?" Annie asked aloud. "Oh, yeah. So there for a while everything was looking great. I even considered having a family. Like a baby. Don't look at me that way! I like kids. Gordon wasn't quite so sure, but he was coming around to the idea when the trip to Mexico went sour."

"What do you mean? What trip to Mexico?"

Annie bounced up off the cushions and spun around in front of the fire. A sudden energy, like an ignited sparkler. "Why am I telling you all this? Nobody needs to know this shit."

"You never told anyone before? At all?"

Annie became an instant cryogenic specimen. Nary a blink of an eye. Her voice was whispered from far away and the lips were motionless, adding ventriloquism to the puppet-doll effect: "Some of it. But not all of it. Only to Chrissie."

"Sit down. You still haven't explained what this all has to do with the climbing accident."

"It wasn't an *accident*, damn it!" Annie burst out. "I'm telling you!"

"Okay. So it wasn't. So now convince me it has something to do with your past."

"It *doesn't* have anything to do with my past. It really doesn't. Or at least it *shouldn't*. But that won't matter. Can't you just take it like that. For what it's worth. I swear to you it's all water well beyond the dam and out to sea. Now just go and find out who really killed them, for god's sakes, so we can both sleep in peace!"

Brandon crossed his arms and remained silent. Annie looked for signs of compromise.

"Bastard!" she hissed. She grabbed a stick of wood from beneath the fireplace and jammed it into the embers. Then she backed up to the bench where Brandon lay until a cushion caught her at mid-thigh, so that she half sat and half fell down beside him again. She picked at her left thumbnail with the fingers of her right hand. The new stick of wood caught in the embers and the yellow flames flickered against her face and sparkled in her eyes. "I told Jerry what I wanted to do."

"Your climbing friend."

"Right. Only we never climbed together again after that European trip. The one where he told me all about the Pipeline. I saw him here at Yosemite in the late spring of '78 and I told him about quitting and he said I should be careful. He acted really nervous about it. Next time I saw him was about two weeks later. He came out here to the house. He told me a story about a courier who had 'jumped the Pipeline', as he called it. I got the impression he'd been instructed by someone to make sure I heard the story in all its gory goddamned detail. By then I was already getting paranoid because of the way he was acting. When I asked him who he'd told about my plans, he said he hadn't told anyone. Got really pissed off that I thought he might not be trustworthy."

"So what was the story about the courier?"

"I'm not sure you want to hear it."

"Try me."

She took a deep breath and made an nasty grimace. "It was about Dolly Frenell. Familiar name?"

"Not really. Should it be?"

"TV journalist. Reporter for NBC. She was killed on assignment in Djakarta. Smothered to death. The media had a field day with it, but they never found out who murdered her. Remember reading about it now?"

"No, but I don't always keep tight onto that kind of news."

"I don't pay much attention to that sort of thing myself, but I remembered her name --- it had only been about three or four months before Jerry came. And after he told me she was with the Pipeline, I looked into it again. I went to the public library next time I was in San Francisco and went through the newspaper files. The official story was that she had been killed by members of an anti-American Communist cell.

"Her body was found stripped naked. She hadn't been sexually molested, and all of her money and identification was right in the room where they found her. Anyway, Jerry told me what really happened to her, and what he told me fit too closely to be made up. He said she was part of the Pipeline."

"Meaning the outfit doesn't specialize in climbers."

"Right. All kinds of people. The more different

professions they tap into, the safer the system. Or so Jerry said. I guess that much makes sense. Anyway, Frenell was trying to get out of the Pipeline. She didn't need the money any more, and she was getting pretty high profile in the television business, so she just wanted to drop it. Only they were afraid she might use what she knew against them. To expose them or something.

"Jerry said she didn't know any more than we knew, but the Pipeline couldn't afford to take any chances with security. He said she was warned, but she refused to take any more contracts. So they decided to make an example of her. She was in Djakarta doing a series on the after-effects of the Viet Nam War on the countries of Southeast Asia or something like that. Somebody put something in her drink, and men --- three of them, according to Jerry's story --- carried her to some kind of tenement room. He said it was obvious they didn't want any information about what she knew or who she'd told about the Pipeline or anything like that, because when she woke up from the Mickey, they had torn all her clothes off and they'd used some of that fast-glue to glue her lips together --- you know, the crazy-glue stuff. It was new, back then. Remember?

"So she couldn't talk. Or scream. And they had glued her eyelids wide open, so she had to watch what they were doing to her. She couldn't close them. You want to hear more?"

"Go on."

"While she was unconscious, they'd smeared glue on the insides of her arms and her wrists and her hands to fasten them tight to her body, so she couldn't move around much. They put one of her arms across her chest with the palm of the hand against her neck and her chin, somehow, so that her fingers were dangling loose over her glued mouth. And they put more of the glue all along between her legs from her knees to her ankles and on the backs of her calves so that her legs were fastened together and her heels glued right up to her ass. And all of this stuff had already set up. And that's how she woke up. Pretty fucking gross, huh?"

Annie's clown face was contorted in a mime expression of revulsion as she spun out the story. "Jerry said they stood a big mirror in front of her so she had to watch what they were doing to her. And they let her live for a long time that way. Long enough for her to gouge and claw and scratch up her own pretty TV personality face with her free fingers when she tried to pull herself loose. And long enough to tear her own skin apart on the underside of one of her arms, and along her side, and on her neck. And long enough to understand that she was being killed. And long enough to understand *why* she was being killed. Which was because 'nobody cuts the Pipeline'. Or so Jerry said.

"So they tortured her like that for hours and then finally they smeared glue on the tips of her fingers and stuffed them up her nostrils and held them there, one by one. She broke her own nose trying to tear her fingers out before she smothered to death. Probably bashed her face against the floor or something."

"Hmmm."

"I warned you."

"Pretty graphic, all right. People always think up such marvellous uses for new technology."

"It's incredible the kinds of details a person remembers. Even of a story you never wanted to hear in the first place. I have nightmares about that one. Sometimes it's Dolly Frenell and sometimes it's me. Years later, after I met Chrissie and fell in love with her, it was Chrissie they were torturing. Great bedtime story, huh? Courtesy of my employer. Which had also been Dolly's employer. Only Jerry didn't have to underline that part of it. I tell you, the message was clear. Very clear.

"I'm a pretty hardy lady, but that story, and that threat

. . . it stuck in my imagination. I couldn't tell anyone. Not until years later when I met Chrissie. Gordon would have come apart if he'd heard it, so I just made excuses to him, and pretended I'd quit carrying."

"So what did you do?"

"What could I do? I tried to travel less and less to avoid the work. But I was afraid to drop out of it completely. I used my teaching job here at the mountaineering school as an excuse. But I still carried. Until the Mexican trip. And sometimes I wonder if they didn't set that up as an 'arranged accident'. Paranoia strikes deep. Right."

"To the best of us. Especially when you keep such terrific company. What happened in Mexico?"

Fifteen

"Mexico. Right." Annie wrung her hands tightly together, shuddered reflexively, and wrapped her arms around herself. She continued to stare, transfixed, into the fireplace. "I was supposed to drop off my carry there. It was a jar of cold cream with something in the bottom of it. Probably in a capsule or something. I'd made the pickup in a store in Bangkok. I was supposed to meet a man named Bill in Enseñada on my way home. I was supposed to go to his hotel room at a certain time and leave the stuff with him on my way to the airport. I'd done the same routine --- with different people every time --- dozens of times and no hang-ups. Anyway, when Bill lets me in and locks the door behind him, I set down my gear bag and my suitcase and I fish through my toiletries bag for the carry. But when I hand it to him, all of a sudden he pulls a gun. Says he's a Drug Enforcement cop. He pulls out handcuffs and makes me put them on myself and then I'm supposed to lie down on the floor while he searches my bags. He was big and he had a gun, so I guess I wasn't thinking. Although I don't know what the hell else I could have done. He didn't act right for a narc, and he never showed me a badge. So I should have known the bastard wasn't for real. Besides, who ever heard of a one-man bust. But I cooperated. I didn't have any drugs on me, of course. I'd been clean for over two years. This was in '80. And as far as I knew there wasn't any law against carrying information. I wasn't trafficking in anything illegal. That's what we always told ourselves, anyway. Fuck, that's what our contacts told us too. So I wasn't worried. Until Mr. Bill goes mental . . .

Annie winced and screwed her face tightly as she probed the memory. Brandon watched her silently.

"After the guy tears all my things out of my bags and my purse, I can tell he's pissed off about something. I try to talk to him, to tell him he's made some kind of mistake, but suddenly he's a bit disconnected. He starts cursing and raging like no cop I've ever seen, and he jerks me to my feet and threatens to beat on me if I don't come across with the drugs. So I really lost my cool then. I started to really tear a strip off of him --- I can get pretty foul-mouthed when I'm pissed off, you know. But he points his gun right in my face and gets all crazy like he's going to actually shoot me, so I told him to back off. To cool down. To check the jar of cream. It wasn't drugs. Never was. I was just passing along information. Nothing illegal, for god's sakes. Man, I just wanted *out* of that room and away from that lunatic.

"So the guy stuffs one of his big fingers in the jar of cream and goops it all out all over the bedspread. And there's *nothing there*! I expected a little capsule or something with microfilm. That's what had been in the carries I'd seen before, but not this one. Nothing but cold cream. There was absolutely *nothing* there! So the guy really goes berserk and throws the jar at me. Real hard. Gets me right in the belly. So I screamed. And he slapped me." As she relived the story, Annie's forehead was sprouting beads of perspiration.

"But you obviously got away from him," Brandon encouraged her. "How?"

Annie rolled her big eyes and frowned in caricature. "I wish it hadn't happened. Not that way." She squinted her eyes hard again, as if trying to make out something in a blinding light. "He smacked me on the side of the head so hard my ear was ringing. I fell onto the bed. All I could think of was that woman with the crazy glue all over her, and I figured this was another Pipeline lesson for carriers who made noises about leaving the fraternity. I guess I knew he was going to kill me.

"He was saying something to me, but I couldn't hear him. I started screaming bloody murder and he hit me again. This time he hit me with the hand that had the gun in it. I put my arms up to protect myself and his arm cracked hard against my elbow, and the butt of the gun got hooked on the handcuffs or something. Anyway, the gun was knocked out of his hand. We both grabbed for it. He was already all over me, so he could see better where it was, but the mattress on the bed was one of those too-soft kind and his knee was braced on the edge, so when he lunged forward his knee slipped off and he fell to one side. Anyway, I came up with the gun and kicked him as hard as I could to keep him away from me. He grabbed my leg, but he was still off balance. He was big, but not all that well coordinated. I don't know how I managed it, but suddenly I was on the other side of the room, pointing his own gun at him.

"He just stared at me and laughed and cursed and said I'd never shoot a government agent. I told him he was no fucking cop and there was no way he was going to fool me that he was. If he didn't give me the key to the handcuffs I was going to blow his fucking head off and get the key myself. I must have convinced him I meant it, because he fished into his pants pocket as if he was going to get it, and suddenly he was jumping straight at me. Came right across the room. He was *really* big, Brandy. And I guess I was just off guard. But not *that* off guard: there was nothing else I could do." Annie took a deep breath and huffed it out before she added, quietly, "So I shot him."

Annie took another deep breath and sighed, eyes now fixed on the opposite wall. "You know how hard it's supposed to be to kill somebody with a single shot? Like a lot harder than the Westerns and the cop shows always made it look? Well, I'll admit it took a lot more strength than I thought it would to actually squeeze the trigger. I'd never fired a big gun before. But when I did, he flipped over backwards and fell against the side of the bed and died right there and then. One bullet. I don't know if it hit him in the heart or what, but he was definitely dead. One bullet.

"I froze up. My ears were ringing. My mind was racing a hundred miles an hour. I remember wondering if he was really down or just waiting for me to get near enough so he could jump me again. But then there was some noise outside, and I figured people would be coming any minute. So I got brave enough to check and see if he was alive. But he wasn't. So then I searched through his pockets until I found some keys. I was shaking so hard I could barely get the key into the locks. It seemed like forever before I got out of the handcuffs. I had to find out who he really was, so I checked through his suit jacket on the chair. Wanna guess what I found?"

"No idea."

"A badge. He really *was* goddamned DEA! I'd killed a government agent. Shit, that scared me! I threw my things back into my purse and I ran to the door. But there were people out there, making noise. Not like they were coming in or anything, but hotel guests. You know. So I went to the door to the balcony. I slipped out and around the back of the motel and I walked a long way. Then I caught a taxi and I was all the way to the airport before I started thinking. I realized that I'd left the gun in the hotel room and there must have been fingerprints all over it, and I got even more scared. I had stuffed the handcuffs and the keys into my purse, so I washed them off in a bathroom sink and then threw them in a garbage can. Dumb move, probably, but I didn't want to be caught going through customs with *those* in my purse."

"So you made it back here . . ."

"Yeah."

"And then what?"

"Then nothing. I didn't hear from the FBI or the DEA or anybody. I can tell you, it was a long mother of a week back here at the ranch in Foresta, pretending everything was normal, planning what I was going to report to my sonofabitch Pipeline contact about it. There wasn't anything about it in the papers, but considering it happened in Mexico, and considering how the DEA works, I wasn't too surprised about that. They don't usually go public unless they have something to gain from it."

"Whoa! If your prints were on the gun, you can bet that the Federales would have had you ID'd pretty fast, m'dear. And my guess is that they would have turned the case over to the Americans in a few days."

"That's what I figured, too. And every time the phone rang for the next month, I jumped. I wasn't sleeping too well, either."

"I imagine."

"But they didn't call."

"And what happened next?"

"I finally got a call from someone named Cory. Pipeline dude. I'd talked to him once before, and he knew the code. I started up by telling him what a bitch-up the Mexican drop-off had been, and he cut me off. Said he already knew. Said the DEA had bought off Bill --- the real Bill --- and had put one of their agents in his room, to make what was supposed to be a big *drug* intercept or something. Some informant must have screwed up. Anyway, the Pipeline had been suspicious about Bill, and this Cory claimed that somebody had gotten to Bill's hotel room just after I left. Cory described the room and the dead cop perfectly, so I knew he was for real. And Cory says the Pipeline man picked up the gun and wiped the room clean. Found one of my earrings from my purse, even. So basically the Pipeline had covered my ass.

"I told him I wasn't doing any more carrying of information, and I expected a fight, but he said the Pipeline thought that was smart, too. Too much heat around me and they didn't like that. So I was being retired.

"I thought maybe it was all a big put-on. I wondered for a couple of days whether Cory had been part of a government plan to sew me up, but I figured if they knew the Pipeline contact codes, it was Game Over anyway. God knew what else they had."

"So what happened next?" asked Brandon.

"Next? There *was* no next. I didn't hear anything from anybody about it. Not about Mexico, not about the Pipeline, not about carrying."

"Given all that you've told me about the outfit, doesn't that strike you as a bit odd. I mean, first they make it clear that carriers retire feet-first or not at all, and then they're offering no-hassle retirement packages?"

"I guess they felt pretty safe that I wouldn't be talking to anyone about anything."

"But how could they be sure?"

"Because I'd killed the Fed in Mexico."

"But you couldn't be linked to what happened in Mexico, it sounds like."

"I wish."

"What do you mean?"

"Cory told me, right after the Mexico disaster, that they were holding onto some insurance. The only other time

I talked with him, which was yesterday . . ."

"Yesterday? You mean you still hear from them?"

"First time in almost ten years. I swear. That's what's got me so fucking scared, Brandy. And they know it. Because Cory reminded me again. He told me the Pipeline had heard about Chrissie and Farmer and Phil Lesyk, and they wanted to make sure that I didn't forget how important it was to keep the Pipeline out of any police investigations. When I asked if they had anything to do with this, he seemed surprised and said 'of course not'. Just that they get nervous whenever the police start asking questions around any of the Pipeline's former associates."

Annie's face warped into a pitiful prune of an expression. "He didn't have to come out and say what he said to me. I know that the police can't have any part in this or I'm one dead little Raggedy Ann doll. The Pipeline still has the DEA agent's gun. Sealed. Protected. With my fingerprints on it. Dusted. A couple of years ago, I asked a cop who climbs here from time to time just how long fingerprints could stay on a surface. Forever, he said. So I knew they were right. They have their insurance."

Sixteen

Brandon walked slowly to the sliding glass doors and looked out through them, beyond the reflected yellow glow of the porch light, deep into the macabre black-on-grey of late afternoon snow-covered forest floor. A forest is a complete enigma when viewed through glass. Were there things out there staring back at him? In amongst the tree trunks and the shadows? He couldn't see anything, but there was a sense of presence. Maybe there were wolves out there, or some smaller, more benign critters. Or maybe there were humans out there. Unlikely, but who could ever be sure? Here stood Brandy in the backlight of Annie's living room, and out there in the homogeneous darkness of nature as night approached . . .

"Brandy, I'm really not a murderer. I swear to you. It was self-defense. I wouldn't have shot that guy if he hadn't attacked me. What else could I have done?"

"Reported it."

"In Mexico? Jesus Christ! They pop people in the rat prisons there for *stealing*, never mind murder. I never would have seen daylight again!"

"You could have reported it back here in California when you returned."

"And end up like Dolly Frenell? I don't think you realize how vicious these people are! Thanks a lot for understanding. And thanks for the *big* fucking lecture." Annie leaped to her feet and thrust a well-used poker into the fire. Her facial expression was half anger and half pout, a combination which looked nearly comic on her mime clown features.

"*Small* fucking lecture, m'dear."

Annie burst into tears. She didn't try to hide it or turn away. She just dropped the firetool from her hand and stood in the center of the room, sobbing. "Damn it, didn't you ever do anything you regretted? Do I have to pay for the rest of my life? It was self-defense when I killed that drug agent. But who the hell would ever believe me? Or care one way or another, anyway? They're just going to lock me up and throw away the key. I *know* that's what they'll do. And I just couldn't bear it."

Brandy stared grimly at Annie. After a few minutes, the flood eased. She wiped her face with the sleeves of her coveralls and pushed her damp hair back off her forehead.

"If it's any consolation," Brandy said plainly, "I'll help you."

Annie was incredulous. "But you said . . ."

"I told you what you should have done. But you didn't. And now you are in a hole. So I'm willing to help you out of the hole."

Animation and glimmerings of reawakened hope swiftly came to Annie's face and voice. "You mean you'll find out who killed Farmer and Chrissie? Without going to the police?"

"I'll do my best. But only on certain terms and conditions. I have to have *everything* you know. No withholding anything. If I ask, you tell. It's hard enough working without benefit of police resources, and on a three month old trail, to boot.

"When I find out what happened up there on the mountain, we're *both* going to go to the police. Together. And if I find I'm getting nowhere, same thing. And if that means busting open the whole Pipeline thing, including your ten-year-old secret, then so be it. But I want *you* to give them the story about your suspicions, *you* tell them about the climbing equipment, and *you* explain why you waited a whole week before coming forward with any of this."

"A week? You mean you expect us to go to them next week? What if it takes longer than a week for you to find out anything?"

"My definition of going nowhere is one week without an answer. 'Kay?"

Annie shuddered. "I don't know. That's not very long."

"Take your choice. If you prefer, I'll do nothing at all. You can take it directly to the police tomorrow."

"You bastard!"

Brandon's brow furrowed deeply. Something broke loose. "Criticism from *you* is rich. Annie, you have always been one selfish little girl. And this thing is no exception. Let's take a look at what you're asking. You want me to bury knowledge of a multiple homicide until whatever trail there is grows very cold and useless to the police, all to cover your own sweet ass. You want me to risk my license as a private investigator both here and in Canada, all playing on a long-standing friendship and any faith I might have as to your basic honesty, all evidence to the contrary. And *then* you want me to forget on a permanent basis that you are living under the perpetual cloud of a manslaughter rap. The smartest thing for us to do right now is to march into the Park Rangers' office and tell your friend Dave all that you suspect about the deaths of Farmer, Chrissie, and Phil, and for me to swear that I just realized that the sling he showed me earlier was something I saw at the base of the falls, under Chrissie. 'What do you know, Ranger? After you left I thought about it and remembered.' It's a lame call, but it's safe. So instead, right now I sit here in a really awkward position, which you put me in, and you call *me* a bastard?"

Annie was stunned by the tirade. "But . . . but . . . oh, shit, Brandy! I'm just . . . scared and pissed off and . . . what the fuck do you expect?" In frustration, she thumped her fist down on one of the bench cushions. "All right. I accept. I accept it all, if that's what it takes to get out of this mess. So what happens now? What do we do?"

"You tell me everything you know about all the actors in this game. All that you know of, anyway. Then for the next few days, you stay in the valley and proceed with Business As Usual, taking inventory at the shop and keeping your ears open for anything that might be of use, and generally acting like the world isn't a very fair place, but that accidents *will* happen. Meanwhile I'll go back to Vancouver and see what I can find out about Farmer's business connections and personal life.

"I also want to find out everything I can about Phil. I'm not so sure his involvement was as peripheral and spontaneous as you seem to think it was. I'll need to look into Chrissie, too."

"Chrissie? But nobody would have wanted to kill her! Chrissie didn't have any enemies. Everybody loved Chrissie!"

"Yeah. Everybody loves everybody. But somehow, more than twenty-three thousand of these loving, friendly residents of this beautiful, utopian U.S. of A. will be murdered during this very calendar year. So just humor me. I want to spend tomorrow morning picking your brain clean. Everything you know about everything, including Chrissie.

Got it?"

Annie nodded agreement. Resignation and relief at once.

They didn't speak about anything to do with the deaths for the rest of the afternoon. They took a long walk in the soft crunching surface of the snow-lit woods together. Then Annie whipped together another Earth Mother meal, and they cruised back to the hearth to curl up in front of another warm fire. Psyches need rest, too.

Annie was back in her regular uniform --- fuzzy slippers and coveralls --- but with the evening cool she brought out a soft comforter in which to be swaddled. Raggedy Annie in a wrapper. Soft haze in the aftermath of a long needed confession. Tension having found desperately sought relief. Forgive me, Father. Forgive me.

"Annie, don't you get hot wearing coveralls with your clothes all the time? You know . . . inside?"

"Inside?"

"Yeah. Inside." Brandon glanced around at the flickering images on the walls, silhouettes cast from a rebuilt fire. "This is a snuggy cabin. Unusually so, for an A-frame. You manage to keep it quite warm in here."

"Oh, I see what you mean," she giggled. "*Inside*. I thought you meant something about the *clothes* inside, that I'd get hot wearing coveralls *over* my clothes, and . . ." she giggled again, "I haven't worn a thing under my coveralls for years!"

She looked up at his quizzical expression.

"Nothing at all?" he asked incredulously.

"Nothing. Not even underpants. Want to see?"

"No!" Brandon snapped, firmly.

Annie's lip shot out to pout. "You really know how to kill a girl's self-image as a sexual animal, don't you?"

"Not intentionally," Brandy smiled. "But I know how to keep a horny man from getting out of control."

"You too?" Annie replied gleefully. "And I thought it was just me!" She reached out to unbuckle the belt of his trousers. "What about if we . . ."

"Annie!" Brandon grabbed her wrist and held it. It had always been a special challenge for him to say 'no' to a lady. Especially here with Annie, when it seemed so natural to indulge in a good roll in the loft. A public service, in a way. Sexual release and respite from the sorrow of her loss. A good old friend. A once-upon-a-time lover.

Adding to the temptation, Raggedy Annie was one of the finest sexual partners Brandon had ever known. Selfish though she was in every other setting, she was a delightful creature when she was making love. Fingernail tracks on the back and deafening of one ear. She could take it in and give it out all night and all day. And no matter when or where you started or stopped, she gave the impression of being infinitely, blissfully satisfied. She convinced you time and time again that you were the best lover ever to plant feet on the Earth. She was pure magic in bed. Making love had always been her medium. And the imp in her big eyes told him she was probably even better now than he remembered from long ago.

His hands still restraining her wrists, he lowered his voice and said carefully: "It's been a long day, Annie. And I have a zillion and one questions to ask you tomorrow morning before I go back to Vancouver. So let's just cruise quietly for another hour or so and call it an early sleep."

"Fan-*tas*-tic!"

"In *separate* beds."

"Awww . . . But don't you remember how we used to . . .?"

"All too well, Annie. I don't want to find myself still here in your bed a week from now, no further along toward helping you figure out what happened up there under Yosemite Falls."

Annie made her prune face again. "Are you in love with somebody or something?"

"Not that I know of. Can't you imagine a man *not* wanting to go to bed with you?"

"Not *this* man. But I guess you know best," Annie shrugged. "Thanks for the recovery, anyway. I mean, for a moment there I thought maybe you just weren't interested in me. You said 'No' so easily."

"Anything but easily, m'dear, I assure you."

"That's nice. So, thanks again. I guess I'm pretty fragile right now, and it probably wouldn't take much to send me into a nose dive." She sighed. The wind was picking up outside enough to be heard in glissando crescendoes above the crackle of the fire in the hearth. "I'm not a very brave person, y'know. I never have been."

"Except when it comes to climbing, obviously," added Drake.

"But that's different. That's my element. Up there. That's where my home is. But down here, I'm terrified of . . . of so many things. That's why I can't imagine having to deal head-on with the Pipeline. Can't even imagine it." She made another clown face into the empty space in front of her and held it.

Slowly she turned and brought her gaze to focus directly on Brandy. "I'm sorry," she said, matter-of-factly.

Brandon was silent for a while, but Annie didn't seem prepared to complete the thought. "About what?" he probed.

"About being such a schmuck. I guess I've been pretty nasty to you. And I hate even more what I haven't been to you. I mean for all these years. Ever since Berkeley. I'm selfish and because of that I'm one hell of a poor friend. I guess that's just the way I am. The story of my life. Annie Selfish Bentley." She looked up at him with a twinkle in her eye. "And I'm sorry that I didn't chase you until you couldn't say no. When we were at Berkeley. We were *terrific* lovers there for a while, weren't we?"

Brandy smirked and gazed back down to the comforter-cuddling Raggedy Ann. "A *short* while," he edited, "but I'm glad you remember it that way, too."

The next morning, an emotionally raggedy Annie pushed her nose against the glass of her back door and watched Brandy's rental car bump and bounce along the road away from her cabin. The moisture from her breath spread on the cold November pane as the car twisted and disappeared through the maze of pines and boulders which littered the Foresta floor. Annie couldn't get rid of that slippery, queasy feeling in her stomach. It was the same sensation she got whenever a jumar jam ratchet was wearing to the point where it no longer grabbed the climbing rope crisply, so that you wondered whether you were as safe as you really should be.

Maybe she should have told him everything. She'd never trusted anyone with everything she knew about the goddamned Pipeline. Sometimes she wasn't sure in her own mind what was fact and what was fiction. Most of what she'd told him was true. And the few exaggerations and omissions surely wouldn't matter, so long as they didn't keep Brandy from finding out who killed Chrissie.

Annie was certain that the deaths of Farmer and Chrissie had nothing to do with the Pipeline. And Annie was *sure* she didn't have any part in their deaths. Bad enough feeling guilty that if she'd just gotten back from Nepal three days earlier, Chrissie might have been in bed with her instead of going up on that climb with Farmer. No sense having Brandy suspicious about the wrong things.

Still, her uneasiness just wouldn't go away.

Seventeen

All the way down to the Bay Area, Brandon kept seeing the hulk of Ranger Dave on the road ahead, kept hearing his pleasant baritone. "Knight errant of Yosemite? Friend of grieving ladies?" The Ranger hadn't actually said it out loud, but the look on his face had said as much.

Knight erring, more like it. Idiot non-savant.

Brandon drove and drove until he reached the Bay Area once again. He cruised past Candlestick Park, through The City, and on through particularly heavy traffic north over the Golden Gate Bridge. The Oakland Bay Bridge was not yet back in service, but according to the radio the major traffic routes of the area had otherwise been restored in the short interval since the quake. So Brandy could have gone the North Bay route through Richmond, but whenever opportunity presented, he crossed the Golden Gate. Pure romantic. No doubt about it. Brandy had always held a special love for the Golden Gate. As he swooped across the great Bridge, he admired the barren Sausalito hills and Mt.

Tamalpais, coming naked to greet him. As if he could still believe that there were open and unsullied spaces near The City. As if the Marin Headlands would serve as the last bastion standing to protect the citadel of the great American dream.

Even for a diehard romantic, though, it was getting harder and harder to pretend that San Francisco hadn't become grossly over-congested and citified. Like every other city in North America. Like every other city in the world. The knowledge that the Bay Area was still shuffling the rubble from the Big One three weeks earlier helped sustain the illusion that the congestion of the freeway routes was really only the after-effects of the quake and not a chronic condition from which the Bay Area and his beloved San Francisco would never recover.

Part of Brandy wanted to think that the staunch independence and bizarre mentality which he'd first experienced in the Bay Area during his university days in the Sixties would go on forever. Somewhere. But another part of him knew that if that kind of free spirit ever really existed at all, San Francisco was certainly no longer worthy of carrying the banner into the next century. Not the San Francisco which had yielded to skyscrapers and freeways. Not the San Francisco which had let itself become just another workplace metropolis to be despoiled by common bedroom suburbanites of the East Bay and beyond.

Brandy drove north to where Old Highway 1 exits to Mill Valley. He sought relief. He yearned for release from the pressures of fast foods and high tech. The whole Golden Gate area bears many pockets of influence from long ago when the Conquistadors came to North America and spread their culture and influence up the coast of what is now California. Now the area has yielded to the New Conquistadors, driving their Volvos and Bimmies, spreading the influence of their microwave mentality and their hot tub

heavens over the same landforms as the Spanish had conquered centuries earlier. Yuppies.

Mill Valley once was a somewhat isolated town with
a unique, docile identity, not a bedroom suburb of San
Francisco. The more Brandy saw what was happening to his
favorite spots in America, the more he was confirmed in his
wisdom of moving north to North America's own crow's
nest. It was bad enough to witness the progressive
disintegration of All Things Bright and Beautiful, but it was
far worse to have to actively *participate* in that process.

The drive down memory lane was pushing him too
close to the edge. He had to get to his old friend's house
before he "lost it" altogether.

At the top of a long curved driveway was perched a
contemporary architect's sprawl of what often passes for
Spanish colonial. Undeniably, Badger Beeley's Twentieth
Century hacienda was a cut above the rest for interest and
taste, but it still cried out "Yuppie Mansion." Even Badger
Beeley, in spite of the many thousands of dollars he'd heaped
onto the specialness of his home, couldn't escape the curse.
It was what the real estate agents and home reviewers would
have dubbed "a gorgeous Mill Valley executive rancher."

As Brandy stared into the depths of the
basketball-court-sized sunken living room with the drive-in
fireplace, it sobered him to realize how easily this might have
been *his* home and *his* commute and *his* situation, had he
chosen to stay in the Bay Area instead of going north to the
beckoning frontier of Canada. Fate and its fickle finger.

Footsteps announced the arrival of Brandy's old bud
Badger. Brandy stood statue-still and sniffed the air noisily.
"Methinks," he began his salutation, "that your new abode
reeks of opulence, old friend. Investigation work continues
to agree with your pocketbook, it would seem."

"I'm sure as hell you didn't take the drive up here just
to storm my feeble mind with bullshit about my Dunn and

Bradstreet rating, so *please . . .*"

The two men clasped hands and then pulled one another into an energetic ritual bear hug.

Badger Beeley, of Cranston and Beeley, Mill Valley,
California, was always casual. That definitely enhanced his
mystique of ever-ready savvy amongst clients and potential
clients. Badger was the closest friend Brandy had ever had
in this strange business. They had worked together on four
separate investigations, one of them personal. On two of
those they had actually been working *against* one another.
That is, they represented clients who were determined to
sue one another with the information gleaned from the private
investigations. But Brandy and Badger were already good
friends, and they both had great reputations for getting
straight information on marriages and affairs and business
irregularities and ripoffs --- all those wonderful things people
spend money doing, and then finding out about, and then
suing one another about.

The first time they met, they had been paid by the
same client, a certain Gerome T. Webber of San Francisco, a
cruiseship mogul who had been extending his entrepreneurial
expertise along a broad beam of diversification. Brandy had
been hired to find out if Gerome's wife's lover was being paid
by Gerome's principal business rival. He didn't mind her
having the lover --- knew the man well as a family friend, in
fact --- but what Gerome *did* object to was the thought that
whatever she murmured in his ear in the sweaty interlude
between rhythmic heavings might go beyond small talk to
include strategic information about Gerome's takeover
intentions. That would have been inexcusable. Rules are
rules. Gerome had been in the creative habit of regularly
cogitating about his business plans with his wife-as-
sounding-board for the entire twenty-three years of their
marriage. It was part of their routine, and they both milked
the rewards of it. Gerome had had no reason to suspect

anything had changed in their relationship lately. But there was the inescapable anomaly of two bitched deals which blemished an otherwise pristine track record of Gerome's corporate raiding, and Nadine's lover was one of only two logical explanations Gerome could come up with.

Badger was on the Webber payroll to find out about the *other* logical explanation: Gerome's own mistress, an otherwise bored socialite who had been happily rubbing Gerome the right way for nearly two years before the business distress began. It frosted Gerome to think that anyone might be using his private life to undercut his business prowess. It was dirty pool.

Because both Brandy and Badger were thorough enough to look more broadly at the situation than their client may have wished, they soon discovered the real situation with the family hanky-panky. It had taken Brandy and Badger less than ten minutes of comparing notes to discover that there was something a little too coincidental about the fact that sizable checks from the same corporate ghost bank account were being deposited to the personal accounts of both Gerome's mistress and Nadine's squeeze. Discreetly they presented their findings to their mutual client.

Once Gerome understood the game, he and his wife dealt with it together. Very-very-wealthy people often react with a special non-emotional self-discipline and decisiveness when they realize that others have been slipping hands into the family cookie jars. In their finest hour, Gerome and his wife both made short-notice dates to meet their two lovers for a one-week cruise on a cruiseship bound for Alaska. They had underlined the special need for discretion, including planned last-minute arrivals and the need to use false identities for coming on board. The lovers were each given specific instructions to come to the Webber suite *only* after the ship had embarked on its voyage. The ship was already out to sea, according to plan, by the time the two lover-conspirators made their separate ways to the supposed Webber suite, which they found occupied by complete strangers. The two lovers were accosted by the ship's staff, and advised that their rights of passage had been revoked for registering under assumed names. They were required to share cramped, damp, makeshift crew's quarters below decks, and were put off the boat ignominiously in Skagway, the first port of call, where they were forced to fend for themselves with completely unsympathetic U.S. Customs and Immigration officers until they could arrange for money to be wired for their return passage to Seattle.

Looking around the Mill Valley home, Brandy had to admit a certain envy that Badger had done so well for himself. Badger explained that his wife was out shopping, but would be returning at lunchtime because she hoped to see Brandy before he left the area again. Badger assembled two late-morning coffees and the two friends settled themselves onto stools on a flagstone-floored breezeway which looked out over a swimming pool. The pool area was cloistered by the wrap-around arms of Badger's home. "Okay, Brandy-boy. Amuse myself with the story that you have brought to entice me into helping you do something."

"Badger! You're so . . . commercial."

"No. I'm direct. You used to say that was what you most appreciated about me. Change your mind? So, talk to me."

"Don't you want to talk about price first? Whether my client is on welfare or living in a penthouse, at least?"

"Wouldn't matter. When was the last time I ever got what I wanted out of you for *anything* we've worked on together?"

"Except fun."

"Of course. Otherwise, my address would be unlisted.

To *you*, at least."

Brandy grinned. Badger lolled his head from side to side in futility and warned, "Some day, my friend, I'll surprise you. You'll come looking for me to ride shotgun on one of your escapades and you won't find me here. I'll desert you. No forwarding address. Ha! Then you'll know you should have taken better care of your old friend Badger. Ha!"

Brandy squinted his eyes in mock menace. "I'd find you, Badger. No matter where you went. You know that?"

"Yeah, I know. Now get to it. I've got to get back to the slave camp in another hour and Connie and I were going to have a nooner as soon as she got home. Don't look so shocked. We're not too old to enjoy sex, y'know."

"That wasn't what surprised me. I'm just remembering Badger Beeley, the workaholic."

"High blood pressure. Heart palpitations. Empty nest syndrome looming. Hell, Brandy. I watched myself whizzing by too many rats in the race. Not that the money and the glory are bad things. It just struck home one morning that the only thing you get by running faster is the pleasure of passing rats. Who the hell needs it?"

"Don't get me wrong. The sense of balance becomes you."

"Maybe I was just kidding, for Christ's sake. Tell me about your goddamned case, will you? What's this all about? Sometimes you're so goddamned melodramatic . . . The way you were talking on the phone, I might have guessed somebody was murdered or something." Badger tilted his head and raised an eyebrow at his old friend's poker face. "And . . ." he continued, feeling his way through their all-time favorite game of Intuitions, "I think I might have guessed right."

Eighteen

The Vancouver homecoming was so quiet and uneventful, Drake had to remind himself that the drama in California was still real, that two people had, very likely, been murdered, and that he was trying to tread the ultrathin line between investigation and obliteration of the trail.

The lunchtime brainstorming session with Badger had been just like the old days. Their talks had allowed Brandy to dissect the case, to root out the impossibles, to explore the improbables, to examine the possibles and the likelies. At one point, Brandy speculated aloud that perhaps Chrissie Peacock had agreed to some kind of misfired hit on Farmer. Perhaps it had been intended for Farmer to die, but the plans had just gone sour and Chrissie was somehow pulled off the rock face. It was a nasty accusation, and not one to be shared with Annie, but it had to be considered as a possibility.

What if Chrissie made an unscheduled appearance to join him in the final climb and let him anchor himself with one of the buggered slings and . . .? No good. Yosemite is not a nook-and-cranny climbing complex. It's more like grand theater. During the summers, spectators are often watching groups of climbers on the massive north and south rock faces. So many possibilities of people seeing them, either before or during the climb, or of people seeing her coming down after the fall.

Far safer to make it happen on a regularly scheduled climb. Accidents happen all the time. She wouldn't have had any trouble selling that kind of story. And if it had been intended to look that way, why would Chrissie want to incur any suspicion by *not* being registered for the day's climb? Any way Brandy looked at it, it seemed most unlikely Chrissie was aware of the rigged climbing gear.

The sessions with Badger gave the Californian all he would need to know to tap his sources and gather certain state and federal police information that Drake needed. Badger would probably be able to accomplish in the next few days what would have taken Drake weeks or months to uncover, if he could have gotten it at all.

After unpacking into his condo, Brandon called Annie early in the evening and checked on her first day's progress.

"It was a long mother day," she sighed, "but I think I've already got most of what you want. I've got paper cuts on my hands and I'm mean as a rattlesnake from the eyestrain and the frustration at Phil's fucked-up bookkeeping system, but I already found the sales slip for the slings. Dated one day before Farmer and Chrissie's climb."

"Good girl. Which one of them bought the stuff?"

"There's no name on the slip. It's marked 'Climbing Equipment', but it's exactly the right amount for the six slings. To the penny. Like I said, there's no name on the sales receipt, but there's a VISA number. It's not Chrissie's: *that* I know. She never even *had* a VISA card. She only used cash.

Always. Can you find out if it was Farmer's?"

"Easily," Brandy confirmed. "Anything else?"

"Yeah. The telephone records. It was pretty much what you thought I might find." Annie paused. The tinkling of ice in a glass said she was drinking something. "Two calls were placed to Vancouver, Canada, from the Shop, to the same number, a week *after* Farmer and Chrissie disappeared. The number is 604-734-6979. I looked over my old phone bills --- here at the house --- and found out that there were three calls to the same number from here, placed three weeks earlier --- about two weeks *before* they were killed."

"Good work, Annie."

"Yeah, well I couldn't wait to find out who it belonged to, so I called there myself late this afternoon. I hung up as soon as the phone was answered, because I didn't want to mess anything up."

"So? Don't keep me in suspense."

"The receptionist answered 'Ergologic Enterprises'. Isn't that the name of Farmer's company?"

"Yes, it is. Very interesting," Brandon mused. "I guess I could understand the calls from your place, if Chrissie and Farmer were making some final plans before he came down there from Canada, but who would have called up there *after* the two of them went missing? And before they were found? Phil?"

"I don't have any idea."

"His being at the slide site looks very strange, especially with the broken sling in his pocket."

"He must have been curious about Hobbs' widow being in the valley, you know. Maybe her name attracted his attention," Annie speculated.

"Yeah, but remember . . . Julia was posing as my wife, so Phil wouldn't have made any associations to Hobbs."

"Oh, yeah. Then I'm back to my first theory about Lesyk's role in this thing. That he followed you up the trail.

He probably just had the hots for Julia, and was drooling along after you two, hoping to meet her 'accidentally' up on the trail. Didn't you tell me he was trying to split her off from you for the climbing lessons? If Phil was involved, there would have been plenty of the touchy-feely while the lessons were on, let me assure you. Julia would have been learning a few more things than just climbing rocks. Lesyk was a lech and a nosy Parker to the extreme. When he saw all the commotion and found the bodies, he must have recognized the significance of the broken sling, and he was such a glory-monger he probably wanted to be the first to show it to the Rangers and solve the riddle of the missing climber."

"Climber*s*."

"All the more reason for him to come unglued. So he probably followed you down the trail, staying as closely as he dared, but something happened and everybody got caught in the sandslide." She paused. "Well?"

"An awful lot of coincidence in that sandslide. And I find it hard to imagine he would have followed us all the way up the trail just to watch a lady he assumed was my wife."

"You didn't know Phil . . ."

"Okay, then. Tell me why would Phil have been calling Farmer's business number right after the accident?"

"That I don't know."

"I'm going over to the Ergologic offices in the morning," Brandon informed her. "Maybe I can root out some answers there."

"I still think someone wanted to kill Farmer. That *he* was the target," Annie declared. "And you know, those slings could have been fussed with before they were sold from the shop, or it could have been done afterwards by anybody with balls enough to break into Cam's cabin while Farmer and Chrissie were away. Like while they were having a dinner together here in the valley or something. I don't see how you're ever going to find out who set this whole thing up. It all seems so hopeless. How can we be sure who was involved and who wasn't?"

"I'll just have to start making educated guesses and poking into other people's business. We have to hope somebody pops out of the woodwork before he realizes how easily he can cover his tracks."

"Or *her* tracks," added Annie.

"Meaning?"

"Women murder, too, you know."

"And you think . . ."

"I don't know what to think. But you certainly can't rule anything out yet, can you? We've just begun. Can you give me a call and tell me as soon as you find out about any of the other things we talked about? Okay?"

"Yes, ma'am," Brandy reassured her.

Augusta Traynor had become the most sought-after social arbiter in Vancouver. Augusta could only be reached by telephonic voyagers who were willing to traverse six levels of answering machines, call-backs, pagers, and intermediaries. The Ask Augusta column in the Sun was only an afterthought. It was merely a mechanism for informing the Simple Folk about what the Royals were doing each week. Three-dot journalism at its snootiest. The real Augusta (if there really was a *real* Augusta) was far too busy happily keeping herself informed to care much about what the commoners out there knew. She would have been the first to tell you. If you were rich and influential enough to get to talk to her to ask her.

But to Brandon Drake she owed an old debt. Or so she insisted. And each time Brandy had to ask a small favor of her, she refused to close the books on that debt, always insisting she still owed him something. Brandon had once protested the claim. Then he gave up. Nobody won arguments against Augusta. The best anyone could hope for was a draw.

Augusta's husky voice shredded the speakerphone on the wall of Drake's sunroom-cum-office with its pronouncements of his success in having finally reached Herself. "So what brings Brandon Drake to the threshold of society, might I ask? I hope it's not a sudden change of heart about grasping for social status. You're one of the few honest hold-outs I know, Sweetheart."

"No, no. That's strictly your domain, Auggie. I couldn't begin to move in the trendy lane. I don't have enough money, for one thing."

"So what brings you to Aunt Augusta?"

"Information about a Vancouver woman."

"Aha! Planning on getting married again? Want to check one out for booty?"

"Nope. Just need to find out whether someone is for real and even if she's who she claims to be."

"Yes? Go on. No suspense. I don't have the time for suspense."

"Julia Hobbs. Name ring any bells?"

"My dear sweet boy, very few names associated with family fortunes or with incomes higher than half a million a year do *not* ring bells for me."

"So what can you tell me about her?"

"What do you want to know?"

"I don't want to lead you. Just see what you can find in the way of background. Whatever turns up. Family connections. Marital history. Friends. Financial status."

"I can give you some of that right now. Off the top of my head. I thought you were coming to me for some *really* juicy details. That's what most people are interested in, you know."

"And do you have any of those on her?"

"No, but I'm always happy to put out feelers if you

think it might be fertile ground for tilling. Remember, I make my living on knowing how everyone fits together. Like pieces in a giant jigsaw puzzle. Or a giant bedroom puzzle, more times than not, what?"

"The Society Puzzle?" Brandon laughed.

"Don't knock it, my boy. The people I concentrate on --- the biggest pieces of the puzzle --- also account for over eighty percent of the domestic capital in this city."

"So what can you tell me to get me started?"

"Let's see . . . Julia Hambleton Hobbs. So let's start with the family. Hambletons are --- or I should say *were*, originally --- Okanagan real estate money. In cahoots with the Barrett empire. Daddy Hambleton spent a great deal of time in court about fifteen years back on a couple of buy-up conflict-of-interest things. They would all be covered in the papers, if you're interested in that. Nothing too exciting, otherwise. They moved here to West Van right after that. Those were the days when *everyone* was moving here. Two kids, I think. Julia was a real spaceball. Not at all socialite material. Too long in the boonies, maybe. So she opted out of it. Ignored the money options. Did a career thing." Auggie snuffled. "If you call that a career."

"What do you mean?"

"She worked at a number of things. For a while she even worked as a witch."

"Beg pardon?"

"You know. Astrological delineations, psychic readings. New age crap. Only she took money for it, too. Embarrassed the hell out of the family, I gather. Ol' Gilly Hambleton was a conservative old fart, and I'm sure he took a good dose of razzing at the Victoria Club about it.

"Now, let's see. What else can this poor, over-taxed mind remember? Oh! Of course. Julia has been obsessed with painting, artwork. A lot. That plus the astrology nonsense is what she's spent most of her adult life doing, but she's never had any recognition for her art."

"Is she good?"

"Frankly, my dear, I haven't seen much of it, but from what I *have* seen, I find her work so much color and noise."

"Meaning you don't think too highly of it?"

"I think it's abysmal! But that's only one woman's opinion. I've never touted myself as an art critic. Two or three of her things actually sold. For a reasonable price. Out of one of the smaller places --- a Harrison Gallery showing, maybe? But more than that I couldn't say. It's a good thing she has independent means, because if she had to live on what she could make as an artist she'd simply *starve*."

"Never were very generous about other women, were you Auggie?"

"I have many women I like, my dear. Just so long as they know their places. That's all. Now, what else can I tell you about this glamour-glommer? In the early eighties --- I'll get the exact date for you later if you want --- she was married to Hobbs. Hobbs . . . from Calgary. Funny first name --- it'll come to me. Into computers or something like that. Odd fellow. I met him once in town."

"At a party?"

"God, no! They weren't the type for parties! Not my kind, anyway. No . . . it was at the Market. Granville Island. To be honest, I thought she was someone else. I never forget a face, but I don't always put the right name to it. Bothersome problem at times, but I always manage to fake my way around it. And I never pass a friend on the street without saying hello. Which is why it takes me four hours for a simple trip to pick up a few odds and ends at the Market. But I have fun, I can assure you.

"Now let's see . . . funny name. I just saw it again last week in the papers . . . Fernfoot? Farnsworth? Farmer! That's it! Farmer Hobbs. He was killed in some sort of mountain climbing thing. Some months ago, in fact, but they didn't find him until last week. Apparently the body had been out in the weather the whole time. *That* must have been a grisly sight. No torrid details about his death, except . . . and maybe you already know about this: *she* found him. Julia, that is. She and some friend had gone to wherever he disappeared, and Julia was the one who found his body. The newspapers didn't say who her travelling companion was, but I'm sure I could find out for you if that were important."

"Don't bother. How are her finances?"

"That I'll have to look into, but I can't believe it's any problem. I mean, unless she donated it to some Maharishi somewhere, she probably couldn't spend all her father has given her if she wanted to, especially considering her tastes. Talk about plebeian! Anyway, ol' Gilly knew what a flake his daughter was, so I'll bet he's set up long term trust funds or the like. He may have made his booty on a slightly crooked path, but I gather he's been very careful to invest it honestly. The two kids should be set.

"The son went away to school in the late sixties. To the States. UCLA or something like that. As far as I know he hasn't come back to Vancouver on a permanent basis. He's probably building Hambleton Empire South. I gather he was more like Papa than like his sis."

"So you don't think Julia would need the insurance from Farmer's death to survive?"

"Oooo . . . so that's our line, is it?"

"I wouldn't have guessed so," Brandy interjected, "but I'm looking for reassurance."

"Dunno for sure, B.D. I'd find it hard to believe, too, but I'll check into it."

"How do you remember all this stuff, Auggie? You really do amaze me."

"Thank you, my dear. You can tell that to some of my many jealous detractors, most of whom *swear* I've had Alzheimer's for years. In fact, you can come tell *me* again, any time you like." She forced a low-octave chortle. "But only if you'll promise to stay for lots of wine. It's no wonder I've never been able to entice you into my boudoir. You hardly ever come by, you never stay long enough when you do, and you never drink enough to allow me to help you forget about all the *unimportant* things in life."

"I think I've just been propositioned."

"That's just the intro. Listen, when do you need this gab on Julia Hobbs?"

"Yesterday."

"Oooo . . . I have a monster of a party to put on tomorrow night. Everybody who ever dreamed of being anybody in this rain-drenched Mecca For Madmen will be here. I have to spend most of tomorrow setting up the final details of the party with the caterers, and I have to get my poor aging face and hair decorated properly. I just don't see how I could possibly . . . oh, well . . . I'll see what I can find out during the day. But I'm leaving at five a.m. the very next morning for a fashion spectacle up at Alta Lake. I won't possibly have time to get back to you until after I get back from Whistler on Thursday. Unless . . . You're probably the only one in town who doesn't know about *The* Party. Am I right?"

"Of course."

"And you're probably the only one in town who wouldn't commit murder to get invited to my party. You rogue. So, I'm going to make you a special offer you don't deserve. I'm going to give you a rare opportunity to pretend that you're interested in being socially acceptable in this city."

"Do I have a choice?"

"Not if you want to get the skinny on your little lady. Now, you can be my special guest at The Party. I won't have but a few minutes to huddle aside with you, but if you want this lurid stuff so fast, that's about all I can do for you."

"You're a schemer, Auggie!"

"I knew you'd be grateful. Seven o'clock. Black tie. Come early. Stay late. Ta-ta for now!"

Nineteen

Morning dawned on one very lonely A-frame in Foresta. Brandy had left yesterday, right after dawn; but at least *yesterday* he'd been right here in the house to reassure her that the world had a few warm spots in it. Not this morning.

Only the perfect, frosty clarity of this morning, and the fine fluid blue of the sky between the cathedral valley walls, and the relative sparseness of the valley population in winter, saved Annie from complete despair.

Last night, Annie resigned herself to spending the early hours of this Yosemite morning at the Mountaineering School, before the village stores opened, continuing to wade through the flotsam and jetsam which were the personal and business remains of Phil Lesyk. But as she walked from the Visitor Parking area past the Post Office on her way to the shop, she wavered.

Her beloved monoliths of granite beckoned to her. They begged to be scaled by her special collusion of grace and art. Raggedy Annie on granite walls was transformed into a lithe ballerina, performing the most amazing pirouettes and pliés as she spun her way up along invisible cracks, thousands of feet above the valley floor.

There were a few routes in this valley which Annie had climbed, which no other woman had ever attempted. There was even a certain climb which no other climber, man or woman, had yet mastered. It was a solo, up the South Chimney on one of the Brothers. Annie's record would probably be cracked soon --- all records eventually were --- but not easily. Then someone would try to free-solo it. That was the trend of the decade. If you can't do a tougher route or a more challenging face, then you give yourself handicaps. You climb without a partner. Or you climb technical climbs without any equipment except your boots and your chalk and your wits.

Soon there'd be no new climbs to be conquered. Not in Yosemite, at least. They'd all be tagged as free-soloed, by both men and women. And then what? Blindfold climbing? Nude climbing? Annie smiled inwardly. *That* was already being done by a small group of faddists, though it was certainly not recorded well. Yet.

Annie grinned up at the sheer walls, in deepest trance, until she suddenly remembered why she had risen from the coziness of her Foresta nest so early this morning. It wasn't for a lovely climb. It was for intellectual bivouacking. All day long Annie was sentenced to spend her time behind the locked doors of the Mountaineering School, working on inventories and cleaning up, putting some semblance of order to the shop so that the concession could quickly be resold by the Park's Curry Company, so that there would be no shortage of mountaineering support when the droves returned to Yosemite in the springtime. Annie also had to find out if there could possibly be anything interesting about Lesyk. But, mostly, Annie had to stay busy so she didn't go crazy. She'd considered running away for a while. That had worked for her in the past. But now that Chrissie was gone, there was no one to come home to, and the running just didn't make a lot of sense. If it ever did.

Annie had promised Brandy she would look further into the telephone records and the sales records and anything else that might give some more clues as to what went on up there at Yosemite Falls in July, or what went on the night three people were eaten by a sandslide. The night the mountain spit two of them back out. The night that Phil Lesyk had been consumed.

Bob and Shirley had already been helping Annie with the inventory. She appreciated the companionship and the lightening of the load with the endless counting and the books, but she couldn't do too much snooping into records when they were there. So, until she discovered whatever it was Brandy thought he needed, she would be getting in early and staying late each evening. With Chrissie gone, there wasn't much pleasure in hanging around the house, anyway. It just reminded her of how final the last good-bye had been.

Annie thought she knew a lot about Phil's business until two days ago. Now all she knew for certain was that Phil Lesyk was a miserable excuse for a bookkeeper. Phil kept books on everything. Absolutely everything. But there was no organization to what he kept. It was all such a hopeless snarl of notes and bound books and ledgers that Phil might as well not have bothered. It was painful to see such a futile tangle of mismanagement consuming a business which deserved better. After all, the Mountaineering Shop had to take care of the basic needs of the climbers.

This morning was clouded with a certain relentless gloom as Annie dug deeper through another of the many locked four-drawer filing cabinets which Phil had packed into the storage office. This cabinet was labelled "OLD SALES RECEIPTS AND TAX INFORMATION". The top drawer and second drawer were as full of dust and mustiness as they were of records, so Annie couldn't help but notice that the third drawer records were almost dust free, as if that drawer had been accessed frequently. She bent down and looked closely at the fat file folder labels. "Taxes --- 1975", "Taxes --- 1976", "Taxes --- 1977". The stiff edges of a spread of photos protruded from one of the middle files and caught her attention. Photographs in a tax file?

She pulled the file out and dropped it open onto the desk. It wasn't tax records at all. It was a collection of yellow-brown envelopes with photographs in them. Nothing but photographs! She spilled the contents of one envelope onto the desk in front of her. There were several dozen black-and-white prints of a homely adolescent girl with ruddy skin, holding a cigarette in some parody of provocativeness, stretching herself this way and that into pseudo-erotic poses, too staged and unnatural to be enticing to any but the most undiscriminating of viewers. These were coarse documentations of artless young girls who were pretending what they thought was alluring sexually. But someone had gone to the trouble and expense of taking these pictures, developing them, and filing them carefully. Perverse in the truest sense.

Annie opened a few more envelopes and thumbed through them. Each was for a different roll of film. Negatives were in a fold of wax paper in each envelope, and a piece of writing paper was stuffed in next to the negatives with one or more names --- presumably the models' --- and a date. Some pictures were dated directly on the back. The handwriting was Phil Lesyk's unmistakable scrawl. Most batches of photos featured different girls, alone or in combinations of parodied lesbian encounters. Although a few faces and young bodies starred in several of the first batches Annie opened, one heavily tattooed young girl was a favorite of the photographer for 1978.

Annie didn't recognize any of the girls in the first file. Almost all of them seemed to be under age. Annie cringed. She could imagine Phil behind the camera, drooling over each of these not-so-sweet young things. She glanced through a few more packets of the pictures and then returned the first file to its place between the others in the drawer. She stared at the dusty, open drawer for a few moments of silence in order to catch her breath and regain her composure. It wasn't shock at the blatancy of it all: she'd travelled too many miles to be shocked by naked bodies posing for cameras. It was the mindless commonness of the collection. That someone had spent so much time and energies (not to mention money) filming and collecting such photographs was something between pathetic and pathological.

She examined a few more of the old "Tax Records" in the drawer and found more of the same. The dates on the photographs were accurate to the year-dates on the files. More recent years were packed tightly near the back of the drawer, but the most recent was still over three years old. Annie opened the bottom drawer. A few of the large envelopes were held in place, upright at the front, by a large shoebox full of batches of unfiled photos, grouped with rubber bands. Behind the shoebox was a large old leather camera case. Annie slowly pulled the drawer out to its maximum extension and eased the camera case out. It was very heavy, and it contained an array of lenses and paraphernalia for photographic work. Annie frowned at the signs of heavy wear. A camera which had been pointed at a lot of young, naive, and probably stupid, girls. The camera said Raccor. Not a brand she'd ever heard of. She wasn't a photographer, but this stuff looked very professional and very expensive.

Annie lifted the shoebox from the drawer and flipped though more photos. Many of this series were in color, although there were still a few rolls of black-and-white interspersed. A few of these models were older women, and some of them had partners. And the poses looked a little more natural, although the vantages were quite odd. Overall, the photographic quality was particularly poor. Some of the faces looked almost familiar. One young girl looked like someone who'd worked as a sales clerk for Lesyk two summers ago, but Annie couldn't be sure. The angles made it hard to see her face, for some reason. Some showed glare spots and reflections, as if they were shot through glass. There were more of the posed shots of young girls, sporting current hairstyles, but otherwise the new collection was every bit as sordid as the photos from the Seventies files. The coarseness and baseness were not relieved by the shift to color film. In fact, most of the girls had an unhealthy yellow tinge to their skin. The close-ups had all the glamour of color plates in a gynecology text. All in all, there was a macabre Fellini-like grotesqueness to Lesyk's private collection. His still-view of sex had every bit of the art and sensitivity of the mangled remains of a dead animal in the middle of a highway.

Annie flipped on to another batch in the box. Suddenly her heart leaped and pounded. She heard herself making a kind of squeaking sound as she gasped for air. Squeaking but distant, as if made by someone else. Repressed by the momentary suffocation you feel when you've had the wind knocked out of you, she panicked. Her lungs were almost empty and she couldn't get air in. She slapped the batch of pictures down in front of her and strained to equilibrate. Finally the air wheezed in. She labored to hold onto it, as if this breath might be her last.

Her hand trembled. It was too ghastly to be true, but it was in front of her eyes --- right in front of her --- as real as could be. The ultimate insult. She stared helplessly at the pictures.

There was Chrissie, lying on the bed, wide-legged

and casual, the way she always did. Naked, the way she waited when she was waiting for Annie.

Horrified, yet mesmerized, Annie flipped to the next picture in the series. There she was. Annie herself, beginning to slip out of her coveralls. And then the two of them were lying together in bed.

Annie tried to imagine how anyone could have managed to take such photographs. As she slowly and grimly continued through the collection, she realized that the photos must have been taken with some kind of special lens, through the glass of the windows of her house. Her own house. The son-of-a-bitch had been out there in the woods with some kind of special camera taking pictures of their private lives!

She searched the box for more pictures of herself and of Chrissie. There were two more sets which featured the two of them. One was filmed just after Annie had last had her hair permed, so it had to be almost a year ago.

The last few rolls were devoted entirely to Chrissie, apparently taken while she was living alone at Annie's, right after Annie had left for the Himalayas this year. The most recent roll was in an envelope dated March. It included a series of outdoor climbing prints taken with a telephoto, mixed with more photos through the large glass sliding doors which led from the bedroom in Annie's house onto the upper level deck. No one had ever pulled the drapes on those doors. It had never occurred to them that there might be eyes in the forest.

The camera angles were bad in some of the last set, but it was nonetheless easy to ascertain that Chrissie was pleasuring herself. Even in some of the candlelight photos, the film was fast enough and the lenses good enough that Chrissie's facial expressions were painfully recognizable in all their lascivious glory. Picture after picture Annie dropped onto the pile in her lap, covering them with her hand to make the images go away. It was horrible. Annie's insides were solidified in a wild mixture of jealousy and anger and horror and revulsion, and her hands were trembling so violently that by the time she reached the last photo, she was no longer able to see the pictures clearly.

She angrily stuffed the photographs back into the shoe box, packed the camera equipment back into its case, and dropped the case back into the back of the drawer. The world was operating in Fast Forward. Everything seemed off kilter. The pictures probably had nothing whatsoever to do with the murders, but they were likely to be something Brandon would expect to be told about. She knew that, but she knew that she wanted to destroy those pictures and never let anyone see them or know anything about them.

Ever.

Especially the pictures of Chrissie.

Especially the pictures of Chrissie.

Twenty

In Vancouver, Brandy's early morning was spent poring over the results of his database searches of the business and financial affairs of Ergologic and its partners, both before and after the death of their star inventor, Farmer Hobbs. He looked at credit ratings, product releases, press coverage of company business, and everything else which might give more texture to the emerging picture of a company which Farmer Hobbs had propelled to a consistently high level of success in the instant-riches, instant-bust world of high tech.

At nine o'clock sharp, Brandon made a telephone call, using a pseudonym, to the receptionist at Ergologic, offering to sell the company some life insurance for its executives. The receptionist smoothly deflected his attempts to break through to the executive level with his sales pitch by assuring him that Ergologic's insurance needs were already well looked after by Hollyburn Associates.

Brandon then called Hollyburn, posing as the business manager of a new accounting firm. He said he'd been referred to them by a friend at Ergologic and wondered which company Hollyburn might recommend as a carrier for key-person insurance for the executives of his new account-ing group. He was passed along to an officious agent who unequivocally recommended Minnesota Mutual. "First and only for the past three years since they reinstated the double indemnity for accidental death. Best company, best dollar. You say you know someone at Ergologic? Who might that be?"

"Uh . . . Dave Wendel," Brandon muttered after glancing about at the notes strewn across the top of his desk. He hoped he had faked a common casualness.

"Dave? Well, then you probably know that I've handled the Ergologic account since they were incorporated."

"So he said. Minnesota Mutual, eh? Is that who's insuring their people?"

"For three years, now."

"How is Minnesota Mutual with their claims? I gather Dave had to make a claim on the death of one of his partners. That climbing accident thing that was in the news again last week. How has Minnesota Mutual managed that?"

"Well, of course I'm not at liberty to disclose any details . . ."

"Of course. I was just curious as to the insurer's responsiveness. A company's promises don't mean dick if they don't come through when it counts. I mean, *that's* what we're paying for, isn't it?"

"Yes. Well, Mutual hasn't paid out yet, of course."

"But I thought the accident was *months* ago!"

"Yes, but if you've been reading the news, you'll recall that they hadn't actually found Mr. Hobbs' body until just a few weeks ago. Any insurer will always have to have a copy of a death certificate and assure itself that there is no question as to cause of death. But, let me tell you, as a man who has spent his career working in the insurance industry: you can bet that the claim will be paid out by Minnesota as fast or faster than it would be by any other insurer in the world. They really are super. I can't praise them enough."

Brandy smiled to himself. "I see. Well, Minnesota certainly sounds like the kind of company we're looking for. Do they do private life insurance policies, too?"

"Of course. In fact, their corporate packages all come with a private beneficiary option for all executives at *very* attractive rates. Can we make an appointment to show you all the programs and figures, and to arrange for your insurance needs, Mr. Sagan?"

"Yes, but I need to check with a couple of other agencies first. Company policy. To avoid conflict of interest charges at Board level. You know."

"Of course. Well, at Hollyburn we handle most of the major West End firms. We're the oldest and largest in Vancouver, you know."

"So I've heard. I'll get back to you in a few days," Brandy assured him, and rang off.

It was a reasonable guess that Farmer had arranged to purchase a policy for Julia with the same insurance company as Ergologic had used to insure him.

Brandon ran a few other probes, by telephone and by modem, on financial records and business connections and made a few other phone calls before putting on his MBA army fatigues: his thin blue wool-blend three-piece suit, black leather dress moccasins, and a crisp white-collared shirt, featuring a suitably dull tie.

Brandy selected from among his standing collection of professional calling cards one which he often found especially useful.

The receptionist at Ergologic was as smoothly

helpful and impenetrable in person to Brandon Drake, Insurance Investigator, as she had been smoothly impermeable on the telephone to Carlos Sagan, the insurance sales agent.

"I realize that Mr. Wendel isn't expecting me," Brandon explained, "but if I can speak to him for just a few minutes . . ."

"That's quite impossible. He's in the middle of an important board meeting. I'd be happy to make an appointment for you, but the soonest I can make it for is Tuesday afternoon."

"Please. I know it's inconvenient, but I just had an urgent request from Minneapolis Head Office for me to see him for just a few questions. Something related to the release of insurance proceeds related to Mr. Hobbs. I'd guess that Mr. Wendel wouldn't want anything to delay that. Can you at least ask him?"

She hesitated a moment, looking politely annoyed, before picking up the phone and connecting herself to someone elsewhere in the building, to whom she murmured a few key elements of the matter. She winced as she listened to the reply. When she hung up, she looked up at Brandon with a raised eyebrow.

"Mr. Wendel says to make yourself comfortable. He'll be able to spend ten minutes with you if you can wait until they finish this meeting. About eleven-thirty."

"That'll be fine. Thank you. Is there somewhere I can use a phone?"

"Of course. Come with me." Seemingly resigned to the special status of the unscheduled visitor, the receptionist led Brandon through the busy maze of blue-spectrum fluorescent hallways which were Ergologic's head office. En route, she offered him some coffee (which he refused) and tea (which he accepted). She led him to a small conference room where she said he would be able to wait. "Space is always at a premium around here. This is a very busy company."

An engineering student sat at an overcrowded carrel in the corner of the room. "This room was *supposed* to be unoccupied," the receptionist said menacingly, making no attempt to mask her annoyance.

The student cowered as he tried to rise from his seat, only to trip over a stack of computer paper. "It was the only free terminal in the building," he stammered. "I . . . I have to finish my . . ."

"You'll just have to take your coffee break now," she commanded the young engineer sternly, "so that Mr. Wendel can have a place to meet with his visitor. It shouldn't take all that long. They'll be finished by noon. The main board room is already in use and . . ."

"Yes, yes. I . . ." he picked up another stack of fanfold printouts and scurried across the carpet toward the door. "I'll just review these over . . . okay. Sorry."

The receptionist rolled her eyes and motioned to one of the chairs next to the small conference table. She placed a telephone beside Brandon and was gone for a few minutes before she returned with the cardboard cup of tea. "If there's anything else you need," she said in a voice which suggested she hoped there wouldn't be, "just push the 'O' button."

Brandy hated tea in cardboard. He looked at his watch. Twenty minutes. It seemed worth a chance. The computer terminal on the carrel was networked to the company system and the engineering student had left it in an active mode. Too much temptation for an information-hungry computer jockey to resist.

The company telephone list was obvious on the main menu screen. When Brandy scanned for the number which Annie had provided him last night, he found it listed as the private direct number for Farmer Hobbs. The list obviously hadn't been updated since Hobbs' disappearance, or the number hadn't yet been reassigned.

The company telephone list had a submenu which used the function keys and which offered access to the "Telephone Usage Log". Brandon entered a null code and was asked "Month?". The July log appeared for Farmer's number. It showed very heavy usage for the first two weeks but no calls thereafter. There were half a dozen calls to the Yosemite area code, but none were to the Mountaineering shop. Four were to Annie's house. Logical enough. The others were placed just two days before Farmer left Vancouver, and were to a number Brandy didn't recognize. He grabbed a notebook from his inside jacket pocket and scribbled the unknown number and the times it was called.

There had been no telephone calls at all beginning the week before the climbing accident. Logical. Farmer was already in Yosemite. But the mystery remained. Why would someone from the Mountaineering shop be calling Farmer's personal business line a week after Farmer and Chrissie had been killed?

Brandon keyed in "WENDEL" and checked the area codes on his personal line during that same month. Two calls had been placed to Annie's cabin, three days after Farmer had arrived in the valley, which made it less than two days before he died.

Noises in the hallway reminded Brandon he was intruding on dangerous turf. He tapped the escape key to backtrack screens to the main menu and briskly swung himself back into the seat at the conference table. The hallway conversation crescendoed, then subsided. Brandy listened carefully to Ergologic's white noise. Nothing special. He looked back over at the computer.

He'd already learned more there than he had the right to expect, and there was nothing else specific he really wanted to find out from it, but a computer hacker has difficulty leaving somebody else's terminals alone. He bit his lip and decided not to push his luck. He decided to review his cover story and wait for Wendel. He looked back over at the terminal, bothered by the thought of what other goodies might be pirated from the network. He was about to yield to his curiosity when the conference room door burst open.

"I don't see why I have to account for my time," Wendel grumbled. "Especially now that they've turned up the body. But if you must know, I was up at the Harrison Hot Springs for a three-day conference." Wendel was peevish. He sat heavily in an empty chair on the far side of the conference table, fondling a small, cordless mouse which he nervously withdrew from his pocket. Brandy looked carefully at the device each time it emerged into view. He hadn't seen anything exactly like it before, and wondered if it were a prototype Ergologic was currently working on.

"I was making product presentations at the NASCOM show," continued Wendel, obviously oblivious to Drake's curiosity about the device, and resentful of having to provide answers to Brandon's questions. "Smith was overseeing the manufacturing division people, at the plant, in Port Moody. They were working on Farmer's latest brainstorm. His last project. The one which damn near sank this ship, I might add. Unfinished symphonies sell much better than unfinished computer hardware, let me tell you. Now, why the hell is Minnesota Mutual suddenly asking all these Back-To-Go questions? Why don't you people just release the insurance money and be done with it? I mean, they found the body more than two weeks ago, for god's sakes!"

"Minnesota Mutual is still concerned about a few of the details," Brandon offered in his flattest monotone. "Please bear with us, Mr. Wendel. Were there any competitors who might have been willing to . . . how shall we say? . . . to help dispose of Ergologic's most valuable property?"

Wendel stopped fiddling with the mouse. "I beg

your pardon?" he asked.

"If I must be more blunt, sir . . . Is there anyone who might have put out a contract on Farmer Hobbs?"

"A *contract*?!" Wendel's eyelids flapped in consternation.

Brandy intercepted his protest. "It's a standard line of inquiry we always make whenever an insured dies under any mysterious circumstances."

"Mysterious circumstances? Are you crazy? The man died in a climbing accident, for god's sakes. The only mysterious part was that they weren't able to find his body for three months."

"Why are you reluctant to answer my question? It's perfectly routine, Mr. Wendel. Quite routine. Although it does occasionally bring out some, er . . . interesting reactions, doesn't it?"

"I think this whole damned thing is preposterous!"

"He was insured for an unusually large sum by your company, Mr. Wendel."

"Not at all, when you consider what an enormous part of our research and development clout he represented. The amount is no more than Ergologic earned in the past two years as a result of his inventions. I'm not sure it's any of the insurance company's business at this late date to address the issue of how *much* we chose to insure him for anyway, so long as we paid our premiums. Which we did. I can only assume that Minnesota Mutual is looking for excuses not to pay the . . . "

"How is Ergologic's current cash flow situation, Mr. Wendel?"

Wendel became very red in the face. His hand began tapping the mouse against the table so hard that Brandy thought the device might break into pieces as they talked. "Mr. Drake, I resent what you are implying. The payments of insurance benefits to all the beneficiaries, including

Ergologic, have been held up long enough. The body was found, and the cause of death is perfectly clear to the police, I understand. If Minnesota Mutual is unwilling to pay immediately, we shall have to begin legal action. Is that clear?"

"Perfectly. You must understand. I *have* to ask these questions whenever . . ."

"You're trying my patience, Mr. Drake."

"I'm sorry. Perhaps I've acted out of habit, tactlessly. But I gather from the California investigation reports that there are still some unresolved issues in the death of Mr. Hobbs."

Wendel looked concerned for the first time.

Brandon continued on the offensive. "Telephone company records of calls placed to the Yosemite area from your company's lines during the time your partner was there, include two placed from *your* personal line, Mr. Wendel. Would you care to explain what those calls were about, and to whom they were placed?"

"I resent your intrusion into personal affairs of the people of this company and its business! These are the kinds of questions I might expect from a policeman, not of an insurance agent. Whoever said you could go asking the telephone company about . . ."

"I didn't think you would have anything to hide, Mr. Wendel," interrupted Brandon.

Wendel glared at him and spluttered nonsense sounds for a few moments until he could compose himself. He expanded his chest with a forced deep breath. "Those calls were to Farmer. From me. To check details on our then-current hardware project." Wendel was aware of Drake watching his reaction and he blurted, "I don't see what anything you've asked about here can possibly have to do with us, except to slow down payment of insurance monies which you owe us. And I won't tolerate that kind of bullshit. You tell your bosses *that*. Is that clear?"

"Minnesota Mutual is not my 'boss'. I represent many insurance companies as investigator for this region. But I'll report to the head office in Minneapolis exactly what you've told me. They should be getting back to you within a few days. Thank you for your time."

Brandon grinned his way to where he'd parked Red Dog, his ruby-throated old Kharmann-Ghia. Brandy had been just nasty enough with Wendel to jiggle some buttons, if there were any to jiggle, but just polite enough before he left to give Wendel a sense of gratification for his righteous indignation, so that if he was not involved in the murders, hopefully there'd be no complaints going to Minnesota about the non-existent representative in Vancouver.

Now it was time to sit quietly and wait and see.

Twenty-One

In the afternoon, Brandy ran a credit check on Julia Hobbs' charge cards. He gave the numbers he'd copied when they were in Yosemite together, and he used the cover which was kindly provided him as a standing agreement by Ed Lawson's credit agency. Her credit rating was in great shape, with an upper limit of thirty thousand dollars on each of two cards.

"Thirty thousand?" shouted Brandy into the telephone at the surprised banker, who thought he was talking to an insurance lawyer. "That's not a credit card allowance; that's a complete *line* of credit."

"She *is* a woman of some means, Mr. Drake," replied the banker politely in his mild British accent. "And I must say, she hasn't disappointed us yet. Is there some reason for which we should be concerned?"

Mastercard told him the same. Her financial and personal analysis all checked out quite well.

Some back-door calls from Brandy's lawyer-cum-agent-cum-information-pimp Teddy Swedholm told him that

Farmer had assigned very little of his estate to Julia, apparently at *her* request. His will left almost all of his assets to his brothers and their children. There was no mention of Farmer's unborn children. Unless Auggie dug up something new, it looked clear that Julia stood to gain very little from Farmer's death, especially compared with the money she had inherited after her father's death two years ago.

Inwardly, Brandy breathed a sigh of relief, but when he realized what that sigh implied, he was troubled. Drake Rule Number Sixty-Nine said that an information agent, like any other type of private investigator, should never get emotionally attached to his clients. Perhaps Brandon's feeling of relief that Julia was checking out clean was simple sympathy for a woman who had been through so much all at once. Perhaps.

Badger checked in during the late afternoon with some early returns on his own diggings.

"You asked about this Pipeline organization," he began. "Well, I certainly ran into some interesting responses here. People definitely sit up and pay attention. It's a nasty corner of the store you're sweeping in. But my sources say the Pipeline has nothing to do with drugs, so it seems like your informant was right about that much. Seems to have been a very successful operation set up to import and export heavy-duty industrial information. I mean *really* successful. State boys worked with Washington trying to bag one end or the other of it . . ."

"Why?" asked Brandy.

"Why what? You mean why all the interest in this group? Well, the Feds always get a bit nervous about successful information channels. Afraid they might start moving DOD type information next. Nothing ever confirmed, at least as far as the California state boys know. They were very near to popping the bubble on it when it shut down."

"What do you mean?"

"Okay to go on?"

"Completely. As far as I know, my line is clean. And I'm alone here."

"Okay. Just wanted to be sure. What I mean is that the whole Pipeline just sealed up. Closed off. Out of business. And nobody knows why. You don't expect a successful Big Money international ring to just close its doors, but that's what seems to have happened here. The State file is still open, but there's been no record of Pipeline activity for about three years. And no active investigation of the file in over a year.

"Right before it shut down, the Feds had arrested one of the Pipeline's couriers, and they were going to work uphill. But somebody got to the guy -- the courier, that is -- right there in the L.A. county jail. They found him dead in his cell. It was called a suicide, but insiders say it looks like the guy had help. Only the county didn't need the embarrassment of that kind of publicity when it wasn't clear cut, especially about an investigation they weren't at all sure they could solve without the guy's information. The Feds already knew a few other things, but nobody has ever been able to finger the organizers. The telephone contacts had pointed to the L.A. area and *that* is all the further they've ever been able to get.

"They figure their investigation must have tipped off the brass of the operation. Or that the Pipeline had a well-placed informant in the State ranks. Or that there was only one chief honcho and that something happened to him. There are one hell of a lot of annoyed State agents who hate to have any of the Bad Guys cheat the gallows this way. Know what I mean?"

"I can imagine."

"By the way, there's nothing linking the Pipeline with

the Frenell murder in Djakarta. My sources would have been able to tell me if there was any suggestion of that kind of connection. Sounds like somebody was taking credit for it to keep somebody else scared."

"That doesn't surprise me. How big is the current agency interest in the Pipeline?"

"How big? By what measure?" Badger asked.

"State only? State and federal? What?"

"Federal and state both. And both FBI and CIA, at one time or another. The file goes back over eight years, and they think the Pipeline may have been operational before then, but they can't close the loop on anything. Like I said, the investigators haven't been able to do anything on it for over a year. But they'd love to know more. Whatever you can tell them."

"Which is *nothing* for the moment," said Drake, firmly. "Did they pressure you? Did you have to link the names I gave you?"

"Brandy! Give me a break! Who do you think you're dealing with here?"

"Sorry, fella. I just couldn't imagine how you could have gotten this much without . . ."

"Which is why my nickname is 'Badger' and why *you*, Brandino, are no longer in the cops and robbers business."

Brandy laughed. "Okay, okay. But seriously, where can I go from here? Anything else you can find out for me?"

"Yeah, there might be. DEA didn't have any record of agents who were killed on assignment in Enseñada. That inquiry required special care, as I'm sure you can imagine."

"Yes, indeed. I wouldn't want *anyone* but you going after that one."

"I accept the compliment, you two-faced S.O.B." Badger growled. "So if you want anything more on that, I'll have to have an exact date on which the agent was supposed to have been killed. *Or* I could get at it by knowing his full name, maybe. 'Ensenada and 1980' just isn't specific enough. And 'Bill' could have been part of a pseudonym. Right?"

"I'll see what I can do. Anything else turn up?"

"The names you gave me ---Phil Lesyk and Christine Peacock. No known connection to the Pipeline. The Peacock girl had no police record in this state. I can check on other states, if you want, but that could take some time and might raise a bit more dust than the kinds of things I do here at home, if you know what I mean. Would the Park Rangers be running that stuff down? I mean, are they looking as closely at her as you are?"

"I don't know. I doubt it. Why?"

"Because I would be able to pick up the information off the Interagency Bulletin Board, *if* it's already been requested, and then I don't attract any attention doing it."

"Badger! You surprise me! *You* using a computer database? Can this be?"

"Okay, smart-ass. I never said the day wouldn't come. I just always said I wouldn't help it come any sooner than it had to . . ."

"Would you like me to joggle your memory as to *exactly* what you always said about it?"

"No, I would *not*! Now, where were we? Oh, yeah. Peacock woman comes up clean. She had no fixed addresses for the past four years. Paid taxes each year, though. Listed herself as a mountain climbing instructor. Reasonable income, but nothing to write home about. Married for a couple of years when she was in her early twenties --- 1975-1977. Divorce uncontested. No children.

"The Lesyk fellow, on the other hand, is a real sweetheart. Has a small collection of offenses going back for nearly twenty years. All kinds of things. Petty, mostly. No felonies. None that stuck, anyway; but then, my sources on this won't show all the ones which *didn't* stick. If you want to know about those, we'll have to get a little more public. Anyway, there's plenty on record to let us know he wasn't always a good little boy."

"Any specialties."

"Lesyk? Yeah. Peddling pornography. Public nuisance charges. Corruption of minors, but he never served time for most of them. Only for a few of the public disturbance things. Otherwise mostly fines and wrist-slaps. His brother owns a nightclub together with him in Los Angeles. Earl Lesyk."

"Partners?"

"Yeah. The brother calls himself Big Earl Lesyk. Pretty cliché, huh? Seems to have a certain clout with the local justice, but definitely small time all the way. The nightclub partnership must have been in name only. *Big* Earl seems to have run the club pretty much solo. Oh, and the brother was part owner of the Yosemite business you told me about, too. You may already know this, but Phil Lesyk had a rented cabin up in Yosemite Valley, and some kind of apartment or mobile home or something on his brother's place in Redondo Beach. It's hard to make out from the zoning description exactly what it is. He also owned a place in Las Vegas. Anyway, he seemed to like a lot of addresses. And his taxes were fairly hefty for a lowly shopkeeper of a small national park concession, but with the nightclub revenues, I guess it's not too surprising. The money part all seems straight enough. At least, he managed to pass an IRS scan four years back."

While he sat at his sunroom desk and listened, Drake alternately typed some notes at his computer keyboard and scratched on the foolscap pad at his right.

"You remember a guy in forensics here named Ferry Johnson?" Badger asked.

"Not really."

"I wondered. He must have come to the S.F.P.D. just

after we did the Wiegelstrom case. You wouldn't have forgotten the name, I'd guess. Ferry is a most unfortunate name for a man living in the San Francisco Bay Area. I mean, as far as I know, he's straight. Anyway, he really knows his stuff. I called him about your fingerprint problem and he says *yes*, prints can survive perfectly well on a surface and could be useful evidence for lifting years later. Indefinitely, he says, if conditions are right. But the object would have to be kept out of the weather and away from high heat and humidity. Says it's been done a couple of times before. Twenty-five years was the longest time on record for lifting prints from a surface."

"Good to know. That jibes with what my man with the Mounties here says, too."

"Sounds like somebody would have to go out of their way to do that for a gun, though."

"Yeah, well, from what I gather, the desire is great."

"Okay. Well, that's about it, I guess. You still want to get me some more specifics on the DEA thing?" Badger asked.

"I'll see about the name and date."

"Sounds smart. If I go back to Sacramento, I'd better have some facts to make it a direct computer-type check. Even then, we may start to attract some attention and I don't think you want to do that. Am I reading you right?"

"That's a roger."

"Okay. Talk to you tomorrow."

Brandy shifted his gaze alternately between his telephone console and his computer screen, trying to digest the scanty details which Badger had provided. The phone rang again.

"Are you alone?" Annie's voice began.

"Who wants to know?"

"Smart-ass! That's what you always ask *me*. I only wanted to know if you could talk right now. I just couldn't wait until whenever the hell you called to tell you what happened this afternoon."

"I'm glad you called. I have to have the full name of the DEA agent you shot. And the exact date you did it."

There was a dead silence.

"Annie?" Brandon persisted.

"I . . . I can't possibly remember any more details about the guy. I've told you everything I know."

"I thought it was engraved on your memory forever?"

"The incident is engraved. Not stupid fucking details like what was written on his ID. I told you. He was DEA. What else does anybody need to know?"

"A lot, in order to look into it."

"Well, I don't want you looking into it. I already told you that has nothing to do with the murders of Farmer and Chrissie."

"Then you shouldn't mind my keeping my ears open." Brandon waited. Still no response. "We still have our agreement, don't we? I have to know everything straight, Annie."

"Yeah, yeah. I just don't know anything more to tell you about the Mexico thing. It's history, anyway. Okay?"

"What month did it happen in? What month in 1980?"

"Jesus, how should I remember . . ."

"Annie!"

"April. Okay. It was April. Hey! But get a load of this. Wait until you hear what happened today."

"Okay. Shoot."

"We opened the Mountaineering Shop for a few hours this afternoon. The Park people were worried that some climbers might be scrimping on supplies they'd counted on buying in the valley. The nearest backup supplier is in Mariposa, and some dummies would rather go on up without the supplies than make the drive. They try to fake it. Dumb bastards!"

"Sounds like self-correcting behavior to me," said Brandon acidly.

"Yeah, but even if they do a righteous head-plant at the base of the face, the cleanup and follow-up gets expensive for the government. Anyway, they asked us to open doors for a while.

"I'd taken an early lunch and Bob and Shirley were still gone on their break. Bob was delivering things up to Badger Pass, while Shirley ran some errands in the village. And so I was there alone when this guy comes charging in. I'd never seen him before, but he looked and acted like he owned the shop. Weird right off the bat. He was one of these people who, whenever he said something, made it sound like it was an order. Know what I mean?"

"Go on."

"He was a non-stop cigar smoker. Kept this short stub of chewed-on, slimy Havana stuck in the corner of his mouth. Talked with it there, everything. Like it was a part of his breathing equipment. The whole shop reeked of old cigar smoke before he spoke his first word. And it stayed disgusting for the rest of the day, too. Really disgusting. And it takes a *hell* of a lot to disgust me, as you probably know."

"So who was he?"

"He didn't give his name at first. Until I demanded it. It was Earl Lesyk. Phil's brother. 'Big Earl', as Phil always called him. Now I know why. The guy is *big*: taller than you and about two-seventy-five pounds, maybe."

"What did he want?"

"Said he came to pick up all of Phil's 'personal stuff'. That he'd already been by the cabin on the other side of the Valley."

"And?"

"I told him there wasn't anything personal of Phil's in the shop, except his King-Of-The-Place sign and a few odds and ends from the desk I'd gone through in the last two days, but if I found anything else, I said, I'd set it aside. Or mail it to Earl, if he preferred."

"And?"

"He ignored me. He barged right on back to the inner office. I could tell by the way he beelined around the shop that he'd been there a few times before. He started going through Earl's desk, pulling things out of drawers and stuffing them into an empty box he'd brought with him. He obviously didn't want me there watching him, but I wasn't about to leave him in there unattended. Then he started getting so obnoxious I couldn't stand it. I had to leave."

"Too obnoxious for the famous Raggedy Annie? That must have been *some* kind of obnoxious. Sorry I missed the performance."

"Yeah, I'm sure you would have *loved* it. He invited me to his club in L.A. Pike's Peek, they call it. Phil used to brag about owning part of it. I gathered it's a two-bit strip joint in a sleazy part of town. And the way Big Earl talked, that's definitely what it sounds like.

"When I said 'No thanks', this asshole comes back with, 'Shit, baby, I'll even kick in a free drink or two for you. On the house, like. Know what I mean?' Then he gives me this big, repulsive, dirty-old-man look, like he's seeing me standing there naked, and then he says, 'We have the best exotic dancers in California. The best. Big boobs and perfect asses, too. Every one of them. They're really something else. Take my word for it. I hand pick 'em. And you'll feel right at home there. Hell, we have lesboes comin' in all the time.' That's what he really said! Just like that. Lesboes! The bastard!"

"Sounds like Phil and his brother must have been on speaking terms, at least."

"Barely. From some of the things Phil used to say. Anyway, Brandy, I swear to god, I didn't know whether to hit him or puke on him. I think I wanted to do both. But I have to admit . . . I was a little afraid. I mean, the guy has this *look*. Like he's crazy. Phil was crazy, too, but he was pretty ineffectual about it most of the time. This guy Earl comes across more like pathological. Real scary. From the way Phil used to talk, I always figured he was afraid of his brother. And now I understand why. This Earl is a ruthless sonofabitch."

"So he just came in to clear out Phil's things, eh?"

"Yeah. Only I kind of had the feeling he was there to watch me, too. Know what I mean? I left him back in the back office, 'cause I'd just finished going through everything back there this morning anyway, and I knew I could tell right away after he left if anything important was missing. But after half an hour or so he came out to the front desk and started to ask a lot of questions. Started to get real mean. Wanted to know where else Phil could have put his things there at the shop, or whether somebody had been going through Phil's things already. He was even more obnoxious than he'd been before. Really insulting.

"I was kind of ashamed I didn't have any nasty comebacks for him. The kind I'm so famous for. But this guy made me feel just like a little girl when the school bully is coming down on her. Like I was *supposed* to feel humiliated.

"Anyway, when I told him there was nothing else of Phil's in the shop, he went and turned the back office upside down again. And then he rooted around the main shop, too. He made a hell of a mess. I didn't try and stop him. I don't think I could have, anyway, unless I called the police. And the guy probably has some rights, since his brother was the one owned the concession and all.

"Anyway, Shirley came back, and he had the same effect on her as he did on me, even though he didn't say all that much to her. Then Bob came back and Big Earl left. I don't think it was because of Bob, really. Earl just must've figured he wasn't getting anything more out of us. He said I should call him if anything else of Phil's turned up. I'm pretty sure I know what he was looking for. And I know why he didn't find it."

"Find what?"

"A collection of pictures. Only I found them earlier today and I hid them."

"Pictures?"

"Yeah. This morning I found a couple of file drawers full of porn shots. Little Phil's secret photo collection. It is *so* pathetic, I can't begin to tell you. I was so revolted by them that I'd more or less decided not to tell you about them at all. Until this Earl clod came along and made such a nuisance of himself."

Annie elaborated for Brandy, omitting only the most embarrassing details. "Like I said, I wasn't *planning* to tell you about the pictures --- that's how outraged I was --- but after Earl's little show, I guess I just got pissed off. For all I know, Phil may have been selling those things through Earl's goddamned strip joint! God knows there are probably enough sickoes out there in the world to buy them. What amazes me is that I *never* knew about any of this stuff."

"Is there anybody there in the valley who's big into photography who might have done the technical work for him?"

"Nobody with as little class as this stuff has. Even the lowest of the people here in the valley wouldn't go near this shit. Not to mention, this was really poor quality. Technically. And in every other way, too."

"I wonder where he kept his darkroom," Drake thought aloud.

"Not at the shop. Maybe at his cabin. I wouldn't know."

"Could we get into his cabin, some way? That might

be highly instructive."

"Might have been. Before Big Earl graced the valley with his visit. I talked to Ranger Dave --- goddamnit, Brandon, now you've got *me* calling him that. I talked to Dave after supper, and he says Gary Severence gave a call wanting to know who the hell turned Phil's place upside down. Gary owns those cabins and he was planning on boxing up all of Phil's stuff at the end of the month. He already had it re-rented. Dave figures Earl must have cleaned the cabin out before he came here to the shop."

"Yeah. Well, it does add an interesting twist to what we know about Phil."

"I gotta tell you, this whole thing is giving me the creeps. I made sure he didn't suspect I'd already taken the photos. If I hadn't been rummaging through those old files . . . Three hours later and Earl the Goon would have been taking pictures of Chrissie and me back to L.A. to show his friends. Maybe to sell. Shit."

"You've given me an idea there. Did you or Chrissie ever get any weird phone calls or anything like that?"

"From Phil, you mean?"

"Maybe. I don't know. It's not an uncommon pattern for porno freaks to have other kinks, too. I just wondered."

"No heavy breathing stuff, if that's what you mean. But I can tell you, I've thought a lot about it today. I remember the way Phil used to leer at Chrissie when he wanted to piss me off. He knew Chrissie was my weak spot. He knew that would really get under my skin. The madder I got, the filthier his looks, and the more perverse his attempts at jokes. Lots of men do that kind of thing, but Phil was always so weird about it. Which, in a way, is why the picture thing shouldn't surprise me."

"But obviously it does, Annie. Or you wouldn't be giving it so much air time."

"Okay, okay. It's just that . . . I mean, the little fart

must have spent hours and hours just sitting out there in the woods outside our house . . . Like some kind of fucking Peeping Tom!"

"I've got a few snarelines out to find out more about his background. It sounds like it might be useful for me to have a talk with Brother Earl, too. Maybe a visit to L.A. would be fruitful. Meanwhile, if you think of anything else, let me know."

"I don't like thinking about *any* of this. And I'm not sure it's such a swift idea your getting in touch with Big Earl. I doubt he knows anything about Chrissie's and Farmer's climbing accident, and he's definitely not anyone I'd want to have pissed off at me."

"I imagine. But he might be holding onto some clues as to what happened to Phil up on the mountain."

"Maybe. You know, Brandy, I've been thinking about it from every angle I can imagine, and I still don't think anyone was after Chrissie. Farmer *had* to be the target. But I'll also have to admit that after I saw the pictures I couldn't help but wonder if Phil wasn't out to get Farmer for something to do with Chrissie. It sounds crazy, but that could explain a lot of things, couldn't it?"

"Maybe."

"Have you found out anything up there in Canada which points in any other directions?"

"Nope. Not so far. Widow Julia had nothing to gain. She checks out okay. I'm less sure about the partners in Farmer's company, but I've poked a stick in their nest, and nothing seemed to come swarming out.

"All in all, Farmer doesn't seem to have been an especially likely target. Are you *sure* Chrissie didn't have any enemies? Any spurned past lovers? What about her personal things? Any recent letters or notes? Anything at all?"

"Not really. What are you getting at?"

"Okay. Well, you keep your ears open down there, Annie. And rattle your brains about Enseñada. I have to have more details."

Twenty-Two

A few lengthy long-distance calls to public libraries in San Diego located one which carried the past fifteen years of regional newspapers from Baja California. After much prevarication, a little cajoling, and the application of every bit of charm he could muster, Brandy was able to unearth three reports about the shooting death of an unidentified male tourist in Enseñada during the month of April, 1980. Brandon ran the credit-card gauntlet for fifteen long-distance minutes until the librarian finally agreed to ship three articles, pre-paid, by fax.

It took about an hour to rasp the rust from seven years of mostly unused high-school and university Spanish reading skills, to confirm what the librarian had told Brandy by phone. An unidentified male was found washed up on a private beach south of Enseñada. He had been shot in the chest. Fingerprints had been dissolved in the salt water. Condition of the body made identification unlikely except by dental records. The second and third articles were shorter and further from page one. If an identification was ever made,

it was not evident. But the good news was that at least
Annie's story seemed to be based, at some level, in fact.

      Brandon was dressed for Auggie's Party of the Year,
and almost out the front door to cruise for a Big Mac for a
tiny bit of hold-me-over sustenance, counting on the
likelihood that there would be a good selection of foods to
eat at Auggie's house, when the phone rang again. He was
prepared to let the answering machine take care of it when
he recognized the voice of Laura Meister, his travel agent
extraordinaire, trying to leave a message.

      "Hallo?" Brandon called, flopping himself into his
desk chair as he intercepted the message.

      "Hello? Brandy?" Laura responded. "You *are* home.
Your answering service guardian-goddess wasn't sure
whether you'd be home until late tonight, so I asked her to
put me through to leave something on your machine. I have
the information you asked for. You said you were in a hurry.

      "The airlines' computers coughed up the itinerary
you wanted late this afternoon. United keeps them for a
year. I wasn't sure if you wanted them faxed to you tomorrow
morning. Or I can send them to you right now."

      "Go ahead and send them along now if you will."

      "I hope it's what you need."

      "I'm sure it will be. You're an angel."

      "One who survives on m'lord's commissions."

      "M'lord is ever in your debt."

      "Stand by for delivery."

      "With bated breath."

      By the time Brandon had finished reading the dates
and times and flight numbers Laura had shipped him, he was
already starting to feel hot flashes in his neck. After he had
studied the printout for a few more minutes, he pounded his
fist on the desk and hissed a curse to himself for his

continuing naiveté in the realm of his trusting dealings with his friends. It was time to call Annie again.

By the time Brandy connected with her at home in Foresta, he had steadied himself. "Annie? A couple of quick questions. Okay?"

"Sure. What's up?"

"How often did you say you'd heard from the Pipeline in the past three years?"

"Wait a fucking minute!" she growled. "I said there was no digging into that side of things. None! So let's just keep away from it."

"You might like that, Annie, but I need to know some things if I'm going to keep helping you."

"Look, I told you I was contacted by one of the couriers from the Pipeline who told me the Pipeline had nothing to do with any of this. Period. And that's all the information I need about *that*, and that's all you need, too."

"Annie, listen up. Carefully. I have good reason to believe you probably haven't heard from *anyone* with the Pipeline for a couple of years. And I think you know that. There's something fishy going on."

"I told you once, I'll tell you again. It's a very big organization which . . ."

"Which has been disconnected and fully out of operation for a couple of years now. Now maybe you didn't know that, but I don't like being lied to! Nobody from the Pipeline called you after the bodies were found, did they, Annie?"

Annie was silent for a long pause. "I don't get it. What are you saying? Of course I was called. You think I'd make up something like that?"

"Annie, I can't help you any longer. First you tie my hands and then you lie to me. I'm out of this investigation. Effective this minute. Right now. And I give you twenty-four hours to go to Ranger Dave."

"Wait a fucking minute, Brandy? What the hell are you talking about?" Annie's voice seemed to move up a full octave in pitch as she spoke. "I don't know what your angle is, but if you tell the police anything, they could stir up the Pipeline thing and a certain pistol with my fingerprints could suddenly show up. Holy god, Brandy! You tryin' to scare *me* or something? They'd probably have it looking like it was me who killed Farmer Hobbs and Chrissie. Everybody around here knew Chrissie and I were lovers. And it didn't take too much imagination to know that Chrissie and Farmer were going at it. I mean, what they might start figuring it was all a jealousy thing."

"Did you, Annie?"

"Kill them?"

"Yes?"

"You could ask me that?"

"Before, no. Now, yes. Did you?"

"You know I couldn't have done that. I told you already. I was in Nepal when they died, Brandy."

"No, you weren't. Your travel itinerary from the airlines says you were in San Francisco for at least four days before you returned to Yosemite."

There was cathedral silence on the line. "Brandy, I can't believe you're fucking saying this! How could I kill my own lover?"

"In anger? Anything is possible. Even accidentally. Maybe it was Farmer you planned to kill. Maybe you hoped Farmer would be climbing alone or with another partner when he used those slings. Maybe you were the one who challenged him to go for a solo. You certainly had access and enough expertise to convince him and to do what was needed to get him killed." Brandy's anger pierced through his voice, "Why did you lie to me about where you were when the two were killed? What else have you lied to me about?"

The Yosemite end of the phone was a garble of choking gasps. "I . . . I didn't think you'd believe me. But I didn't have anything to do with it! I couldn't have! I wouldn't have hurt my beautiful lover." She sobbed for a while, then steadied herself to continue. "If I *had* killed them, why on earth would I have called you up and told you about it? You or anyone else? Remember, if it hadn't been for me, this whole thing would probably have faded into history quietly."

"Probably. I don't know, Annie. I really don't. But I do know that any bridge of trust between us has disintegrated."

"Okay. I lied about being in San Francisco for a few days before I returned to Yosemite. But I can account for every minute of it. I was . . . I was with a friend. A close friend. I . . . I can prove it. But I don't think she'd ever want her husband to know we were together that way. Or the other city council members, either." There was another silence, which Brandon allowed to simmer. "Shit, Brandy! What could I do? I was scared. I'm still scared. Scared shitless! Can't you understand that? But everything else --- everything --- was fact. I really did get a call from the Pipeline. It was exactly like I said. Please believe me, Brandy. Please. You have to. And you have to help me, too. I'm just so scared. Please help me!" She broke into frantic sobs again.

Brandy took a deep breath. Let it out as he considered the situation again. Wondered how the hell this whole thing had slipped so far out of bounds. "Okay. I'll run a few more things to ground before I flick in the towel. But no more 'off-limits' areas of information. Understand?"

There was a long silence. "Okay."

"Was the Ensenada story you told me real? All as told?"

"Exactly."

"Do you remember the exact date?"

"Look, I don't see what this has to do with . . ."

"Annie!" Drake warned.

"Okay. April 1st, 1980."

"Are you sure about that?"

"It's a nightmare imprinted on my memory. I know it better than I know my own birthday. That was the year I got to know the real significance of April Fools' Day. *I* was the April Fool."

"You remember the name of the drug agent? You said you saw an I.D. badge?"

"Yeah. A card. With his picture. Agent William Moffat."

"Are you certain Phil Lesyk had no connection to the Pipeline?"

"Phil? God, no. The Pipeline couldn't trust anyone like him. He would have been skimming after the first week. He also didn't travel. Except to and from Las Vegas and Los Angeles."

"How much did Chrissie know about your Pipeline connections."

"Almost nothing. We never talked about that. Except once, and then I told her I was getting out of it completely. I was afraid to tell her most of what I knew. I was afraid for her. Brandy *please* tell me you don't need to go stirring any of this up. Please?"

"I'll talk to you tomorrow."

"That's it?"

"Yep."

"It's just that . . . oh, shit. Do you know how scared I am? I used to tease Gordon that I had never done an unselfish thing in my whole life. It was more like confession than teasing, I guess. I think of Chrissie, dead, and I know I don't deserve to think about myself so much. But maybe after forty years, I'm just too old to stop being anything more than the selfish, self-centered little bitch I've always been. Is that really so wrong?"

"Psychoanalysis isn't my department, Annie."

"Yeah, I know. Besides, maybe being that way isn't necessarily all bad. Maybe it's just that selfishness that makes me want to know what happened up there on the mountain last summer. I'll do whatever you want me to do, Brandy. Whatever it takes. Just find out. That's all I ask. Just find out who killed my Chrissie."

Twenty-Three

Red Dog ran through the remnants of rush hour cross-town traffic into the staid, treed hollows of Shaughnessy. The rapidly darkening grey of early winter evening lent a particularly welcome coziness to the long, curved walkway leading from the streetside parking to the large, brightly lit house. There were no front driveways for any of these homes. The garages all face unlit, narrow backlanes behind and between the main streets. Palace rows alternating with shantytown alleys. It is a typical Vancouver anomaly that a home which costs two and half million dollars might have only scraps of street parking available for the owners to offer their guests.

Drake was being followed. He couldn't spot anyone, but he had the sense of the shadow, off and on, all the way to Augusta's. He stood for a while near his car on the street and watched the passing cars. Still he couldn't confirm the eerie feeling, so he shrugged and walked on in to join the party.

Within the first six minutes of his arrival at Augusta

Traynor's house, even Brandy had recognized no less than a dozen of the city's movers and shakers. He'd seen them in the newspapers, or babbling at the cameras on the evening newscasts. City Hall, Big Business, the Young and the Restless, the Wild and the Crazy, the Fruits and the Nuts, the Shallow and the Shallower, and anyone who preyed on financial riches either to move them along the Great Gameboard or to alleviate their boredom. Here they all were. Pieces of Augusta's Society Puzzle. Trying to fit together. In ones and twos and sometimes in larger numbers. But it didn't seem to Brandon to be working. Not for many of them, anyway. And no wonder. Some of the pieces seemed to be defective.

As soon as he could break free of the clutches of Auggie's assigned Greeting Hostess, Brandy set out in search of Augusta herself. Everyone had seen her, but nobody knew where she was, and the risk of asking anyone was that whomever he asked wanted only to check him out, to find out what section of the puzzle Brandon Drake fit into, to find out which of the other people at the party he fit together with. To determine whether he was a threat to be avoided or a resource to be exploited. Or a romp to be enjoyed.

He had spent three long minutes with a lady who sucked relentlessly on the olive from her otherwise empty martini glass before and after she responded to each of his questions. Brandy wondered if agreeing to come here had been such a swift idea. He was tired and feeling jet-lagged, even if that didn't make any sense. California was only a little more than a two hour flight away and it was in the same time zone as Vancouver. Maybe he was suffering from culture shock. Right.

Just when Brandy's head had started to buzz the same way it always did in the shopping malls after half an hour or so, and just as he was deciding he would probably have increased his odds for success by trying to reach Augusta by phone again, a husky voice from the second floor railing above the far end of the living room where he stood exclaimed, "Brandon! My god! You *did* come! Come up here at once, my dear man." Then she promptly disappeared.

He wound his way up the back stairway and saw her white satin dress whisking through the open doorway of a room. Like a befuddled Alice, he followed it into the unidentified room. It was a guest room, and Augusta was rambling off orders to a white-coated caterer, who then scurried away and closed the door behind him.

"Brandon, Brandon!" she wailed, as if his arrival in the room were a complete surprise. She opened her arms wide and gave him a big hug and a small polite kiss on each cheek. "Thank god you've come early, before the *hordes* arrive. I have to make a proper entrance soon, and if you hadn't come here now I might never have managed to greet you properly before midnight. Dear, dear. I don't know why I ever even stage these . . . these *carnivals*." She had a twinkle in her eye.

Brandon stared back at her. Tough woman to read. Probably impossible. Which accounted for part of her success at her unusual art form. "What did you learn about my lady?" he asked.

Augusta looked shocked. "My goodness! Not *now*, dear. I don't have time to talk about all that. How about after all the Brave and Thwarted leave this palace. I'll be run ragged, a useless remnant of humanity myself, but at least I can give your problem my *full* attention." The twinkle returned.

Drake grimaced. "Sorry, Auggie, but I can't manage it. Have to meet someone at ten-thirty. More information. Most of my friends don't keep regular hours, you know." He smiled. "Like you."

"Well, at least you consider me a friend. So what can we do? You could come back?"

"Another time. Sorry, but this was the best I could

do."

"Snubbing Augusta? Coming and going? I should have you thrown out!" She laughed affectedly. "Okay, but let me tell the headwaiter what to do when the paté arrives from Markham's. He's quite good, but a little simple. It's only intended for the palates of certain guests, but he's just as likely to serve it to *everyone*. Wait here."

Augusta returned about ten minutes later, huffing and puffing and muttering to herself. "Sounds like a too-worn cliché, but you really *can't* find reliable help these days . . . Okay. Now if you insist on being so rude about this, and I could only tolerate such treatment from *you*, Brandon Drake . . . But then I do still owe you. Ut-ut! Now don't bother saying it. I *know* whom I owe and whom I don't. So! You have to take the condensed version of what I found out. If you want the long version, it may cost you a bottle of wine and a private evening."

"When was the last time you had a private evening? With anyone?"

"Don't be any ruder. It's an occupational hazard of mine to be so public. So! Guess what?"

"Shoot. I'll just listen."

"Your Julia Hobbs is every bit as sound financially as I told you she was. In her mid-teen years she was a real hellion, I'm told."

"Weren't we all at that age?"

"Maybe, but Gilly --- her father, remember? --- was so embarrassed by her antics that he quit taking her out in public. Big disappointment to Daddykins, but he couldn't handle having a sweet, beautiful, and unfortunately very intelligent 16-year-old daughter who said exactly what she thought whenever she thought it. It's quite enough to have to deal with the social jackals on the *outside* of the inner circle; nobody needs Cassandras inside the house, too."

"I guess I don't understand. What you're describing

sounds like normal adolescence. What was the big deal?"

"You're really interested in this one, aren't you, Brandy? Woo-woo! I haven't seen you like this before."

Brandy felt himself flush. "Don't get too excited, Auggie. It's just business. I need to find out more about the lady."

"Sure." Auggie smiled patronizingly. "Well, she insulted the Mayor of the city in front of TV cameras, for one thing. The old fart made the mistake of letting them turn the cameras on him as he plunked himself down next to the Hambleton girl at a big benefit do, so that he could look trendy with the younger set. Probably wanted to show how up-to-date he was. The mayor waited until the microphones were in close and then greeted her in some palsy-walsy way, like some wonderful good-buddy uncle. You've seen it all before. It's the older version of baby kissing. Usually good for a few thousand votes in the next election. So sweet Miss Julia looked at the camera, then at the Mayor and said something like 'What's on your mind? Back to try to put your hand under my skirt again?' "

Brandon burst into laughter. "She said that? What did the mayor do?"

"What could he do? He had to hope they wouldn't run it on the six o'clock news. Needless to say, he wasn't too happy with Gilly's daughter. Or with Gilly. Apparently that wasn't the only episode. She was just as likely to talk about her sexual fantasies at the dinner table as most people were to talk about the weather. And this was mid-Seventies Vancouver, remember. The Sixties were long gone. So you see why she was cut out of the pack. And *fast*."

Brandon was smiling, but said nothing.

"Since then she's led such a dull, dull life by all counts as to be almost untraceable because *nobody* wants to gossip about a stone. Know what I mean? No scandals. No public embarrassments. Nothing recent, anyway. She did a stint of modelling before she was married, but nothing more than fashion faces. I already told you about the witch thing, but even that has been a bore in the long run. She doesn't do readings for anybody any more, as far as I can tell.

"She's had almost no men around since she and her husband were separated and, near as I can tell, she hasn't been with anyone since hubby disappeared in the summer. Lots of men have tried to get at her, I'm sure. Money attracts that. Usually she's seen either alone or not at all. *When* she's seen. In spite of all the exhibitionist tendencies from her teenage years, since she married she has always behaved like the perfect married woman. Probably just an over-reaction from adolescent rebellion. No reason to believe there's anything going on with that lady which is any more exciting than watching cement set. I can't even imagine why you thought there was anything there worth knowing. And I called in a few extra favors of my own to find out some *real* gossip, but there just isn't any.

"She locks herself up for weeks at a time and paints her mediocre oils and acrylics --- and I'm not the only one who finds them without redeeming artistic value, I assure you. She reads, she goes to the beach, she takes care of her home, and she dabbles in other artsy things from time to time. Nobody seems to know if she even does any of the witchy things on her own any more. She shops, she rides horses once in a blue moon, and . . . that's it. Period. Can you imagine anyone so *bo-ring*?"

Drake smiled broadly. "Thank you, Auggie. I knew if there was anything out there, you could find it. No news can be good news, even in my business. If only you can explain to me how she magically found the remains of her husband after the finest Mountain Rescue units in North America turned up nit-all for three months . . ."

"Maybe the fellow who was with her when she found him could tell you more. But good luck finding out who it

was. Even _I_ couldn't come up with that tidbit." Auggie
scowled at Brandon. "You're smiling like the proverbial
canary-eating cat. You know who he is?"

"I do. But his account matches hers exactly."

"You've talked with her about it? Well, how did she
explain finding her dead husband?"

"She said she just had 'this feeling'."

"Well, she _is_ a witch, don't forget!"

"Surely you can't buy into stuff like that, Auggie."

"Can and do, my dear man. I know a lot of individuals
who thrive and survive and have made great big fortunes on
cultivating certain senses the rest of us will never
understand."

"It's still a pretty hard coincidence to accept, her
finding him like that."

"I suppose it's possible that her travelling companion
is in some kind of pact with her about it, that they agreed to
lie about what led them to him."

"Well, I know for certain that he's not lying." Auggie
watched Brandy and the twinkle returned to her eye as he
continued, "Part of me can't understand it, but another part
wants to."

"Listen to the part that says 'accept it', my dear,"
said Augusta. "Life is full of things we don't understand. It's
not really surprising that we don't understand them. What's
surprising is that we manage to survive in this dreadful world
in _spite_ of not understanding so much!"

Brandon brushed back his hair with the backs of his
fingers and looked at Auggie seriously. "Thank you, Auggie.
You've been a big help again. As usual. One of these days,
maybe I'll convince you to take some of the money my clients
so happily lavish on me to procure information for them. You
know they'd never find out who was paid for it, and I would
feel much less guilty for coming back to you so often . . ."

"I've said this once, and you'll probably make me say

it again. But not often, please, because humility doesn't become me. You may feel that I have helped you again, my dear, but I shall *never* be able to repay you. If it hadn't been for you . . . well, what can I say? I treasure the fact that I'll never need to seriously contemplate what *could* have happened if you hadn't come to my rescue Way Back When." Augusta suddenly smiled. "But if you're trying to say I can have some sort of *bonus* for a job well done . . ."

"Whatever you want, Auggie," Drake laughed.

"Hah!" she said with a vampish gleam in her eye. "Lot of good that will do me. Before I'd get what I want from *you*, I'd die of unrequited love."

"You're good for the ego, Auggie."

"You, too, you rogue. Now get out of my party before I have you arrested for crashing it and being a misfit. I know how you hate being here."

Drake took her hands in his and gave her a quick kiss on the lips. She blushed deeply and looked at her diamond-studded evening watch. Right on the brink of gaudy. Like everything else about her. But consistent unto herself. She pursed her lips, troubled by the strains of her schedule. "I'm late, thank you very much. Call me if you need anything else, dear. Ta-ta for now." And away she raced.

Drake went straight home, circling a few blocks at one point to confirm the empty sense that he wasn't aware of being followed any more. Since he'd left the party, no one had been erratically changing routes or driving any more strangely than Vancouver drivers normally drove.

There was nothing out of the ordinary for a Monday evening. Nothing at all. But, then, there hadn't been anyone there when Brandy *did* have the sense of being followed on his way *to* the party, either. Eerie. Disquieting. Maybe Auggie was right. Maybe it's not really surprising that we don't understand some of the things that go on around us. Maybe what should surprise us most is that we manage to survive in *spite* of not understanding so much.

As he worked his way back across town, Brandy cogitated on what bits and pieces of the murders were beginning to fit together and just what pictures were emerging. Based on what he had found out about Julia, she seemed all the less likely to have been party to the murder of her husband. That ugly suspicion had been niggling at the back of Brandy's brain since the strange discovery of Farmer's body. If she *had* been involved, surely she wouldn't have wanted to draw such attention to herself by making such a bizarre scene at the Falls with Brandon.

Quite to his annoyance, Brandy felt a most definite relief in any reassurances that Julia was not involved with the murder. So much for objectivity and Rule Sixty-Nine.

For the time being, the fingers of suspicion pointed elsewhere. Brandon kept wondering about Phil Lesyk and his porn collection. Phil's role in this whole affair definitely merited more follow-up. Brandy had a hunch Phil was more than the luckless souvenir hunter Annie had thought he was. The phone calls between Phil's shop and Farmer's business partners were especially difficult to explain.

The closer you looked, the more loose ends this fabric had. Usually that was good news, but for the moment Brandy felt as if he were fading further and further back toward the end-zone to receive a pass, only to find out that the quarterback had fumbled the ball. Or that the game was long over.

Back in his Burnaby suburb, Brandon parked Red Dog at the nearest street spot, a half block over from his condo. Wondered if the time had come to pay for reserved parking. Decided it wasn't worth the fee. He had a negative reaction to anything which could let people know where he was or where he wasn't. This way, at least, people who were watching him had to work at it a little. Security wasn't as much of a problem since he'd given up the garden variety PI work, but caution was an old habit. And one Brandy saw no reason to change.

He locked his apartment door behind him and went immediately to check for messages on his answering machine. Two blankoes and one long one from Karen, signing off for the night and telling him to call Annie Bentley after eight o'clock in the morning. Drake smiled that Annie had used her maiden name.

Brandon put his rent-a-tux away on its hanger in his bedroom closet and turned off the lights on his way to the kitchen. He liked the tactile familiarity of his home. He never had to grope around, even in the darkest depths of the darkest night. There was always some glint or extraneous light reflecting from some familiar object or surface. Occasionally he would completely close his eyes and move through the apartment, although he had to hold his hands out in front of him for safety when he did that. It was a game he had played since childhood. And winning it was how he knew when a new house or apartment had truly become his home.

He made a PB&J sandwich by the light of the refrigerator, filled a big mug of orange juice, and ambled lazily toward his moonroom-cum-office. The new moon limited the heavenly lighting, but his eyes soon adjusted to the pleasant background glow from the reflections of the streetlamps along the next block.

Feeling fat and sassy, Brandy leaned back quietly in his desk chair and munched his grand repast. He felt the pervasive cool of the evening, but decided to stay in his underwear and contemplate Things In General. His mind tried on a few explanations and a few stories, and a few fantasies.

But he must have dozed, because the next thing he heard was the intrusion alarm. Not his electronic alarm --- that one was armed only when Brandy was away from his apartment. What awakened him from the midnight drowse was his low-tech alarm. Kept next door. The best kind. Hard to disable. Easy to care for. The elderly couple who had inhabited 203B for the past three and half years owned an Irish Terrier named Vic. Vic always warned Drake --- and everyone else on the floor, if not the whole building --- of *any* intruders, whether invited guests or not, who stepped into the common hallway outside the second floor elevator doors after "lights out" in his own apartment.

Vic was not an especially big dog, but when Vic growled, it sounded like someone had just revved an unmuffled, well-tuned Jaguar V-12. Some of the neighbors complained about Vic from time to time, but Brandon appreciated the pooch. It was worth having sleep interrupted from time to time for other people's late guests when it saved you from concern about unscheduled surprises from your own unwanted visitors.

Another series of barks. Vic usually desisted after three or four rounds, provided the intruder moved out of the hallway and into someone's apartment. In the silence there was a metallic slide and then a click and a door opening and closing, and then Vic released another salvo.

Adrenaline coursed in quantity.

The opening door had been Brandon's own.

Twenty-Four

Drake sat bolt upright in his desk chair and rolled onto his feet. His nocturnal drowsiness dissipated in moments, replaced by adrenaline clarity. He stood statue-still in the near darkness of the office and felt the emergency unfolding. He felt the tension in his scalp as his ears were drawn as high on the sides of his head as the muscles could lift them. Every sound was magnified, every thinking moment expanded.

The only conventional weapon Drake owned was the pistol in his bedroom closet. He was still licensed to have it, but he never carried it. As part of his campaign to take charge of his professional life, that had been one of the key groundrules. All his new clients got the same speech: "If I have to carry a gun for this contract, find another turkey."

Footsteps were moving across the living room carpet toward the door at the east end of the office. Barefoot, Brandy slipped quietly along the conservatory windows to the door which led into the kitchen. He moved quickly across the dinette and toward the front door, circling around behind the intruder.

Whoever it was was carrying a small flashlight. Not much more than a penlight, but with an intense beam. Brandy could make out the silhouette clearly in the glow. The person was short and dressed in dark clothes. Moved like a man.

Decision time. Break and run through the front door? Or confront the intruder? Common sense said "To hell with it. Get out of here." But curiosity and indignation blended to repel the impulse to beat a retreat. Not just yet, anyway. Next to the front door was Brandy's practice jo, his wooden aikido staff. It was only a hardwood stick, a make-believe weapon about four feet long, but it did offer a certain measure of control, if not protection. It was unlikely that the burglar was armed with anything more than a knife, anyway. Not in Vancouver. Not usually.

So Brandy crept through the darkness in pursuit of the burglar, guided by the reflections of the burglar's own flashlight beam. The intruder shined the light into the bedroom. It gratified Brandon's sense of justice to realize that the unslept-in bed might be a false reassurance to the intruder that the condo was empty.

The intruder crept back out to the office. Moving to a safe vantage behind the door to the living room, Brandy could watch in the reflection in the broad expanse of office windows just what went on in the flashlight glow on the other side of the wall, in the next room. Cat and mouse.

Brandy heard his file drawers being opened, one by one. He never locked them, except when he was away for very long trips. The filing cabinets held routine business papers. The only important information was encrypted on Drake's computer.

The cat, stick in hands, watched the mouse playing for some time. This was not a routine money-and-jewelry burglary. The intruder seemed to be interested only in some sort of information.

Brandy slid his hand gently along the wall just inside the door, ready to flip the overhead light switch. He wanted a chance to talk to this mouse before he called the police. A car drove past on the street below. The intruder froze, panned the flashlight around the room hastily, clicked it off to listen. In a few moments the flashlight came on again. By its light Brandy saw what he'd hoped he wouldn't see: the unpleasant outline of the butt of a small handgun on the near side of the intruder, at the waist. Shit. Drake reconsidered retreat. Considered a dash for his bedroom closet, too. Weighed odds against both moves. The game had just become a survival play. The best solution seemed to be to watch and wait. Get him on the way out, maybe? As he came back through the door out of the office?

The paper fumbling in the file cabinets spoke of rapidly increasing frustrations and time pressure. The intruder turned off the flashlight and looked out the window again.

And then the intruder did the unthinkable. With a click and a whirr and a burst of cathode ray color, he switched on the power bar master switch which activated Drake's computer. For Drake, the gut feeling of rage outflanked his fear response. Indignation of a special order. You can steal a man's car or break into a man's home, but don't ever *ever* mess with his computer. A New Age adage. Wherein may lie the key to Yuppie chivalry.

The computer's memory check tocked though the motherboard's resources. In the bright light of the initial full-colour pop-up menu screen, the intruder's face was fully illuminated. Using the relative light-blinding to his advantage, Drake peered around the corner through the open doorway to glimpse directly the puffy, chalky, intent face of the small burglar. No one Brandy recognized.

It was time for the move.

Jo firmly in hands, Brandy stepped quickly down into the office, pivoted, spun, and brought the jo down solidly with a crash on the desktop just in at the base of the key-board. The well-planted blow fell directly on a startled pair of hands. The intruder screamed. His flashlight bounced off the desk with the rebound. As he leaped back from the desk, the man fell over the chair in which Brandy had been sleeping just minutes before. He was scrambling to regain his feet and groping at his right waistband when Brandy, who had already hauled the jo back and spun it over his head for another well-aimed thump, landed his coup-de-grace on the burglar's near shoulder.

Emitting another animal yowl, the man dropped to the floor. The handgun bounced across toward Brandy. He quickly kicked it away behind him. The burglar was immobilized. He just rolled back and forth on the floor with his arms wrapped around him, shouting "Help! Help! Somebody help!"

Brandy switched on the light above his desk. Vic was in 203B, barking with gusto again. The man on the floor saw the lanky six-footer dressed only in his boxer underwear, towering over him with the big stick. "Get away from me!" the man blubbered hysterically, "Get away from me! I'll call the police. I'll . . ."

"Oh, for god's sakes," Drake snapped, "Shut up!" The intruder was shocked to silence. Drake heaved a deep, adrenaline-purging breath and huffed it out. His hands still held the jo threateningly over the intruder, who lay trapped on the floor, wedged between the chair and the wall. He tried to sit up, but Brandy raised his jo and the man cowered.

Drake reached for the telephone.

"You broke my fucking fingers, you!" the burglar complained. "And I think you broke my collar bone, too! Hey, what are you doing?"

"Calling the police. You're burglarizing my house. What do you expect? Free medical coverage?"

"No. Wait! Wait. You mean this is *your* place?"

"No. I'm a security man, and I always patrol this building in my underwear. Of *course* it's my house."

"Wait. Don't call the police. I wasn't trying to steal anything. I . . . I just . . ."

"Tell it to the police," said Drake. He dialled 9-1-1.

"No, really. I can tell you who hired me to come here. I can tell you all about 'em. But I don't want any police trouble."

Brandon dropped the telephone gently into its cradle, shifted his jo in his hands and leaned against the edge of the desk. The man on the floor was short, with wiry hair whose journey from black to graceful grey was being retarded by zealous applications of some sort of hair dye. There was too incongruous a homogeneity to the shading and too heavy a mixture of grey in the midnight facial stubble to leave any doubt. He had big ears, one of which was held back by his navy stocking cap.

"Can you get me some ice, man?" the intruder whined. "Shit, this hurts!"

"My heart bleeds. What's your name? Speak!"

"Jimmy Cantor. Like the singer. You prob'ly heard of me."

"Can't say as I have. Who sent you here?"

The short man narrowed his eyes, considering Drake carefully. "Name Wendel mean anything to you?"

"Dave Wendel?"

"Yeah. Him and his partner. Only I don't know the partner's name. They said you was asking some funny questions about them, and they wanted to know why. Said they'd give me a big bonus if I could find out within a day. Twenty-four hours exactly. So . . . this was the best way I could figure this one."

"Pretty direct way of finding out. Direct, but dumb."

"See, I kind of guessed you'd stay at that big party a while longer. You couldn't have been there an hour! I guess I got careless." He doubled over his hands and made no attempt to rise from the floor. "Jesus, this smarts!"

"What are they so worried about?"

"Who?"

"Wendel and his partner. Remember? Your employers?"

"Oh, yeah. Hey, are you gonna call the police? Because if you do I'll lose my license. I'm a private investigator, see, and . . ."

"You're kidding."

"No, only I didn't know you were, too, until I see your stationery here on the side of your desk a few minutes ago. You *are* some kind of P.I., ain't you? Just like me?"

Drake rolled his eyes. "I hope to god there's no similarity. Look, clown . . ."

The man frowned and winced and then focused on Drake's jo. "Damn. What *is* that thing? Some kind of lead pipe? You didn't have to hit me so hard."

"You didn't have to break into my home, either."

"Okay, okay. Hey, can't we negotiate? I do something for you, you forget this happened."

"Just what do you think you could do for me?"

"I can probably tell you whatever you wanted to know about Wendel. I've worked for him a lot before. I know a lot about him."

"Like?"

"Are we dealing?"

"You've *got* to be kidding. I can't imagine you have anything to offer me except your assurance that you'll retire from investigation work before you disgrace us all. Look, Mac," Brandon said, "I do straight contract work. Today it was for an insurance company. I ask questions. People give answers. My clients are happy. No twenty-four-hour deadlines. No B and E's. No broken fingers. Just a few facts. You see? So you were wrong. We don't have much in common."

"Only maybe you didn't *get* the facts today. Whatever you asked about, maybe Wendel fed you lies."

"Give me an example."

Shorty squirmed. "I don't know. What did he tell you?"

"You, my friend, are a loser." Drake picked up the telephone again.

"Hey! You want to know about those guys or don't you?"

"Nothing more than they already told me this morning."

Shorty began to babble a mile a minute. "Wait! It was something about their partner. The dead one. Right. So they didn't have anything to do with how he died. I mean, he died in a fucking climbing accident for god's sakes. What the hell can be suspicious about that?" Shorty was still on the floor, doubled over his hands, sweating bullets.

Holding the telephone handset back from his head, there was a tiny, comic voice emitted from the telephone earpiece to the pair in the room. "Police --- Sergeant McCreary speaking."

Shorty's eyes bugged out. He rattled out in a whisper, at lightning speed, "Okay, okay. So I lied. I'm not a P.I. Now hang up the phone so we can talk. For God's sakes! Please!"

Brandon sighed and dropped his finger onto the disconnect switch. "One more chance."

"Like I said, I'm not a P.I."

"That much was obvious."

"But that sort of makes us even, doesn't it?"

Brandy raised an eyebrow. "Come again?"

"You're not an insurance investigator, either. At least, not for Minnesota Mutual. We called them to find out. That's really why I came here tonight."

Brandy pursed his lips and narrowed his eyes as he blended observations with hunches, "Which probably makes you Smith, Farmer's other business partner. Jerry Smith?"

"Gerald. But that's right. So if you don't mind telling me . . . what's your game, Drake?"

Drake looked through the man for a moment before answering. Time to rattle cages. No time for the slow route. "I have a client who suspects that Farmer Hobbs may have been murdered."

Smith unwound from his pain and sat sharply upright in genuine surprise. "Murdered?!"

"There's no hard evidence, so I'm looking into a few questions to see if there's enough to take to the police."

"Murdered? Jesus! But . . ." his eyelids fluttered frantically. "Who'd *ever* want to kill Farmer? Even his enemies were his friends. That may sound strange, but if you knew Farmer, you'd know what I mean. I can't imagine anybody who'd want to kill him."

"That's what we're trying to figure out, too."

"It couldn't be anybody in the computer business. Shit, even our competition profited from the inventions Farmer came up with. He was always trading ideas with them. And everybody knew him . . . I mean, Farmer may have been lost in his designs half the time and a little aloof the rest of the time, but . . . he was a really good guy."

"I've heard rumors," said Brandy, "that Farmer was planning to leave Ergologic and take his inventions to another company next year."

"Yeah, well we were hoping it would happen even sooner. Because Farmer was such a square shooter that he'd already given us a guarantee that we would get 15 percent of his royalties on whatever his next three years' inventions earned outside Ergologic. And the way we figured it, that was worth even more to us than what our present cut came out to, after the legal and patents bills we had to cover while he was still with us. We'd over-extended on our diversification plans last year and we've been cash-strung to make ends meet. Farmer was our best bet no matter which company he was inventing for. Then the only thing which could have screwed us *did*. Farmer's disappearance almost drove us right out of the ballgame. If the insurance money comes in before the next interest calls, we may manage to pay off enough of our debts to survive. Maybe. Shit! And then it'll still be touch and go. It would have been a hell of a lot easier if we could have just finished the keyboard he was working on and gotten it to market in August like we'd planned. We'd be cruisin' right about now. Shit."

"So who stood to *lose* from his leaving the company?"

"Only *he* did. I tell you. Everybody respected Farmer. He had to be one of the few men I've ever met who didn't know the meaning of the word 'greed'. No bullshit. He didn't mind the glory of receiving credit for his work, but he always had more money than he knew how to spend. He didn't need to screw people out of their shares of the profits. All he did lately was work and climb mountains. Work and climb, work and climb. But mostly work. He loved it. He was just that kind of guy." Smith looked down at the floor and screwed up his face. "Murdered? Jesus!" He looked back up at Brandy. "You mean killed and then left under the waterfall where they found him? Or do you think somebody cut his rope or something? I don't understand. Wouldn't the police have been able to tell those things?"

"Unknown. But let me give you some advice. If your company is as desperate to get that life insurance check as you and Wendel have led me to believe you are, you'd best keep everything I've told you to yourself. Because insurance companies get very testy about paying out when foul play is suspected. Hear what I'm saying?"

Smith nodded quickly. "Sure. But what are *you* going to do about it?"

"If I can't substantiate my client's suspicions, I'll do *nothing*." Brandon watched Smith for any reaction, but the man just listened. "But we'll turn it over to the police if we *can* prove anything."

"Yes. Yes, of course." Smith rose unsteadily to his feet, still nursing his right fingers in his left hand. "By the way . . . who hired you?"

"That's none of your business." Brandy picked up the Saturday Night Special from the floor. Mint condition. "What were you planning to do with this?"

Smith lowered his head embarrassedly. "Uh . . . nothing, really. There aren't even any bullets in it. I didn't want to hurt anybody. I just wanted to scare them off. I guess I just felt safer having it with me."

Brandy checked the empty clip and shook his head incredulously. "Well, you were wrong. You're more likely to get yourself killed when you carry this kind of thing around. When people see you have a gun, they don't usually wait around to ask you whether or not it's loaded." He handed it back to Smith, who stuffed it in his pants pocket with his left hand.

At the front door to the condo, Smith turned back to Brandon and pointed at his jo. "Is that some kind of martial arts thing?"

"It's an aikido jo. Just a stick."

"Yeah? If you're into that kind of thing, then how come you didn't do any fancy stuff? How come you didn't break my neck or something when you found me in there?"

"Because aikido doesn't work that way."

"But what if I'd been sent to kill you or something? I had a gun. You didn't know it wasn't loaded!"

Brandon rolled his eyes. "As my first aikido sensei once told me, a skilled martial artist never has to fight with anyone. He just stands quietly in the middle of the universe and keeps his balance."

Smith wore a blank expression. "I don't get it."

"Neither did most of his students. Including me. But

he was right. And it's lucky for you that he was."

Smith frowned again, and squinted at Drake. "I gotta ask something else. Why the change of mind? Why did you level with me? What makes you so sure Dave and I didn't have something to do with Farmer's death?"

"Because if you were actually involved in the murder, I don't think you would have risked coming anywhere near me."

"Oh, yeah. I guess so."

Drake examined the doorframe and the door as he opened it. "My turn for a question. How did you manage to get past a deadbolt so easily?"

Smith looked embarrassed. "I worked as a locksmith's apprentice for two years. Nights. While I was getting my MBA. I . . . I guess I learned to do *something* right. Listen, I'm sorry about the . . ."

"Good-bye, Mr. Smith," Drake cut him off. "And take my advice on a couple of things. First, go straight to the hospital and get an x-ray of your hands. Second, and more important, get rid of that gun before you get yourself killed."

"Yeah."

After the front door was closed, Vic unleashed a farewell salvo until well after the elevator doors clanked shut behind Mr. Smith.

Brandy would have to confirm what Smith had told him about Farmer's business associates, including his Ergologic partners. But Smith seemed scared enough by his botched snooping job that Brandy thought he was probably telling the truth about Farmer's relationship to the company. It looked less and less likely that anyone in Vancouver had been instrumental in the death of Farmer and Chrissie.

Twenty-Five

Early morning light was streaming through the
venetian designer blinds, making diagonal
light-stripes across the tall, fit, lean body flaked out across
the king-sized mattress. The mattress sat directly atop the
raised tatami which covered most of the bedroom floor.
Remnants of a spate of interior decoration following a
Japanese binge. Brandon had even gone so far as to sleep
on futon for a year or so. Until a strange assortment of back
aches and back pains sent him packing to a series of
orthopedists and chiropractors. And after three agonizing
months with only sporadic relief, he bought a firm, padded,
king size mattress. The problem disappeared within a week.
Some people just weren't made for futon.

A green call light began to flash on the telephone
console on the wall above his low bedside table. The silent
digital clock on the console showed "7:06 a.m.". Shortly, the
green light remained on, and from the console was broadcast
a telephone conversation.

"Good morning," chimed a bright professional

receptionist's voice. "Drake Information Agency. Karen speaking."

"Good morning," a more distant voice replied. "May I have Brandy Drake, please?"

"I'm sorry. Mr. Drake is not in his office at the moment . . ."

"Mr. Drake is not *alive* at the moment . . ." Drake groaned to the otherwise empty room, still unable to animate his depleted body after the long night.

"May I have a number where the call can be returned?" Karen continued, unaware of the elemental struggle which was ensuing in Le Château Drake as she spoke.

"This is Don Beeley here," the caller replied. "I'm calling long distance from San Francisco." As soon as Beeley identified himself, Drake laboriously began to push, and then pull, see-sawing himself toward the side of his mattress, first supporting his head against his fists, then leaning heavily against the wall, finally managing something almost seated, with his face buried deeply in both of his palms.

"Is there a number where he can be reached now?" Badger continued. "I'm going to be out of my own office for the rest of the day, and it's important that I reach him."

"Just a moment," Karen replied. "I'll check."

Next to the green console light by the bed, a red one began to flash.

"Mr. Drake?" Karen's voice inquired. "Mr. Drake? Are you there?"

"Yes," Drake replied in a deep rasp, still immobile at the edge of the bed.

"This is Karen. Do you want to speak to Don Beeley?"

"Ask him if I can call him back," Brandon droned, "in about ten minutes."

Brandy pushed himself unsteadily to his feet and staggered through the doorway to his ensuite.

The red light was replaced by the green light, which

flashed intermittently as Karen's voice passed the message along to Badger Beeley. Then the red light returned, bringing Karen's melodic, "Mr. Drake? Mr. Drake? Did you catch that? Mr. Beeley will call *you* back in about five minutes. It's the only chance he'll have to reach you today." She waited for a response, but none came. "Mr. Drake?"

The first part of Brandy's reply came as a hollow echo of acknowledgement, combined with the sound of a flushing toilet. He heard a girlish giggle.

"For Christ's sake, Karen," Brandon continued, pulling a terry robe about him as he re-emerged into his bedroom. "You can use my first name. I'm hardly likely to be entertaining guests at this hour."

"After the Big Party last night, who could guess who might have followed you home, Boss Man?"

"I wish."

"Well, I wouldn't want to be presumptuous, would I?"

"That's never bothered you before." He tied up his terry robe, and with a tired smile on his face walked out to his kitchen to mix up some frozen orange juice to sustain him until after the call from Badger.

No sooner than the first glass was poured, and before the first awakening sip could wet his lips, the doorbell began to ring off the wall. As if someone were leaning on it. By the time Brandy had muttered his way into the living room and put his sleep-logged eye to the peephole, the racket finally let up. Through the fisheye lens he could see a woman. Frizzy hair. Raising her fist to knock on the door. For cryin' out loud! Couldn't she hear that the doorbell was working?

In a single fluid action, Brandy whipped the door open. The room was filled with a peculiar aura of déjà vu.

Julia straightened up from the surprise of having the door jerked out from beneath her knuckles. She charged in.

"Good morning," she announced. "Hope I didn't wake

you." She spun around, took in a full panorama of the room, and then paused to consider Brandon. He was standing by the open front door in his bathrobe with a large glass of orange juice in his hands. "Have you already had your breakfast?" she persisted.

"Uh . . . no. I was just starting it. And if you don't mind, let's make an appointment for later in the . . ." The ring of the telephone interrupted. It seemed especially loud. Why was everything ringing so insistently this morning? If he'd had anything to drink the night before, Drake would have assumed he was suffering from a hangover. But he hadn't. So it had to be a simple case of early morning input overload. Right. "Listen, Julia. I really can't talk with you now. Maybe you can come back." The telephone rang again. Drake motioned her toward the open doorway.

Julia whisked to the door, obediently, and closed it firmly. Brandon rolled his eyes in helplessness as she whipped off her sweater and said, "Don't be silly! I don't mind waiting. You go answer your phone and I'll fix the breakfast. Eggs over easy? My specialty." She beamed a Happy Face smile and scuttled toward the kitchen before a surprised and rattled Brandon could object.

He shook his head in disbelief and hurried into the office to pick up his call on the phone next to the computer. "Hello! Badger?"

Badger answered. "You sound like hell. Did you party all night?"

"Not exactly." Then Brandy paused. "I couldn't say *why* I expected your call, Mr. Beelo."

There was a pause at the other end of the phone. It was an old routine. A code from their San Francisco escapades together, when too often they had reason to suspect that lines were being tapped or their rooms bugged. They'd once dubbed it a Hokey-Code, because it seemed so awfully unsophisticated and hokey. But it had never failed

to work, so what the hell? Drake knew that his conversation
with Badger might be stilted by his self-consciousness at
having Julia within earshot in the kitchen. This way, at least
the detective would expect Brandy's query pattern to be
unusual.

"Should that go for *both* of us, Brando?"

"Nope. You sound fine. And for me, it'll only be from
time to time."

"Well, that's good," Badger proceeded, "because I
need to talk to you and I've got a whole *slew* of questions for
you."

Still in his robe, Brandy plunked down into his desk
chair. The office was brightly lit with morning light through
the panorama windows which had been the original
inspiration to convert the architect's planned sunroom into
the only real office Brandy maintained. To the north he was
afforded excellent views of the nearby slopes of Burnaby
Mountain and of the Coast Range on the north shore beyond
the inlet. Early winter snow had not yet begun its build-up,
but the permanent snow-cap on the highest of the Coast
Range brought the distinctive High Alps look for which the
Pacific Northwest is suitably famous. To the west it was
possible to see parts of downtown Vancouver and, when it
was *very* clear, Vancouver Island beyond.

As he spun around slowly in his chair, Brandy's eyes
came to rest on the nicely framed Japanese silk-screen, a gift
from a very special lady who had chosen self-exile to the
Islands of the Dragon in preference to a life with Brandon.
The print adorned the wall above the computer desk, and
lobbied for simplicity in the too-often crazy world of Drake.
With the widow of a murder victim in his kitchen and hot
information on the line, that plea for simplicity seemed all the
more appropriate at this moment.

"You there? You ready for the questions yet?" Badger
pressed.

Brandon laughed. "Carry on. And don't worry, Badger my Badger . . ." Julia began singing to herself in the kitchen. Brandon lowered his voice to a coarse whisper and continued. ". . . because last night I think I managed to eliminate a few characters from the play and I'd say it looks like we're dealing with a murder where the murderer is already 'past tense'. I think it was probably this Lesyk dude. He seems to have been a real psycho. And it's my guess that when he died in the slide, it was the Fickle Finger of Fate. I'm guessing he somehow managed to set off the slide, maybe trying to kill Julia Hobbs and me because he thought we'd seen something that might implicate him in the murders. How's that hit you?"

"Sounds pretty far-fetched to me, Bran."

"C'mon, Beeley," Brandy said, raising his voice in irritation. "It wouldn't have been too tough for Lesyk to dump a boulder off the top of the switchback. But something screwed up for the guy. Justice dealt out by Mother Nature. With a beautiful touch of irony. What's wrong with that?"

"Well, then, somebody sure seems cheesed off at Mother Nature's decision."

"Meaning?"

"That's what I was calling about. *If* you'd shush up long enough for me to get it all out. Seems you got some great admirers out there, Brandy my friend."

"Badger, I must be half asleep or something, but I'm just not tracking on whatever it is you're trying to tell me."

"We were hit last night, Brandy. Broken into. Ransacked."

"We who?"

"Cranston and Beeley. The agency. In peaceful little Mill Valley, California. Where crime does not occur. Well . . . anyway. I'm pissed off. Can you tell? And I want to know who your friends might be, so we can open a few wounds on this one. Not to mention you now owe me a little *more* for this one, guy."

"Hold on. You mean you think that whoever broke into your detective agency offices had something to do with . . ."

"I am *not* a man of speculation, B.D. In this case, I am a man of certainty. It was related to those queries I put out for you. And I found your answers. Or at least as much in the way of answers as you're likely to get. But it's obvious that someone has some very good informant chains, to react so fast and to be able to trace those inquiries back to me. But facts is facts. And the facts *is* that someone turned files upside down here and searched what they could of the computer records, too."

"I still want to know what makes you think it had to do with the Yosemite murders. Don't you all have any other cases on the go which could bring people out of the woodwork?"

"Sure. But this mess was *yours*, baby. All yours. Period. Which is why I feel free to call and awaken you from your beauty-rest and give you a suitably hard time at seven o'clock in the morning."

"How long ago did all this happen?"

"About four hours ago."

"Was there a lot of damage?"

"Well . . . no. Not really. Mostly just bruised egos around here. Nobody likes to think some second-story man can just waltz in to an office specializing in sensitive private investigations and have a boo at anything he wants without permission. It's . . . it's *humiliating*, that's what it is!

"The story goes like this: our junior partner, Kyle Dornuth, comes in this morning, first thing after an all-nighter following some clown down in The City. He sees broken locks on the filing cabinets, and the burglar alarm is jammed. Nobody's here, and the place is a mess. Before he calls the police, though, he notices that the phone in Harry's office is not solid in the cradle. So Kyle's clever enough to pick it up real carefully, just in case there are prints on the phone --- which, it turns out, there weren't. But Kyle is even sharper, and he wonders if the burglar has maybe made a call from the phone while he was going through the place. So before Kyle calls Law-and-Order's Faithful, he presses the auto-redial button and finds out where the last call on the system was headed. Know what I mean?"

"Sounds like you caught a rare bird with this Kyle guy. Does he always think like that?"

"Often enough. That's why we offered him a partnership last month. But don't distract me. I'm enjoying being righteously pissed off at you. And I know from experience it's likely to be the only compensation I get for what we've been through last night. Want to know what Kyle found out?"

"Of course."

"The last call from our system was to Los Angeles. To the Police Department." He paused. "Which happens to be where I got my hottest of hot info for you yesterday."

"So it wasn't the burglar at all, then. It was your own call?"

"Nope. The burglar's. The last number dialled on the phone Kyle checked was to LAPD's main switchboard number, but *I* had used direct lines into homicide. And, furthermore, I hadn't dialled those numbers since just after you and I talked early yesterday! And there were dozens of calls placed during the day on house lines --- including Harry's line --- by Harry and by the other three of us, too. We've checked it out, and there's no doubt, Brandy. Whoever broke into us called the LAPD. And yours is the only inquiry involving that office that anyone has made around here for nearly four months."

"Have you told the police all about this?"

"Brandy!" Badger rebuked. "Give me a break. Kyle

and I talked and we decided to leave that bit out for the moment. We can always tell them later, if it suits our purposes. They dusted and took a few photos and laughed and left. There's still no love lost between ourselves and the local blues, you know. And I was sure you wouldn't want anyone knowing about the leak until I talked to you. But I gotta tell you, I don't think we're going to get anywhere further than we've come already on finding the source of our leak. The LAPD switchboard receives hundreds of calls day and night and I don't think there's a rat's chance in hell of our finding out who our burglar contacted there."

"Can you tell if the burglar got any information from you? Anything that could tie it to any of the people we talked about, or to me?"

"I don't think so. I don't have any files on what you've asked for. Only a few scratch notes I was carrying in my briefcase in case you decided to call me at home last night or something."

"And on the computer?"

"Nothing useful. I think the guy came up empty-handed, which was maybe why he had to call L.A. To recheck his info, or to report in . . . something like that. But, all in all, it was a fairly professional job. And whoever sent him has one hell of a solid intelligence network to find out about me asking those questions. Some really good inside ears."

"It's a pretty safe guess what this is all about, right? This whole thing fits the M.O. of the Pipeline operation, doesn't it, Badge? It must have been the Pipeline inquiry that sparked the break-in. Your Sacramento inquiry must have roused a sleeping Pipeline."

"Except that the leak was *not* related to my Pipeline inquiries. Which I made to the Feds. Via Sacramento. *Furthermore*," Badger continued, "to make it more maddening, I find out about an hour ago that someone also

has a full inside track with my DEA sources in Sacramento.
When I checked to find out if there were any more action on
my Federal queries, I was told that there had been another
inquiry about current intelligence on the Pipeline. And ours
were the only two outside inquiries on that file in nearly a
year. Same day as my investigations. Funny coincidence,
huh?" He paused. "Only it's even better than that. The query
came from --- can you guess? --- also from Los Angeles
Police headquarters. More than that is unclear. So now I
can't trust the security of any of my sources in Sacramento,
either."

"Aha!" Brandy exclaimed. "So your burglary *could*
have been related to the Pipeline."

"Nope. I was just told that the other Pipeline query to
the Feds in Sacramento came in the middle of the night, over
an hour *after* we were hit here. So whoever it was couldn't
have known from Sacramento sources that we were shopping
in the same department."

"Unless the *burglar* found out what you were into."

"Which he could not have done. There was no record
of any of that here. And he couldn't have used the same 'last
call' system that Kyle used, because my Sacramento call
was, as I said, in the middle of the day."

"That doesn't make any sense."

"That's the strangest part of it, for sure. The only
way I can make it is this. The burglar phoned the LAPD
sometime before he left. Which is where the Lesyk inquiries
had been made. So I think whoever came here came because
of the Lesyk questions."

"Maybe. Can you find out any more about who else
is asking about the Pipeline? Through your sources in
Sacramento?"

"The ID given for the Pipeline query was a general
one for the L.A. Homicide and Assault teams."

"Couldn't something be traced?"

"Not very likely. There are too many contacts routinely from those numbers. And whoever is searching could be using a remote Out-Line --- one in somebody else's division --- to avoid detection. That much I'd bet on. It could be that the Pipeline still has police insiders, though I'm a bit puzzled how that links into this climber murder. And why they would suddenly begin asking questions right when we do."

"It's a long shot, but could the L.A. police have sent people to search your place?"

"No way, Brando. I always give them whatever they want direct. I touched the Lesyk button and somebody jumped. Why? Maybe there's something else you'd care to enlighten me about?"

"Once I figure it out myself."

"As usual . . . Okay. I'll see what I can stir up from here. After I clean up the mess, that is. The dust the lab clowns left around, trying to lift their goddamned prints, is worse than the mess the burglar left."

Julia switched songs in the kitchen, and turned up the volume. Her voice was quite good.

Brandy continued in a low voice, "One more item. The guy we talked about yesterday afternoon? Named Bill Moffat. Died in Enseñada on April 1, 1980. I need to know if he was DEA and if he was ever linked to the Pipeline."

"More Pipeline stuff?"

"Security couldn't be any worse than it is already, could it?"

"You sure ask for a lot! What'll this net me? A car bomb?"

"I thought you were convinced the break-in had nothing to do with the Pipeline queries. Besides, you're always complaining I never give you any challenge. If it's too warm, you can always get out of my kitchen."

"Cute. I was just kidding. I have a right to be pissed off this morning. You should see our offices. Frankly, Brando, I don't think the Pipeline is related to the murders. I just think you've started stirring in two pots and so you shouldn't be surprised if you start getting reactions from both of them. That both leaks are related to Los Angeles doesn't mean a whole hell of a lot to me. The LAPD has always had a reputation as a security sieve anyway.

"Mostly, Bran, what is surprising me on this case is *you*. I mean, Pipelines and Mexico are pretty big numbers for a lowly, high-tech information agent, aren't they? What happened to the ol' if-you-gotta-carry-a-gun-find-another-turkey rule?"

"Still stands. I promise you, I'm not carrying a gun these days."

"Okay, but Lesyk's brother --- or whoever the hell is interested in his case --- may well be carrying a weapon. And from what I've turned up about them, I can pretty much guarantee you that this Pipeline outfit isn't going to be playing by your nice-guy rules. Know what I mean? If what we're running into now is representative of the company you're starting to keep, maybe you should *carry* a piece. I don't want you to wind up in a morgue somewhere with a John Doe tag hanging from your toe. Y'hear?"

"Quit worrying, Badge. You're starting to sound like somebody I used to be married to."

"How soon do you need to know the stuff about the Mexico killing?"

"Later today. if possible."

"I'll put out calls, but don't expect answers until tomorrow morning sometime at the earliest. The government works at a snail's pace and it shuts down at 4:30."

"Even the databanks?"

"Don't get pushy."

"Whewee! Getting a bit testy, aren't we?"

"Comes with the sleep deprivation. When can I reach you tomorrow?"

"From what you've just told me, it looks like I better think about heading back down to California. I'll call you, Badge, okay?"

"You're coming back to The City?"

"Nope. What you've just told me convinces me I should be going to Los Angeles. If I can get a plane this afternoon, I'll pick up the puzzle down there. You've been great, Badger. I'll call you later."

"Wait a minute, friend. I want to put in my two bits."

"I thought you already had."

"Not completely. Mostly, I've just been spinning out the facts. If I thought that your murders had anything whatsoever to do with this Pipeline outfit, I'd suggest you clear out of the matter and turn it over to police a.s.a.p. Even with my all-time low opinion of them. What I *really* think is that you'll find your answers nestled under this Big Earl clown. And I have a personal interest in that part of it now. So I want to make a proposal. Let's work a quick hustle on him. Start with a B & E search of his place and then poke at him and see if he jumps. Just to see what comes of it. If we get answers, great. If not, either we decide he's clean and leave him alone or we really put him in the pressure cooker. Like we did Halstron a few years back."

"We?"

"Look, it was my office somebody busted into. It's a matter of principle!"

Brandy thought about the proposal for a few moments. It had been a long time since the Drake-Beeley team had worked together. "There were three of us working on Halstron. How are we going to work a shill game like that without a female accomplice? Melanie told me after she had the twins she was out of consideration for any more undercover stuff."

"I know. I asked her last year for something similar."

"You have another female detective type on the line, maybe?"

"Nope," Badger grunted in frustration. "Maybe we can rework the hustle. I don't know. We'll figure something out. We always have. Hell, I haven't felt this much adrenaline in years. Tell you what. I'll meet you in L.A. tomorrow morning. If this Earl Lesyk knows who's behind the hit on my company here, I want to have a little chat with the dude before the police arrive."

The singing paused. Brandy looked up to see Julia, on tiptoes, a plate of steaming breakfast balanced on one hand, a paste-on smile, raised eyebrows, pointing at a clear spot on the desk in query. Brandy shook his head in the negative, pointed back toward the kitchen and put up his index finger to signal "one minute".

Brandon paused a moment until he heard her in the kitchen again, whistling the same tune she'd been singing before.

"If you're so certain about Lesyk," Brandy continued, "why don't we let the police take the whole thing from here? You could just wind 'em up, and point 'em in the right direction, and let 'em go."

"Because they'll get so tangled up in the technical legalities and search warrants and Mirandizing and all that shit that they'll give him everything but a written text of what to say to cover his ass better."

"Okay. Try this one on. How about if we tell the Feds that Earl's tied into the Pipeline? They're usually swifter about getting in on something, aren't they?"

"Because the Feds'll need some kind of proof of the

connection. You got any?"

"No, of course not. And you said . . ."

"Well, I don't think you're likely to get any, either. And when he turns out *not* to have anything to do with the Pipeline after all, we'll wear egg on our faces. The Feds are very helpful people to me from time to time. I don't want my welcome to wear thin with them. I'm telling you, let's go to L.A. We'll find a way to squeeze him. But we have to work fast."

"Let me think about it. Can I get back to you in about half an hour? I'll need to set up my flights, anyway. You said tomorrow morning?"

"Connie has the kids in San Jose tonight at her sister's place, so I'm going to do a little stakeout here at the offices with Kyle. We think our visitor may not have found what he was looking for. That he may have been spooked off in the middle of his search. That he may get the cute idea of coming back tonight."

"You have a real problem calling on the police, don't you?"

"Look, Bran. Are you just goading me? Even if we could convince them we're still a target, buddy boy, you know as well as I do they'd just screw it up. I don't mind admitting, I am turning out to be one cynical red-neck when it comes to my lack of respect for the efficiency of the police in this country. They've had their balls cut off by the lawyers and the courts, and so they've become about as slack these days as the rest of our legal system. That's only an opinion, I'll grant you, but it's *my* opinion."

"I know, I know. Not much different here in Canada, either, I have to admit. Anyway, thanks for your help so far, Badger," he said into the phone. "You're a champ. I owe you, again."

"Care to know exactly how *much* you owe me?"

"Not really. Let's wait until we've finished this. Okay

with you?"

"Does it matter?" Badger began laughing.

Brandy hung up the telephone and ruminated on the new input. Did someone hire Lesyk, and begin to get panicky now that there were inquiries coming down the line about him? And what about the coincidence of the Pipeline query? The whole affair had shifted from strange to clumsy.

It wasn't so much the sense of missing key pieces of the puzzle. It was more like the pieces on the table belonged to two different puzzles.

Twenty-Six

Brandy carried his thoughts to his kitchen and sat down distractedly to breakfast with Julia. At the table in the sunny corner off the kitchen, he took his first good look at her since she'd barged through the door before the phone rang.

"Something's changed," he declared.

"Is it that obvious?" she beamed.

"Unless you're starting to dye your hair green," Brandy said, reaching out and flipping her paint-glopped green curls with his fingers.

Julia laughed. "Oh . . . *that*! Yeah. Something's happening. I'm not sure what, but it's *something*, at least. Since last week I've been painting non-stop."

"That's a good sign?"

"Oh, the *best*. I'm still turning out mediocre stuff, but at least it's starting to flow."

"Congratulations," he nodded.

Julia had a frown on her face. "That thing you did in Yosemite. At the cabin. When I was having the miscarriage?

With your hands?"

"Yes?"

"Where did you learn to do that?" Julia asked.

Brandy wolfed another forkful of scrambleds. Julia waited patiently, poised, elbows on the edge of the table. "I've done a few years of aikido practice. About six. Do you know aikido?"

"Only that it's some sort of martial art."

"That's true. But it has a lot of other applications, too. It's based on a philosophy that conflict equals an imbalance of energies in the universe. In practice we learn about how to rebalance those energies. Against physical attacks and against other kinds of conflicts, too. And in the process, during the physical practice, it's easy to get bruised and cut and broken up. So I've had to learn how to take care of myself and a lot of my own injuries. Sometimes I've been able to help other people, too. What we did at Yosemite is a lot like a form of self-hypnosis. Some people it doesn't help at all; some people use it like magic."

"It sure saved me a lot of pain. So, thanks," she said.

Brandy smiled. "Not to look a gift horse in the mouth, and I *do* appreciate your visit, but I think I deserve an explanation, Mrs. Hobbs. Why are you dropping in, unannounced, to make me breakfast at seven in the morning?"

Julia looked around for a clock. "Is it really only seven o'clock? I didn't know it was *that* early. But then I didn't sleep much last night. I was too excited. You see, *I* think he was murdered, too. I mean, *they* were murdered. Anyway, once I figured it out I didn't want to make another move without talking to you first and finding out what we're going to do to find out who killed them."

Brandon eyed the widow coldly. "What are you talking about? Who said anything about murder, Julia?"

"Nobody *has* to, do they? I mean, it's obvious. I

thought so the moment we found the bodies up on the mountain. And I guess I'd been wondering about it for most of the past three months since Farmer disappeared. Only I couldn't imagine anyone doing that to him, and I was hoping he was still alive, so I didn't take it any further until . . . until you showed up at Wendel's yesterday asking questions. Well, I just *knew* then that you thought he was murdered, too."

Brandy opened his mouth to object, but Julia curbed him and forged on ahead. "Dave didn't guess it, of course. And I certainly didn't tell him what I thought. When he called back later to tell me that you weren't working for the insurance company, and to warn me not to let you into my house if you showed up, I asked him why he thought you were asking us questions. He said he figured you were one of those hucksters who shows up after an obituary is listed in the paper, the kind of con man who wants to help the bereaved families and friends invest their new monies. I don't know if he believed it. He sounded kind of worried, but I think that was more about delays in the insurance payments to the company. They're cutting it close since Farmer died. Anyway, I played dumb and thanked him for the warnings, but I *knew* what was happening. And I decided then and there to help you."

Brandon rolled his eyes.

Julia frowned. "Listen," she offered, "I'm going to try to tell you something. I tried to tell my doctor, but she doesn't have any children of her own, and she never had any miscarriages so I don't think she understood. Please eat your eggs before they get cold. I'll talk, and once I finish my little soliloquy we can turn this into a real conversation again. You want some jam for the toast? You had some strawberry in your fridge, but it looked like Fleming's original penicillin colony. You have another jar some place else? Like on a cabinet shelf somewhere?"

"I'm fine," Brandy began, "but . . ."

"Then don't interrupt. Please. I'm only telling you so that maybe you'll see why I've decided to help you find out who killed Farmer. Not because he was my husband --- which he was. And not because he was the father of the baby I carried around inside me for three months --- which he was. Even though the baby wasn't born: that doesn't even matter. In fact, it had to happen that way. I knew in my heart before I came to see you last month that once I found out for sure whether Farmer Hobbs was alive or dead, I would make the decision as to whether I could --- or would, or should --- carry his baby alone into this world. Am I running on?

"That night after we found them, after the avalanche, after you and I got back to the cabin . . . I think *that* was when I decided. Miscarriages and still births don't just *happen*, you know. At some level, women *decide* what is best and just do it. That's what I think, anyway. And I think that the decision to end my pregnancy and to set that little spirit free was the most important decision I've ever made. Ever. And this may sound really weird, but I had the sense that the baby and I made that decision together.

"Oh, sure. I had a juicy bout of depression after it happened. Four or five days of hell. And I don't know if I told you right then how much it meant to me that you were there for me. But after I got back here to Vancouver, what I most wanted was to be alone. I didn't know how much of it was grieving for Farmer and how much was grieving for the baby, and how much of it was just plain feeling sorry for myself. I suppose it's natural.

"Then two days ago the cloud lifted, like the whole process had been sped up to its conclusion, driven along as if there were an important reason for it to be past. Even though I didn't know what that reason was. Then suddenly I got the call from Dave yesterday morning and I *knew*. Everything made sense to me. Everything in the universe has suddenly bounced back into balance, like a weigh scale just after you step off of it. Everything except having Farmer's killer out there loose. Which is why I have to help you --- and I mean *really* help you --- find Farmer's killer.

"And while I'm being perfectly open about everything to you --- I guess I'm on a real roll, eh? --- I want to reassure you that I'm not playing Joan of Arc, rallying the troops for a Crusade. I'll admit that some of my thoughts about helping you on this are what objective observers might call . . . less than exemplary. But at the same time, I want to make it *perfectly* clear that my decision has nothing *whatsoever* to do with my sexual attraction to you."

Brandon looked up from his plate and blinked several times, startled.

Julia's eyes were looking down and to the right. She squeezed her thumb tightly with the fingers of her other hand as she rambled on. "I'll admit it has been a distraction for me when we've been together, but I'm used to that. I've often had these kinds of feelings for the men around me. Ever since I can remember. Since I was a little girl. But I want you to know that I never acted on them while Farmer was alive. Never. Not in any physical way, anyway. I was always careful to protect my relationship with Farmer. One-man woman and all that. Even after we started living separately. I guess it's just an old-fashioned streak or something."

Julia pursed her lips tightly and continued looking down at the table as she continued. "Fidelity is such a prissy word, and I never felt *that* way about it, anyway. And it never really bothered me that Farmer must have had affairs with other women. Like this Christine. I mean, I saw her pictures in the newspaper. I can understand what he saw in her. I could see it in her eyes, even in the pictures. But that had nothing to do with me. And he never flaunted that at me. I never even knew about her. Until afterward . . .

"Anyway," she said, making direct eye contact with

Brandon, "I was faithful to Farmer to the end. But that's over. Mostly, what I guess I'm trying to say is that I don't have to wear black. Not for Farmer and not for my unborn baby. Black is what you wear until you've finished your business with someone. And I have a strong sense of completion of that phase of my life. I feel free to go where I want to go and do what I want to do. Perfectly free. But what that *doesn't* mean is that I'm here to cling on to you or to seduce you, Brandon Drake. So you can get that out of your mind." She examined his face for clues as to his reaction. "Okay?"

Brandon waited a while to make sure Julia was finished, that the question wasn't another midpoint rhetorical. It wasn't. His hand still held a now-cold forkful of scrambled eggs in midair in front of his mouth. He set it down carefully on the edge of his plate before speaking.

"I'll . . . I'll have to think about some of that," Brandy fumbled his way uncertainly. "I don't usually get such speeches at seven o'clock in the morning. Or at any other time, if the truth be known. I . . ."

Julia looked alarmed. "You think I'm strange, don't you?" she blurted out.

Brandy smiled reassurance. "You *are* strange, Julia."

He resumed eating his breakfast, providing some relief from the tension between them.

Julia squinted her eyes, as if to pierce into another cosmos. "So, where are we? I mean, on finding out who killed Farmer. You know, I can be a big help to you. I have this special sense about the people around me. I'm almost . . . psychic. At least when it comes to people I know. I can't see what's going to happen to *me*, really, but for other people I can do it. That's how I knew *you* were the one who was going to find Farmer. And that's how I knew I had to be an important part of it." She looked at his face to see if he thought she was talking nonsense.

He was watching her, expressionless, so she

continued. "And that's how I know you'll find out what really happened to Farmer and that lady." She frowned. "What do you already know?"

Brandy was stone-faced.

"Look," Julia persisted, "I don't want to have to force myself on you. And I don't want to threaten you that I would go to the police to find out why you're asking all these questions about Farmer and his company. Because it would probably mess up whatever you've already done. But I won't be left out of this, either. Especially when I know I can help you."

"You're not too subtle, are you?"

"I don't intend to be. Does that Annie lady know about this, too?"

Brandy sat up, surprised. "Why do you ask?"

"I don't know. Even during that one meeting there in the valley, in front of the Ranger station, I could see in her eyes that she was a pretty shrewd little woman. Just another intuition, I guess. But she seemed like she thought something was wrong. She said all the nice, right things to me, like she was just another sad lady who was really sympathetic to what I was going through, but I was in a real state, and when I'm like that, I'm especially tuned into other people's feelings. So I wondered, even then, what was on her mind. I just figured then that it might have had something to do with what had gone on between Farmer and her friend, and that she was worried about saying something tactless to me by mistake. But since then, I wondered about other possibilities, too. Well?"

"Okay. She's suspicious. She wasn't when you met her there in the valley, as far as I know, but things have changed."

"I thought so. So, now what?"

Brandy made a quick decision. Julia had to be on board. Not that he was going to give the whole investigation over to psychic flakiness, but he was prepared to believe that Julia's help might come in handy. She'd checked out all right. Brandy had to remember countless times past when he'd made breakthrough discoveries as if he were guided by some aberration of Fate, confounding the rules both of random coincidence and of applied logical processes. There was no way to be certain about Julia except to stay close to her and watch her. And she was right about being able to mess up what little of his investigation was still under control.

"Can you dig up Farmer's personal charge account records for the last two months of his life?" Brandy launched in. "Do you have access to those?"

"Yes," Julia replied eagerly. "What else?"

"Can you be ready to travel on short notice?"

"How short?"

"I don't know yet. Tonight, maybe."

"Of course," Julia blurted excitedly. "Where are we going? Back to Yosemite?"

"No. I think we may be going back to California, but not to the mountains," Brandy said, watching Julia closely for any reaction. "I can't give you any details, yet, because I'm not sure myself at this point. I have a few more calls to make, but I have a hunch that a lot of answers are waiting to be found down there."

"Whatever you say!" Her response was genuine. Enthusiastically spirited, but unforced. "When will I hear from you?"

"I'll call you this afternoon. We'll have to leave this evening or first thing tomorrow morning, Julia. We may be gone for two or three days. I'll let my travel agent handle the tickets for both of us."

Julia was positively beaming. "And what will I be doing to help you?"

"Don't know, really. I thought you were the psychic? You tell me!" Brandy grinned at her worried expression, "If nothing else, you can cook breakfasts."

Julia swooped out of Drake's condo much as she'd swooped into it. Spinny, flaky lady, with green splotches in her hair. A unique woman, Drake reflected. Absolutely unique. And in a way, he couldn't help but like that. Deep within him, he was sure he'd made the right move to trust her. Time was running short. Sometime soon the whole investigation would have to go back into the laps of the police, no matter what the Drake-Beeley team discovered in L.A.

Julia's presence had reminded him that no matter how clever he thought he was, if he couldn't wrap the investigation up quickly now, Drake's covert investigation would have no privacy left in it at all. As Mama Drake had always said, macabre sage that she was, "A secret is only good between two people when one of them is dead."

Twenty-Seven

Drake's database work of the mid-morning was slim pickings.

Annie had left a message with Karen while Drake had been connected to the ethereal info-world. Brandy reached her at the shop. "How are you doing?" he asked innocently.

"Just peachy," she grumbled.

"Right. Sounds like it, too. What's wrong?"

"If you must know, I'm going fucking stir crazy! I haven't spent this much time in this valley without climbing for over ten years. And I don't like it. Especially with all the weird stuff that's been happening. At least it hasn't been boring . . ."

"I got a message that you called."

"I'd been thinking about what you said yesterday about weird phone calls. And, like I told you, I don't remember anything special there. But last night my beady little raggedy-brain twigged into some weird mail Chrissie used to get. I don't honestly think it's got anything to do with this, but . . ."

"What kind of mail? Hate mail? Threat mail?"

"No. Not hate mail. More like love mail. And it's ancient history. Goes back a few years. There was always the secret admirer stuff. Chrissie got a *lot* of that. Off and on."

"Really? Tell me more."

"Well, anyone as good-looking as Chrissie gets used to her share of admirers. Same pattern, usually. Most of it was pretty out in the open, and they sent presents and flowers and finally they just happened to include their names on one gift so she'd know who it was, and then she'd shut them down. She was always kind about it. But she got the occasional notes or letters where she never knew who sent them.

"Chrissie wasn't a saver, and she especially made a point of trashing those kinds of letters. She always threw them away after she showed them to me. I dug around this morning in my storage boxes, and I came up with one of them. There were more, but I guess this was the only one I managed to save."

"Can you read it to me?"

"There wasn't anything really sick about them, if that's what you're expecting . . ."

"No. I'm just curious. It might fit a pattern."

"Something to do with Phil?"

"Or with someone who saw Phil's pictures. Someone who bought from him, maybe."

"Bought pictures? Of *us*? Of Chrissie and me? Oh, sweet Jesus . . ."

"You were the one who suggested it, Annie. And it doesn't sound too far out to me.

"I guess. Shit. If I thought . . ." Annie paused. "Here, let me read this to you. 'Darling Christine, . . .' It's typed, by the way, on an old typewriter. At least, I think that's what it is. Pretty uneven, anyway. 'I really like the way you walk and talk. I like the way you move your hands, too. I'm sure every-body knows when you walk into a room. And I bet you could make any man happy with just a touch of your soft hand or a smile from your soft lips.' And it's signed, 'Your admirer'. Pretty soppy, huh?"

"That's it?"

"That's all. I told you."

"Where was it sent from? How did it arrive?"

"Always by mail. And they had different postmarks, usually U.S."

"Could it have been Lesyk?"

"I don't think so. Rub-'em-dub-'em secrecy wasn't his style. He would have told her to her face any time he wanted, or at least made enough suggestive remarks to cue her as to his interest. He was always doing that with other women in the Valley, too."

"Did he ever do that with Chrissie?"

"Yeah. He did right after she came here, but then he gave up on her."

"Except in the candid camera department."

"Don't remind me."

"Yeah? Well, I want to see the letter you just read me."

"Really? Okay. If you say so. How should I send it to you? Should I mail it?"

"Nope. Fax it. Got a fax machine in the village?"

"Yeah. I think so. At the Ahwahnee. But won't they get to see what I'm sending? I couldn't let those nosy bastards over at the hotel see anything like this. I've never sent a fax, and . . ."

"You tell them it's private. You tell them you want to send it yourself. Have them show you how. If they won't do that, then photocopy it and send me the original by the fastest express mail or whatever special delivery services come up to Valley."

"You think it's *that* important? It's a couple of years old, at least. You can't think it's related to the murder, can you?"

"Maybe not. But you never know. There aren't too many solid clues here. Besides, the clock's ticking and I'm having to rely on gut responses more than usual. I want you to see if you can find any other letters like that at home."

"I'll look again, but I don't think so. Chrissie was really careful to take them back after she'd shown them to me, and I know she always got rid of them right away. She was like superstitious about it or something. Even when she knew who'd sent her a letter."

"Okay. Well, send it along and . . ."

"That's not all," Annie interjected, her voice more animated. "One more mystery has been solved. And this one *is* important. About how Chrissie wasn't signed out on the climb with Farmer? One of the customers who came in this afternoon was one of our Sacramento regulars. Full of talk. Really excited about the climber deaths. He'd just gone to the Ranger Station to report what happened to him this summer. Came up here yesterday with a group of Boy Scouts --- teaching a basic climbing safety course. And he was reading about the climbing accident in the valley newsrag. He saw the pictures of Farmer and Chrissie, and he recognized her.

"Seems he was up here with a friend this summer, climbing the same week Farmer was climbing. The guy and his friend had been driving down from Tuolumne Meadows to the Happy Isles parking area at the end of the Valley to meet a climbing group to do the Half-Dome Arcturus route. They gave a lift to a blonde girl hitchhiking off of Big Oak Flat Road. She had climbing equipment."

"Chrissie?"

"That's right. He was sure it was her. And it would have been the morning of the final climb. He said she was really anxious to get to the base of the Yosemite Falls trail because she had to intercept a friend who was going to climb alone. After he saw the picture and the articles in the paper today, this guy guessed that the man she was going to meet must have been Farmer. It never twigged on him back when he saw the stuff about the solo climber lost in the summer. Chrissie never actually mentioned Farmer's name to the guys. The scout guy was sure he and his friend would have remembered it if they'd heard a weird name like Farmer.

"He said Chrissie was really upset. Angry that her boyfriend had been conned into doing a solo he wasn't ready for. He said she'd changed her plans, that she put off some trip to South America so that she could catch up with this guy. The fellow says he remembers thinking that whoever this guy was, he was pretty lucky to have this lady caring so much about his welfare that she'd postpone a trip to South America. A real looker, he called her. And the guy remembers thinking that whatever fun this man was planning on getting from his solo wasn't likely to compare with the treat of getting chased up the wall by such a gorgeous lady. That may not sound like much of a compliment to you, Brandy, but from a climbing addict, there couldn't be a much bigger compliment.

"He remembered that Chrissie was carrying full solo gear, a chalk bag, a loop of hardware, and her hammer. She was so agitated about catching up with her boyfriend, the guy says, he and his buddy went out of their way and drove around and dropped her off at the foot of the Falls trail, at the Lodge. So she must have intercepted Farmer there at the Lodge or on his way up, and talked him out of the Arrowhead Spire solo. So they went up to climb together instead."

"Conned into a solo? By whom? One of the other climbers earlier in the week?"

"Dunno. Neither did the scout guy. I asked him about that. Maybe that was just talk to pass time with the ride."

"Where'd the second rope go? There was only one

with the bodies."

"Stashed, maybe. Or maybe still up on their last be-laying point before the fall. I don't know. But don't you see? It means Chrissie couldn't have been the target of the murder. She wasn't even supposed to be up there that day."

"Not necessarily. And why didn't she take part in any of the climbs earlier in the week? She could have posed as his instructor or something, right?"

"Yeah? Well, this guy claims she mentioned about how she had sprained her ankle the week before, while she was bouldering, and so this was her first time up in a week. That was why she said she hadn't realized what Farmer was planning until she called into the registration desk at the Visitor Center. Which is also probably why everybody was sure Chrissie had gone south already. They hadn't seen her during the week climbing, and she and Farmer must have been keeping a low profile out at Foresta. Discretion, god bless her . . . Anyway, it all means she *wasn't* the target. Right?"

"We still don't know she wasn't supposed to have taken those slings to South America with her. Maybe she had Farmer buy them for her while he was in the valley. Maybe she was the one who brought those along with her to that final climb."

"Shit, you've got a devious mind! I still think Farmer was the target and Chrissie just happened to be in the wrong spot at the wrong time."

"Okay. If so, then who did it, Detective Annie?"

"Maybe Phil?"

"Motive?"

"Jealousy?" Annie hissed out a frustrated lungful of air into the telephone. "Pretty weak, huh? I don't know."

"You work on it," Brandon replied, "I'll work on it, too."

Twenty-Eight

On examination of all that he knew so far, Brandon was beginning to agree with Annie that her Pipeline connections were probably unrelated to the murder of her lover. But it bothered him to have to rely so much on guesswork.

The Lesyk connection looked more and more suspicious, which meant that the trip to L.A. was definitely in order.

Brandy and Julia might be able to carry off some blitz probing to find out what Lesyk's brother knew, or at the very least might turn up something useful if they could poke around at Phil's other residence, the one which he shared with his brother. The Park people might have gone through Phil's Yosemite cabin before Earl got to it, but without an open investigation, the L.A. police would not have been likely to search the Redondo Beach home. It was time to shake, rattle, and roll.

A fax groaned in just before lunch. It was the fan letter Annie had read over the telephone, typed on an old manual typewriter, judging by the unevenness of the density of the print. Maybe an old Underwood or a Royal. Probably a real collector's item. It was on standard note paper. Otherwise, nothing special except a very crooked, small case "e", twisted about forty-five degrees clockwise. A defective die on the hammer, probably.

Drake's trusty travel agent, Laura Meister, was able to get two people on a flight to L.A. on the five o'clock afternoon special, arriving at seven fifty-eight in the evening. Laura apologized she couldn't get any better than the twenty-five minute layover in Portland, but it was the best she could do on short notice. A Budget rental would be waiting at the Los Angeles airport.

Brandy called Julia and asked her to pack "light, but versatile". She replied that she'd already packed her city clothes. Whatever that meant. He would pick her up on the way to the airport.

None of the messages left on Badger's machine were returned by three o'clock. Beyond waiting for Badger, there was nothing much Brandy could do to pass the time.

He wasn't very hungry or thirsty. He was mostly exhausted from the long previous night and from the anticipation of the trip south with Julia, so he shelved all the seemingly endless bookwork and paperwork, postponed the curse of quarter-end taxes, and the unread E-mail updates on the four database searches which related to standing retainer contracts, all of which had hung in limbo while he had attended to Annie's problem. Thus reluctantly resigned to rapid encroachment of limbo into yet more domains of his existence, Brandy turned in for a short nap.

And it *was* short. He was awakened just before three-fifteen by the buzzing. He groped wildly for his bedside travel alarm, fumbling through his recovery from the first dip into REM-land. It wasn't until he held the travel-clock in his hand that he realized that what had awakened him was his telephone. He stubbed his fingers going for the buttons on the wall phone. This had all the hallmarks of the beginning of what was bound to be a terrible, no-good, very bad evening.

"My friend! Glad I caught you before you went south. We have business to attend to!" Badger's voice.

Brandy tried to focus on the digital readout of the clock on the telephone console, but couldn't make the numbers unblur. He rallied himself to shake the clutches of his sleep and to respond with some semblance of energy to Badger's salutation. Brandy heard the groggy slur of his own words, but heard the slur fade quickly as he persisted. "Whassup? What've you found out for me?"

"I got through to both of my Federal contacts in the middle of the morning's muddles. For once, the government was faster than I expected. You know your man in Ensañada?"

"Right?"

"Well, there's no record of anyone by the name of Bill Moffat ever being with the DEA, no record of any DEA people killed in the line of duty in Enseñada at *all*, and no agents killed anywhere during the particular month you gave me, or within two months either side of that. That, in and of itself might not be so significant except that my other Fed sources came up with a match for both the name *and* the circumstances.

"They have records of a Bill Moffat washed up on the beaches south of Enseñada on April 3rd of that year. Looked as if he'd been in the water for a couple of days. It's a closed file, but never solved. The Mexicans do that when they don't expect to find out anything. Improves their statistics. Cleans up their caseloads. He was linked with organization courier activities, but only as a strong-arm. Beat up a few union people in strikes back in the early Seventies. Some petty stuff. No leads. Pistol registered to him found by

Mexican authorities in a garbage heap in Enseñada. No prints on it. Ballistics tests of slug found in him checked out. His own gun had killed him. Happened in Mexico, so it's assumed the matter was linked to some kind of disagreement with local muscle. Or some kind of gang disposal that went wrong. Could have been working for the Pipeline, but that wasn't anywhere in the record."

"A suicide?"

"Not unless he was clever enough to dispose of the gun and then throw his own corpse into the ocean afterwards.

"How sure is all that?"

"Absolutely no room for error. My info chain on that is rock solid."

Brandy contorted his face as he blinked a few times to get the residual sleep out of his eyes. "You sure the leaky sources couldn't have changed some records?"

"Well, I've done some thinking about that, too. And some checking. I don't think there was ever a leak in Sacramento. They're just a little too careful with security there. Turns out they routed their questions through LAPD. Which leads us back to our suspicion that the Pipeline has ears there."

"And which means that the hit on your offices could have been Pipeline related after all."

"Could be, but I doubt it. I'm still putting my money on your sweet boy Earl Lesyk. But I'll admit there are a few too many coincidences unfolding here."

"So you're still okay with the tomorrow plan?"

"Yep. My plane gets in at noon. Can you pick me up in front of United?"

"You bet."

"I'm looking forward to shakin' tail with you, again, Brandy-iron. This could be fun. Especially if this is the bastard who ordered the break-in on my shop."

"I'm going down in another couple of hours. We'll

pick you up at LAX."

"We?"

"The widder-woman done joined up."

"You don't waste much time, do you?"

"Hey . . . It's not like *that*, Badge."

"Yeah, buddy. I know. It never is. Heh, heh." He cleared his throat. "So she's not going to get in our way?"

"You said you wanted to work on Earl Lesyk like we worked on Halstron way back when. If so, we can do it best with a woman there. She's not a bad actress if you give her all her lines. It's only when she gets extemporaneous that it starts to get scary."

"If you say so. I'll work on a script for her tonight during the stakeout. See you tomorrow. I'll be the guy who walks off the plane looking for a place to get some sleep, but just ignore the bitching. It's worth it for me to hang around the office here tonight just in case whoever it was tries again. I want to be right here to get off a swift riposte, while the perp is least expecting it."

Twenty-Nine

The time was getting tight. Julia would be standing on the curb, bag in hand, in another twenty minutes. But the news from Badger was significant enough to warrant another call to Annie. Brandon tried the shop. No one there.

Then he rang her home. A man with a French accent answered, rather informally. "Oui. A moment . . . An-NIE!"

After a lengthy muffled pause, Annie picked up the phone, breathless as if she'd run from somewhere. "Hello?"

"Drake."

"Oh . . ." she huffed a few breaths. "Did you get the letter?"

"The fax from you? Yes. Who answered your phone?"

"Ooo! Are you my social chaperone, old buddy Randy-Brandy? If you must know, that's Jean-Claude Laffont, my old climbing buddy. He arrived here this afternoon to do some climbing with me, only I thought I was going to have to keep it to climbs here inside the house --- if you know what I mean, wink-wink nudge-nudge --- because of all the goddamned *work* one of my dearest old friends, one Brandon Jennings Drake, is making me do at the shop. And I hope that makes you *prickly* with guilt reactions! I'm so fucking stir-crazy with all this office stuff, I think I'd probably climb the outside of the Transamerica Teepee with him if that's what Jean-Claude wanted. I swear to you, all my muscles are turning to flab and my mind is turning to Jello. I've *got* to get out of here soon for a couple of days, or it won't matter what the hell we've found out!"

"Good, because that's what I want you to do. It's up to you whether or not you go climbing. I just want you out of touch for a few days. Is this a good time to talk?"

"You mean 'Is Jean-Claude listening'? Hell, no. He couldn't possibly hear *anything*. The way I've got my thighs wrapped around his ears? I've got strong legs, Sweetie. Remember? Short, but strong." She giggled. "Oops! I promised not to do that to you again, didn't I? You don't really mind. Do you, Brandy? Listen, I've had a little wine, and I'm feeling a little pissy at you because of how helpless I feel. So tell me what you called about. Jean-Claude *really* can't overhear, but it's only because he just went to the can to take a pee." She giggled again.

"Annie, You're incorrigible! You probably don't deserve it but I've got some good news for you."

"What kind of news?"

"Best news you can imagine. The Pipeline has nothing on you."

"Beg your pardon?"

"The Pipeline. The gun? Remember? The DEA man? He was not a Fed. *Not* DEA. He must have been hired by the Pipeline. It was probably part of some kind of scam or set-up to scare you into keeping quiet during your retirement, but I daresay they hadn't counted on the guy bitching it up so badly. They *certainly* hadn't counted on his getting killed. And after their cleanup man discovered the body in the hotel room and disposed of it, they must have decided to capitalize on the situation as best they could, and hoped to control you with it anyway."

Annie's voice dropped a few levels to flip-side sobriety. "Wait a minute. You mean . . . but I *killed* the man. I'm sure of it!" She was having trouble tracking. Whether it was ethanol or surprise, Brandy couldn't be sure.

"Annie, just listen to me. You don't have to be afraid of them. You killed a man in self-defense. The gun was found and there were no fingerprints on it. They've never officially solved the case, but the Mexican police consider it closed. Finito. They could never make a case against you now unless you went forward voluntarily. Get what I'm saying?"

"Yeah. I get it," she replied grimly. "The police are no threat, but what if the Pipeline finds out that they don't have anything on me? Then I'm dead meat! Great news, Brandy!"

"That's why I want you to be careful, dear --- *very* careful --- until after I sort out the rest of the details about what happened to Farmer and Chrissie. There are still a few mysteries, but I don't really think you're in any immediate danger. For the time being, I want you where no one is likely to be able to find you. Understand?"

The nervousness continued to permeate her voice. "Just tell me one thing. Do *they* know that *I* know about this? The Pipeline?"

"I don't think so, but we're not sure. That's another reason I want you to be careful. You understand?"

"Goddammit, Brandy. I have that icy feeling I used to get after those nightmares. What if . . ."

"There are no 'what-if's now. I'm just concerned that if we don't deliver the whole platter to Dave soon, he may look into things you'd rather not have opened up. Even if you can't be convicted for them. Okay?"

"If you say so. It takes a bit of the glamour off of any climbing trip, though . . ."

"I imagine," Brandy soothed. "But I want you to go ahead and take two days to go wherever you want. Just make sure you go where no one will find you. And when you come back, give my Vancouver number a call before you go back to your home."

"Before I go home? You mean . . .? You really know how to instill confidence in a girl . . ."

"I'm just being super-cautious. It's probably unnecessary, but if for any reason you can't reach me directly, go to the Ranger Station in the Valley and contact me from there. You can tell Dave everything you know about Chrissie and Farmer and Phil. I'll fill in the details when I get there. Clear?"

"But . . ."

"Clear?"

"Sometimes I think I should never have opened my big mouth. I should have let it ride. I should've let Chrissie and Farmer rest in peace."

"But you didn't. And if you hadn't called me, the murderer would be sitting pretty."

"Which he probably is anyway."

"Not the way I read it. We'll know for sure in another few days. Anyway, Annie, I'm proud of what you did. It was very . . . unselfish."

"Bullshit. It was as selfish as it gets. I was scared and I was pissed off."

"Suit yourself. But I'm telling you most people would have stuck their heads in a hole and hoped everything would pass."

"Maybe I wish that's what *I* had done. Where are you going to be if I need to get ahold of you in the next two days? If J.C. and I come down early, maybe."

"I'm on my way to L.A."

"Why L.A.?"

"Well, I'm pretty much at a standstill here. All the

hooks are coming out of the water empty. We might as well do some digging in this Brother Earl's back yard while he's still figuring out where little brother hid the Rogues' Galleries. I want to look more closely into Earl Lesyk's setup. The things you've turned up in the past couple of days should help me shake his tree a little harder."

Annie's voice went gravelly. "Be careful, Brandy. That bastard is mean. You can see it in his eyes. And I've known a lot of mean ones to compare to. If you got killed, I know I'd be next in line. I'd be so afraid, I don't know what I'd . . ."

"I'll be careful."

"What happens if you don't learn anything from Earl?"

"Then you and I will go to the police and let them take over with it. At least you won't have to be concerned about the Enseñada connection any more."

"I don't like to think about any of this . . ."

"I'll be in touch as soon as we get back from L.A., unless I hear from you first. Okay?"

"We? As soon as *we* get back from L.A.? Who else is involved now?"

Shit. He hadn't meant to do that. "Uh . . .yeah. Hobbs' wife is going with me, too. She came to me today, convinced something was wrong. She was convinced that Farmer was murdered." Why did he feel such a compulsion to explain this to Annie? "She can help with the Farmer angle like no other person could. It's also a dandy way for me to sound her out for any inconsistencies in her own stories. Not that I have much doubt about her, but . . ."

"Look out for widows," Annie interrupted. "They go for the throat."

"Oooo . . . are we catty?"

"No. Of course not. I have direct knowledge of the widow mentality. Remember . . . I *was* a widow once."

"I know."

"And I don't like her knowing so much about this."

"Nor do I. But she does, so we might as well have her on side."

"Just make sure you keep her on her *side*, big guy," Annie chimed in, " . . . not on her back or on her knees." She began to wine-giggle again.

"My goodness, our claws are long."

"Just hers. Don't kid yourself. I really don't see why she has to go with you."

"She doesn't have to, but she certainly has vested interests in finding out who killed her husband. And she may be very helpful. There are many times when a man travelling with a lady is able to get at certain kinds of information which people are less likely to unload on a lone male."

"Right. Face it, Randy-Brandy: you have always been ruled by your gonads! And this is no exception. You can't fool me. *I* know why you want to have her travelling with you. You bastard!"

"Have a good time on your climb, Annie. And be careful."

"Careful? Hell, the safest place in the world I know is up on those granite faces."

"It wasn't for Chrissie."

"Yeah. Well, believe me, I've checked my equipment. Twice. And I can't tell you how much I need a really tough climb --- a sweat-rolling, scratches-and-bruises, dusty-mouth, muscle-puller of a climb --- to sort me out."

"I bet. Well, call me superstitious if you wish, but listen: don't sign the register for your climb this time. Don't let anyone know where you're going."

"You're really putting a scare in me. I thought you said everything was okay now."

"I think it is. But why take a chance until it's all in the bag?"

"We'll probably head up one of the long cracks in El Cap. There won't be any people up there this time of year. There's hardly anyone crazy enough to brave the kind of cold and damp we've got now up on the North Faces. We won't even go all the way to the top. Just a couple of days on the face."

"You're sure this Jean-Claude guy is a safe climbing partner?"

"That depends on whether you might be worried about my safety or my virtue?"

Brandy laughed. Welcome back, Raggedy Annie. "You're not likely to go too far astray, I guess. There's hardly much you can do while you're dangling off the side of a rock face sleeping in those spider net gizmos."

"Wanna bet?"

Thirty

After they picked up their baggage and the car, and wended their way through the maze of high-speed madness which surrounds Los Angeles International, Brandon and Julia went directly south to Redondo Beach to check in to a hotel. Brandy wanted to get settled as close to Big Earl's home as possible. He hoped to scout the area out a bit, now that it was dark, to make tomorrow's set-up with Badger that much easier. Julia listened earnestly when Brandy discussed the plans.

The motel on Sepulveda was barely a one-star. The exterior was in moderate need of Spackle and the pool wanted cleaning, but the rooms smelled clean and smoke-free. And the location was perfect: less than a mile from Lesyk's.

They registered under their own names into separate rooms.

"The suites are adjoining. That okay?" asked the woman at the desk, looking carefully from Brandon to Julia to gauge any reactions.

"It doesn't matter," replied Julia flatly.

"Never know," chatted the desk clerk. "Some folks travellin' on business are real picky. Don't want to be near their work-mates. Others want connecting. You never know."

"We've had to make do with the *same* room once," Julia said, matter-of-factly. "You get used to it when you travel a lot."

"What business you in?" asked the clerk. She extended her arm to put one of Brandy's business cards into focus and squinted to make sense of it. Brandy finished filling in the registration form and scooted it back across the counter at the woman.

"Taxation review," Brandy answered, deadpan.

"Oh," the woman frowned. "We pay *our* taxes. Probably a few other people's taxes, too, judging by the amounts we hafta pay. Humpf. Rooms 236 and 234. Up the stairs. The bellboy is off, so you'll have to handle your own gear." She stapled Brandy's calling card to the registration card, dumped them into a numbered slot at her side, and shuffled through an open door where she pivoted and whumped her derriere down into a form-fitting old Laz-E-Boy. A familiar, yet disjointed, dance. Her expressionless face flashed neon and blue from an unseen television. End of conversation.

Julia and Brandon looked at each other, shrugged, and moved their bags to their rooms.

Without unpacking, they took a short drive to the Lesyk house. They drove by it and parked on the next block. As they walked in silence along the sidewalks, weaving through the cars as they crossed over-full driveways, they realized how few other people were out walking. Los Angeles. Home of the four-wheeled illusion.

The neighborhood was an older settlement, full of ranch-style houses from the Fifties and Sixties. Lesyk's was a two-story rebuild. On a larger lot than most of the others, and set back from the street a bit more. Even in the dimly streetlit darkness, his house showed urgent need of maintenance. Movement and lights suggested someone was home. Brandy checked his watch. Around the side of the house, near the back, stood an old trailer. Darkened. Raised on set-up blocks.

A dog from a street or two away barked in alarm at something. Other dogs set up a serial howl, until the whole neighborhood sounded as if it were under canine siege.

Brandon slowly led Julia past the Lesyk house, until a tree and some bushes blocked out the nearest streetlight. He squinted to adjust his eyes to see better in the darkness where the trailer stood. The wooden cross-blocks on which it stood were recently placed, judging by the torn-up weeds and several stacks of what looked to be old skirt-panels in front of the garage. The trailer was being readied for transport.

When Drake had seen all he could from the road, he motioned silently to Julia to wait in the shelter of a low, large loquat tree. He stole quickly along the old cross-link fence and worked his way to the front edge of the trailer. The house next door was completely darkened. Brandy saw movement inside the Lesyk house and ducked behind the trailer, partially obscured by the dense weeds which had grown up between the trailer and the fence.

At the off side of the trailer, Drake climbed up onto one of the temporary support-block pilings and pulled himself carefully up to one of the darkened trailer windows. He clicked on his penlight to see inside. Filthy screens obscured most of his view, but he was able to make out a clutter of boxes and papers stacked in disarray. The screens smelled musty and dusty. He eased himself back down and looked closely at the pilings. New wood. The weed pattern offered confirmation of the recent raising of the trailer. Probably within the past few days. Somebody was getting ready to move it away. Brandy considered trying to get around to the other side, to sneak in the door and have a look inside the trailer. Phil's trailer, if Badger's intelligence was right-on. He got down on his hands and knees and began to crawl across the barren patch of ground which had been sheltered from sunlight by the trailer skirt, but which was now exposed to Earl Lesyk's house nearby.

A dog barked. From inside the Lesyk house. A big dog, judging by the deep throttle of its growl. Dogs nearby set up another chorus howl. Brandy withdrew to the weed line and waited. A light went on at the side porch of the house, across the driveway from the trailer. A door creaked open. Brandy held his breath, ready to leap the fence behind him if the screen door opened, or if a dog came his way. He couldn't make out a face behind the screen door because of the reflected glow of the yellow porch light, but someone was there, looking out and around.

After a few moments, the neighborhood canine chorus faded. The door was re-closed. The light was turned off. Brandy worked his way back past a large propane tank, grazing the side of his head on the unseen copper hose which still connected the tank to the trailer. He cursed softly and sneaked away, back along the fence line, back to where Julia waited.

They walked swiftly and silently away, down the street.

"What happened?" Julia whispered after they had passed just beyond the first streetlit corner.

"Nothing. Unfortunately. Except that now I have a pretty good idea of what Badger and I will need to break into the trailer."

"That's good," said Julia, encouragingly.

"But I don't know when we'll get an opportunity to search it. Or whether there's anything in there worth the risk."

"Maybe it's better to call the police?" Julia suggested.

"That concept would have my vote except that we

can't give them enough for an arrest, probably not even for a search warrant, so Earl would have time to destroy anything incriminating he hadn't already disposed of. If there were any such things in his house. Which seems like a long shot. For now."

"So what will we do now?" she asked.

"Eat," Brandy replied, unlocking the car door for her. "I'm hungry."

The choices of establishments for dinner cuisine tend to two extremes after ten o'clock at night. At one extreme they are pricey, and at the other they are greasy. Brandon chose pricey. In nearby Manhattan Beach they found a wooden platform cantilevered over the ocean which justly claimed specialty status in seafood. The dinner went well into the midnight hour, and the restaurant was nearly empty when the two tired travellers headed back to their motel. The dinner and the drive back were strangely reminiscent of the dinner at the Ahwahnee Hotel in Yosemite. They spoke of Things That Matter. They made long, unembarrassed eye contact. They smiled for no real reason. They acted like old friends. Or like seasoned lovers. Even though they really weren't either.

Back at the motel, Drake escorted Julia to the door of her room. They paused. Caught on a cusp of uneasiness. Julia made a fuss of finding her key in her purse.

Brandy sighed.

"May I ask a favor?" he said.

"I . . . certainly," Julia replied, expectantly.

Brandy started to speak and then bit the inside of his lip. Embarrassment was not a familiar emotion for him, but his earlier conviction at dinner was suddenly overcome by an atypical reticence. Time for a recovery. "Did you bring an alarm clock?" Julia looked puzzled. "I forgot mine and I'm not too confident about the reliability of the motel desk."

Julia nodded agreement. She seemed momentarily relieved by the distraction of such inane planning.

Brandon prattled on: "Could you set your clock for no later than nine o'clock? That should give us time to get out to the airport to pick up Badger. I've got a little nosing around to do by telephone before I have breakfast. Okay?"

"At your bidding, Kind Guardian." Julia curtsied. "Well . . ." she tried. Then she actually shuddered with the excesses of her own energies, like a happy, wet duck shaking off excess water. "What do I say now?"

"Maybe . . . 'Good night, Mr. Drake?' "

"Good night, Mr. Drake."

Brandon smiled and gave her a brotherly hug and a kiss on the cheek. She responded in kind, but she seemed to vibrate. Or maybe it was only his fertile imagination. Damn.

In the silence of his own room, Drake listened. For what? For the sounds of the spontaneous combustion engine next door whom he had just kissed good night? He heard nothing. He smiled to himself. Maybe it was his imagination, but he could almost feel the vibration through the walls. What an incredibly energetic woman!

As he pulled off his clothes and looked at the amber face reflected by the low-wattage bulbs into the mirror above the dresser, he frowned at the gaunt, shadowed features of the old cynic he saw there. What a crystal palace of fantasy his mind could build on the foundations of a passing scent of perfume, or a hint of an arched eyebrow, or an imagined entendre in a simple good night from the sister of an old friend. Brandy wondered if he would ever reach an age at which he would be free of having his fantasies sweep him from hour to hour, from woman to woman, from thought to thought, from rush to rush. Sometimes he felt like a boy adrift in a small lifeboat nearing a rocky coast in a storm. Sometimes he felt as if he were safely at a distance, *watching* the boy being tossed about in that boat. Did everybody find themselves so obsessively, albeit usually pleasantly, distracted by their sexuality? Good thing he managed to keep it all in perspective. Otherwise he'd never get any work done. Right.

Elsewhere in Los Angeles, there were men who were otherwise obsessed. But not with sex. No. They were obsessed with some of the other preoccupations which so frequently compete with sex for mental machination time.

And the name Brandon Drake was among others which surfaced in *their* thoughts. Not that Brandon could have done anything at that moment to avoid their obsessions. The best Brandy could do was to keep watching the boy in the boat.

Thirty-One

Drake took a long, hot shower. The searing, sublimating kind. The thinking kind. The water-trance kind. The kind which draws deeply from the almost unlimited supplies of hot water from the gigantic tanks of even the most elegant establishments. In the tinnitus-hiss of post-shower silence, in the steam chamber effect which turns wall-filling mirrors into barely translucent backdrops for the dense, swirling clouds of warm fog, Brandy towelled himself kindly and hedonistically. Showers always felt so *deserved*.

His thoughts had drifted still further to hedonistic tracks, following from his fantasies of his comely neighbor, when he heard a noise from beyond the bathroom door. The noise of movement. Of intrusion. He froze. Listened. Waited. Strained. But there was still nothing. Naked, he reached out with his long arm to flip off the light and the fan. He strained to hear more, but there was nothing. He wrapped a towel tightly around his waist and tucked it into itself. He could hear only the sound of his own arterial blood pulsing through his middle ear. Then there was the muted ker-clunk of a clos-ing bureau drawer. An acoustical trick? A sound from an-other guest's room? Only one way to know.

Seizing the doorknob tightly in one hand, he pressed his shoulder firmly against the door to allow the latch to dis-engage noiselessly. His heart pounding, Brandon eased the door open and put an eye to the crack to peer at the room beyond.

It was Julia. In a nightgown. Neatly smoothing the contents of his suitcase into the middle drawer beneath the mirrored dresser.

"Julia!" Brandy exploded, swinging open the door and marching into the bedroom, clad only in his towel. "You scared the hell out of me! What in god's name are you doing?"

Julia dropped the shirt from her hands and stared at him in embarrassed surprise. "Uh . . . scaring the hell out of you, I guess. Sorry."

"How did you get in here?"

"The connecting door was unlocked."

Brandon grabbed his terry-towel robe from the foot of the bed, shot his arms into it, and pulled it around him with its sash. He undid the towel, dropped it and stepped out of it, picked it up and tossed it back through the opened, darkened bathroom door.

"What's the matter? What's going on?" he asked, plunking down on the end of the bed and bracing his arms behind him against the firm mattress.

Julia stood at the bureau, continuing her steady eye-contact. Groping for words, even making shapes with her lips, but unable to begin speaking, she eventually seemed to give up altogether on replying. A few moments later she managed to break her own spell. Carefully she began to enunciate, "I . . . I don't want you to think it's just because . . ." Her voice tapered off into nothingness. Only the eye contact continued.

Brandon sat up and stuffed his hands into his bathrobe pockets, cocked his head to one side, and waited. Patience had often been his strongest suit.

Eventually Julia looked away long enough to take a deep breath and burst forth, "I want to say something. Listen . . ." She floundered again, searched his face, and finally picked it up in a tone of voice more appropriate to a rehearsed sermon than to a casual bit of late-night conversation. "As regards sex, there are four types of women."

Drake raised his eyebrow. Julia paused for a response, but he wouldn't have interrupted now if there were a fire in the building.

"The first type sees sex and lovemaking as a chore." Julia walked back and forth next at the foot of the bed as she continued, carefully punching her right index finger in to the palm of her left hand to emphasize each of her points of discourse. "If she is creative in her life's work, it's usually a result of the rechanneling of her repressed sexual energies. You follow? I know that sounds hackneyed, but it is so true. I've never been able to really sympathize with that, but I do understand them, I guess, at least as far as *why* they probably got themselves into that fix.

"The second type of woman has an average sort of sexual desire and is able to be pretty choosy about whether or not she wants to have sex and about who she wants to partner up with. A lot of my friends claim to be in that category. Which makes sense, I guess.

"The third type of woman wants sex all the time, and will track on any man in sight. It doesn't matter if she's married or single, or whether she's got a man on her arm at the moment or not. She usually goes through her life branded a 'pathetic hussy' by the women around her and a 'nymphomaniac' by the men. No one leaves her alone. People either run *toward* her or *away* from her, but they can't be neutral about her.

She's always a victim to her own appetites, which she senses to be constantly in need of feeding. Fortunately I'm not in that category, although I've had my moments of doubt from time to time."

She paused and stared at Brandon. "You still with me?"

"Almost wishing I could take notes. Please proceed."

"You make this sound like a speech."

"Well," smiled Brandon, crossing his arms, "*one* of us certainly does."

Julia blushed and self-consciously flicked a lock of frizz from her forehead. Her nipples were noticeably erect beneath the wisps of her thin nightgown as she continued to speak. "Then there's the fourth category. Those are the women who are *ready* for sex all the time, but don't *have* to have it. They fall in love very, very easily but very, very deeply, too. They are very direct about love and sex. They come right out and tell their men what they want, but they are willing to work out compromises and figure out ways to make their relationships work out because they have an interesting facet of their personality that demands a high level of exclusivity: they are outrageously monogamous. Not out of guilt or fear, but out of pleasure. They choose a partner carefully and then they compulsively reserve their charms for him. Paradoxically, their creativity isn't an outlet for repressed sexual energies; it's a complement to their sexuality. When they are mated, they blossom in every one of their pursuits. They go wherever their man is, whenever they can, and enjoy every possible moment of their sex lives together. It's not a dependency. It's a creativity obsession. And that's me all over.

"I've known I was like that since I was fifteen. For the entire five years of my marriage to Farmer I was totally faithful to him. And it wasn't difficult, either. Oh, I've always enjoyed *looking* at other men and being in their company. But after I beamed in on Farmer, I wouldn't *sleep* with any other man. You know what I mean? Sometimes Farmer and I would have to go for a week or two apart, like when he was throwing himself into a design project. And I didn't mind or resent it. That was just the way he worked. I was so much in love with him, I'd paint and paint and just be happy and sexy and in love. We'd wait until he was available and then we'd lock ourselves into our house and go crazy for a day or two with each other. That kind of stuff doesn't leave much room for a heavy social life. Not if you're married to a workaholic.

"If we had an argument, which only started happening before the separation, I just couldn't paint. Nothing but junk turned up on the canvas. And after Farmer disappeared, I couldn't paint a stroke. I was like some lost dog looking for its master's hand for a pat, shunning all others. I guess I must have known what happened all along." She frowned at Brandon's bemused concentration and took another a deep breath. "Why aren't you saying anything? You think I'm crazy or something?"

"I didn't have a prybar," Brandy replied. "And this is the first time you've taken a breath since I asked you why you were here. About halfway through, I was prepared to say 'Are you trying to tell me you're horny?' But you were on a real roll. Again. That was quite a dissertation. Do you do that kind of thing with everyone, or did I just win some kind of lottery?"

She flushed. "Too strong again, eh? Type Fours do that. But only about some things and only about certain people. Some people don't even know how to respond to this kind of conversation. Know what I mean?"

"The thought had crossed my mind."

"You have a *very* dry sense of humor, Brandon Drake."

"Thank you. Not too many people appreciate it."

"I bet. Anyway, you don't *have* to respond to me in

any particular way. No obligations, because this wasn't a proposition."

"'Wasn't'?"

Julia's eye contact was unwavering, but her smile reflected some uncertainty. "Neither of us has to do a thing about it, you know. But I *did* want to level with you. Otherwise you might have misunderstood some things. Understand?"

"No. But I feel like I've just been complimented."

"You *have* been. And you don't have to respond in any way, shape, or form. I just wanted to explain. So you'll understand. And so you won't think I'm too strange . . ."

"But you are, Julia. As I told you this morning, you are probably the strangest woman I've ever met."

"Do you mind?"

"Not at all." Drake watched her eyes. They were deeply sincere. Not a frivolous flicker. "I'm fascinated. And more than a little flattered. What man wouldn't be?"

"Plenty, as I recall. From long ago and far away. Maybe I'm too direct."

"So you've done this with many other men?"

"This? You mean coming right out and telling you what I want and how I feel? Not for many years."

Neither of them moved. Julia began to blush deeply. "I . . . I promised I wouldn't let it get in the way, didn't I?"

"Yes, you did."

"Oh." She looked down and continued in a quiet whisper, "I'm sorry. I . . . would you like me to leave now?"

When she brought her eyes up to where Brandon still sat on the end of the bed, he remained as inscrutable as he had been throughout her speech. Slowly, resignedly, and almost artistically, he gestured with his hand toward the connecting door through which Julia had come into his motel room. The door stood wide open. "I think you should probably go back to your room . . ."

She nodded acquiescence to his unfinished request, squared her shoulders proudly and turned to walk back to her own room, when she heard Brandon's smooth voice from behind her, " . . . and bring back your alarm clock. Just in case we can't hear it from here in the morning. We can't afford to miss getting to the airport at noon to meet my friend."

She looked back at him and frowned. He had a quizzical smile on his face.

"Meaning?" she asked.

"Meaning, my dear Type Four lady . . . I want to sleep with you. Lots of soft wonderful hugs and cuddles and rubs. And I want to hear from you that it's okay if that's all we do. Just sleep together. And if later we decide to make torrid, passionate love together, that would be okay, too. Type Four love, maybe? I don't know. But since you're into the lecture mode, how about if each of us begins by telling the other *exactly* how we most enjoy making love."

"Really? Just like that?"

"Why not? It might let us by-pass First-Time Disappointment Syndrome and maybe even let us roll through Second Time Doldrums."

A recharged Julia whisked off into her room and moments later bounced back through the connecting door with a travel alarm clutched in her hand. Electricity radiated from her wild frizz of hair. "Well?" she demanded.

"Well what?" asked Brandy, pulling back the bedspread.

"Who goes first? Who talks and who listens?"

Drake grinned from ear to ear and shook his head in amazement. "This is undoubtedly the strangest seduction I've ever been party to. I wish I knew who was seducing whom. Somehow I'm guessing it probably doesn't even matter."

Julia rubbed her earlobe gently between her thumb

and the side of her forefinger, and nodded wordless agreement.

"Since you're on such a roll," Brandon continued, "why don't *you* tell *me* how you most enjoy your lovemaking."

Julia was positively beaming. "How about if I *show* you instead . . ."

Thirty-Two

Julia and Drake slept in. Sometime in the early morning light, Drake looked at the quiet, low-voltage, resting frizz sleeping in the warm hollow of the soft pillow next to his.

He watched Julia take a deep, slow breath, and sigh. He smiled. For a woman who had been through a lot of turbulent times in the past three months, a woman who operated at high revs and fast pace, a woman who had lost both her man and her baby in less than three weeks, there was a certain peace she emanated. Maybe not "in spite of". Perhaps it was "because of". Sometimes the resolutions of the mysteries, however dramatic, are easier to absorb than the uncertainties of waiting.

There were times like this, with a beautiful, aromatic body draped loosely over you, limbs sleepily entwined --- the perfect fit --- when you couldn't help but speculate that the inconvenience and work of having a private, special, full-time partner again might be worth it. There was no doubt, ever since those first strange nights in the Yosemite Lodge cabin, even in the separate beds and in the iron grip of her deep anguish, that Julia had been very comfortable to be with. Not restful, perhaps. And certainly not casual. But comfortable. And that was an unfamiliar feeling for Brandy.

He had been on his own for sixteen years, more or less. Living alone had its advantages. At least it was *always* better than living with someone you didn't like very much. One round of that game had been quite enough. But maybe it didn't always have to be that way. A few couples Drake had known closely had managed to cultivate the magic for years on end. Damned few. But enough to lead him to the suspicion that it *could* be done.

There had been a lady named Mikki, and one or two others who had graced the morning cool with him, and many others who had been engaged in the short-term, frenzied, sweaty trades which are the frequent fare of lonely singles who need clinging fixes to keep them strong in their resolve to maintain their singleness. He had fed, and been fed, such fare.

But sweet sights like Julia here, now, offered so much stark contrast that Brandon couldn't, struggle as he might, remember participating in one-night stands. And maybe this wasn't anything more than a one-night lonely-persons' liaison drenched in the deep hormone balance of the morning after. A dreamy bubble waiting to be popped when they began their first conversation of the morning.

There was a special freshness to Julia which transcended her flakiness. Brandon was pondering it, trying to identify it, stepping outside to look upon it objectively, when Julia's closed eyelids fluttered. She sighed again, rolled over, and sensuously backed up against the comforting solidity of Brandon's body.

As she rolled and then wrapped herself in the warm bedclothes, her vaporous aromas wafted up and surrounded Brandy. He loved them. She smelled absolutely delicious.

Even more delicious than she had last night, because this morning she also smelled like him. Take one part Brandy and stir gently into one part Julia. Mix thoroughly several times, in rapture. Simmer, in Julia, and enjoy.

With nothing planned for the morning, they ordered in a room service breakfast and fed it to each other as they made love again.

At noon they were waiting at the airport to meet Badger. Brandy was looking forward with amusement to how Julia and Badger might get along with one another. Acid and base, he guessed, but it is one of life's ultimate puzzles that you never knew for sure how two of your friends would actually hit it off. Julia was alternately glowing and fidgeting as they waited.

But there was no Badger. After the plane load emptied, and after all the other passengers on his San Francisco flight had come and gone from the baggage carousels, Brandy checked with the airline and weaselled from them the information that Mr. Beeley had not reported for his flight. Perhaps he would be taking a later commuter flight, they suggested, but there was nothing scheduled for him at this time.

Drake couldn't raise anything but a Pacific Bell disconnected service message at Badger's home, so while Julia paid a visit to the ladies' room Brandy called Badger's office in Sausalito. His call was passed along immediately.

A faraway voice said, "Hello? This is Kyle Sommerfield speaking." There was a weird echo in the line. Not enough to warrant a reconnection. Just enough to give you the feeling you were speaking to someone at the bottom of a mine shaft.

"Hello. Brandon Drake here. I'm trying to get a hold of Badger. Maybe you know where he is. He was supposed to be meeting us here this morning and . . ."

"I've been trying to reach you all morning," Kyle interrupted. "Mr. Drake . . . uh, I'm not sure how to say it, but . . . Don Beeley was killed last night."

"He *what*?"

"He was murdered. I didn't know where you were staying in L.A., so I couldn't get word to you. I'm sorry to have to break it to you this way, but . . . I'm not sure if there's another nicer way anyway." Kyle's voice was unsteady.

"What the hell has happened?"

"Somebody tried to break into his home and they bushwhacked him when he tried to tag them. Then they burned his house to the ground. Possibly to confuse the police; maybe it was an accident. We're still trying to work out the details, but most of it looks pretty clear as to what went down."

Drake's confusion and shock were genuine. The mine shaft echo suddenly seemed especially appropriate.

"Badger left Lou and me on the stakeout," Kyle explained, "at about midnight last night. I think he knew something was about to come down, though I doubt if he knew just what it was. He always had a special sense when things were about to go wrong. He filled me in on what he was doing in this case with you. All the details. And I was puzzled why he was telling me. It didn't sound like emergency stuff to me. So I asked him what he wanted me to do about your case, and all he said was, 'Be ready.' He said that a lot, and it usually meant 'Don't ask me any more questions. You'll figure it out when the time comes.' "

"But if he knew something was up, what happened? Who . . . ?"

"They broke into his house and were going through his study. The mud on the soles of Badger's slippers was from the garden outside the study windows, which is near where they found him, so we're guessing he had slipped outside and was looking in through the windows at who-ever had broken into his house. So it looks like Badger could have gotten away, but for some reason he didn't. And it's hard to be sure exactly what happened next. His youngest boy, Greg, came home --- the only one still living at home, you know. He's a college student at UCSF. He was sup-posed to have gone down to San Jose with his mother, but he didn't.

"Greg had forgotten his key, so he rang the doorbell. He rang again, then he heard a crash and that was followed by some gunfire. Badger might have been worried it was Connie coming home unexpectedly, or maybe me at the door. Anyway, he would have wanted to make sure he got to the intruder before the intruder could get to whoever was at the front door. So it looks like he kicked in the big picture window to create a diversion, and whoever was inside just opened fire at Badge right there and then. Either that, or after the doorbell the intruder looked outside through the window and saw Badge there. We'll probably never know for sure."

"What about Greg? What did he do?"

"Badger trained his kids well enough to know when to stand their ground and when to run like hell. Greg tore off to a neighbor's house. Before the police could get to Badger's place, though, the house burst into flames."

"You're saying whoever killed Badger shot and killed him before Badger could fire back? Didn't Badger have a gun? He was always Mr. Safety First."

"Yeah, I know. He had a gun all right. They found it near him in the shrubs. But the perp had an automatic rifle. One of the assault machines. AK-47 or something like. I guess the guy must have pulled the trigger and made his sweep. Badger just didn't luck out." Kyle and Brandon shared a spontaneous moment of long-distance silence. It is one thing to be accustomed to tragedy. It is quite another to be touched personally.

"Greg feels like shit," Kyle said. "Blames himself for his father's death. But I've told him that he did the absolutely correct thing, that he couldn't have saved his father, that he probably saved his own life. Hell, the kid didn't even know that any of his family was in the house. He said he just rang the bell on a long shot before he went out back to dig up their emergency key. If he'd known his dad was in there when he heard the shots, he said . . . well, you get the idea. You can't blame him for feeling pretty badly, I guess, but I'm still going to work on making sure he goes through the rest of his life knowing he did the right thing. Nobody needs that kind of guilt load, do they?"

Brandy felt the tears trickling from the edges of his eyes down his numb face.

"Who would have done this?" Brandy asked.

"Well, I'd kinda thought you might be able to let me in on that. It looks like the same entry pattern as the previous night's hit on our offices here. Only this time they must have hoped to find something at Badger's house, and they must have gone prepared to torch it to cover up the entry. Hard to tell if they knew he was there, too, or if that was a surprise. I'm guessing it was a surprise."

"You think it was related to the investigations *we* were doing?"

"It looks that way to me. Let me give you some more info --- a few things Badger was planning to tell you himself this morning."

Julia was sauntering from the ladies' room to where Drake stood at the telephone cluster. As she approached, she saw the pained look on Brandon's face and quickened her pace toward him. She drew near him and waited for an explanation. Her expressions mirrored Brandon's as she listened to his part of the conversation and strained to pick up a sense of whatever had happened.

"Let's see," Kyle proceeded, "where do I start? This

morning I received the confirmation from one of Badger's
Federal insider sources that your DEA man definitely *wasn't*.
I guess Badger was already pretty sure about that yesterday. Now it's for absolute. But something is really cooking
with this Pipeline group. Lots of inquiries. Lots of calls. Lots
of Los Angeles, too. Does that make sense?"

"I suppose. As much as it ever has."

"Badge told me last night that he was using fresh
information channels --- something about his regular sources
being contaminated. He said that he had the Feds do a scan
on all incoming calls from LAPD yesterday, and that the
name Brandon Drake showed up on one of them."

"My name?"

"Yep. Does *that* make any sense?"

"Less and less. Anything else?"

"Apparently, none of the Yosemite people were on
the LAPD inquiry list --- at least not from yesterday --- except
for the Lesyk fellow."

"Which one? Earl or Phil?"

"The dead one. Phil. That I know because I saw it on
a printout early this morning. And I had a real challenge
trying to get any more information from Badger's contact at
Social Security. Especially when he heard why it was me and
not Badger who was following up on it. He got real nervous
about the fact that Badger had been hit. I had to give him a
hell of a lot more than my mother's maiden name to convince
him to talk to me over the phone."

"Social Security?"

"Yeah. Believe it or not. I'm going to have to do a lot
of work to try to re-establish any of Badger's strange links.
And I figure I'll be lucky to find or retain even ten percent of
them." There was another protracted silence before Kyle
carried on. When a friend's death is recent, the past tense
references seem all the more painfully obvious. A ringing
bell that can't be stilled. "When do you want me to send the

police your way?" Kyle asked.

"You mean you haven't yet?"

"No. I guessed that that might blow apart whatever you and Badger had going. If it could have been taken to the police, I figured Badge would already have done that. Was I wrong?"

"No. You were right. I'm just . . . I just need to think for a bit to put it all together. I figured when you told me you thought there was a tie-in to this case, and then about Badger . . . I'm just impressed with you, Kyle. There aren't too many young investigators as shrewd as you are. Badger had told me about you, and it's obvious that his instincts were right. Once again."

Brandy looked at Julia, whose facial expression showed the limbo in which she would have to hang until Brandon finished the telephone call and could bring her up to date. "How long do I want?" Brandy mumbled aloud to himself. "Do you think you can give me one day of shelter? Until tomorrow morning? It all seems to be working out bass-ackwards, and I'm really not sure how much I can do down here, but I think I need to sort out this thing with the Lesyk brothers before I can let the authorities start ripping the Pipeline out of the ground. On second thought, can you wait until I call you before you sick the police on me?"

"Sure thing, Mr. Drake. Whatever you want. You want me to come down there and help you track down the people who killed Badger?"

"Thanks, Kyle, but I'm not even sure I'm on the right trail here."

"Well, for what it's worth, Badger thought so. He told me last night he thought the people who were involved in the Yosemite murders were somehow tied in with the Pipeline. He always talked about your instinct for being in the right place at the right time."

"I wish I shared his certainty right now."

"Well, he never doubted it. And frankly, that is the quality I most admired about *him*, too. In spite of what happened this morning."

"Shit!" Brandy hissed, helplessly. It wasn't a particularly illuminating remark, but nothing else expressed the frustration.

"Badger always said you were the very best, you know," Kyle offered tentatively.

"No. I didn't know. Funny how mutual admiration societies get started. And it's Brandon. Okay?" Brandy could almost feel the smile burrowing through the undoubted sorrow on the face of Badger's young protégé. Full circle.

Brandon hung up the phone and stared helplessly into Julia's face.

"Is your friend ill or something?" she asked.

Brandy started to explain in everyday words, but every word that tried to emerge got choked off. "Killed" was all Brandy's constricted throat could manage to enunciate. He needed to let out something awful which had seized hold of his insides, but it hurt too much to cry. Instead he gave Julia a rib-compressing hug and smoothed the hair on the side of her head as he felt his own tears stream down his face. He whispered in her ear, "We'll shake trees until they fall out. Whoever killed Farmer and Badger. Don't worry. We'll find them. I swear to you."

Thirty-Three

By the time Brandy and Julia had returned to the motel, Drake had formulated an outline of a plan. First he called the Mountaineering Shop at Yosemite. Annie's friend Mary was minding the store.

"Annie is gone for a couple of days," Mary reported. "She said you might call, but she didn't leave any message."

"She didn't say where she was headed," Mary continued, her gregariousness evidencing slow times in the early winter climbing scene, "but Doug heard some scuttlebutt that she has a visiting climber friend. He's from Switzerland or somewhere. Small and blonde --- I guess that's just perfect for Annie, huh?" she giggled. "I haven't seen him, but you know how the rumors fly. Someone told Doug they were headed up the Dihedral Wall. El Cap. They're probably working on a new speed record, if I know Annie. And if anybody can do it, Annie can. Even with the pitsy weather. Still, if they go all the way up, it'll be Thursday or Friday before they can get down. I think she really needed to get out of here for a while. She must have been pretty excited about it. Doug just came back from the Visitor Center and he told me she forgot to sign out. Can you believe it? This is her first climb since she lost her friend Chrissie, you know. Poor girl. Want me to leave a message?"

"No. That's okay. I'll try back again in another day or two. Thanks."

So Annie was safely up the great granite walls, out of the easy reach of harm. Even if everybody seemed to know exactly where she was. Brandy marvelled at what a tiny, inbred clique world class climbers were. No secrets were allowed.

Next Drake called the Yosemite Valley Ranger Station for Ranger Dave, but Dave was "out of the valley for the day. Can anyone else help you?"

"No," Drake replied. "I'll call again tomorrow. Can you tell me what time you expect him?"

"Who's calling?"

Brandy considered the exposure. He wanted to have Dave all ready to take charge of protecting Annie if something went wrong in Los Angeles, but there was every reason not to get Dave engaged too early. As with so many things in this world, timing was everything.

"Fred Markham," Brandy lied. "Santa Rosa private investigator. I have some information for him."

"I expect him to call in later today. Can I take your number?"

"Not really. I'm on the move. What time tomorrow?"

"Try 8:00 in the morning."

Brandy and Julia spent nearly two hours shopping in hardware stores. The big mall stores don't have the right kinds of tools and the little general stores --- the kind that stock just a few of nearly every damned thing anyone could *ever* want --- are nearly impossible to locate in mega-sales

America. Drake finally found all the odds and ends he thought he might need to get into Lesyk's place for a search.

      In the mid-afternoon, the Vancouver duo cruised by Lesyk's house. All was quiet and there seemed to be no activity around the mobile home at the back of the driveway. It was tempting to run a frontal assault, to knock on the door and pose as a travelling salesman if anyone happened to answer, or to do a straight daylight B & E and search if no one answered. But there might be problems. Too many risks for the possible gain.

      From a gas station payphone Brandon called Lesyk's unlisted home phone number --- the one Big Earl himself had pencilled in on the business card he'd left for Annie at the Mountaineering Shop. An ancient answering machine hissed and beeped, and offered the sticky-sweet voice of a common-sounding young girl who pretended erudition, but got all of her who's and whom's reversed, like Marilyn Monroe was famous for doing on-screen. Sticky-Sweet gave out only a telephone number --- no name --- and then instructed the caller that the answering machine's recording mechanism was hoping to glean a name and number from the caller.

      Uncertain as to whether he had called the correct number, as to whether Sticky-Sweet was really responding for Big Earl, Brandy phoned Earl's club and demanded to speak to him.

      "Who *is* this?" answered a gruff man who could have subbed in for a WWF announcer. There was a lot of noise in the background: clanking and clacking and stereo speakers with too much bass playing out-of-date honky-tonk R & B.

      "Jeremiah. Out at the track."

      A long pause. Gruff cupped the phone and growled at someone nearby. He returned to Drake after a confused pause: "Earl's out of town 'til late this afternoon. Would you like to speak to the assistant manager Derksen? He usually handles the pony calls."

"No. This is private. Lesyk said I should only talk to him personally. Will he be into the club tonight?"

"Probably. Depends on when he gets back. Wanna leave a message, I'll have him call you soon's he gets in."

"No. No message." Brandy saw an opportunity to confirm the other number. "All right I should give a call to the other phone? He gave me an unlisted number --- 265-7781. Is he there maybe?"

"He gave *that* number to you? Jeez. This must be something big. Yeah, that's his home. But he won't be there either. I'll tell him you called case he checks in here first. You got a number where you are?"

"Yeah, but he already knows it. Bye."

Brandy and Julia had an early dinner at a fast food fly-through. All through the meal, Drake found himself wondering if maybe Big Earl were returning from a quick trip to the Bay area, wondering if he had had an unscheduled meeting with a private investigator named Badger. The clenching of teeth didn't help the digestion. Brandy kept reminding himself that there was no proof Earl had anything whatsoever to do with Badger's murder, but too many coincidences were coming together for Brandy to quietly ignore some very ugly possibilities. By the time they were leaving the speed-feed, Brandy had promised himself that if he hadn't shaken anything loose before tomorrow morning, he was going to call Ranger Dave to look after Annie and to ask Kyle to go to the police. They didn't have much, but it was beginning to look like the Good Guys were outnumbered and outflanked by the Bad Guys.

Brandy and Julia dropped by the motel and changed to clothes they guessed would be suitable for a visit to Earl's club: an open collar sport shirt and dark polyester pants for

Drake and another set of light-up-the-world Day-Glo's for Julia. She seemed to have an endless supply, and she was one of the few women Brandy had met who was as attractive as she was striking in such attire.

The drive through the last few blocks in the heart of East L.A. was an eye-opening reminder of the socio-economic contrasts which deeply divide the good ol' U.S. of A. Groups of homeless street-dwellers huddled around streetfires at every corner. But in the fading dusk, past the sidewalks strewn with unconscious derelicts, drove a continuum of brand new cars filled with the beautiful people of L.A., in their tuxedos and evening dresses, on their ways to exciting evening entertainment which they hoped would distract them from their workaholic hangovers.

Brandy searched very carefully for a safe parking place for the car. It was hard without knowing the neighborhood. There was a valet sign leaning up against the wall beside the club entrance, but nobody stood outside who might make good on the offer. Furthermore, it seemed prudent to avoid anything which might unnecessarily catch the attention of the club staff. Discreet exits were much harder to manage when a car had to be fetched by the people you were running from. On the third pass through the nearest grid of the neighborhood's best lit sidestreets, Brandy found a parking spot just around the corner from the club.

Even Julia at her spaciest was not oblivious to the high level of danger on these streets. Her persistent spinniness was suddenly sobered by the dim-lit, graffiti-scrawled grunginess of the inner city. As she stepped from the car and caught a waft of a nearby pile of over-ripened garbage, recently pawed-through for any overlooked edibles, drinkables, or pawnables, she latched onto Brandy's arm and offered no resistance when he steered her away from the unlit building entrances and alleyways. Urban No-Man's Land. Far removed from the grizzly-inhabited wildernesses of the northern reaches of the Canadian Rockies. But much more similar than different. And far more dangerous.

The Lesyk's club was a study in tackiness. Posters and crude eye-catchers in exaggerated girlie shapes were pasted all across the streetside walls. A garish neon sign announced the club's name in big block letters: "PIKE'S PEEK". A backlit fluorescent signboard beneath flashed on and off, advertising "What's new-d at Big Earl's?" also in black block letters. Immediately below that the answer pulsed in another rhythm: "Everything that's worth seeing!!!" Bump and grind hard rock rattled the doors and vibrated the street in front of the entrance. All that was missing was a hawker with a cane.

"Climb On Up" read another, smaller flashing sign above the three steps in front of the door. Brandy wondered how many exiting drunks had pitched headlong down those steps. Wondered if some sharp lawyers hadn't already tried to make Big Earl's bank account a hell of a lot smaller with a few negligence suits. Or maybe the rules were different in East L.A.

The entryway was dimly lit, a darkly painted cave that smelled like old cigarette smoke and stale beer. It opened into a foyer from which steps led up into the flashing strobes of the club proper. The smoothly worn carpet in the foyer had once been dark red, probably coordinated to a previous scheme of lighting and paint. "Pike's Peek or Bust" proclaimed bumper stickers everywhere in the shape of bikini tops.

Along one wall was a glass-fronted marquee box. Tacked up on the corkboard behind the locked sliding glass were the publicity pictures of the week's 'stars' and announcements of special activities.

One sign read, "Don't forget! Monday night is Amateur Night. Make yourself a star. Make your lady a star!

Some of California's best exotic dancers got their start at Pike's Peek!" Another sign read, "Auditioning Nightly for the Amateur Talent Lead-in competition. Just see the Maiter Dee or Club Manager for details."

A short, burly fellow ducked down the steps from the main club and approached Brandy and Julia. He wore a dark, poorly fitted sport jacket over a gaudy, Hawaiian print shirt, and he had a gold chain necklace to emphasize his carefully cultivated deep tan. Likely the Bouncer. Or "Maiter Dee", as he seemed to be called here.

"Welcome to Pike's," he rasped in the same gruff voice Brandy recognized from the telephone call earlier. Hopefully the man didn't have any special talents when it came to voice recognition. "Help you find a table?" he croaked.

"Sure," Brandy replied, following the man up the steps, "but not too near the stage. We want to have a little privacy, too."

The Bouncer glanced back at him and then gave Julia a once-over appraisal before flicking Brandy a sleazy grin and replying, "No problem. Listen, the regulars already grabbed the seats near the front anyway, but every seat in Pike's is a good seat. Know what I mean? Just follow me."

With a practiced flourish, the Bouncer led the way up the steps and across a railed aisle to a table at the front of the upper level, just above the stage and looking directly over the main seating area down below the stage. A low countertop was built around three sides of the stage, so that all the patrons on stools there had the stage floor at their eye level. Behind that were half a dozen small tables, about half full already. There was some sort of control room behind the stage, separated by a runway by which staff and dancers could get to and from the stage itself.

The Bouncer pulled back a chair for Julia and pointed to the adjacent one for Drake. The music was loud enough that the Bouncer had to raise his voice almost to a shout in order to be heard. He leaned close to Julia and rasped: "You folks change your mind about gettin' closer to the action, jus' give me a shout and I'll see if anything can be opened up down in front. Okay? Have a good time." He gave Brandy a wink and then cock-walked back to his station at the entrance.

Julia looked at Brandy and raised an eyebrow, but said nothing.

Brandy carefully looked around the club to explore its layout and personnel. His eyes were adjusting better with each minute to the darkness. Things seemed to be just getting started for the evening, but there was already a smoky haze.

A T-shirt-and-shorts-clad waitress appeared to take orders for the first of the compulsory two drinks, and returned in less than two minutes to trade weak drinks for eight dollars.

The first two dancers established the club routine. There were four numbers in each set. Each dancer started from fully clothed in some sort of costume, and removed progressively more clothing during the first three dances until she was completely naked by the beginning of her fourth dance. Then she would drag a blanket or a rug from the edge of the raised stage to the center and writhe about on it in a parody of eroticism, presenting herself visually in as many creative poses as she could to the glazed eyes of the sweaty beer-guzzlers right up next to the stage. Gynecology Row.

The first dancer had a sad-puppy face that suggested a hard and humorless life unrelieved by whatever pleasure she might have managed to garner from the occasional approving whistles and salacious compliments of the various bolder members of the audience.

The second dancer, an overly plumpish ginger-haired stripper, had moves which were more gymnast than dancer. She had a perpetual haughty expression, as if no one in the audience was good enough to see her dance, much less to see her naked, so that what she was conferring on them was a nearly majestic gift. For most of her fourth level number, she remained in steel spike heels alone, rolling around and undulating her torso and her hips on the fluffy but slightly overused synthetic rug which she'd taken to the edge of the stage at the beginning of her act.

The customers showed their first real enthusiasm when the carnival barker, whose face was barely visible through a narrow panel of grey glass in the dark control room behind the stage rasped into his microphone, "Hey, everybody! How about sending Sweet Cindy to the shower. Hey! She won't go without some help, will she? Let's hear some noise if you want Cindy Baby to get *wet*!"

The glasses clinked and the cheers came and the shouts and the catcalls and the whistles. At the response, Cindy looked around the audience in mock surprise that was supposed to say, "Why, do you mean *me*?"

A worker appeared from the control area with a large turkish beach towel and handed it up to Sweet Cindy on stage. She hung the towel over a bar beside a suddenly brightly-illuminated plexiglass shower stall, which had been hidden in the dark recesses of the far corner of the stage, and opened the door and stepped inside. Music pounded forth as she cranked on the water and played with the shower head. Howls and hoots competed with the sounds of the shower as the booze-mellowed fans watched Cindy get clean.

Brandy was mesmerized less by Cindy herself than by the audience reaction. What other species would spend money to watch one of its members wash itself?

Julia pushed her face close to Brandon's ear. "What are you going to do now?" she asked. "How are you going to put the squeeze on this Earl fellow?"

"I'm not sure."

"Not sure? I thought you had a plan."

"I have a series of plans. I'd like to get a look at this

guy first, and from then on, we'll have to fake it."

"But I thought detectives always planned everything down to the tiniest details. Nothing to chance . . ."

"Number One . . . I'm not a detective. Number Two . . . when I *was* a detective, I didn't usually plan to the tiniest details, because the people I was up against seemed not to read the same script. So it got too dangerous to keep following the plan. And furthermore I always seemed to miss the best opportunities when they appeared but hadn't been planned for."

Julia's eyes glittered. "I see."

"Mostly, I'd like to check out that trailer of Phil's in Redondo."

"Well, why don't you? If Earl is here tonight, there's probably nobody there. Right? Doesn't he live there alone?"

"As far as Badger was able to determine. But that may be dated information. And right now we don't even know if Earl is here."

"If he *is* here, is it worth a try to get a look in that trailer?"

"I'd have to make damn sure I don't have any interruptions."

"Need my help for the search?"

"No. I don't want you anywhere near the place when I'm searching."

Julia looked around her, squinted her eyes in consideration as she performed a systematic analysis of the various characters around the club.

"Done," she declared, with startling finality.

"Done?"

"Give me half an hour. Just stay here and enjoy the show," she added giving Brandy a pat on the shoulder as she slid off her stool and picked up her purse from the counter.

Brandy grabbed her arm. "Wait a minute!" he shouted

above the din of bump-and-grind bass. "What are you do-ing?"

"We're faking it," she whispered, leaning close to him. Then she drew back and shouted, "I'm going to see if I can get a job here. I used to do a little modelling. I hear they're looking for new blood." She laughed at her own phrasing. She leaned close for one last whisper, "If this Earl character isn't here at the club, I'll be right back. But if he *is*, I'll occupy him for as long as you need him out of circulation. Watch for my signal. That'll mean you have a couple of hours. Which means you should go straight on back to his house and do your thing."

Julia did an about face, but Brandy grabbed her by the arm. "Wait a minute. You can't do that!"

Julia grinned broadly. "Trust me. I know what I'm doing." She shrugged free and headed straight for the bar.

Brandy lunged after her and caught her by the arm again. "You can't do that!" he shouted above the clamor of the music. "I won't let you!"

The Bouncer had watched the disagreement brewing between the tall guy and his frizz-haired girlfriend. He started across the floor to intercept Brandy the moment Julia had pulled away from him again. Seeing the man coming toward her, Julia turned to face Brandy and, without hesitation, swung and slapped him hard across the flat of his cheek. He drew back, stunned, as she spun and strode defiantly away toward the bar with a sassy sway and a streetwise grin. Julia Number Five.

"Hey, Buddy!" the Bouncer grunted. "What's the problem?"

Brandy glared at the Bouncer. "Nothing," he growled. "I . . . I just think my lady has had too much to drink. I think we'd just better take her on home and . . ."

The Bouncer turned to watch Julia swinging her hips as she approached the full bar at the side of the club near the kitchen.

"Looks to me like she's doin' just fine. This is the New Millennium, Jack. How's about we let *her* decide when it's time to call it a night, huh?"

Brandy reluctantly returned to the table. The Bouncer slowly made his way over to where Julia sat perched atop a bar stool trying to get the attention of the busy bartender.

"Everything okay?" the Bouncer asked her.

"I wanna enter that exotic dancer contest," she drawled in a very convincing, if slightly liquor-slurred, East Texas accent. "And *he* says I can't cause we're only in town for a week." Petulant, she pointed up to where Brandy sat sulking. "I think he's afraid I might win and want to stay here in a new career and never go back to Texas with him. Where's Mr. Big Earl Lesyk? The bartender says he owns this place, and I wanna dance for him. Soon as he sees me, he'll want me to go on tonight."

The Bouncer slowly looked Julia over, from head to heels, as if he were inspecting a used car. "Tell you what, honey. Mr. Lesyk don't usually do the auditions, but I'll talk to him personally, and I might get you on tonight's line-up. C'mon with me and lemme see what I can do." He looked up to where Brandy sat watching them and grinned at him.

Brandy watched Julia follow the Bouncer along a low walkway which disappeared behind the bar and the control room. The Day-Glo cross-banding on her skirt was chameleon attire here. She strutted along radiating the same confidence that she had that first night in his condo in Vancouver. Crazy woman.

The Bouncer escorted Julia down a few steps to an unmarked door along the passageway from the bar to the stage. Brandy felt the tension mount as the door closed. Crazy woman. What the hell did she think she was doing? Blowing every bit of cover again. *That* was what she was doing!

Another dancer appeared. An older woman, twenty-seven, maybe twenty-eight. She moved like a professional, and the crowd responded to her entrance as if they recognized her. Star status in East L.A. But her heavy make-up and leather-like tan could not obscure an obviously hard lifestyle.

Exotic dancing seems to be one of those professions which abuse women more readily than others. Maybe it's the hours. Maybe the heavy makeup and the hot lights. Maybe the expectations of the patrons and the owners of the clubs. Travelling is part of the game, and you can't have your managers there with you to protect your best interests every hour of the long days and nights on the road. Or your boyfriends. Or your husbands. And sometimes it is less hassle to go with the flow than to fight it.

The corners of the older dancer's eyes showed a hard cynicism about life and its missed opportunities, and her body went through its moves as if by dull, uninspired rote. An overworked old plough horse in familiar traces, plowing the same old fields in exchange for her daily hay and the occasional new pair of shoes. Given her total contrast to Sweet Cindy, the crowd predictably simmered down. What the older dancer offered in the way of experience and smoothness over the pubescent bubble who had preceded her was more than reversed by her complete lack of luster. After she had completed her obligatory four-dance set, the mandatory cheering contest sent her to the shower. She didn't even feign any surprise.

Brandy continued to keep one eye on the still-closed black door, but no one passed through it in either direction. The old stripper had dried herself and gathered a short robe around her, and slipped back into her spike-heeled sandals. Alone on the stage she piled and gathered her blanket, her towel, and the remaining parts of her costume into her arms to step carefully from the stage, out of reach of any alcohol-inspired customers who might want to handle what only their eyes had touched. The spacer music, slightly lower in volume than what was played during the sets, clanked forward in a heavy-bass pulse designed to bring the wallets forth, to make the booze flow, and allow time for the sexual frustrations to be converted to cravings for the over-greasy, overpriced food from the club's kitchen. Four of the T-shirt-clad waitresses scurried forth, right on cue, to gather in the orders.

Brandy's belly was in knots. It had been almost half an hour since Julia had gone off with the Bouncer. Just when Brandy was about to launch his contingency plan to make an Irate Boyfriend scene, the black door opened. A giant hulk of a man emerged, followed by the Bouncer who'd taken Julia into the room and another strong-arm type whom Brandy hadn't seen yet. The door closed firmly. So where was Julia?

The big man was large in all visible dimensions. He looked like a human balloon which had been overfilled with air so that it was evenly overstretched. The clothes were well fitted to the bulk, but were of the same Big Man In Cheapside fashion which the Bouncer was wearing. There was a panther's watchful aggressiveness in his eyes as he surveyed the customers in the club on his way along the passage toward the main floor. A cigar glowed between the fingers of his left hand. The big man had to be Earl Lesyk.

Brandon stood up next to his stool for a better view of the black door off the passage. A waitress stepped up beside him. "Something else to drink?" she asked. Brandy glanced at her. Back at the door. The big man was approaching the steps to the floor of the club and a table was being cleared near the stage for him. He moved with a certain economy of motion, but showed a surprising agility as he surged up the few steps.

"Yes," Brandy replied to the waitress, still watching the black door. "I'll have another dark draft. Say, isn't that

Earl down there?"

"Mr. Lesyk? Why yes. You a friend of his?"

"Uh, yes. An old friend. I heard he owned this place, but I never expected to actually see *him* here."

"Yeah. He's here most nights. You want I should . . .?"

"No, no. I'll go talk to him later. Maybe after a few more sets. Better surprise that way. Does he usually stay for the whole evening?"

"Not usually. He pretty much leaves the closing down of the place to Greggie Tyler. 'Cept when new girls are being tried out or something. But it's hard to say. With Mr. Lesyk, you never know. Greggie's the manager. The guy sittin' next to him down there."

"Right. Thanks."

Brandon sat back down on the stool and looked all around the club. What the hell had happened to Julia? He was in a real bind. Decided to wait until the distraction of the next set was underway and then go have a talk with the bartender.

He was constructing his story when the D.J. announced, "A real treat, ladies and gentlemen. A real treat. Monday night is our usual amateur night, but tonight Mr. L. has decided to give you a special treat. She's Sally Forth, an exotic dancer all the way from little Waco, Texas. Sally *just* got into town and it seems she's one cowgirl who's just r'aring to go! So let's have a big hand for a lady going to show you how they dance in Texas!"

The volume knob was turned up and a raunchy rapper tune crunched its way into every corner of the room as a costumed dancer skipped along to dump a big red imitation fur rug at the edge of the stage next to the stairs. As she pulsed her way up the steps onto the stage in time with the music, Brandy realized that the woman hiding behind the considerable poundage of makeup was Julia.

Thirty-Four

The fit of the costume wasn't bad for a hasty borrow, and she carried it with a model's familiarity. The effect of electric Julia on a stripper stage was spell-binding.

The background noise in the whole room was hushed. Even the tinkle of glasses behind the bar was temporarily suspended as the employees watched the newcomer. Rapper music in space, Julia in the middle. Her moves were good and fresh, her manner both coy and seductive. The hush of the crowd soon turned to appreciative cheers and howls and by the end of the first song in the set she had the whole house with her. By this time she had dropped her red sequined dance dress to reveal the line of her full breasts and beautiful hips clad in a next-to-nothing bikini.

Lesyk raised an eyebrow as the two men with him at his table muttered what seemed to be compliments about the new talent on stage. He sucked on his forefinger as he watched Julia, and Brandy noticed that the big man had occasionally to rearrange himself in his seat for comfort.

Sexy Julia. Crazy Julia.

As Brandy focused on Julia's sensuous dancing, she continued stripping to the second, slower number. He realized that her slow nods as she looked up at him through the veil of bright lights and smoke were the signal she'd promised. He was supposed to leave now to go to Lesyk's house to search it. Right now.

Part of him wanted to seize the opportunity which Julia had created, to zip to Redondo and search the home and trailer. But another part of him was reluctant to leave Julia until the end of the dance set, reluctant to leave her unchaperoned and unprotected. That part of him said to sit tight until he was sure everything was under control.

Brandy gritted his teeth and pursed his lips tightly in frustration. No question about it. The dilemma was more complicated than it should have been. What Brandy had first seen in silhouette in the rented cabin at Yosemite, and which he had enjoyed and savored to the fullest all last night and this morning, was now going on display to the customers of East L.A. Brandy felt himself reacting in a clearly proprietorial way. At the very least, part of him had to stay here to . . . to *protect* her, for god's sakes. And then what? Was he going to hang around until she was safely out of this den? And then try to explain to her why he had not trusted her to be able to look after herself while she set him up to do the job they had come to L.A. to do? The Lady or the Tiger. Damn!

Brandy closed his eyes long enough to avoid the animal distraction. Julia had called the shot on this one, and Brandy should now take care of the search. Let her take care of her own setup, all by herself. Right.

With difficulty, Brandy pried himself away from his seat, put down enough to cover the bill, including the new, untouched beer, and slipped toward the stairs to the foyer before the second dance was finished. In his intense concentration on Julia, Brandy had not noticed that the Bouncer had left Big Earl's table to return to his station at the top of the stairs which led down to the club entrance.

The Bouncer saw Brandy approaching and flashed a mean grin. Brandy burrowed his head and prepared to go right on past him, but the Bouncer stepped to the side to block the exit.

"What's your hurry, Jack?" he rasped loudly. "I'll bet your girlfriend looks real good without any clothes on."

Drake strained against his inclinations, strained to maintain an expressionless face and an even tone of voice. "I'm sure she does. Now please get out of my way."

"Oh, really? A little sore, huh? You wouldn't want to leave before she gets to the best part, would you? Man, I'm gettin' a hard-on just thinking about it. I think you should go back to your seat and watch the customers enjoy her some. Don't want to be too selfish about it, do we? You ain't goin' *anywhere* yet!"

He grabbed the sleeve of Drake's shirt at the shoulder to spin him, but Brandy's reaction was aikido instinctive. His left hand snapped to the Bouncer's closed fistful of fabric while the heel of his right came up hard to control the man's elbow. The Bouncer swung round with a right hook, but Brandy smoothly applied a wrist-locking nikkyo so that as the Bouncer's punch came around the leverage was multiplied against his own arm. In the fraction of a second in which Brandon was supposed to have gotten a broken jaw, the Bouncer gasped in surprise and collapsed to his knees in pain instead. Because he'd been standing at the top lip of the stairs when he intercepted Brandy, the Bouncer lost his footing as he went down, and tumbled down the five steps onto the foyer floor.

He rolled over onto his feet, coming up on the attack as Brandy arrived at the bottom of the steps to meet him. There was no one else in the foyer. All attentions in the club above them were riveted to Julia's act on stage. The Bouncer lunged forward, this time grabbing onto Brandy's lapels with his left hand to get the best leverage for his straightarm right punch. Brandy stepped aside, latching onto the incoming left hand, spinning nimbly around to keep the heavier man off-balance. As the Bouncer spun around to try to connect with his flailing right fist, Brandy stepped back and folded the left hand over itself in a classic kotogaeshi technique which sent the Bouncer crashing to the carpet. Brandy held on to the controlling left hand and immobilized the Bouncer with a standing pin of his arm, so that Brandy's weight was free to bear against the Bouncer's shoulder joint.

The Bouncer was in a spitting rage. The more he struggled against the arm lock, the more it hurt him. His sounds weren't words, but more like hisses and gurgles.

"You've made a mistake, asshole," Drake commanded, maintaining his low, even tone and a crystal clear enunciation. "You say one more derogatory word about my lady-friend, and I'll see to it that you aren't fit to sell pencils for a living."

"You got a lucky break on me, you sonofabitch," the Bouncer growled, his cheek pressed into the dirty carpet as he tried to speak. "If I hadn't slipped up there at the top of the steps . . ."

"Then we'd be having this little conversation up there where everyone could see you, instead of down here," Drake interrupted.

The Bouncer gave a great twist to break loose, and the agonizing effect on his shoulder was recorded in his distorted face. When he caught his breath, the Bouncer demanded, "You let me up, you bastard, or I'll call George."

"Great idea! I'll bet a club bouncer who can't manage to toss out a lone patron really gets promoted fast, right?"

The Bouncer groaned.

Brandon glanced across to make sure his exit to the door to the street was clear. "I'll be back to pick up my lady a little later. And when I do, I want you to address her as 'ma'am' and me as 'sir'. Got it?"

The Bouncer grimaced, gave another deep-throated growl and spat, "If I see you again, Motherfucker, I'm gonna . . ." Drake leaned against the Bouncer's extended arm and the man gasped again. "Okay, okay . . ." he groaned.

"Sir . . ." Brandy corrected.

"Sir," the Bouncer agreed reluctantly.

"That's better. Thanks for the hospitality."

By the time the Bouncer pushed himself to his feet and looked around, Brandon had disappeared through the front door, and the Bouncer wasn't sure he really wanted to chase him anyway.

Brandy rolled his eyes and shook his head as he sped in the rental car toward Redondo Beach. There had been no planning of whether he should return for her after the search. Or would she take a cab? Should he meet her back at the hotel? Julia, Julia.

It was probably a stupid move, dropping the Bouncer, but Brandy couldn't handle the combination of the comments about Julia and the physical assault. Now the Bouncer could report to his boss about how Waco Sally's irate boyfriend became unpleasant and had to be escorted to the door. It might be something Julia could use to her advantage to occupy Big Earl for an hour or so longer. It was academic, now, anyway, Brandy reminded himself. Water over the dam. Right.

There was some clever Breaking and Entering to be done. But all Brandy could see in his mind's eye was that the final dance was just beginning and Sally Forth would by now be dancing completely naked for all those "ladies and gentlemen" to admire and lust after her body. "Hey, everybody! How about sending Waco Sally to the shower. Hey! She won't go without some help, will she? Let's hear some noise if you want the Texas Baby to get *wet*!" Big Earl probably had special plans for Waco Sally. Any other woman, Brandy would have probably been worried about. But Julia was different. Crazy woman. It was almost too much. But from his brief exposure to this lady, he had every reason to believe that she would walk away unscathed. That she would arrive back at the hotel about the same time he did. Her plan had certainly worked so far. Crazy woman.

Thirty-Five

Brandy stopped the car less than a block from Earl's house. It was completely dark outside. He donned thin gloves, picked up his tool bag from the afternoon shopping expedition, and walked along the street in front of Earl's house. There were no lights on in either house or trailer.

At the front door of the house, Brandy rang the doorbell. A dog was loose inside. Big, judging by the bark. A Doberman, probably. Earl seemed the type. Brandy rang again. No humans reported, and no neighbors responded to the racket. They were probably inured to it. After the third insistent series of rings brought no more than growls and snarls on the other side of the heavy door, Brandy unwrapped a canine offering of raw hamburger from the plastic ziplock bag in his pocket and laced it with the contents of two capsules of a sedative. If he correctly guessed the dog's weight, the animal would become drowsy enough to sleep through the inspection of the house. If the dog were still active when he returned from the search of the trailer in a few minutes, Brandy could deliver another dose by the same route.

Brandon dispensed the offering through the mail slot carefully, so as to avoid adding his fingers to the tastiness of the raw meat. He heard the dog sniffing and then chomping at the medicated feast. Brandy headed for the trailer with a wry smile. That was one thing they could almost *never* train a guard dog *not* to do.

From the edge of the wooden front porch which stood propped up against the raised trailer, Brandy employed the simplest of tools to pry open the window screen next to the front door. He reached through the screen and unlatched the door. Once inside, he was engulfed with the sealed stench of mustiness, dustiness, and rotting food. The small propane refrigerator was propped open with a piece of scrap trim veneer, to air out. An open box of wooden matches lay on its side between the stove and the refrigerator, matches spilled on the countertop behind. There were small clusters of unwashed plastic dishes distributed across the countertops of the kitchenette area between piles of boxes and papers. Moldy dishes also filled the small sink, with months-old dried food caked onto most of them.

By the light of his small flashlight, powered with fresh longer-lasting non-rechargeables, Brandy began a methodical search of the trailer. He held the flashlight in his mouth, interrupting periodically to snuff its glow by pressing it tightly to his shirt while he surveyed through the windows for any activity on the nearby driveway.

The boxes in the kitchen were from Phil's Yosemite cabin, likely. They had just recently been added to the dust-and-grime-covered contents of the trailer. The second box through which Brandy pawed held a jumble of papers and letters, most addressed to the Mountaineering Shop.

At the bottom of this box were several batches of photos of young, lifeless girls in strained poses, grotesque caricatures of sexuality. The poses were self-consciously and embarrassingly unsexual, and it was difficult to imagine why anyone would want to photograph them, much less keep them. There were no negatives and there were small, odd numbers of photos in each envelope, as if they were excerpted from larger collections.

One of the most recent sets in the box, judging by the condition of its envelope, was in quite a different league from the others. These photos featured a thin, blonde, blue-eyed woman whose distracting good looks were obvious in spite of the poor lighting and setting in which she had been photographed. It was unquestionably Annie's friend Chrissie, and she had been filmed through a big bedroom bay window of some cabin. It wasn't Annie's place, and Brandy couldn't be sure, but he guessed it was Cam's house. In spite of the acute angle and the fuzziness imparted by the telephoto lens, her partner was unmistakably male, and unmistakably Farmer Hobbs.

Even the poor resolution of the photos could not mask the reality that in pose after pose, Farmer and Chrissie were making the most passionate love. Part of the series was shot by incandescent light and part of it was shot in candlelight, presumably using a very special and sensitive film.

A headlight swept by on the street in front of Earl's house. Brandy cupped his flashlight quickly and scrambled to the nearest window. The car passed by. So far, so good, but he was reminded of the need for haste.

Brandy worked his way down the trailer's short hallway and into the bedroom at its end. The room stank, a musky odor of cheap cologne and never-washed bedclothes. Brandy grimaced as his olfactory memory registered the cologne as the one Phil had worn in the shop. The living confer ironic memorial to the departed.

The double bed was unmade, and the sheet grimy

and tangled with a holey spread. At one corner where the bottom sheet had pulled back, the mattress showed large splotches of dark stain on the basic yellow-brown discoloration of body oil, perspiration, and dirt. A sliding closet door of aluminum-framed veneer tilted askew from its broken hinge, revealing bent hangers and a few poorly hung clothes. A pile of dirty laundry bulged out from the bottom half of the closet. A small chest of drawers stood half open nearby. The stench of the disturbed filth was magnified as Brandy poked through the debris.

Wads of Kleenex, dirty socks, and scraps of paper were scattered about beneath the edge of the bed and around the night table. In the small drawer of the night table fastened to the wall next to the bed lay one of Phil's special treasure troves. Assorted foil wrappers sported many colors and textures of condoms, and a big jar of Vaseline, sans lid, still bore the grooved impressions of anxious finger-swipes. There were assorted old photos, polaroids, and cutouts from magazines. Phil's bedtime browsing.

Most of the photographic material was well dog-eared, and Brandy noticed that over half of the collection featured Chrissie. Some of the magazine clippings were professional climbing shots taken by a commercial photographer for the Yosemite Park concessions. They had been carefully cut from advertising and promo literature. The special attractiveness of Chrissie was clear in these photos. In the middle of the drawer was folded a homemade cut-and-paste collage, featuring Chrissie lying naked, except for the climbing boots and ubiquitous chalk bag, on a ledge high on a granite face. The graininess of the shots suggested they had been the combined efforts of a very high magnification lens and a lot of darkroom blowup work. The pictures were totally unposed, so it appeared that she was climbing *au naturel*. Brandy was impressed. This group represented work which was really not bad quality stuff. He clenched his teeth as he reflected grimly on the obvious phrase: a labor of love.

For a brief moment, Brandy could almost understand Phil Lesyk's obsession with Christine Peacock. She was as lanky and flat-contoured as Annie was buxom and hippy, but very graceful and *very* beautiful.

At the very bottom of the drawer of the bedside table, there were two more relatively recent, unposed photos of Chrissie and Farmer Hobbs. One had been shot in the valley village, right in front of the Mountaineering Shop. The other picture was a telephoto taken from the woods, looking into the same house Drake had seen in the kitchen box, presumably Cam's house. Farmer was naked and barely recognizable because of the angle. Each of these photos had a large, red feltpen scrawl, a big red "X" marked over the image of Farmer. The message, like the evidence, was obvious.

Brandon closed the drawer and moved to a tiny window in the hallway from which he could scan outside for activity. Still clear.

He quickly but unfruitfully searched the bathroom and a small storage area which had probably originally been intended as another bedroom. In this room had been piled empty suitcases and old sports equipment: skis, racquets, a dismembered bicycle. Brandy was backing carefully through the junk when he spied a set of narrow wooden shelves near the door. On the middle one, beneath the hulk of a small television with a broken screen, was wedged an old manual Underwood typewriter. Brandy pulled aside the television and lifted the typewriter carefully away from its ledge to inspect it. He gently pushed the letter "E" and lifted the die. The final indictment: the lower case "e" was set on a tilt which matched the slant of the e's in the letter Annie had faxed Brandy.

There seemed to be plenty of evidence in the trailer to suggest Phil's involvement in the murders of Farmer and

Chrissie, but with Phil already dead, such an investigation could only hurt Annie.

Drake returned to the boxes in the kitchen, wondering if the search were worth continuing. A box of financial books sat atop the propane stove next to the sink. Thumbing quickly through the contents of accounting books and financial records, Brandy was struck by the cryptic entries which filled them.

He reached for his reading glasses, but they weren't in his pants pockets. Damnation. What a time to be without them. The financial script was quite readable when held at arm's length, but it still annoyed him to have been unprepared for such a problem. The entries were readable; they didn't make any sense, but they were readable.

Accountant mentality took over. Brandy looked at the categories of entries. He wondered why the Accounts Receivables and the Salary and Expenses payout items for the Mountaineering Shop should have been entered into the ledger without clear identification. As an accountant he had been accustomed to people using some level of shorthand for their frequently entered account categories, but this ledger was nothing but three-letter codes! Brandy looked through several of the books for some sort of decoding legend, but found none. Very peculiar.

The handwriting looked like Phil's, and Phil had seemed a basically simple person, so the code was probably fairly simple, too. On a hunch, Drake checked through the "Expenses" section of one of the older ledgers. If the entry codes were initials of people paid, then Annie's should be among them. She said she had earned some coin in the Mountaineering Shop, off and on. She might be AB for Annie Bentley, or ABC if she were using Cruikshank, or ABG if she were using Gordon.

Sure enough, there were sporadic entries for ABG in the '76 to '79 period, but there was nothing after 1979. The books spanned a period from '72 until a few days before Phil's death.

Drake performed a few simple calculations and realized that the Salary entries alone amounted to nearly a quarter of a million dollars during 1987. He checked back to the 1978 ledger and discovered that salaries during that year amounted to nearly $650,000! For a Mountaineering Shop in Yosemite?

Brandon's curiosity was further piqued. The most active years were 1976-1985. And the Expenses were more than double the Salaries in almost every year. Toward the end of one of the first ledgers was a list of foreign countries and category entries for expenses associated with each country. Mexico, Thailand, Burma, India, Switzerland, Turkey, Morocco.

Brandy stared at the list, and then something clicked. These weren't the accounting books for the Mountaineering Shop at all. These were the accounting books for the Pipeline!

His heart pounding with the excitement of the discovery, Brandy rifled through the ledger containing the most recent entries. There had been very few expenses and salaries paid during the past two years, and only three different sets of initials were featured during the past year. The only one of those which meant anything to Brandy was JCL. But why? What possible switches could have been jiggled by those initials?

Brandy squinted into the flashlight halo and tried to mobilize the neurons to find out what was so recognizable about JCL. He ran through the list of names Annie had given him related to the Pipeline, but everything came up blank.

He flipped to the cover page of the previous ledger hoping to glean something further, wondering if there was any advantage in continuing here. Maybe he should take the ledgers and go directly to the Feds, or maybe it would be smarter to take a chance on leaving them here, in hopes of implicating Earl Lesyk more deeply in the crackdown.

The discovery of the Pipeline books was absorbing. Too absorbing. Perhaps if a dog had been awake in the main house, it might have barked to warn of someone's approach. But the dog was peacefully sleeping off its sedative snack.

Thirty-Six

Brandy stood at the counter in the kitchen, pawing through the papers in one of the stacked boxes, his mouth cramping with the unaccustomed effort of holding the flashlight. He heard a creaking sound behind him, from the front door, and at the same instant that the light was flicked on inside the trailer, a deep, smooth, fast-speaking basso voice boomed, "You pick some mighty odd bedtime reading, shitface."

Brandy snatched the flashlight from his teeth and tucked low to a defensive posture as he spun around, but it was too late. The big man was part-way though the door, and when the pistol in his hand cracked sharply, Brandy was slammed hard in the left shoulder by its small caliber bullet and thrown back across the top edge of the countertop.

Big Earl's voice remained even in intonation and pace, as if it were a casual and negligible matter that he'd just shot a man. "You try anything like that again, shitface, and I`ll fuckin' kill you outright."

Brandy peeled his right hand away from his left

shoulder slowly and saw that it was covered with blood.

"Raise your hands up high now, shitface. You ain't gonna bleed to death."

Brandy lifted his hands as ordered. His collar bone didn't seem to be broken, but the lancing pains in his neck and left shoulder were tremendous.

Something must have gone wrong with Julia's plans.

Earl squeezed himself the rest of the way through the small front door. The tiny wall lamp inside the front door flickered uncertainly and the big man reached up to steady it by tapping it with the back of the same hand in which he held his cigar. Cigar ash snowed down as the dim light steadied.

"You must be that Drake fella," Earl said, without any doubt in his voice. "I figured if I sat tight long enough you'd show up. Now supposin' you just tell me what the fuck you're doin' here, breakin' into my trailer and lookin' through my things."

Brandy watched how casually Earl held the pistol, and wondered if the direct shoulder hit had been just a fluke. Drake had long ago learned that anyone who shoots you once will, unless he's wearing a badge, probably do so again soon, if he's provided an opportunity. Earl fiddled with the light a bit longer. At its best, the small, faded, yellowed lampshade permitted passage of only the most hideous light to the dark recesses of the grimy trailer.

Brandy glanced down beside him among the litter of dirty plastic dishes on the chipped formica top of the kitchen counter and spied one heavy, once-white, thick porcelain coffee mug lined with brown stains of long-since evaporated dregs. He estimated the distance to the coffee mug, and the distance to where Earl stood. The range was right, and though Brandy didn't like the odds, he guessed they wouldn't get better with time. There was something about this guy. Annie had called it right. He was one of the mean ones.

"I suggest you go ahead and call the police," Brandy bluffed, as casually as his fear and the pain in his shoulder allowed. "They already know I'm here, anyway."

A neighbor's dog barked a quick salvo. Earl leaned back to cast a glance out at the driveway, through the ripped screen next to the door.

Drake took advantage of the distraction, seized the coffee mug, and hurled it at Earl's head.

Some fat men lumber, and some are quick. This one was quick. Earl skilfully ducked the ceramic projectile, but it was so thick that rather than shattering on the laminate wall behind him, next to the door, it ricocheted and careened into the dim lamp. The lampshade started a one-and-a-half gainer to the floor and, with a tinkle of bulb-glass, the room blanked out.

Drake threw himself low, toward the tiny dinette table, twisted and rolled to draw the most inaccurate pops from the pistol. The flashes from the muzzle made horrible fireworks, and each one sounded like someone with a large industrial broom stick was whapping it at random on walls and counters around the room.

Drake heard three reports before the one that got him. In mid-lunge toward the last spit of fire from the gun, in his surge to knock the weapon from Lesyk's hand, Brandy's world took a wrenching spiral twist in the opposite direction and his feet went out from under him. The bullet had only grazed the side of his skull, but on his way down Brandy's head cracked into the edge of something hard. He saw a complete spectacle of stars and white light and then he lay on the floor and wondered who had won. He tried to move his arms, but nothing worked.

Another dim light went on over the sink. "Boy, you are just plain dumb unlucky, that's what you are," said the huffing basso voice, wherever he was. As Brandon's vision began to clear, he could just make out Earl standing over him, the pistol still in one hand as he stooped to pick up something with the other. "Made me drop my ciggie, shitface. I don't appreciate that."

Brandy tried to raise himself to the sitting position. Everything was in slow motion. "Not so fast, there!" Earl boomed again. Brandy saw the side of the automatic pistol coming his way, but he felt powerless to react in time to do anything about it. It hit him in the temple and he crashed to the floor again.

Brandy tried to shake his head to clear it, but it hurt too much when he did that. He tried to sit up again. He wasn't thinking too clearly, but somehow it seemed important to sit up.

"You don't listen too well, do you, shitface?" Earl growled, sounding annoyed. "Guess you need a li'l softenin' up."

With that began a beating which went on for longer than Brandy could consciously keep track of. Inside him, a little voice kept asking "When will that guy just go ahead and kill me? It shouldn't take this long. Aren't there any more bullets in his gun?" Brandon couldn't keep track of where Earl was standing. Every time Brandy tried to lift himself up, he was clobbered in the head. And when he lay still on the floor, he was kicked again and again in his back and his belly and his shoulders, until he would try to raise up to avoid the kicking.

Brandy had been in a few brawls before, but never had he been beaten so relentlessly. He found himself hoping he'd pass out, but guessing that his survival might depend on maintaining a thread of consciousness, no matter how thin it seemed, he tried to hold on. He felt himself losing his grip until all at once, every bell in the world simultaneously clanged, and then everything went still.

It was scary and disorienting. Out of the silence, Brandy became fascinated by the weak background beating of a deep jungle drum. He recognized the rhythm and the timbre. It was just like the sound of his heart. Only slower and weaker. He tried to take a deep breath, but his rib cage felt constricted and horribly sore, as if he were locked inside an iron cast. As the fear returned, the jungle drum quickened. It *was* his heart.

By the time Brandy became aware again of a dim light in the trailer, the tugging pain and restriction of his arms and legs was unbearable. He attempted to open his eyes several times before the internal light show backed off enough for him to make out where he was. He tried to remember if he'd lost consciousness. He tried to take a deep breath, but almost passed out from the sharp pains in his chest and the nauseous smell of some sort of industrial solvent. He strained to focus his eyes on himself and his surroundings, to get a status report. A damage report. Anything.

Brandy tried to move, but he felt completely frozen up. He saw that his shirt and pants had been pulled off and the insides of his calves and thighs and been smeared and stuck together with some sort of glue. Shit! He'd been crazy-glued! His forearms had been lashed to his thighs with multiple wraps of silvered duct tape. Very tightly. His hands, which were held fast against the outsides of his knees, were already starting to turn blue from the compromised circulation.

The situation had too many echoes of the story Annie told him. He hurt all over and he couldn't move. His face was pushed into the kickplate at the base of the ticky-tack particle-board kitchen cabinet below the sink. Somewhere a dog quit barking.

Brandon turned his head to one side as far as possible. When he blinked his eyes he felt the stickiness of a slow-oozing cut somewhere near his eyebrow. If his nose wasn't broken, it was at least so badly battered that it felt twice its normal size and so congested that he couldn't breath through the left side. Maybe blood. The situation was not good.

Brandy could make out the silhouetted hulk of Earl sitting on the edge of a chair which he had turned around from the dinette table. With his free hand he was delicately rolling a fresh cigar in his fingers, licking it all over. When he'd finished the wetting ritual he nipped off the end, spat out the tip, and clenched the fresh cigar heavily between his big jaws. He reached into his pocket, withdrew a lighter, flicked its flame gently back and forth in front of the end of the cigar and sucked heavily to draw flame for lighting it.

Whether a figment of his dazed state or in reality, Brandon couldn't be sure, but Earl seemed to be weaving his pistol through the air with the same motion used by a symphony orchestra conductor during an adagio. Earl began huffing in slow rhythm through his cigar so that for each huff, the cigar tip glowed red beneath the nerd of ash.

Earl noticed Brandy's movement and said slowly, "I guess we can talk a little easier now, can't we, shitface?"

Brandy kept silent. Earl stepped over him carefully, and kicked Brandy squarely in the kidney from behind. The sharpness of the kick knocked Brandy's breath out with a cough.

"Speak up, compadre! Haven't got too much time before I have you hauled outa here!"

Brandy tried to roll over to look up at Earl, but was too restricted by the bonds of duct tape and glue. The smell of the glue was almost as strong as the smell of the cigar. Earl stepped over Brandon again and flicked ash on him.

Brandy squinted up at the big man, who continued to weave the air between them with the pistol. It was only a Saturday Night Special, but it obviously had enough oomph to put a hole in a shoulder and a nasty gash somewhere on the side of Brandy's skull. It felt like the second bullet had nipped just above the top of his ear, but Brandy couldn't be sure what was bullet and what was from the fall and what was from the pistol whipping.

"I expect us to be interrupted soon," Brandon croaked, "unless I report in to a certain LAPD lieutenant within the next hour or so. You've got some explaining to do."

"Cut the crap. The police don't even know you're in town."

"You're sure of that?"

"Pay a certain radio clerk a lot of good cash to be sure of everything the LAPD knows and does, sweetheart. And Li'l Suzie performs real well for us 'cuz she knows what happened to the last pair of ears when there was a screwup. It's an expensive service, but it pays. And it's a must-have item, in my business."

"The nightclub business or smuggling?" Brandon asked, bluntly. His situation was beginning to come home to him. It had moved from being terrifyingly unreal to terrifyingly real. He had to do something to shock Earl, to keep him talking, to play for time. If there was any chance at all of rescue, it depended on Julia sending the police to Earl's. Brandy wondered where she was, and when she would figure out that it was time to call for reinforcements. Meanwhile, he had to keep Earl talking and he had to radiate enough confidence for Earl to keep wondering what else Brandy knew.

Earl frowned and then sighed and relaxed. He chewed and rolled his fresh cigar between his teeth from one corner of his mouth over to the other before he answered, "Both." Earl's breathing had steadied. The effort of the beating had taken its toll on him, too. Precious little consolation.

Earl stared at Brandon for a long minute. "You sure seem to know a lot more than I thought you would, Drake."

"I don't think you understand, Lesyk. You've lost the

ball game. Your overpaid informant at LAPD messed you up on the Federal side. And they sent me to find out more about Phil and the climbing murders. That was something we couldn't understand."

"You pretending you're a Fed now, ace? I'm supposed to believe the Feds would hire a Canadian?"

"I'm not working *for* them. I'm working *with* them."

"And I'm supposed to go light on you because of that?" Earl chuckled.

"No. You're supposed to understand that it's all over. And you don't need to piss them off with another killing. You do that and they might bring back executions especially for you."

"Cute. First off, I wanna know what makes you think Brother Phil had anything to do with any murders."

Brandy was so badly beaten that he hurt at any attempt at movement against the tape and the glue. The side of his head was jammed hard against the bottom edge of the baseboard. It was everything he could do not to let himself be consumed by panic.

"We know he did it," Brandy declared. "What we haven't figured is the motive. Was it supposed to have been a Pipeline hit? And if it was, why Farmer and Chrissie?"

"You want to know about that, do you?" Big Earl puffed on his cigar and flicked ash on the table. He didn't seem to be in any hurry. "Well, it don't matter none now, anyway. It was a mistake. One big, dumb move. Phil, god love the perverted sonofabitch, had a real thing about that skinny blonde bitch. The lesbo. Shacked up with your friend, the dumpy climber broad up in the Sierra. But I guess you knew all that, didn't you? Saw the dumpy one a few days ago. Jeez, I don't understand why they don't make laws about that kind of shit. Dykes are the lowest thing I know. Lower than queers, even. A real waste. Know what I mean?

"But the climbing accident was a real bind for us. We

couldn't afford to have any police looking too closely at either of us, so I just told Phil to be cool. He'd already called the guy's company out in Canada, or wherever the hell it was the guy was from. Just to be sure he'd got him. I mean, after they couldn't find any bodies, Philly he got just plum freaked out. Know what I mean? Dumb move. Really dumb. And so I told him to cool that, too."

"So what went wrong? Sounds like your brother ignored you, didn't he?"

"My brother was okay. He did the best he could, bless him."

"Trying to kill two more people and then getting himself killed? Is that your idea of being cool? What happened?"

"You asking *me* what happened?" Earl huffed angrily on his cigar. "That's rich! Best I can piece together, *you* killed Philly, you sonofabitch. He called me right after you and the widder of that climber came into the shop. He musta' followed her to the other side of the village after you left his shop. Phil was like that. Saw a nice piece of tail and he'd just track on her. Brazen bastard. All he usually got to drill on was the young stuff, but you had to give him credit for tryin'. Hell, he'd have hit on the Queen of England if she'd turned his crank.

"Seems he recognized the widder's name on a credit card slip she left at some village store. He sure as hell was shook up about it. He musta nearly puked he was so shook. So he called and told me about it. About the wife of the dead guy being there and all. Said he couldn't figure out why you two were in the valley, giving false names and some cockamamie line about being married and interested in climbing and so on. Didn't make sense. He was worried maybe you knew something. He'd been plenty worried already since three months when the guy's body never showed up. It was spooky like, for him. Poor, dumb Phil."

Earl took another drag on his cigar and then asked Brandy, "So, tell me, did he ever know he'd killed the blonde bitch too? Or did you kill him before he found out?"

Even in his compromised state, Brandon reacted viscerally to the accusation. "I didn't kill him, friend. I didn't even know he was up on the mountain until a week later when they found him. But putting a few things together with what you've just told me, it's more than a casual guess that he tried to bring the mountain down on *us*. By getting above us on the trail and rolling a few boulders down through the switchback walls onto us. He could have expected to make our murders look like another accident. He was big on the 'planned accident' concept, wasn't he? Maybe he slipped, or maybe the ground shifted and gave way beneath him."

Earl snorked to clear his nose and, without making any attempt to take his perpetual cigar from his mouth, spit a big mucous wad onto the grimy lino squares of the floor beside the table. "Shit. You're lying through your fuckin' teeth."

"I've got no reason to lie."

"Coulda been like you say. Another dumb move on Phil's part. But it coulda been another way, too. Maybe you had an argument with him up there on the mountain and twisted him around a little. You're a lanky hoser, but you also kinda look like you could be pretty tough from time to time, maybe. And Phil scared easy. So I figure it you cornered Phil and threatened to bash his head in, and he spills what he knows about our Pipeline operation to save his skin. You already know the dumpy lesbo. Right? The one who used to carry. So it fits for me that you might have tried to squeeze Phil, once you see he had something to do with killing the climber guy."

"It might make sense. But it didn't happen that way. I didn't know anything at all about your courier outfit until later. We think your brother was just so blown away to discover he'd killed *two* people, especially the girl he had such a big obsession with, that he panicked."

Earl raised the barrel of the pistol and pointed it at the center of Brandy's chest. Brandy could hear the whistle of a freight train many miles away. God knew where. Earl sneered and waited to see how Brandon reacted to the scare. "You're an unlucky fucker, you know that? But you got guts, too. Real staying power."

"What did you expect me to do now? Say goodbye and walk out the door?"

Earl grinned again and lowered the pistol. "You're right about one thing. Phil must've had one helluva surprise when he found out they was *two* of 'em died in that climb. He never said nothing about killing the girl, and I don't think he woulda done her on purpose, so I guess it was another screwup. Fact is, first time he told me about it, it was right here in this trailer, one night he was falling-down-drunk, and he was bragging how he'd set this guy up for climbing alone by telling him about how Miss Skinny Blonde couldn't have no respect for a pussy-assed climber who didn't take no chances like climbin' alone. Actually I was kind of glad he got into a jam when they couldn't find the body. Cause the longer it went, the scareder he got. He stopped braggin' about much. He was real close-mouth for the whole summer after that. Best coupla months me and Phil ever had. But then when he finds out about his blonde lesbo, I'll bet he just came to pieces. Some kind of screw-up, all right. But you didn't have to go and kill him."

"Lesyk . . . think about it. If I'd killed him, why the hell would I be here now?"

"To put the squeeze on *me*. I know you been asking some questions about me and Phil. You see, I got the kind of connections to follow the trail back to you." He sucked on his cigar and let a thick cloud of smoke slowly plume up around his head. "Via San Francisco," he added, carefully

measuring the response in Brandy's eyes. "That's right. You
think you got a lot of friends, don't you? But not as many as
Big Earl. That slick dick in Mill Valley was some kind of hero
type. If he'd have come home a little later, maybe he coulda
told us what we wanted, but the way he comes chargin' in,
guns ablazin', or so they told me, they didn't have no choice
but to drop him and to torch the place. Only they gave me a
call and read me the names from a personal phone book
they lifted before they torched the place. They only had to
go as far as 'D' and . . . Bingo! Your name struck a mighty
fat coincidence from the list of people signed up for climbing
lessons at the shop that day Phillie bought the farm."

Brandon reflected glumly that Earl was not as dumb
as might have been hoped. But he seemed to be on a talk-
talk streak, and Brandy had to keep him going. More time,
better chances.

Earl tapped his forehead with the thick middle finger
of his right hand. "I got a good memory for names, y'know."
He grinned. "Nobody was at your apartment up there in
Canada today," he continued, "so I'm wondering what the
fuck you was up to. It was real sour for me all day today 'til I
guessed you was probably coming this way.

"See, on this Pipeline shit we were smart enough to
quit while we were ahead," Earl explained. "But I almost had
to strong-arm Phil to keep him from setting it up all over
again. He was a little too greedy. Anyway, after we retired
from the courier business, we didn't need no attention to
what it was we used to do."

"So now there are all kinds of things going wrong.
Why don't you just flick it in?"

"Meanin' what?"

"The screw-up with Badger Beeley was a bad mistake.
Because you've got a big problem now. That's what got me
together with the Federal people this morning."

"Look, shitface, you can quit with that bullshit,

because I don't believe a word of it. If you was chummy with the Feds we'd be swimmin' in spotlights and tear gas now, so just knock it off."

"Believe what you want, but the temperature is getting a tad too high here for you. Me alive you cannot afford. But explaining me dead is even tougher."

"Stiffs don't talk about much worth explainin', ace. So I don't plan on worrying about it."

"And how are you planning to explain what a Canadian investigator is doing here at your place? The police will ask a lot of nasty questions about that, won't they?"

"Maybe it's not so bad. I figure I got a way to turn any kind of lemons into lemonade. Hell, the way I see it, if you hadn't of started nosing around, I mighta been caught with my pants down. Maybe you done me a hell of a favor."

"So what now?"

"The plan I liked best was I just put you right out of action and do what I shoulda done last week when I come back from the mountains with all these little boxes of letters and pornie pix Brother Phillie saved. I stick 'em in my car and I drive out into the desert where I have a little bonfire and then I bury the ashes. Then I come back and arrive just in time to see the big fireworks." He grinned. A hateful grin. "And the official story goes like this. A burglar breaks into my brother's trailer while I'm at the club. He accidentally sets off a fire from the propane tank behind the stove. Fuckin' explosion to rock the shopping center three blocks over. You know the kind?"

"I can't believe you're that dumb, Earl. How are you going to explain the bullet hole in the corpse? And that the burglar is an information agent from Canada, who just happened to be the guy who was on hand to discover two climbers your brother murdered?"

Earl pushed to his feet, jerking his cigar from his mouth and turning beet-red in the face. "There ain't gonna be no bullet holes, asshole!" he roared. "I'm really a very smart guy. I put together the whole Pipeline show, y'know. When all the others were doing drug running and shit like that. And you can bet on one thing. For sure, there ain't gonna be no evidence to link nobody to nothin'. When the police tell me who you are and ask, my guess is maybe you come here lookin' for something valuable of Phil's. After maybe you killed him in the mountains. Hey, at least they start wonderin' the truth about all that, too. Don't they? Right? After these papers is destroyed, nobody can prove nothin'. It don't matter what they look into. *If* they even identify what's left of you."

"Oh, they will. Because a couple of people already know I'm here."

"Don't count on it. They're taken care of. That Frisco hardnose is already dead, right? And the only other one knows you're here is as good as dead. I've arranged for her to die *real* neat."

Brandy cringed at the news. Wondered what had gone wrong for Waco Sally. Cursed himself for letting her try such a half-baked stunt. "Hey, but you know . . ." Earl squatted back down onto the chair by the curtained window and waved the pistol in Brandon's direction as he continued to plan aloud, "maybe you give me an idea, there. You really set my creative juices to flowing, shitface. Maybe there is a better way to do this. How about you join me when I take my little drive down south into the desert and *that's* where you disappear? I can still have my bonfire and burn all of the papers my dumb brother saved. You see? Lemonade. Shit, if all this hadn't happened, if Phil hadn't tried to zip the climber, and if you hadn't come along, Phil might've been busted again sometime for contributing to the delinquency or something, and that Pipeline shit in his filing cabinets up there in the mountains mighta been discovered and made some state DA real happy. I couldn't believe he still had that shit. I thought it was all long gone until I searched his stuff, but Phillie was always like a packrat for anything he collected."

Earl looked at his wrist watch and muttered to himself, "Now where the fuck *is* that boy?" He shuffled over to stare out the window of the trailer, then shuffled back around to where Drake lay helpless. "Look, I don't have any more time or energies to sit here and shoot shit with you, dickhead. So its time we say adios while I check and see what you did in my house." He ripped a short piece of wide duct tape from a roll --- the same kind of tape he'd used to bind Brandy's ankles --- and slapped it across Brandy's mouth.

A dog nearby started to bark. Earl went back over and peered out the cruddy window again. "Garry?" Earl hissed out toward the driveway. "Garry? Over here. In the trailer."

There was a thumping of boots on the wooden steps, the screen door screaked on its tinny hinges, and the hollow front door swung inward. Whoever it was in the doorway didn't see Brandon lying against the counter until he was all the way in.

"What's goin' on, Boss? What're you doing out here?"

"Playin' with myself. Can't you see? Where the fuck you been? You were just s'posed to take that bitch to her hotel, not to give her a damned sightseeing tour of the city! You been so long, I figured you prob'ly jumped into the box with that peeler and was tryin' to set some kind of new marathon record for humpin' her. So now you can deal with this P.I. dick burglar who thinks he knows something about ol' Phil . . ."

"One of Phil's friends?" Brandy recognized the voice of the Bouncer from the club.

"Not exactly. This guy killed Phil, far as I can tell, and he can't prove different. And he thinks he's some kinda expert on Pipelines, too. Sit your ass down and watch him. I'm gonna go check the house. I want to know if he went through that, too."

Brandy buried his face into the kickplate of the cabinetry, to keep from being recognized.

"For all I know," Earl rambled, "he might have brought somebody with him. My sources say 'no', and I think he's working alone, but I have to find out for sure. If you see anybody or hear anything outside here, just sit tight and get ready to bag 'em when I come back out."

Earl clonked off the porch and headed toward the house. The Bouncer crept through the dim trailer light. He stooped beside Drake and rolled him back from beneath the counter, grabbed him by his belt and flopped him over onto his other side to take a good look at him. "Boss! Hey, Earl!" he shouted.

Heavy footsteps clunked back up to the wooden porch. Earl poked his head in the door, and hissed in a loud whisper, "Jesus, Garry! You trying to wake up the fucking neighborhood? What the hell you want?"

"This is the sonofabitch I was telling you about. The one who hit me from behind and ran out of the club tonight."

Thirty-Seven

The Bouncer glared down at the bound and bloodied victim on the floor of the trailer, and launched a vengeful kick squarely to the center of Brandon's exposed shins. The Bouncer seemed especially delighted by the explosive gasp his kick brought from Brandy's blood-occluded nostril.

"Sorry you're all taped up at the mouth, jackoff. I'd love to hear you *scream* a little!" He turned back to Earl. "This is the guy who came in with that Sally Forth piece."

Earl's mouth dropped open. Then he snapped it shut and screwed up his face and worked the cigar in his mouth as he considered. "Go back and get her!" he ordered.

"The stripper?"

"Yeh. Where'd you take her?"

"To that motel on Beach. The Budget. Only I don't think she was staying there, maybe. It was like she didn't want me to know where she was rooming. Not the first lady I've known to do that, y'know. But she's prob'ly stayin' near there, cause she acted like she recognized the area."

"Go find her. Fast. Too much coincidence them showing up and her tryin' to keep me in irons while this guy goes through my house. I'll stay with him until you get back. Hurry!"

"I'll find her, all right. There are three motels right there together. I'll check them all." The Bouncer glared down at Brandy again. "After I get back, Boss, can I have a few minutes alone with this guy? We have a matter to settle."

"Just get the girl. Get movin'! I don't want her talkin' to nobody."

The Bouncer ran down the driveway. Earl stooped down next to Brandy and yanked the duct tape from most of Brandy's mouth. "What's with the girl?" Earl demanded. "Who is she?"

Brandy remained still. A kick to his kneecaps shot electricity all the way up to his right hip.

"Talk, god damn you!" Earl roared. Through the pain, Brandy took a small pleasure in witnessing Earl losing his cool. Brandy braced for a lot more pain, but without apparent reason Earl suddenly stopped himself and sat down in the plastic-covered dinette chair.

After only a few minutes, there was a noise outside the trailer. Someone shouting. A woman. Brandy tried to signal whoever it was: "Help!" he screamed. "Call the police! Help!"

Earl kicked Brandy hard enough in the chest to knock the breath out of him, and slapped the tape back over his mouth while he was still gasping for air. Earl grabbed the gun from his belt, dowsed the light, and stepped quickly to the door. Beneath his swollen eyelid, Brandy could see Earl's silhouette at the torn screen window, pistol in one hand, his cigar still in his mouth.

The screen door was jerked open from the outside and banged against the wooden handrail of the porch. A thrashing, kicking, tousled mass of Julia Hobbs was propelled through the door, her arm held behind her back, the Bouncer's thick hairy forearm clamped around her neck. She was struggling and trying to shout but she was being throttled so tightly that she couldn't get out any words.

Inside the trailer, Big Earl was still in confusion. "What the . . . ? Where the hell did you find . . . ?"

The Bouncer steered Julia forward into the living room and threw her down onto the couch beyond the door, partially obscured from where Brandy lay in the kitchen. Julia fell to a half-sitting position and grabbed at her throat and gasped for more air and made more choking sounds.

"I didn't have to go far, Boss. I noticed somebody prowlin' around the front of the house when I left, so I stopped the car a little piece up the street and doubled back on foot." Julia, still heaving for air, looked very frightened. "She was lookin' in the back windows over at the house. I almost didn't catch her. She's quick. Damn quick!"

Earl grabbed a big handful of Julia's hair, dragged her to her feet, and jerked her head back so that she was looking right up into his face. "Sally baby! You're just in time. Maybe you can tell us why *he's* here." He jerked her around to see where Brandy lay in his underwear on the lino of the kitchen floor, bruised, bloodied, taped-up, and impotent to do anything but watch them.

Julia let out a shriek when she saw Brandy. Earl jerked hard on her hair, like a dog-owner pulling on his dog's chain. She tried to spin and flail her arms at him, so he cracked her behind the ear with the butt of his pistol. The placement and sharpness of the smack had a clinical precision, and Julia's legs buckled beneath her and the screaming stopped as she sank back to the couch.

"Get smart, girl! Time to start talking!" Earl pulled her to her feet again. She was stunned and confused.

Julia's first few words were slurred, until her head began to clear. "What . . . what are you talking about? . . .

What *is* this?"

"How's about you start talking to me, gal, or we just start thumpin' on you some more until you start makin' sense? Or maybe it'd cut more ice if you got to watch us thumpin' on your boyfriend here instead? Whatever it takes, I'm gonna get a lot better informed in the next few minutes." He switched his cigar to the other corner of his mouth and jammed his face into hers. "Understan', bitch?"

Julia looked from Earl to the Bouncer, who had planted himself squarely in front of the only door. She pointed at Brandy. "Him? Go ahead and thump him. Why should I care what you do to that creep?"

"Funny," Earl said, "but *something* musta brought you here looking for him . . ."

She shook her fist at where Brandy lay on the floor. She played her part well. "Give me a club and maybe I'll *help* you pound him. Guy left me alone at your club. If it hadn't been for you two I woulda had to get home alone."

"So you just happened to come around my house looking to get even with him? That what I'm supposed to believe, Sally? Why do I doubt that?"

"Look, him and me are staying together. When this bouncer of yours drops me off, I find this note in our room saying the guy's coming here, so I . . ."

The Bouncer interrupted. "Here's her wallet, Boss. She musta drove here or taken a cab or something to get back here so fast. Lucky I just seen her there, huh?"

"Sure, Garry. Security is what I'm paying you for, huh?" Earl looked carefully at the Bouncer for the first time since Julia had been brought in. "Why are your arms all tore up like that?"

The Bouncer self-consciously rubbed the scratches and gouges on both of his arms and one side of his face. "She sure put up one hell of a fight 'til I chopped her one!"

Earl rifled through her cards. "Canadian . . . eh?" He

grinned. "You gonna tell me you just met this man here in L.A.? Just coincidence that the two of you comin' all the way from Canada?"

Julia stumbled on her reply. "Uh, no. No, of course not. I met him last week in Vancouver. He, uh . . . he promised me a freebie weekend here. A good time. A real good time. Oh, yeah! Second night here and he takes me to some slum and dumps me in your club." She glared at Drake and hissed. "Buddy, I hope your wife finds out and cuts off your cojones for this one!"

"Nice try, but don't bother, Sally. Or should I call you . . ." Earl drew his head back to focus on the credit card in his hand. "Julia. Let's see . . . Julia what? Julia . . . Hobbs. Hobbs? Shit! No fucking wonder!" Earl directed his attentions entirely to Julia. "Now maybe you're gonna tell me you're the dead climber's mother, sweetheart? Or is that just another coincidence?" Julia stared at him. "What's your game, bitch?"

She stared back silently. Cornered.

"Look, bitch, I'm gonna find out what game you and your loverboy here are playing. So how do you want it? Easy or tough? Doesn't matter to me, 'cause as soon as you tell us what's going on, we'll just cruise on over to your hotel and help you clean up and disappear back to Canada. Come on, baby. Be smart."

Julia took in a deep breath, as if she were about to scream again.

"Eh-eh! No more screamin'," Earl warned her. "It might disturb some neighbors. And it won't help anything, 'cause this is one *well*-insulated trailer. And most of all . . ." he wiped a sweaty hand on his shirt and puffed cigar smoke into her face, "it annoys me!"

"I wouldn't trust her to keep quiet, Boss. I tell you, she's a hell-raiser. I bet she screams again."

Without looking away from Julia's eyes, Earl's face contorted into an ugly distortion of a smile and he said, "No more than once. And then I might just be *so* annoyed, I'd get the urge to just dispose of you and your friend here *real* quick. Get it?"

Julia's voice quavered. She discarded her Southern accent and asked, "How do I know you aren't going to kill us anyway?"

"You don't. But you do know *this*. I'm a mean sonofabitch. And I don't like people breakin' into my house and looking through my things. And if you *don't* do what I'm telling you, I'll guarantee you're *very* dead meat and I mean right fucking now! Both of you! You understand me? As long as you play Big Earl's game, you can stay alive. You do want to live a little longer, don't you? You know . . . hope springs eternal and all that bullshit?"

Earl instructed the Bouncer, pointing his cigar at Brandon, "You stay here and make sure ol' sticky-legs stays put, while I take Sweet Lips here over to the house for a little interview. I don't want them comparing notes any more than they probably have already. Now, don't mess him up. You hear? I didn't know this bimbo was here with him and I'm kinda beginnin' to wonder just how many more people are involved. I'm gonna have to come back over here and talk to him some before I can give him to you. You understand me?"

"Sure Boss. And if you need any help with *her*, Boss," the Bouncer said, licking his lips and crinkling his thick eyebrows in a parody of seduction, "just give a call."

Earl shook his head disgustedly. "I think I can handle her just fine. Just sit down, Garry baby, and take a load off. You can take out your frustrations later, on *him*. But not yet. No screwups. Okay? I want him alive and talkative when I finish with this one. I think he still knows a lot of shit he ain't lettin' on. Anybody comes up to the drive or there's any problem, you let me know fast."

Earl dropped his chewed-on cigar butt to the floor, smeared it out on the linoleum with the heel of his shoe, and hastily relit another one from a case in his pants pocket.

Then, with the suddenness of a snake striking, he snatched a fresh fistful of Julia's frizzy hair, hauled her to her feet, and pulled her along to the door of the trailer. She gasped and squeaked, but withheld any scream. Earl waved his automatic pistol in the air toward the Bouncer. "You got your piece?" The Bouncer groped at the back of his belt and pulled out a snub-nose police special.

Earl pulled Julia's head back and down enough that she had to struggle to get her feet under her, to keep from falling backward into him. "Come on with me, sweet-ass. You were pretty convincing at the club tonight. I'm in the mood for a private performance. Let's see what you can do for ol' Earl." Julia's eyes showed new terror. She pulled back to try to free herself from his grasp, but Earl cuffed her on the ear. He let go of her hair and she spun around, dazed. He grabbed her by the upper arm and spun her around again. She weaved loose in the joints, like a ragdoll learning how to dance. "When Big Earl says 'Come', sweetheart, you gotta learn to move. Come *on* now!" He laughed and pushed her out the door.

The Bouncer sat down next to Brandy and gloated. "I'm sorry you ain't freed up and ready to go a few rounds with me, asshole. But real soon we can settle up for the stuff you slipped by on me down at the club. That some kind of martial arts shit? Never seen it, but it sure came fast."

Brandy tried to sit up. The Bouncer kicked him in the side and knocked him over. "The Boss said not to lay a hand on you, but I don't recall him sayin' nothing about kickin' you."

Someone turned on a stereo over at the house. The volume was turned up. "I seen your eyes when Earl took off with the woman. That wasn't an act, was it? You wanted to kill him for takin' her over to his own cozy bedroom, huh? Shit. And here I thought when you jumped me at the club, you were just pissed off at her. So I guess you musta forgave her for going public tonight, huh? Or was that part of some plan you cooked up to put one over on Big Earl. Which you fucked up, I might point out."

Through the blare of loud music from the house, and through the muffle of the insulated walls of the trailer, there penetrated the awful sounds of a woman being beaten. Pitiful protestations and pleading were followed by thumps and muffled screams. The Bouncer pricked his ears to hear better, and smiled at the pained expressions on Brandy's face. "Sounds like ol' Earl's helping himself to your lady. She'll come around and cooperate real soon. They always do, don't they?"

Brandy wiggled his fingers and twisted his arms against the bonds as surreptitiously as possible, but the Bouncer noticed and laughed. "Go ahead," he growled, leaning forward and shaking the barrel of his pistol at Brandy. "Go for it. Do something spectacular so I can tell the Boss I didn't have no choice in the matter. That I just *had* to blow you away."

The Bouncer grunted and stood up again. "You're in my way, clown, and I wanna take a piss. You're in the way. Sit up and get outta my way."

"Sit up, now, y'hear? You can do better than that. Didn't you hear me? Or did I forget to say 'sir'?" Brandy struggled to sit up again, but with his forearms secured to his thighs, he couldn't quite make it. He hovered unsteadily, chest forward to his knees. The Bouncer stepped across his feet and walked to the bathroom.

Brandy heard a sigh of release as a stream of urine hit the water in the toilet. Hopelessly, Brandy scanned the kitchen area in the dim light. No miracles. No magic. Nothing.

He took a deep breath through his swollen nose and

leaned precariously against the stovefront. The back of his head banged into hard knobs on the stove. Insult to injury. He pushed back against them to straighten himself more and heard a very faint hiss. Damn stovefront gas knobs.

Gas. Gas?

An infinitely long shot. And probably suicidal at best, but in the absence of *real* choices, foolish choices begin to seem tenable. All Brandy could think of was that he had to stop whatever was going on over there inside Big Earl's house. The thumping had desisted but the music continued to blare. Brandy didn't know if that was better news or worse. He leaned back against one of the knobs and waited for several minutes to let as much gas into the trailer as he could.

The music paused between numbers.

Brandy pushed up hard with his head against the gas valve, uncertain whether he could turn it enough to lock it in an "on" position. He leaned forward and the hissing stopped.

With a flush and a clunk of a seat top, the Bouncer churned back down the short hallway, zipping as he came. He walked directly to the door and used the barrel of his gun to push the loose screen aside for a clearer peek through the window toward the house.

Music began again. Bump and grind bass. Brandy pushed back again and twisted himself to try to get a different angle of pressure on the knob. The Bouncer looked back toward him and said, "The Bossman could be over there *some time.* Once he gets started . . . hell, the girls at the club all say he's an *animal.* Know what I mean? Hell, he could keep her goin' all night. After tonight you prob'ly won't *ever* gonna be able to satisfy her again. Know what I mean?" He laughed. " 'Ceptin' it sounds from what Big Earl says like that mayn't be a problem for neither of you two, anyways. A body don't worry none about satisfyin' sex when it's stone-ass dead, does it?"

He chuckled and looked back out the window. Brandy struggled to sit as upright as his restraints allowed and pushed his head hard against the stove knob again. When he drew his head forward from the stove to test it, the hissing continued. Now he had to count on the combined smells of the trailer, including the pervasive stench of the smoke from Earl's cigars, to obscure the gradually increasing smell of propane.

He took a long, hard breath against the thunderbolts of pain from each of his bruised and broken ribs. Then he breathed another slower, easier breath, a breath both of relief and anticipation. The pain was diminishing. Body Wisdom was beginning. From here on, the timing had to be very good. Brandy forced himself to wait three more slow breaths to fully prepare, and then he grunted as loud an ejaculation of pain as he could through his nose. Eyes wide and fixed, he gave the Bouncer a moment to look his way before making his eyes roll right up into their sockets. He gave two quick choking huffs and a final gasp as he fell over onto his side, limply to the floor.

The Bouncer watched the progress of what he assumed to be some kind of seizure. "What the shit?" He stepped over to where Brandon lay. Now came the hard part. Every ounce of Brandy's attention and concentration were focused on using Body Wisdom to achieve complete flaccidity and non-response. Even reflexes had to be stilled. Blood pressure and heart rate had to be lowered. All systems on pause.

"What the hell *you* tryin' to prove, assbite?" the Bouncer shouted. "Sit *up!*"

A shuffle and a clatter, and then came the expected kick to the ribs. And then another to the kidneys. "Wake up! Come on, you. You sonofabitch, you can't fool me!"

Being trussed up with duct tape and glue made it

easier to make it look like there was no reaction. The Bouncer kicked a few more times to convince himself that Drake was really unconscious. He cursed and mumbled to himself and to Brandon's limp form before he stooped down to clamp fingers tightly around Brandy's throat to check for a pulse. The Bouncer clutched with a fierceness more likely to strangle than to palpate any pulse.

"Shit!" the Bouncer said. "Fucker goes A-rab and passes out on me! Earl's gonna figure I got to messin' around with him and corked him. He'll be damned pissed off. Shit!" He paced to the window and back. Drake lay completely still, keeping his breathing as slow and controlled as possible. Nearly at standstill, but not holding it tight for fear he might gasp if he were kicked again. Dead soft. All to the center of the silence. Dead soft. No response. Absolutely flaccid. Absolutely limp. And the tape ran on . . .

A howl of despair rang through the heavy beat of the music from the house. A man's voice barked something. A woman's plaint faded into nothingness. All lost in the animal beat of the instrumental bridge of the bump and grind.

The Bouncer was in a real state. He banged his fist on the window sill. "Shit!" he growled in frustration. He marched over to give Brandon's body a full swing kick squarely between his taped legs. Right in the groin. The thunderbolt of pain shot straight up Brandy's spine and almost snapped his head right off his body. He nearly lost it, but the stretch of tape near the impact point deflected and checked the force of the kick just enough to let him continue his pretence of unconsciousness.

"God *damn* you!" the Bouncer shouted. "What the *hell* is *wrong* with you anyway, dumbfuck! Damn it all. I'm gonna get Big Earl over here, and if you're fakin' this, you're gonna fuckin' regret you tried anything with me. I'll be teaching *you* a goddamned trick or two, you dumbfuck."

The Bouncer clamped his thick fingers around

Brandy's neck again, hissed another oath, and stomped off through the screen door of the trailer. He stuffed his gun in his waistband and slammed the door with a clattering bang as he left.

As soon as Brandy heard the rapping of the Bouncer's fists on the back door of the house, he twisted and struggled to roll himself over onto his knees. Waves of pain wracked his body, but his fear provided enough anesthesia to keep him moving. The smell of propane was strong as he straightened himself against the pull of the tape-and-glue bonds. He scooted around away from the stove and tried to rock himself up onto his lashed-together feet.

His head was cloudy and buzzing. How much of it was pain and fear, and how much was from the effects of the gas, he couldn't be sure. On the first attempt to get to his feet, Brandy lost his balance altogether and fell onto his side with a loud thump. He lay in the hissing silence for a moment, terrified that the Bouncer might hear him and come running back. There was a distinct sound of rattling of a door, but it came from over at the house. Brandy quickly rolled over onto his knees for a second try at it. This time he teetered on his feet, straining at the taped ankle attachment to maintain his balance. Unable to stand upright, he hopped in his hunched position toward the bedroom at the other end of the trailer. It was all he could do to keep up the rhythm and momentum as he banged into walls and hit his head on the bathroom door jamb, bounced across to the opposite wall and rapped his ear on the thermostat box at the end of the narrow hall.

After another eternity, he angled through the bedroom door into the unlit haze. The gas smell was now suffocating. He hopped around behind the door and butted it with his head to close it. He stumbled sideways onto the greasy, clammy sheets of Phil's unmade bed and rolled himself over toward the end wall on its far side, next to the night

table. With a heavy thud, he fell into the narrow crack between bed and wall, his shoulder wedged painfully between
the metal bed frame and a bowed section of the micro-thin
simulation-knotty-pine veneer which lined most of the trailer.

Brandy held his breath and listened. All he heard
was a ringing in his ears and a racing da-dup-da-dup of the
arteries in his head with each surge of his heart. No other
sound was discernible, neither within the trailer nor outside.
He couldn't even hear the music from the house. If it was still
playing.

Maybe it wasn't in the cards for him. Maybe Big Earl
would return with the Bouncer, smell the gas, turn off the
stove, open the doors and windows to air it all out, find
Brandy trapped behind the bed, realize the intent of the plan,
and watch the Bouncer beat him to death.

For now, all Brandy could hope for was that Big Earl
would interrupt his "interrogation" of Julia long enough to
come see what the problem was in the trailer. And Brandy
had to hope that the rumors about Earl's inseparability from
his cigars was based as much in fact as in lore. He had to
hope Earl would come angrily swaggering over to the trailer,
his whining Bouncer in tow, a lit cigar in his mouth, and . . . It
was logical. And it was improbable. But it was the only hope
Brandy had.

And what if it *did* happen that way? The explosion
would probably kill all three men. Unless Earl had Julia in
tow with him as he returned. Not a nice speculation, but
certainly possible.

The ringing in Brandy's ears was becoming
horrendous. And the amplified noises of his own heart were
now growing into grotesque squishing, whooshing,
pump-like sounds. Still in the da-dub-da-dub cadence but
more horribly invasive now. Nightmare magnitude. His face
ached from being jammed tight against the wall, and the bed
frame dug into his shoulder blade.

The smell of Phil's filthy bed replaced the heavy gas smell. The gas smell was fading. Maybe it was just an olfactory illusion. Or perhaps the propane gas cylinder had been nearly empty and there was not enough in the trailer for even a small airfire.

The da-dub-da-dub became background for a new noise. A clacking sound. A slamming screen door. Probably at the house. A voice. Deep voice. Angry voice. Shuffling of impatient shoes on the driveway outside. Thumping of heavy legs on wooden steps.

The door to the trailer banged open, and Brandy's heart stopped in mid-beat as he felt the full agony of his failure unfolding before him.

There, suddenly, at the edge of the horror, something shifted. It was as if every light in the universe were ignited, every sound sucked back into the Center, and Brandon was hit hard from behind. As if one world had ended and another began in its place. Armageddon. The wall of the bedroom. The wall of the trailer. For Christ's sake! He'd been hit with a wall! Bizarre hallucinations!

If he could just turn his head a little more to see who had hit him and what was coming next, at least he could accept it with some sort of dignity.

In the Deep Pit mode, in the nightmare mode, in the concentration of horror, four trivial items of information danced like puppets on strings at the front of a curtain-box stage, taunting him, teasing him. Four facts. Four suits to the complete deck. Four corners to the square. Did heaven demand from those who would enter the life after death the answer to a skill-testing question? Or was this an information agent's hell?

Four facts. But there's no time for games. Four facts.

Number One: JCL from the account books of the Pipeline. JCL who was paid lots of money. Within the last few months. JCL. But who the hell . . . ?

Number Two curtsied and bowed to JCL, who stepped back. "And the only other one knows you're here is as good as dead. I've arranged for her to die *real* neat." But it couldn't have been Waco Sally he was talking about, because Earl had been genuinely surprised when Julia appeared at the trailer! So who the hell . . . ?

Numbers Three and Four were at Stage Rear, having a private dance. Or was one chasing the other? It was foggy. Or maybe smoky. Hard to tell. They were important, Numbers Three and Four. But why? What difference could it make? Brandy was about to die. Or maybe he was already dead. What difference could it make. Three and Four looked out at Brandy. Wondered why he was bound and gagged and flying. What the hell is . . . ?

Number Three stomped forward to the front of the stage and shook a fist which was wrapped tightly around the black stub of a cigar. His face was a bulldog caricature of Earl. "And he knows that lesbo I sicked the Frog on. Her!" he thundered, pointing back at Number Four.

Number Four was a woman. A short, busty woman with a raggedy-ann face. A true raggedy-ann face. "If you must know, that's Jean-Claude Laffont, my old climbing buddy. He arrived here this afternoon to do some climbing with me."

A marquee flashed its patterns of incandescent letters: "JCL". Then there was a Bugs Bunny cartoon closing. "That's All, Folks!" and a fuzz of snow and a screaming woman with frizzy hair. She kept screaming. Why was she screaming?

Despair became wonder became tomorrow, and all those lights flickered low, and then off, and then on briefly before flickering off for the last time.

As the senses went slack, Brandy wondered if he'd remembered to turn down the thermostat when he left his condo earlier in the day. Or was it yesterday? No, it had to have been today. But when he puzzled over how he would go and check whether he'd turned it down or not, he realized he didn't even know where his condo was. Hadn't a clue. And why was that woman screaming?

Brandy was completely without orientation, completely lost. A little boy in a big department store. With no Mom.

Thirty-Eight

On El Capitan, the weather had soured. Cold November clouds dipped sporadically to enveil the climbers, then cleared away for a few moments. Then back. Warm became cold. And damp became wetter. Nastiness that kept the fair-weather climbers away. Typical early winter climbing in the Sierra, and Annie loved it. Brer Rabbit in the Briar Patch. It was everything she knew and expected.

What she *hadn't* expected was the peculiar behavior of her climbing partner. Yesterday he'd been fine. Yesterday they had climbed more vertical rise and more impossible pitches than Annie had ever packed into a climbing day. Yesterday the muscles and the tendons were stretched and strained to pain and beyond, and the unlikely busty, hippy body that was Annie Bentley Wharton was absolutely glowing. It had been a happy-to-be-alive day, the best in many, many years.

The night had been spent in spider nets --- hanging hammocks suspended from hold-fast pitons and rock slings

--- which the night winds gently swung and rocked until the storm front moved in just after midnight. The winds picked up dramatically and Annie's spider net began banging her so erratically against the vertical spine of the crack to which she had anchored that she decided to move her net another twenty meters along the wall. In the dark, by flashlight and feel, she worked her way along the slippery granite away from the crack where Jean-Claude had holed up.

Jean-Claude was understandably surprised when, by the dawn's early light, he couldn't find his climbing partner where he'd left her when they'd first set up their sleeping arrangements. They had been separated from one another`s sight by a prominent ledge, and her midnight move made her even harder to locate. But during the night, she hadn't wanted to shout out into the wind and disturb him.

Jean-Claude's irritation seemed entirely out of proportion, and it was magnified while they breakfasted on the pseudo-ledge they'd found just a short pitch above their night shelters.

Annie couldn't understand it. Yesterday had been so wonderfully idyllic. Maybe Jean-Claude hadn't slept well. He began muttering and growling and bitching in alternating English and French about the cold and the damp, and cursing in an even greater mixture of languages. By the midpoint of the first full pitch, Annie realized that the fun of this climb had come to an abrupt end.

"Hey, J.C.," she shouted up at him. "Time to go home! Let's start down."

"What?" he whined. "I thought we are climbing to the top tip! Are you accepting the defeat of the weathers?"

"Of course not. But I'm tired of listening to your bitching. Yesterday was great. Let's leave it at that. I've been to the top of this mountain more times than I can count now, so I don't need to set any new records. Okay?"

"If Madame wishes," he replied, uncertainly. As an

afterthought, but with a surprisingly renewed enthusiasm he added, "Let us rappel together to the Transverse Crawl, and then we each take one of the ropes and race to the valley. Agreed? Non?"

"Race? Me? Only if you want to add humiliation to your misery," she laughed.

And so the odd race had begun.

The two climbers made their way down to the Crawl, where Jean-Claude announced his intention to flank west toward the Dihedral Crack itself. Annie knew she could make better time on the Crossover.

While Jean-Claude rearranged his equipment on his waist slings, Annie was off and away. She tied on carefully, rechecked her protection, and swung away from the wide ledge. No sooner had she bounced in from her first graceful, spider-like descent than a huge boulder disengaged from the ledge and started down the granite face after her. She heard it coming and managed to latch onto a spike of rock quickly enough to jerk herself under the cover of an overhang.

She was just quick enough to save her body, but she was unable to avoid getting the third and fourth fingers of her left hand crushed as the stone rolled by. As she pulled free and swung out, she saw Jean-Claude glare down over the edge.

"I'm okay!" she reported. "It missed me!"

"Ah! Bravo!" he returned.

Annie released from the wall and immediately proceeded with her rappel, but during the next drop, she felt vibrations through her taut rope. What the hell was going on up there? On instinct, Annie rappelled in one fast, short sweep to a wide oblique crack just ten feet below her, a good fifteen meters above her target ledge for this rappel. She threw her right fist into the crack. Her feet scrambled to find bumps to latch onto while she jerked on the freeline with the smarting fingers of her mauled left hand.

Her second jerk pulled the rope free. As it fell down past her, she noticed that the rope was still knotted. She anchored and pulled the rope up to examine it more closely. It hadn't been unlocked by her pull at all! The protection had somehow come undone. Which meant that the belay sling had been cut!

If Annie had spent the extra seconds rappelling all the way down to the next ledge, she would have fallen to her death. The message was outrageous, but perfectly clear. Jean-Claude was trying to kill her. She presumed he hadn't cut her rope directly only because of the questions which might have been asked when he got down to the valley floor.

She peered up to see if he could see her. In moments he would realize he'd been unsuccessful. Now that he'd shown his hand, she knew he had to dispose of her quickly. No matter what it took, he couldn't let Annie get down alive. She knew that. What had started as a fun race down the face of El Cap was now a race for survival.

Annie had to seize the initiative. First she would do what she always told her climbing students to do if they got into trouble on a Yosemite rock face and needed assistance. She hollered for help. Often, tourists on the valley floor could hear a climber in distress, and they would summon the Rangers. Even in the winter, there were bound to be a few hikers down there within earshot.

Annie screamed and shouted and called at the top of her lungs. The low clouds along the valley edges seemed to dampen the usual echoes, but she had to hope that some of her calls would be heard down there.

Even as she screamed her repeated S.O.S., Annie was already working her way across the wide crack from which she hung. Cautiously. Urgently. She was without protection for the moment, but she needed to get out from under Jean-Claude. Another rock came crashing by, two meters to

her left. If she could get to the end of this crack, she'd be out
of his range for the moment. He would have to descend to
the ledge she'd passed midway down the rappel, and then
traverse to get above her again. He could do it, but he'd have
to move quickly.

Annie wondered if Jean-Claude were tied into the
deaths of Chrissie and Farmer or, worse, if he were part of
the Pipeline. That was it! This had to be a Pipeline termina-
tion contract!

Despair grabbed hold of Annie and wouldn't let go.
She could feel herself freezing up. She had a sudden vision
of a naked woman, her hand glued to her face, struggling in
utter futility, suffocating to death, while her murderers
surrounded her, watching her.

Annie shuddered. She couldn't let this happen. She
was in her own element, for god's sakes. Jean-Claude was an
impressive climber, but Yosemite was her own Briar Patch.

She got her hips wedged in the corner of a vertical
crack as she reached it, wiggled free, then unhooked two
large chocks from her belt and jammed them in a lateral crack
as anchorage for another rappel.

As she tied on, she hissed under her breath, "Try to
catch me now, you sonofabitch!" Whether it was the
invigoration or the oath which came first was academic. Annie
sucked in a deep breath, and another, and was transformed
to ballerina Annie, flying across her stage. Her beloved
monoliths of granite smiled as they received the touches of
her special collusion of grace and art. Raggedy Annie
performing the most amazing pirouettes and pliés as she
spun her way down along invisible cracks, thousands of
feet above the valley floor.

Even if nobody responded to her emergency call,
even if she were all alone with this assassin on the raw,
monolithic rock face of El Capitan, she was so completely at
peace in her element, she was certain that God himself

couldn't catch her. This was what Raggedy Annie was all about. Annie swooped into the endorphin euphoria she'd experienced dozens of unexpected times before, usually in response to the most severe stresses of climbing. But this time, the high was higher, the feeling lighter, than she had ever felt it before. Strange. Beautiful and strange. She felt as if she could cast off her rope and float across the rock face without protection. Free solo rappel. Free solo flight.

But she knew the realities of this job. Knew and accepted them. She would work the rope and the protection, she would traverse and dodge and tuck and swoop and get safely down this face with the special and unique grace she'd spent most of her adult life cultivating. It was everything she'd trained for. The madman above her didn't have a chance. Didn't have a chance. Didn't have a chance.

This was the ultimate climbing challenge. Maybe they would have to start a new record book for Snuff Climbing. Gallows humor, Raggedy Annie. Gallows humor. No time for that.

Her breathing evened out and she was finding the rhythm of her descent. A football-sized rock hurtled down the cliff, bashing a ledge thirty yards to her left. She tried to catch a glimpse of where he was now.

She dropped and crossed, checking above her every few moments to try to get a glimpse of her predator. To see where Jean-Claude was moving. In her mind's eye was a map of this part of the Dihedral Wall, complete with variations and side routes. Her strategy counted on a bit of luck in the timing as she crossed back under her own path of descent to make the Pillars. That was the most vulnerable spot, where a well-placed Jean-Claude could pelt her with a deadly salvo of loose rock from the wide traverse above. She'd been there once when a clumsy climbing group above her had dislodged a medium-sized boulder which had snagged the climbing rope of one of her students and had sprung three pieces of protection before crashing down the thousand or so remaining feet to the valley floor. It was an exposed section, but there was no avoiding it. She just had to hope that by the time she reached that crossover, Jean-Claude would be so far behind that he couldn't get into position above her, or that he would be close enough behind her that he would be past it.

There had been no sign of Jean-Claude for three-quarters of an hour when Annie had reached the first major fork in the routes of descent. She had ceased calling out to the valley floor for help, in hopes of depriving Jean-Claude of any special intelligence as to which route she had chosen for herself. And there was no reassuring evidence whatsoever that she'd been heard. No gathering group of pointing binocular wearers, no armadas of cars and trucks assembling to begin a rescue. Annie was on her own.

The thickening clouds added to the unreality of the descent. Annie rested for a few minutes as she reached the critical pitch. She looked out across the open expanse of exposed rock face in front of her. As she slid out toward the first secure anchor point, she saw a movement about thirty meters directly above her and pulled back to the partial cover of a vertical crack. A boulder crashed down past where she would have been standing.

Her heart sank. He was there and he was accurate. Before she could think of any contingency plans, another rock came sailing down into the crack where she stood, bouncing just inches away from where her right toe balanced on a narrow granite step. She looked straight up the shaft of the crack. Jean-Claude was edging over right above her. In another few moments he would be able to begin showering her with stones and boulders until he got lucky with one of them and knocked her from her perch.

She looked anxiously for alternative routes. Her mind's map knew of nothing on this section of the face except the exposed traverse beside her. She leaned out and peered down the wall. She was at the top edge of an overhang, at the apex of a cathedral arch. Below was only open space. No ledge.

Far below her, but at the side of the cathedral concavity, was a small knob of rock at a lateral crack. To reach it she would have to rappel into the empty space below her and somehow set up enough swinging action to get over to the knob. Annie made a quick guestimation of the descent and realized it was about 45 meters down. Her rope was a standard 55 meters long, but only half of that could serve the rappel. The other half would be the freeline which was needed to pull loose the anchoring knot to retrieve the rope for the next pitch. On only very special occasions in her career had Annie elected to used a special triple sheepshank lock knot to gain extra descent, almost twice the scope of the usual arrangement for a single pitch.

The triple sheepshank is a solid pressure knot which holds well so long as even, steady tension is exerted by the weight of the climber, but which releases instantly when the tension is slacked. It requires straight, even descent. Any roughness or bouncing against the wall is likely to release the knot, sending the climber plunging to her death. An all-or-nothing knot.

Annie winced as she speculated. The free-space descent below her would be satisfactory for maintaining the even tension required, but she couldn't imagine swinging without slacking the tension as she struggled to latch onto the knob of rock which was to be her target.

Another rock bulleted down the crack from above, bouncing off the spire over her head, sending a foreboding shower of rock fragments over her. The decision was fairly simple. She could stay put in her present position until Jean-Claude homed in on her and knocked her off the mountain. Or she could move out into the open and begin to slowly work across the traverse, making his targeting even easier.

Or she could take the Big Chance and become the human pendulum in hopes of finding another way out from under her assailant.

It would take Jean-Claude longer to descend to her anchor point than it would for her to get to the knob below, although she had no assurances that she could get anywhere further once she'd reached the knob of rock, anyway. It could be a dead-end. Another granite bomb exploded on the rock beside her. Decision made.

Annie tied on at the tip of her rope with the triple sheepshank. Her hands were shaking as she secured and set the knot against her body weight. She waited for the next crash of rocks from above and then launched herself out and over the edge, maintaining the most even tension she could. Another boulder bounced off of the ledge above her as she worked her way down.

Gently, gently she eased herself down the rope. By the halfway point, the walls of the concavity were further away from her than she had expected. She could no longer touch the rock with her feet. Free rappel. The steady pressure of the sling between her legs, which she had always interpreted as highly sensuous, had an especial intensity now as her very life support.

Nearing the end of her rope, she lowered herself until she was dangling directly adjacent to the target knob. She needed a few more feet in order to be correctly positioned for the pendulation.

There was no further rock bombing from above. She hadn't had a shower of rock since shortly after she'd begun her free rappel. Which probably meant Jean-Claude was coming down to what he hoped would be a better position for his continued assault. If he dropped to where Annie had just anchored her rappel, he would be too late to interfere with her swing to the knob and the snap-free recovery of her rope. Better still, there was no loose rock at that point which he might use for ammunition. By the time he might work himself across to a position more directly above the knob, she would have retrieved her rope and be long gone on her next rappel.

Carefully, Annie began twisting to initiate her pendulation. The first time she was able to swing herself to the knob of rock, she realized she was about a meter too low on the rope. With the triple sheepshank, it was too risky to adjust the length while she was pendulating. And there was no way she could grab onto the rock outcropping without slacking rope and risking a fall. She slowed the pendulation and hoisted herself up to have another go at it. A scrabble of rock chips --- not like something hurled down but more likely loose footing dislodged by Jean-Claude during his descent to reach her --- rained down on the facing escarpment to her left, on the opposite side of the arch from her destination knob.

The fingers on Annie's left hand throbbed where she checked her rope. She began to swing again. Back and forth between the walls of the arch Annie swung, like the pendulum of a gigantic grandfather clock. More rock scrabble caused Annie to look over her shoulder. Above the arch and on a quick descent toward the small ledge opposite to her was Jean-Claude. He would make the ledge in moments, and each swing that took her closer to the rock knob on one side of the arch also pendulated her closer to where Jean-Claude would soon be on the other. The action of the swing was beginning to reach the point of momentary slackness at the change of direction. Annie was straining to keep everything steady. Jean-Claude continued his descent to the ledge behind her with smooth technique and, except for the scuffle of his climbing shoes against the granite walls, in deadly silence.

Annie stretched out to grab onto the rock knob with one hand, being ever-so-careful to resist the temptation to lurch out for it, but the swing was not quite large enough. Jean-Claude set himself down at the ledge and scrambled to anchor in to the rock as he side-stepped toward Annie. He threw out a hand to grab at her as the backswing of her pendulation brought her to him. A cat on a windowsill pawing to sink its claws into a mouse on a nearby tree branch as it waved in the wind.

Annie screamed, "Bastard!" as she kicked his hand away. She *had* to reach the rock knob this time!

Throwing all the body English she could muster into the upswing, Annie estimated she was still short of getting an arm on the rock knob. Jean-Claude was anchoring himself for a still better purchase from which to snag Annie on the next swing. He was certain to have guessed what kind of knot held her, certain to know how little was required to knock her loose.

In desperation, at the height of her pendulation, Annie threw her legs up in front of her toward the bulging rock knob. One boot glanced off of the granite uselessly, but the other locked into the crack between the knob and the wall. With a frightening, tooth-rattling jerk, Annie was whipped against her rope. Her left hand was snapped free, but the right held. She was caught in a hammock-like position, slightly head-down. Desperately, she secured her left hand by giving the rope an extra turn around her wrist as she tried to work herself up toward the rock without easing any tension on her lifeline.

Her ankle was locked in such a way that if she bent her leg enough to get the other leg into the crack, she couldn't move at all. She twisted her head back to get an upside-down look at what Jean-Claude was doing. She could see him crouched down, probably searching for something to throw at her. She had to get herself up to the rock fast!

As she struggled to get herself to safety, still dangling upside down from her foot, Annie became aware of the in-

vasion of a thumping sound, the sound of a grouse pounding its wings against the ground, the sound of an ape thumping its chest. Jean-Claude paused to search for the source of
the sound, too.

Out of the thinning clouds below them emerged a
helicopter. As it moved quickly into position opposite the pair
of climbers, a bullhorn honked barely intelligible commands,
which became clearer as the helicopter rose to the level of
the climbers.

The bullhorn voice addressed Jean-Claude by name.
"This is Ranger David Jervis of the Yosemite Park Police. We
know why you are here and we are prepared to use force, if
necessary, to stop you." The barrel of a rifle extended
threateningly from the side of the helicopter. "I want you to
stand up and move slowly to your right, away from the edge
of that rock arch. Do you understand?"

Jean-Claude was as stunned as Annie was. He
nodded robotically.

The bullhorn also addressed Annie by name, telling
her to sit tight. "I'm going to try to put out a pair of Search
and Rescue team members on the ledge below Mr. Laffont.
Can you hold on for another ten or fifteen minutes? Signal
by nodding your head. Annie?"

Annie nodded vigorously in the affirmative and
continued her struggle to rebalance, to pull herself up onto
the knob of rock without slacking tension on her rope. Her
arms were aching with the strain of holding. She was cold
and the muscles were stiff, responding reluctantly. At last
she twisted and turned herself enough to snag her other calf
over the knob and pull herself up over its edge with her
powerful legs. The bullhorn continued barking unintelligible
commands at the Frenchman.

Dense clouds were moving back in. Annie looked
around the lip of the arch and scouted an oblique crack
which would probably offer her a reasonable descent route

just east of the Black Dihedral. She looked down to see where the helicopter was planning to drop out climbers. She could make out Ranger Dave pointing toward an isolated ledge just thirty feet or so below Jean-Claude. It wasn't any more than fifteen feet wide. There was no way they could get the helicopter in close enough to the vertical granite wall to set down climbers without shearing the blades off. The helicopter hovered below them, indecisively, near the ledge, disappearing and reappearing in the thickening windswept clouds. Annie could make out the climbers inside moving to the door, preparing to unload.

While the Rangers were preoccupied with the unloading, Jean-Claude fumbled in his chalk bag and sidestepped back to the edge of the rock arch. Rock chicked above Annie, throwing a shower of granite chips over her. Another rock zing and a ricochet sound. The sonofabitch had a gun! He was shooting at her! Still holding tightly onto her rope for balance, she ducked down behind the knob of granite and steadied herself.

Unsteadily Annie peeked through a narrow crack and saw that Jean-Claude had turned his attentions to the helicopter, now hovering close to the wall. A sudden updraft would blow it against the rock. Any contact of the main rotor with the wall would send it down. In order to get one rail onto the narrow ledge the pilot had to come in on an angle and keep the helicopter poised at a precarious outward tilt. Ranger Dave threw out a grappling line to anchor the bird so that the two climbers could disembark safely.

Annie's ecstasy at being rescued turned to agony as Jean-Claude raised his pistol to shoot down at the helicopter. Before the first climber had leapt from the side door, two shots cracked out above the cacophony of the helicopter engine. The hovering machine lifted and swerved sharply away from the wall, but the rope from the grappling hook tangled over the bird's left landing skid. The helicopter jerked and oscillated horribly as the pilot struggled to regain control on his short tether.

A bullet in the fuel tanks, or even a lucky hit on one of the rotor blades, would spell certain destruction for the helicopter and death for its inhabitants. Jean-Claude lowered his gun, but then the pilot steadied the helicopter and the Frenchman took aim again. Ranger Dave would be unable to shoot back because Jean-Claude was above them, and he would have to fire through the rotor. If he could get a steady enough aim to hit anything. Which looked less and less likely.

As Jean-Claude steadied his hand against the rock beside him, taking careful aim at the helicopter, Annie was clutched by a combination of indecisive fear and protective instinct. If she just stayed put now, regardless of what happened with the helicopter, Annie was safe and Jean-Claude was cooked. He couldn't get at her before the next loads of climbers and helicopters would arrive to surround him. Or he might try to make an escape down to the valley, although it seemed highly likely that he would be intercepted at the base of the Dihedral Wall. Either way, it was all over for him. Jean-Claude was no longer a threat.

"Stop it!" she shouted from behind her rock. "Stop it, Jean-Claude! Put your gun down! Give up!" Why didn't he listen to her? What was he trying to prove? Couldn't he hear her in the roar of the wind and the rotors?

Selfish Annie. Selfish little Raggedy Annie looked back and below her. Looked across at where a madman was now trying to destroy four men and a machine which had come to rescue her. Annie wanted to fly across the gap of the escarpment and intercede. To protect her friend. To right a wrong. But she was scared.

Annie couldn't think what she could do. From the protection of her rock, she tested the knot. She had maintained enough tension on the rope. The knot was still solid. One swing across the gap and she might be able to distract the Frenchman enough to give Dave another chance to free the tangled tether, to get the helicopter up to where they could get off a shot at Jean-Claude. A chance to stop him. But a miscalculation of the smallest order and she would topple and fall to her death, bouncing off the wall like a discarded Raggedy Ann doll thrown from a skyscraper window. She glanced down the granite wall and saw herself tumbling and bouncing and hovering in space until, an infinity below at the base of the rock face, her imaginary self clumped to stillness.

She shuddered. This was the first time since Jean-Claude's intentions had become clear that she'd let herself feel a crack in the façade of her confidence.

The silent calm of woman and rock was paced by the background rhythm of her breathing. The world was suspended and the clock stopped. It was the same magic which had served her so well whenever the climbing had gotten really tough. Certain portals slowly opened in the back of her raggedy cranium, and the answer emerged complete. Her body --- her tiny, funny, hips-and-breasts body --- launched into action with complete precision and direction. Pure intention translated into pure action.

Annie knew exactly what she had to do, as if she'd done it a thousand times before.

Thirty-Nine

The nonsense thoughts continued on, without relief, without transitions, and without apparent pattern. Brandy knew they were nonsense, and he knew he was being assigned the thoughts, one by one, as projects to keep him together. To let him survive. To *make* him survive. And that didn't make any sense either. And it was only after what must have been weeks of such testing that he realized the ones asking the questions all wore pastel blues and whites and greens. Uniforms. Uniformed interrogators. Three fingers. Unless you count your thumb. I see the tip of *that* sticking up next to your little finger. They liked that answer. It always brought smiles.

Bandages all over the arms and the legs. Insides, outsides, all sides. Mummy wrap. Skin on fire. Or no skin at all. Aching muscles and tender bones and tender joints. If this hadn't been a test, Brandy would have tuned into the Conelrad stations --- which quip seemed undeniably hilarious to him until they shrugged and patted him on the shoulder and left him alone again. They didn't understand, but if they'd put themselves in his place they could have understood. Brandy had to say something crazy, something really lunatic, to get them to leave.

Only then did they let him sleep. Well deserved sleep. He'd earned it. All that nonsense. All those fingers. At least they were all counted now. All the fingers . . .

All the fingers in . . .

Brandon awoke in the dimness of evening. Of some evening. The window shades were drawn on the single window of the hospital room. Everything was still. Calm. The machines beside the bed, the monitors and the IVACS and a lot of other magical medical paraphernalia, were all silent and unlit.

He noticed the silence. He *heard* the silence. He wondered how long it had been like that. And wondered if it had ever been otherwise. Perhaps he had died, and it would only be a short while until they discovered it and wheeled him down to the morgue. He wiggled his toes to feel for a tag.

He tried to take a deep breath and felt the pull of bandages. His back and shoulders and sides ached miserably. The left side of his head throbbed enough to convince him that if he'd died, he certainly hadn't made it to heaven yet.

When he awakened again, Brandy was in the same hospital room, and it was still night, and the machines were still silent. There were fewer machines than before.

A nurse was holding his arm, taking vital signs. She pried open his eyes carefully, one at a time. When he blinked a few times and then kept the eyes open, she smiled at him. "Welcome back again, Mr. Drake," she said. It was a friendly and oddly familiar voice, although he was at a loss as to why he might recognize it. Especially because her face did not look at all familiar.

At the foot of the bed were two more people. The frizzed hair of Julia glowed red in the room light. Brandy focused on her until he could make out details.

Julia looked odd. Asymmetrical. Could it be her hair? That was it. Her hair was shorter on one side of her head. Almost shaven. Brandon raised his eyebrows in recognition. Julia smiled broadly. "Brandy?" she asked. "Are you really back? Or is this just another test?"

Brandon frowned in confusion. Words came only with difficulty, but they came. "What . . . do you mean? Back? Test?"

Julia gave no reply. There were tears in her eyes.

The nurse finished and recorded something in a chart. She nodded approvingly and said in the general direction of Julia, "If he feels like talking, please keep it short. I'm going to call in the neurology resident. I'll be back in a few minutes."

Next to Julia stood a man in a dark brown suit. "I should read you your rights," the man said solemnly. He was looking directly at Brandy.

"What? Why?" Brandy asked. "What's happening?"

"I should arrest you," the man replied.

"For what?" Brandy persisted, trying to make sense of the odd welcome. "Who are you?"

"Lieutenant Jim Abbott. Drug Enforcement Agency. Sacramento. I've been put in charge of this case. Federal jurisdiction."

Julia bit her lip and looked away. Was this part of a stage play? Did everyone except Brandy have the script?

"What made you think you could operate in L.A. without a license," Abbott asked, "and without letting the police know what you were doing?"

Brandon looked from the Lieutenant to Julia. "Would

someone please tell me what's happened?" He raised a bandaged hand to touch a tender, itching temple. It too was wrapped in bandages. "Where's Annie?" He looked to Julia for answers.

"You know a Yosemite Park Ranger named Dave Jervis?" Abbott persisted, ignoring Brandon's questions.

Brandon squinted to squeeze forth all the memories before responding. "Yes."

"Well, he became suspicious about links between the avalanche death of a certain Phil Lesyk and the deaths of this lady's husband and his climbing partner. Some fungus on some kind of climbing gear Lesyk had in his pocket matched what they found growing on the Peacock girl's climbing suit. And there was some kind of imprint where she'd been lying on the sling. Any of that make sense to you?"

Brandy looked to Julia again, pointed a bandaged arm at Abbott, and mouthed carefully, "Is he really who he says he is?"

Julia nodded affirmative. "It's okay, Brandy. Everything's okay, now."

Abbott resumed. "Do you remember what happened before the explosion? Does anything I told you just now make sense to you? It's important."

"Yes. It all makes sense," Brandy sighed.

"I thought so." Abbott muttered. "And that's why I should have you arrested. If you had screwed up any worse, we might never have found out who was behind this Pipeline group. As it was, you almost got yourself and your friend here killed."

"Where's Annie Bentley?" Brandy blurted out. "Is she okay?"

"Just a minute," Abbott growled. "If you can keep us waiting around for five days, we can damn well tell you in our own sweet time what you missed."

"Five days?" Brandon asked, astonished.

"Six, if you count the first night," Julia corrected.

"What happened to Lesyk?" Brandon asked. "The brother. Earl."

"Dead," Abbott replied. "You remember anything about the explosion?"

Brandon frowned as he strained to remember. After a few lines of blanks, he gave up. "No."

"I thought not. While you were spinning out your mumbo-jumbo nonsense that first day, you gave us a lot of detail right up to the time of the explosion and nothing after that . . . well, I'm not surprised. You must have been knocked out by the blast. You were thrown damn near forty feet. They found you and one wall of that trailer out in front of Lesyk's garage."

Abbott pointed his thumb at Julia. "You probably owe your life to this lady. By the time the ambulance people got to you, her hair was still smoldering from where she'd been picking you out of the rubble."

Julia shuffled nervously next to the Lieutenant. He glanced at her and snuffled self-consciously before turning back to Drake. "Okay. I guess you owe your lives to one another. I'll leave it to you to sort that out. Anyway, I'll need to take a statement from you. Maybe tomorrow morning, if you're feeling strong enough. There's no real hurry now, I guess. Couple of other people will want to get statements, too.

"There's a list at the nursing station of who you can and can't see. If you aren't sure who you're talking to, give a buzz on your call button and have them check it out. Until yesterday, reporters were thicker than fleas on a mutt's ass around here. Excuse me, ma'am. They seem to have run off to bigger news, but when they find out you're conscious, they'll be back. I'd advise you not to talk to them. And from what I understand of the way you run your business, Mr. Drake, that won't be difficult to convince you to do. Am I right?"

"Yes. I've got to find out more about what happened."

"Mrs. Hobbs should be able to tell you everything." Abbott stepped back from the foot of the bed and nodded. "And I've got to be off to another meeting with the LAPD. When you jerked up this Pipeline rock from the stream bed, you certainly cost this city a fortune in overtime for the internal affairs guys down at police headquarters.

"I'll be back in the morning. Good night to both of you."

"Good night, Lieutenant," Julia said, keeping her eyes on Brandon as she spoke.

The door bumped closed behind Abbott. In the silence of the room, Julia fidgeted at the footboard of the bed. She and Brandon stared at one another.

"Would you please tell me what happened?" Brandy asked her, his driving curiosity struggling to overpower the enveloping fatigue.

Julia answered his queries with a practiced formality borne of repeated recitations of the story for various law enforcement officials.

After her amateur debut as Waco Sally, Julia had tried to keep Earl Lesyk at his club. She had tried almost everything to hold him, but he'd seemed preoccupied with a desire to get back to his house. "It was almost as if he expected something to happen there."

She had successfully fended off the attentions of the Bouncer when he drove her back to the hotel. Not finding Drake there, she immediately called a cab and went to Earl's home to find out if Brandy had completed his search and gotten away safely, or if it was time to telephone the police for help.

When she saw the light on in the trailer, she crept around the back of the house, to see if Brandy was inside. The Bouncer jumped her from behind and dragged her into the trailer and, well, Brandon knew the rest from there.

"What happened later?" Brandy asked. "After I played possum for the Bouncer? He must have thought I passed out on him."

"Passed out? He thought he'd killed you. He came running into the house, frantic. I thought for sure he'd killed you, too, judging by how worked up he was, and I really lost it. I let out a scream and Earl hit me and knocked the wind out of me. The doctors think that was probably when my rib got broken." She touched the rib through her loose sweater with her fingers. "It could have been earlier. My arms and chest still have so many colors on them they look like an art project.

"Earl got really angry with the Bouncer and shouted, 'What the hell am I supposed to do about Drake? You telling me you left him alone over there?' And he started calling the Bouncer names. Earl grabbed me by the hair and dragged me as far as the back door, and left me to the Bouncer to watch while he checked on you.

"He must have noticed something before he got all the way to the trailer --- maybe he smelled the gas or something --- because I remember him stopping in the driveway, shouting 'Oh, *shit!*' and then charging toward the porch of the trailer. The Bouncer threw me down on the floor inside the door of the house and charged on out toward the trailer, too.

"It's a good thing he did, because if he'd taken me outside with him, or if I'd been left standing there in the doorway, I'd probably be dead. Whatever it was, it couldn't have been more than two or three seconds until there was an incredible explosion and the whole world flashed bright lights and flames and . . . It was really incredible! The police figure Lesyk's cigar probably set off the gas."

"Anything left of what was inside the trailer?"

"Not much. They've been sifting through it for nearly a week now. Water damage from the fire people destroyed more than the explosion ever did, but they're still working on it. Maybe Ranger Jervis can tell you more about that."

"He's in Los Angeles, too?"

"Since Tuesday. He should be here any minute. The nurses called him when you started to come around the last time. About an hour ago."

"What about Annie? For God's sakes, Julia, tell me about Annie. I found out when I was in the trailer that Earl had pre-paid a contract for a hit on her and that . . ."

"I know," Julia interrupted. "You talked about that non-stop all during that first night and a lot more during the bad spells for the next two days. And it's a good thing. Because if you hadn't been ranting on so much about that, they figure that the French climber would have killed her and gotten away scot free with it."

"So she's all right?"

Whoever knocked at the door wasn't waiting for acknowledgement before entering. Into the room marched the bigger-than-life hulk of Ranger Dave, almost unrecognizable without his uniform.

"Hello there, stranger," he said to Brandy, amiably. "Evening, Mrs. Hobbs." He walked up to the foot of the bed, to the spot where Lt. Abbott had stood. "I thought you were going to sleep for a hundred years or something," he laughed. Then he narrowed his eyes to inspect Brandy's face.

"He wants to know about Annie," Julia said.

"What have you told him?"

"I hadn't started that part yet. Since you're here, maybe you should talk about that."

The nurse scuttled back into the room and began another check of vital signs. Brandy ignored her. "Well, damn it. *One* of you better start talking!"

Brandy searched from Dave to Julia and back. Their expressions were inscrutable.

"Settle in," the Ranger began, "because this story

has got to be the genuine cliff-hanger of all time. I was there. Less than thirty feet away, and there wasn't a damn thing I could do about the most important part but watch it happen.

"Frankly, if you hadn't continually rambled on about some John Clod, and if Mrs. Hobbs hadn't been here to hear Annie's name, too, we might never have put two and two together, and gotten up there at all."

Dave told Brandon the story of how the police and Julia had unravelled Brandy's rantings a few hours after he had been admitted to the hospital, and about how they had contacted the Yosemite police to reach Ranger Dave. He explained the plan about the helicopter and the attempt to put out the Search and Rescue climbers on the side of the mountain to apprehend Jean-Claude.

"Actually, we almost had everything under control until Laffont turns up a pistol and takes aim at our helicopter. Annie was safe behind a ridge of rock and pretty well out of his reach. Once his game was over, she figured she was home free. She could have gotten the rest of the way down on her own. No problem.

"But Annie sized it up that her pistol-packing friend might have either killed one of us in the chopper or might have brought the chopper down and killed all of us."

"And could he?"

"Quite likely. Helicopters are pretty vulnerable. Anyway, she surprised herself more than anybody else. She moved out of her safe position, did a Tarzan number, and swung right over to him. I was staring right up through the rotor blur, trying to get a good bead on the guy, with the pilot shouting not to shoot until he tipped us more so I wouldn't hit the blades, and my climbers trying like mad to cut the grappling line that was holding us down.

"Annie managed to plant a solid kick onto Laffont's pistol arm. Knocked him off balance from his ledge. He grabs out to her to steady himself, or to pull her down, I don't know which. See, he'd untied his own protection earlier when he moved across the ledge to shoot at her, so he went down."

"Off the mountain? He fell?"

"Over a thousand feet."

"So Annie's okay?"

"Yeah. She shouldn't be. But she is. Couple of broken fingers and a sprained ankle, but she's okay otherwise. But you know what? By all rights she shouldn't have survived it. When Laffont tussled with her, it slacked her off enough that her knot should have broken loose. It was one of those quick-release items they use sometimes to get extra reach on their ropes. Real touchy. When the Search and Rescue people belayed her back up to her anchor point --- it was the only safe way they could figure to get her out --- she discovered she'd mis-tied the knot. It happens to the best. It's easy to do by accident. It was locked in. She couldn't have gotten the rope loose anyway!"

"But she didn't know that when she swung over to Laffont?" Brandon asked.

"That's right. She figured it was a suicide thing." Ranger Dave smiled admiringly as he added, "Crazy stunt! I think she's done a lot of personal soul-searching about it. Annie has always had a generally low opinion of herself. I think that may have changed a little. I hope so."

He pointed a finger at Drake and continued, "I was so pissed off at you for what you did, trying to carry this whole thing along by yourself and damn near getting a few people killed in the process --- including *me*, I might add --- that I wanted to really tear a strip off you when you came to. But the more I learned from Annie and Mrs. Hobbs here, the more I realized there was probably no other way you could have done it. I've been friends with Annie too long, and I think I know what you were up against."

A doctor appeared a few minutes later to examine Brandy and ask a lot of questions. More counting of fingers. Some squeezing of fingers. More reciting of numbers.

"When can I get out of the hospital?" Brandon asked.

"What's your hurry?"

"It was my mother's deathbed wish that I avoid hospitals whenever possible. She always used to say that a hospital was the worst place in the world for a sick man to be."

The doctor gave a tired and lop-sided smile. "She was right. But you're not sick. You're just broken. And you're staying here for the next two or three days, Mr. Drake."

"I'm too tired to argue with you. We'll talk about it tomorrow."

"Very sensible." He put his hand on Brandon's shoulder and added, "See you in the morning."

Julia stood in the corner of the room and watched quietly. She was gone when he opened his eyes again. It was like that for the next two days. Changing of bandages, and statements to police, and filling in the gaps of the missing week.

Julia was there almost all of the time. She was helpful but not intrusive. Conversational, but subdued. Early on, she silenced Brandon's protestations that she didn't have to stay in Los Angeles. That his needs were being well met by the medical staff at the hospital. She said that she had unfinished business, and that she refused to leave for Vancouver until Brandy was mended enough to travel with her. She made it clear there was no room for compromise. Brandy accepted it. He understood that kind of pride. Never to be beholden.

Dave returned to bid farewell the next morning on his way back to Yosemite. "Do you know why the Frenchman was on a contract with the Pipeline to kill Annie?"

"Because Annie had information about the Pipeline

which they thought might hurt them."

"What kind of information?"

Drake paused, cautiously. "I'd rather not say until I've talked with Annie."

"You're good. She already told us she was an information courier for the Pipeline. Told the police everything she knew. I think."

"Then why were you asking me just now?"

Dave grinned. "Just curious to see what you'd say."

"Did I pass?"

"You're a good friend for her. That much is pretty obvious."

"And what's happening to her? Any charges?"

"Not yet. They may come, but I doubt it."

"Why is that?"

"Because . . . technically speaking . . . as an information courier, she didn't violate any laws except by not declaring everything she was bringing into the country. No patents acts. No illegal wares acts. No controlled substances. That Pipeline was a pretty clever operation, from what I'm beginning to understand. Anyway, in light of what we've pieced together about Annie's part in it, I doubt if there'll be charges against her."

Forty

From the police Brandy learned that Big Earl's 'ears' at LAPD had been arrested and charged. The rest, if there was any more to it, would probably never be solved. All the records had been tinder for the Redondo Beach trailer fire, or had disintegrated to paper pulp in the dousing of that fire.

On the second day after Drake regained full consciousness, the tired doctor pronounced him ready to travel.

"What are you going to do now?" Julia asked when they were alone again. "After you get out of the hospital and back to Vancouver?"

Brandon closed his eyes and smiled, luxuriating in the most vivid imagery as he answered, "I have a lovely, lovely cabin up north. Nearly a day's drive from Vancouver. No phones. No power. Gravity-fed water. A wood-burning stove for keeping the three small rooms warm and for heating up the hot-water tank. And no neighbors for about two miles in any direction."

"Wow! That sounds wonderful! And that's where you're going right after you get back?" she asked.

Brandy thought about it. "Starting Monday. That'll give me a couple of days to tie up unfinished business and put any new contracts on hold."

"What about Christmas?"

"I can't think of a better place to spend it. I don't know which I like better. The empty time or the solitude. All I know is that my cabin is one of the most beautiful places on earth." He opened his eyes to suspend the reverie. "What are you going to do after you get back, Julia?"

"Make one or two hundred great breakfasts and then take it from there."

Brandon looked perplexed.

"On Saturday," she continued, "I need to shop for some good winter clothes . . . if you'll tell me what kinds of things one should wear up at this cabin of yours."

"Wait a minute . . ." Brandy objected, "there you go again!"

"I don't have to go, I know, but the way I look at it, I still owe you something. If I'd done a better job of keeping Lesyk and that other fellow out of the way, this never would have happened to you. And besides, you'll be able to get away to that cabin of yours much sooner if you have someone to help with the chores. Right? And I make *great* lunches and dinners, too."

"Julia, you're impossible."

"I could fit right in. I mean to your solitude thing. I could set up my painting in one corner of the cabin and take long walks by myself every day. I'd stay right out of the way."

"No. N-O," Brandon declared. "Julia, you're a wonderful woman, but I'm sure that, even in my all-time best condition of body and mind, I could never handle so much . . . *energy*."

"Does that mean I'm being . . . turned down?" Julia asked.

"How about 'postponed'?" Brandon replied.

Julia drew in a deep breath and slowly let it out. "The curse of the Type Four. We tend to be very obvious about our affections. Sorry. What would you like me to do?"

Brandy bit the inside of his cheek. There was something about the delicate post-case relationship of information agent and client that was not unlike the relationship between doctors and their patients, or between professors and their students. Such relationships needed space and reconditioning before dependencies ensued and people were disappointed. It didn't seem to matter that, in the course of events, Brandy and Julia had spent a wonderful night together. That was eons ago, and this was now. Better to get space and finish healing and then reassess. Or was this just a big juicy rationalization of the Great Distancer.

"I think we will fly back to Vancouver tomorrow," Brandon suggested. "I'll catch up on my business mail and head off to my cabin, and you'll get back into the world of brushes and oil paints. In the New Year, after I return from the North Woods, I'll call you and we'll have a great dinner at the 'Kettle of Fish' and reassess the situation. I think we both need recuperation time right now. What do you think?"

"You're right," Julia admitted, resignedly. "I really shouldn't be so presumptuous. Part of my makeup, I guess."

At noon the next day, Julia drove Brandon's car from the Vancouver airport and helped him into his condo. They called a taxi and when the driver appeared at the door to take Julia home, she gave Brandy a gentle hug, planted an undecorated kiss on his cheek, and left with a smile.

An hour later, as he was settling in, Brandy found an envelope on the seat of the couch in his living room. In it was a check for $25,300 and a note from Julia, which read, "Thank you for everything. Enclosed is a check to cover your fee for the six days you worked on finding Farmer's murderer, and for the eight days you spent in the hospital recovering. Please bill me for any additional costs or expenses you may have incurred. A deal is a deal. Our friendship is too important to me to be cluttered by debt."

Brandy knew he'd done the right thing. Case closed.

He closed his eyes tightly and saw the quiet cabin in the quiet woods in the North Country. 'Tis the gift . . .

EPILOGUE

December 23 --- At a quiet cabin in the quiet woods in the central part of British Columbia, Brandon Drake removed the last of the dressings from the healing scabs on the insides of his legs. The snow was deep on the ground outside, and a new layer of snow was starting to fall in thick, rich flakes. It was good timing that had possessed him to drive Red Dog into town for supplies this morning before the storm began to drop its load. Once a good blanket came down it was often a couple of days before the sideroads were plowed out. Even with the new studded snow tires, Red Dog was a little low-slung to be particularly adept at managing deep snow.

The muscles were starting to mend and stretch and build back past the attrition of disuse, courtesy of the daily rigors of the chopping of wood and the chinking of the new little gaps which the winter air, whistling through the log joints, had discovered.

Brandy smiled as he hoisted the frozen turkey into the cold-box in the wall next to the small nickel-trimmed wood stove he'd picked up at an auction four years back. The stove was a treasure from a ship's galley and dated back to the first decade of the century, complete with a smart nickel-plated railing originally intended to keep pots and pans from sliding off the stovetop as the vessel surged and rolled on the open seas.

The turkey was for Christmas dinner. He'd invited the Cantrells, an older couple from Bog's Bench, to come down and join him. They were some of the few full-time residents of the area. A lot of folks closed up their cabins for the deep winter and went south for a few months. Which created special ties for those who stayed. Now that the storm was on the way, the Cantrells, whose road was barely pass-able at the best of times, would be coming down by cross country skis. They would bring a bottle of good wine, and one of Elaine's special holiday puddings, and they would sit around telling wonderful stories about Bernie's early days working on the railroad which connected Prince George to Jasper. They would report to Brandon about what outra-geous scandals had made the gossip circuits since he had been up last spring, and they would give him a hard time that he still didn't have a full-time lady friend. Then they'd look at one another with a wonderfully connected and loving twinkle in their eyes that gave Brandy some of his few genuine pangs of loneliness and convinced him that he really would like to have a special partner to share his later years with.

Brandy looked out the window at the white fluff starting to build up on the Kharmann-Ghia again, poured himself a big mug of warm milk and hot chocolate from the stove, tossed another small bolt of wood into his Ashley, and settled down with his reading glasses and the top novel from the pile of mindless junk-books he always brought up with him from the city.

A half hour or so later, a car engine whined above the crackle of the Ashley. Brandy damped down the flue on the stove and went to the door. On the road below the cabin, a fairly new Japanese import was gunning and fish-tailing its way toward his driveway. The car revved in just behind Red Dog and shut down. Whoever was inside it was thrashing around to get into coat and gloves and boots before opening the door to greet the cold.

Brandon watched from the porch as a frizzy haired nymph emerged, opened the trunk of the car, hefted a large box, and bounded up to the porch of the cabin.

"Merry Christmas!" Julia announced, handing over the box to Brandy as she kicked off her boots into the tray by the door. "Here you go! This should be enough to last us through Boxing Day. She shook the snow from her hair, and beamed at Brandy with her insistent brown eyes.

She pulled off her coat and gloves and took the box back from Brandy and carried it to the counter next to the stove. Pulling out two bottles she turned to Brandy and announced proudly, "Glühwein! My uncle's Christmas specialty. Have you had it before? Of course you have. But have you had the Hambleton recipe?

"Oh, and here are two letters for you. Your secretary, Karen --- she gave them to me when she told me how to find this place."

"Karen Perrin? But she'd never tell anyone where to find me."

"Yeah. Karen," Julia grinned impishly. "That was her name, all right. She said you had bushels full of mail, but the rest was all junk or business which could wait. But she thought you might like to have these two," Julia said, extending the envelopes. "She sent a note explaining it . . ."

The note from Karen read:

> Brandy, I hope you'll forgive the break in
> form, but this is not a question of business. It's

personal. I'm loyal, but I'm not inhuman. And I don't think <u>anybody</u> could have stopped Julia Hobbs from finding you. I'd hate to imagine what would have become of Teddy if she'd descended on him for directions. If my call was bad, you may fire me. If it was good, you can give me a raise for it. Whatever you think best. Merry Xmas, Boss Man.

Karen

One of the letters was from Kyle Sommerfield. It read:

Congratulations on the closing of the Pipeline case. I have a pearl-handled Ruger .44 which Badger instructed in his will be set aside for you: 'For my dear friend Brandon Drake, in case he ever needs to carry a gun again.' Badger often quoted your rule about not carrying guns, so I'll put it in storage until you decide you need it. I hope you never do. Let me know if you ever need help in this part of the world. I've been asked by Lew Cranston to stay on as a partner. I'll work hard to justify his confidence.

Best regards, Kyle

The other letter was from Annie. On the envelope beneath his Vancouver address, she'd scribbled, "Please forward to the Hermit's Lodge." Inside was a card wishing him Merry Christmas. At the bottom she had penned, "Chop wood, carry water, and make slow passionate love in front of the winter fire . . . but have the decency <u>not</u> to tell me about any of it, you bastard!"

While Brandy was reading, Julia had hung up her snow clothes on the hooks by the door and had inspected the other two rooms of the cabin. She was warming herself by the Ashley in the corner of the living room when Brandy looked up again.

She shivered with excitement. "I want to be fair about this. Since I've all but invaded your privacy."

"I'm reassured you noticed."

Julia made a caricature of a sad face. "Am I being sent away before I can ask my questions?"

"Questions about what?"

Julia beamed. "Oh, about all kinds of things I don't know about you. Like, what kinds of books you read. And what kinds of music you listen to. And whether you put the top back on the toothpaste tube. Things like that. Things That Matter. I was just sitting at home, painting up a storm, and I realized that somehow we had missed all that."

Brandon raised his eyebrow and shook his head from side to side incredulously.

"Well . . ." Julia offered, "could you tell me just a *few* of those things, anyway. Just to satisfy my romantic curiosity? Before you send me away?"

Brandy regarded her carefully for a long moment. "All right if I *show* you instead?"

About the Author

Lance Rucker was born in Louisville, Kentucky. He is the author of four *Brandon Drake* novels, more than 100 magazine stories and articles, and dozens of non-fiction works.

Dr. Rucker and his wife and family make their home in Vancouver, British Columbia, Canada.

Information Agent
Brandon Drake
will be back.

In the information business
there are

Two months in Japan. A good friend. A lover. A death threat. No one was supposed to care much about the information Brandon Drake had been hired to gather. But a cell of Japanese national security agents will kill to insure that the information never leaves Japan.

To reserve a signed copy of the next Lance Rucker novel,
NO SECRETS
**visit the lochenlode.com web site, or
fax the information requested on the next page to**
Lochenlode ◎ Publishers

NO SECRETS

☐ **Please reserve a signed copy of the**
    next Brandon Drake novel   **NO SECRETS**
☐ **Please send me a pre-release announcement of**
      NO SECRETS

Title (Mr., Mrs., Miss, Dr., etc.)
First Name:
Last Name:
Mailing Address:

        City   **State/Province**
   Country   **Zip/Postal Code**
Phone: (   )
Fax#: (   )
e-mail address   **@**

Send to:

         Lochenlode Publishers
         Fax: (604) 433-0111

        Lochenlode ◎ **Publishers**